PRAISE FOR CHA[...]

JOURN[...]

"Ms. Hubbard brings to [...] girl who has many less[...] them she does through the telling of *Journey To Love*.... The romance is sweet and the conclusion a happy one, though it doesn't come without much soul searching and spiritual growth. Enjoy your journey of love with the reading of this novel."

—*Romance Reviews Today*

"This is an interesting historical romance that showcases how different society was just under a hundred and fifty years ago as the sixteen-year-old heroine hopes to marry the man she loves...Charlotte Hubbard provides readers with an interesting mid-nineteenth century journey to womanhood."

—*The Midwest Book Review*

A PATCHWORK FAMILY

"Hubbard delights with the first in a five-book series that is sure to keep readers salivating for the next installment."

—*Romantic Times BOOKreviews*

"*A Patchwork Family* is a wonderful adventure! Each time you think the story has finally leveled out, there is another surprise waiting at the turn of the page and around the bend...*A Patchwork Family* is a Perfect 10 and sure to become a cherished keeper!"

—*Romance Reviews Today*

"A great family story to share, [*A Patchwork Family*] will appeal to nearly every age and anyone who enjoys historical literature."

—Fresh Fiction

VOWS INTERRUPTED

"Dearly beloved, we are gathered here in God's house to witness the sacrament of Holy Matrimony, to join together this man, William Henry Bristol and this woman, Emma Jane Clark."

Eve's throat tightened. She felt ugly and fat and tainted. She had no right to intrude on the bride's special day; no right to expect her childhood friend to come to her rescue, as he had when they were young. It wasn't Billy's fault his brother still couldn't tell the truth or honor his promises.

She swallowed again, battling the urge to collapse with exhaustion or vomit from agitation—or both.

"If there be anyone present who believes this man and this woman should not unite as one, let him speak now or forever hold his peace."

A spasm ripped through her abdomen and Eve cried out. Her knees buckled. As her body slid down the back wall, she saw a multitude of faces turn toward in her horror, and Billy's eyes widening in disbelief.

Angel's Embrace

Charlotte Hubbard

LEISURE BOOKS NEW YORK CITY

For Neal, truly the hero of my life's story.

A LEISURE BOOK®

June 2007

Published by

Dorchester Publishing Co., Inc.
200 Madison Avenue
New York, NY 10016

ISBN-10: 0-8439-5803-0
ISBN-13: 978-0-8439-5803-4

The name "Leisure Books" and the stylized "L" with design are trademarks of Dorchester Publishing Co., Inc.

Printed in the United States of America.

Visit us on the web at www.dorchesterpub.com.

"I cannot think of any need in childhood as strong as the need for a father's protection."
—Sigmund Freud

"Tenderness is a virtue."
—Oliver Goldsmith

AUTHOR'S NOTE

The characters in my "Angels of Mercy" series discuss Negroes and colored men and Indians, because in the 1800s such terminology wasn't derogatory or demeaning. It simply was. The Malloys pray and discuss their faith in public, too, because a strong belief in God was the foundation these homesteaders built their lives upon.

So, at the risk of writing a politically incorrect story, I have told a more authentic, historically accurate one. I applaud my editor, Alicia Condon, for supporting me in this.

To everything there is a season,
  A time for every purpose under heaven:

A time to be born,
  And a time to die;
A time to plant,
  And a time to pluck what is planted;
A time to kill,
  And a time to heal;
A time to break down,
  And a time to build up;
A time to weep,
  And a time to laugh;
A time to mourn,
  And a time to dance;
A time to cast away stones,
  And a time to gather stones together;
A time to gain,
  And a time to lose;
A time to keep,
  And a time to throw away;
A time to tear,
  And a time to sew;
A time to keep silence,
  And a time to speak;
A time to love,
  And a time to hate;
A time of war,
  And a time of peace.

—Ecclesiastes 3

Prologue

April 1876

"Oh, Emma, you'll make the prettiest bride Abilene's ever seen!"

Emma Clark's cheeks tingled as she watched Mrs. Rieckmann measure out yard after yard of frothy lace trim. "Thank you," she said. "I'm glad Mercy Malloy offered to sew my gown, though, because her new machine makes fast work of these slippery silks and satins. Sewing just isn't my talent."

"I don't imagine Billy notices that. He's a fine catch," the grandmotherly clerk affirmed, "and Lord a-mercy, I thought he'd *never* ask you! What took him so long?"

Fingering the delicate lace, Emma bit back a grin. "He's been tucking away his pay from handling the horses there at the Triple M. Wanted to be sure he had enough laid by," she hedged. "What with not really being the Malloys' son, he doesn't want Mike and Mercy putting themselves out on his account."

No sense in letting this old biddy know that *she* had done the proposing: it'd be all over Abilene by sundown, and Billy would be embarrassed. As well he should be! Everyone knew they'd been sweethearts since they were ten, when Billy's mama had abandoned him and the Malloys took him in. Her mother had always said some men needed a little extra time to catch fire. Emma thought of her proposal as lighting the cookstove: Billy made fine kindling, but he needed a flame like her to set things boiling!

Maude Reickmann was nodding, her weathered face creased like old parchment. "Billy Bristol's a giver, not a taker. Very responsible and hardworking, that young man is. Every girl in Dickinson county had her eye on that rusty hair and those blue, blue eyes."

"But I caught him!" Emma crowed, "and just two months from now he'll be all mine! Those other girls will just have to hunt for someone else."

"Shall I put this on your daddy's account then?" She folded the lace tenderly and fetched a spool of white thread from the notions rack behind her.

"Yes, please. And we need some flour and a case of tinned peaches."

"And how's your father doing? Always harder for a man to make his way after his wife dies," the storekeeper mused. "Women deal with the loneliness and the day-to-day living better. They're tougher than their men in many ways."

Emma's jaw clamped shut against an emotional outburst. Just when she thought she could have a conversation without someone mentioning her mother's death—just when she could concentrate on her own happiness for a moment—this storekeeper reopened the gaping hole in her heart.

"Daddy's all right, I guess. Doesn't say much. Goes off to the barn and the fields each morning." The lace on the counter blurred, so she looked away to compose herself. "Comes home to eat and sleep. Tells me how much he misses my mother's cooking. Always finds a way to remind me how I come up short, compared to her."

"That's his grief talking, Emma. That second plague of grasshoppers last summer cost him a lot more than his crops." Maude's face and voice softened. "He'll miss you, too, when you move into that new house with Billy. He just doesn't know how to say so."

Mrs. Reickmann finished the notation in her ledger, and smiled kindly at Emma. Then she walked back to the yard goods table and returned with a small bolt of trim.

"We just got this in yesterday, and the pale blue reminded me of your eyes, dear," she said as she unfolded a length of tiny, shiny ribbon roses. "Sew these on something for your wedding day, or for your new home."

"But Daddy's already fussing about how much—"

"This a gift, Emma. I'd like you to have it."

Nodding mutely, Emma swiped at her eyes. How she hated it that she cried as quickly when folks did her favors as when they brought up the subject of her mother. She was made of tougher stuff! She should be over this by now!

"Th-thank you," she murmured miserably. "These are just the thing for the nightgown Mercy's made for my wedding night. You've been very k-kind."

A weathered hand squeezed hers, and then Maude cleared her throat briskly, to shoo away the gloom that had settled over their transaction. "Let's not forget your mail—and you might as well take the Malloys', too. I'm sure they're busy with foaling and the spring plowing—and all those children! Mercy has her hands full!"

"Yes, ma'am, I'm stopping there on my way home."

The little bell above the door tinkled as she hurried out, determined to quit crying before anyone else saw her. Everyone meant well, but it only made her situation more difficult when people felt sorry for her. Eight months had passed since that hot August day when hordes of grasshoppers hit the ground like hail and ate everything in their path . . . including the green gingham dress her mother was wearing.

High time they all set their pity aside! She was tired of feeling like a charity case, when these weeks before the wedding should be the happiest of her life.

The Reickmann boy was hefting a crate of peaches beside the fifty-pound bag of flour already in the back of her buckboard. Feeling generous, she clutched her precious package of lace to take a nickel from her reticule.

"Thanks, Stephen."

He flashed her a gap-toothed grin, and then wove the fingers of both hands into a step-up for her. She whooped when he gave her an unexpected boost above the driver's seat, making her skirts billow around her—which was exactly why he'd done it.

Emma settled herself on the wooden bench and raised an eyebrow at him. "Watch yourself," she warned. "Your mother'll tan your britches for sneaking a peak at mine. And I'm just the one to tell her!"

"She'll hafta catch me first!" The kid darted off, his snicker trailing in the breeze behind him.

She clucked at the horse, suddenly too excited to be bothered by Stephen's pranks. Two months from today, she would be Mrs. William Bristol! She and Billy could begin the life of her dreams in the frame house her father, Billy, and Michael Malloy were building at the corner where the two homesteads met. It wasn't as big or as fancy as the house on the Triple M, but it looked out over the trees along the Smoky Hill River, and it had plate glass windows and plank floors, and it was all theirs. Their first home!

Smiling broadly, Emma waved at Pastor Larsen as she drove by the church. Once past the livery stable, she clucked to Bessie and gave the mare her head on the open road. Bride-to-be or not, she would always love the feel of speed that made her hair billow back in the breeze and painted roses on her cheeks. Soon enough she'd have babies and all the responsibilities of managing a home, and these rides by herself would be few and far between.

Holding the reins in one hand, she reached into the sack containing her lace and the mail. She'd noticed a few letters—reason enough to be curious—but a much larger envelope had caught her eye when Mrs. Reickmann took the Malloys' mail from its slot behind the counter. Emma pulled it out, scowling at the three large wax stamps with an elaborate *E* in their centers.

They were pink.

When she flipped the envelope over to read the address, her eyes widened. It was addressed to Billy—in very elegant, feminine handwriting.

"Whoa, Bess," she crooned. "Whoa, girl—easy now."

She pulled off to the side of the road and wrapped the reins on their hook. Was it her imagination, or did she smell lavender? Perfume, perhaps? The return address—*E. Massena, Richmond, Missouri*—made her heart flutter because that was Billy's hometown, and E. Massena obviously wanted to get his attention, sending an oversized letter like this!

Emma blinked, her fingers itching. Should she?

She could always say the wax seals had been broken before she got it: mail that traveled by train got crammed so haphazardly into those leather bags, after all. And it wasn't as if she and Billy wouldn't be sharing every dream and secret as man and wife.

Before her conscience could talk her out of it, her finger slipped beneath one pink seal, and then another. With a little gasp she popped the third one, glad the vellum envelope didn't tear with her efforts. Who could possibly be contacting her Billy? He hadn't lived in Missouri for more than ten years! The Bristols had lost their breeding stock to bandits and their home to a scalawag of a banker, so as far as she knew, Billy had nothing to go back for in—

She let out a low whistle. She'd pulled a small painting from the envelope, and it showed an impressive white house with pillars along the front porch. It sat back from the road, and the long driveway was lined on both sides with trees painted at the peak of their autumn glory. In the bottom corner, she made out "E. Massena" in the same perfect penmanship she'd seen on the envelope.

So this picture had been painted by the same young lady who'd written the note she pulled out next.

"Dear Billy," Emma whispered. . . .

It's been such a long time since we've seen each other. I thought you might enjoy a memento of your home place, the way it looked before the war. I painted it from memory, from the times Mother would bring me to visit your mama and Christine. Sad to say, the house and stables are in a state of disrepair that would break your heart.

Emma glanced at the painting again, even though it made her pulse pound painfully. The Bristol kids had obviously lived a very fine life before their wayward mother abandoned them on a stagecoach. No wonder Billy's sister had run off! The log houses here, so dark and plain, must have been a painful comedown for these children of the upper crust.

And if this young woman had painted it from memory, with such detail that Emma could almost feel the comfort of the shade on that front porch, Miss Massena had also enjoyed a privileged life. The only kind of paint they saw out here on the Kansas prairie was the kind used on the walls of houses and barns.

Emma read on, gripping the page so the breeze didn't snatch it away. She suddenly had to read every line this E. Massena had written to Billy, and then fill in her own assumptions between them.

I thought you'd also like to know that I've seen your brother Wesley. He's grown into a big fellow with the same ornery twinkle in his blue eyes he had when we were kids. Still doing his best to find trouble, it seems. Which is why I'm writing you this letter.

"Oh, here it comes," Emma muttered. She read on, as fast as her limited book learning allowed, until the words blurred before her eyes.

There are things I think you would want to know, Billy, so I've decided to come to Abilene this summer to visit with you. If you could send me back directions on how to find you—

"I don't think that's going to happen," Emma muttered. But she kept reading.

—I'll catch you up on all the local gossip in person. I know you're probably still upset at how Daddy foreclosed on your home, but things are very different around here since he hanged himself in the barn five years ago. Mother still plays the organ for church and gives piano lessons, while I teach in the little school—

Impatient, Emma skipped to the very end. What did *she* care about this presumptuous Miss Massena and her mother?

—hope your mama is doing well, but it's you I need to talk with, Billy. I have a very special favor to ask. I hope you're as eager to see me and hear my news as I am to tell you about it. Fondly, Eve.

Fondly? Who did this Eve think she was, demanding a favor of Billy a decade after her daddy had turned them out of their home? Her name alone conjured up images of that snake and the apple in the Garden of Eden.

Emma pressed her lips together hard as she reread the letter. Bad enough that this Eve could paint. She also wrote a pretty hand and probably lacked for none of the social graces Mama had tried in vain to teach her before she'd died last year.

Emma took a long breath, trying to control sudden tears and her runaway heart. Her life hadn't been the same without her mother, and she'd invested every last one of her hopes in Billy Bristol. When she thought of forever keeping house for her father, wasting away as a spinster on the dusty plains, Emma Clark felt a deep, dark desperation wrap itself around her heart like a shroud.

Billy was all she had. She was crazy for him, yes—always had been. No other man had ever caught her fancy.

So without another thought, Emma ripped the letter in four pieces and watched them flutter away like drunken doves, dipping and whirling in the wind. No need for Billy to see this letter, or to encourage some pampered neighbor girl from his childhood, because by the time Eve got here, he'd be a married man. *Her* man.

That's why God had brought him to Kansas, after all.

Emma took another long look at the painting and then ripped it in pieces, too. What purpose did it serve to dredge up the past? Or to resurrect the twin Billy and his mama had figured for dead, after all these years of not hearing anything about him? She could just see Virgilia Bristol hauling her boy back to Missouri, in search of the Wesley who'd been snatched by the Border Ruffians when they ransacked the family's horse ranch.

Who knew when they'd be back? She would *not* postpone the wedding!

And who knew if Eve Massena wasn't using Wesley as bait to lure them back for her own purposes? A banker's daughter who'd been reduced to teaching school—not married yet—had to be pretty desperate, to write such a letter and send it to Abilene. How did she know Billy still lived here? It was a shot in the dark, at best.

Emma took up the reins and clucked to Bessie. A little voice inside her hinted that she'd been wrong to read Billy's mail, much less tear it up.

"But I did it for you, Billy," she whispered fiercely, urging the horse up to speed. What was that verse in the Bible about letting the dead bury the dead? Even Mike and Mercy Malloy would agree that Miss Massena was up to no good.

Not that she'd mention the letter to them. Or to anyone else.

Chapter One

Two months later, in June

"A man might as well fasten a noose around his neck as button one of these dang shirt collars," Billy muttered. Try as he might, his callused fingers wouldn't work the button through its stiff new hole. He was sweating already. Still had to put on his suit jacket before stepping into the sanctuary, in front of everyone he knew.

The organist began to play. It didn't help one bit that Gabe Getty, his best man and best friend, watched him with the smug look of a fellow whose skinny neck never gave him such problems.

"Here, let me try it." Gabe's dark curls quivered with his effort not to laugh. "We'd better show ourselves out front before Emma throws a hissy fit, thinking you've backed out—"

"Now there's a thought!" Billy grimaced when Gabe stuck a finger between his neck and the starched collar. "We could slip out the back way, and I could head to St. Louis with you on the train. You could start your apprenticeship with that lawyer while I—"

"Sounds like you've got a major case of cold feet."

With a grunt, Gabe finally forced the button through the hole, and then stepped back to study Billy's expression. "You've had a while to think about this wedding, and we both know what Emma will be like as a wife. I haven't seen you this skittish about anything since the day we slit our arms with that big knife and became blood brothers."

Billy considered this, wishing he had a clear, decisive response to Gabe's insinuation. "It's just . . . I dunno, a big step. Sure, we've got the house almost finished, and it's not like I've got anybody else in mind to marry, but—"

"Emma has to be the boss. She'll make you toe her line every day of your life, Billy. And you knew that when you asked her."

Billy tugged at the collar to give himself more swallowing space. He could *not* tell his best friend that Emma had popped the question, and that he'd been so flummoxed—with no real reason to turn her down—that he'd gone along with it. He was pretty sure she'd be disappointed with the plain gold band he'd picked out, too, after flat out telling him she wanted a ruby or an emerald.

But he was a ranch manager, not a Romeo or a rich man. He'd bought most of the materials for building their house, believing that was a more practical investment.

Would Emma think it was good enough? Would she think *he* was good enough, after the excitement of this wedding day wore off?

"Come on, Billy. No use in standing back here, chewing your lip off," Gabe said with a good-natured chuckle. "If we wait any longer, they'll send Joel back here to be sure you haven't ducked out of town."

"Yeah, it's now or never. It'll all work out." He shrugged into the suit coat Gabe held for him, shaking his head. "Sure is a dang sight easier handlin' horses all day than tryin' to do everything just right so she won't cry."

"Well, you're the most decent, steady fellow I know, William Henry," Gabe said, slapping his shoulder. "If Emma can't be happy with you, she doesn't stand a chance with anybody."

Not that it's much consolation, Billy thought. Forcing a grin, he locked hands with the kid he'd loved and trusted since they'd both come to Kansas ten years ago, fresh from their own separate misfortunes.

"Blood brothers—through thick and thin," he whispered fiercely, because it would sound girlish to say how much he'd miss Gabe when his friend left for St. Louis tomorrow.

"Blood brothers through thick and thin," the slender scholar echoed. "Still out to right the wrongs of this world, no matter what!"

Billy sighed. He'd been vowing vengeance against the Border Ruffians who killed his father before burning his family's barns, while Gabe wanted justice for his family, killed in an Indian attack. Those were big promises they'd made as little kids.

So why did promising to love, honor and cherish Emma suddenly seem so much more difficult than their boyhood vows?

Once Gabe opened the small door leading into the sanctuary, there was no backing out. People he knew— *lots* of people from around town—were filing into the back of the church. The folks who mattered most in his life sat right there in the front pews, watching him.

Mama flashed him a smile, gripping her lace handkerchief. She looked pretty in a suit the color of summer leaves, seated beside Carlton Harte, her second husband. He wore his usual benign look to cover whatever little dramas he'd endured on the way to the church.

They seemed happy, though. Billy was just relieved that after months of the neighbors' clucking over their living together, his mother had finally married the Pinkerton operative who'd rescued her from a postwar hustler. They had a home in Topeka now, a few hours away. He was sorry the space beside them was empty, but his sister Christine was in the family way again and couldn't make the trip from San Francisco.

The faces beaming at him from across the aisle made him smile in spite of his nerves. The Malloy kids were dressed in their finery and polished to a shine: hard to believe Lily was now eight, all a-sparkle in pink with ribbons in her long, blond hair. He clearly recalled the Easter morning they'd found her in a basket on Mercy's doorstep—and today she was singing for them, so grown up his heart clutched a little.

Beside her, Solace fidgeted with the collar of her deep green dress—he knew *that* feeling! The wedding excited her, but she'd much rather be working the horses with him, dressed in her denim pants. With her dark curls and snapping brown eyes, Solace Monroe was the image of her deceased daddy, Judd—Billy's special girl, because he'd birthed her during a blizzard, when Mercy had no other help but him and Malloy and Asa.

And Asa, bless his heart, sat between Solace and Joel to keep them quiet. He looked older these days, and thinner. But that wrinked, coffee-colored face held all the wisdom of Solomon and the love of the Lord as he gazed proudly up at him and Gabe in their new suits.

Joel was gawking around the church, looking for a way to escape. At eleven, the kid had a restless spirit and he flitted from one interest to the next like a bird darting at worms. He wasn't happy about wearing a shirt with a buttoned collar, either, and Billy suspected Joel would either sneak away—maybe crawl under the pews!—or cause enough ruckus that Michael would usher him down the side aisle for a sermon all his own.

Next to Joel sat Temple Gates, the children's teacher and the Malloys' household helper. Serene and lovely in a gown the color of butterscotch, she kept a watchful eye on her flock—and kept a firm, brown hand at the ready to grab Joel. She was indispensable to Mercy during meals and at bedtime; a model of faith and strength who'd bonded these patchwork children into a family after Mike and Mercy took her in.

The white-haired headmistress beside Temple regarded him regally: Mercy's Aunt Agatha ran the prestigious Academy for Young Ladies that had surely saved Christine from ruination. Her wealth and sense of decorum set her above the humble homesteaders hereabouts, but Miss Vanderbilt believed anyone could better himself—which was why she'd so generously offered Gabe Getty a room in her home while he studied with a St. Louis lawyer she knew.

She'd advised Emma about wedding etiquette, too . . . and graciously held her tongue when his bride-to-be turned up her nose. Aunt Agatha and Mercy had always been his staunch supporters, however, and Billy knew he'd be asking their help and opinions often in the coming months.

And Mercy—how she beamed at him, with such love in her eyes! Because she'd helped Emma with the wedding preparations—and didn't want the bride's side of the church to be empty—she'd insisted their family would sit across the aisle. Just as she'd insisted from the beginning that *he* was part of their family. Strands of silver now accented her chestnut hair, but she sat tall in her new yellow dress, her hand wrapped in Michael's as she smiled at him.

Billy shifted nervously, wondering if this organ song would ever end. Everyone in the church was looking at him, waiting for the bride to make her appearance.

But it was Michael Malloy's gaze that gave him pause. This man who'd assumed the role of father for

Mercy's children considered Billy his son, too—and Billy had been the most concerned about how Michael would react when he and Emma became engaged last fall. He owed Mike Malloy more than he could possibly repay, for the solid foundation he'd provided an abandoned boy who'd been little for his age, and so badly in need of a home and a purpose.

As the owner of the Triple M Ranch, Malloy stood head and shoulders above most of the other locals financially, but his shrewd, progressive thinking—and solid knowledge of horses—had gotten him there. Nobody had given Michael any breaks or handed him this life on a silver platter: Malloy was the most decent, hardworking man Billy knew, and he was grateful he could remain at the Triple M as his manager, where the work—and the company of these fine people—sustained him. It was Michael who'd offered to build them a house, and Michael who'd drawn the plans for it and directed most of the building, all while doing his own wheat farming and raising the finest Morgan horses in Kansas.

Billy swallowed, fingering his collar again as the organ wheezed into a higher registration. Malloy's gaze didn't waver: It was fixed on his eyes, as though asking him, *Billy, is this what you really want?*

And once again Billy was face-to-face with the questions that had niggled at him since September, when Emma had caught him unawares with her proposal. He had some doubts, sure, but didn't every new husband?

He worried because last year's invasion of grasshoppers had wiped out the wheat and corn crops, and their gardens, for the second year in a row. If the insects had laid eggs—and surely they had—folks might have to face a third such devastating event this summer. How would he and Emma have food to put up? She and her daddy had barely scraped by this winter.

And Emma Clark wasn't as stalwart as she used to

be. Watching her mother go berserk and run to the river, while those hoppers ate away her dress, still haunted Emma. And why wouldn't it? Rachel Clark had fallen and hit her head before rushing into the water to kill the horrid creatures crawling all over her. Emma and her father had called to her, running as fast as they could, but their cries were muffled by the racket of those grasshoppers devouring everything in their path. By the time they'd pulled Rachel from the river, she was too far gone to save.

Billy shifted again. He'd prayed on it often, but still didn't have an answer for why God had allowed those bugs to descend like a cloud of death and destruction. He'd asked himself plenty of times if he could be the steadying hand Emma needed, in case those eggs from last year's invasion hatched into a repeat performance this summer.

But who could say?

And who could guarantee them the happiness Michael and Mercy had found together? And what would he do if Emma had dreams he couldn't make come true? Her head was full of female notions these days; even before her mother's death, she'd changed from the solid, sturdy tomboy he'd met ten years earlier. She was a woman now, every bit as temperamental as his sister Christine. And that scared him.

A rustling in the congregation made him look up. Beside him, Gabe straightened, gazing down the center aisle at his cousin, arrayed in a gown of flowing white, peering coyly from beneath her veil.

Emma. A bride—*his* bride.

And when she gazed at him, her hand in her daddy's bent elbow, Billy got a quivery feeling in his gut. Was it love, or was the chicken he ate for dinner about to fly back up his throat? Mrs. Reid, the organist, brought the congregation to its feet with the thundering chords of the wedding march.

Little Grace Malloy stepped and paused with the calculated poise Mercy's Aunt Agatha had taught her, strewing petals of roses and orange blossoms from her white basket. Her pixie face was alight with glee at being part of the ceremony, and Billy had to grin at her. She was six now; born on the day his sister Christine had married and moved to California. Gracie was a pretty little thing, with Mercy's large, doelike eyes and Michael's sandy hair and unruffled disposition.

Before they knew it, *she* would be a bride—but first Billy had to get through today's ceremony. Preferably without tripping over the hem of Emma's wedding gown or doing anything else he'd live to regret.

After a moment of letting her gaze flutter over all the people admiring her, Emma Clark started down the aisle at a stiff, determined gait. Her father looked flummoxed, as though the warm summer day and the financial drain of this wedding were working on his nerves.

Billy knew the feeling. To keep from yanking the starched collar off his shirt, he gripped his fist . . . took a deep breath . . . prayed this was the right thing—the way God wanted him to go.

Next thing he knew, Emma was taking his arm, and Reverend Larsen was making his introductory remarks. Then Lily, the princess in pink, was stepping up beside the organ to sing her first song.

Billy nipped his lip. He had a fleeting thought about slipping away to toss up the knot that rolled in his stomach—

But it was too late for that, wasn't it?

Chapter Two

Eve Massena lumbered up to the door of the mercantile, holding herself. She stopped to wipe her brow, gritting her teeth against a low, sharp pain. Where was everyone on this fine Saturday afternoon in June? Back home, the streets would be bustling with carriages. Servants would be out fetching fresh meat and vegetables for Sunday dinner—at least for those who could still afford hired help and groceries they didn't grow themselves.

But this dusty spot in the road called Abilene was obviously not home. Still, the train came here. The stores looked prosperous enough, and several hotels beckoned to her aching, tired back.

But Eve saw no one. Just a number of buckboards hitched in front of the church, as though there might be a funeral.

She grimaced again and swung the mercantile door open, annoyed by its tinkling bell. The store smelled of grass seed and pickles swimming in a barrel of brine. Bolts of calico along the back wall bespoke home-sewn clothing only poor relations would wear in public. And though she saw quite an array of tinned foods and saddles, candles and hatchets, the items were bunched alongside each other in no particular order.

At the counter sat a rumpled boy of perhaps twelve, surveying her with suspicion as he chawed on a black licorice stick. Eve knew instinctively that he had snitched his candy from the glass jars when nobody was looking.

"Who runs this place?" she demanded. The query came out more sharply than she'd intended, but she had no time for an insolent kid.

"They're down to the church." The boy gawked at her as though he'd never seen a woman before.

"Could you *please* go and fetch someone?" she replied shrilly. "I need to find—"

"Not buttin' in on that service," the kid said with a smirk. When he wiped his mouth with his sleeve, the sight of his black tongue nearly made her gag. "Pa told me to set right here till him and Ma got back. So I am."

Her first impulse was to fish in her dress pocket for a nickel, but she had none. Only a piece of newsprint, old and folded, rustled there when she walked. To bolster her flagging patience, she fingered the clipping.

"How long will they be?" she asked, hoping she didn't have to while away the entire afternoon in this stuffy little store. She wouldn't *last* all afternoon, the way her belly was shifting. Her temples throbbed and her back felt as if somebody was whacking it with a hammer

"No tellin'. Reverend Larsen, he's plenty long-winded when—"

" 'Reverend Larsen' does not require the additional subject '*he*' in that sentence," Eve informed him. Once a school marm, always a school marm, even though her teaching position was a thing of the past.

Not that grammar mattered, when she felt so desperately hot and exhausted and alone in this awful town. If there was indeed a funeral—or heaven forbid, if—

"I hope it's not one of your family being buried?"

The kid laughed, displaying large front teeth smeared with black licorice.

What a stupid question! she chided herself. He'd be at the church himself if—

But her mind simply wasn't working anymore. Eve wondered if her trip to Abilene was her worst idea yet—and she'd made her share of stupid mistakes lately. But she refused to knuckle under. She refused to grovel or cower back home, and she would certainly not let this rude, candy-chomping kid belittle her by—

"You swallow a punkin seed, lady, or you just fat?"

The blood rushed from her head as heat scorched her cheeks. "None of your business, you—"

"So how come you wet yourself?"

Eve clenched her jaw against an outburst that would only fuel the boy's crudeness. It was time to go elsewhere, but a wave of hot, prickly nausea made her close her eyes and stand still until it passed. As if the humiliation of a soaked skirt weren't enough, her belly began bobbing visibly.

"Some cowpoke git in your britches?" The kid leaned on the counter, his eyes burning with curiosity as he pointed his black braid of candy at her. "Plenty of that goes on here, ya know. What with ranch hands comin' into town of a Saturday night—why, if you're lookin' for a man to—"

"Billy Bristol," she wheezed. It felt as if a huge steel hand had just clamped around her belly.

"*Billy* done that?" The kid hopped gleefully onto the counter. "Why, it's Billy down at the church gettin' married! This very minute! Wait'll I tell—"

"You move from that counter, young man, and I'll slap you into Kingdom Come!"

Where she found the strength to say that, and to point a finger as only an incensed school marm could, Eve didn't know. Her exhaustion was suddenly replaced by a fear so desperate—so driving—that she turned on her heel like a bulky ballerina.

If Billy Bristol was getting married, she had not a moment to waste.

If Billy Bristol was getting married, she had no one left on the face of this earth to turn to. Had she driven all the way from Missouri, with just the clothes on her back, in this awful heat, for *nothing*?

Eve Massena refused to accept that.

That blasted bell tinkled above her head as the door slammed behind her. She waddled as fast as her bulk would allow, sweating profusely. Her thoughts churned full throttle as she focused on the church down the street. The slickness between her aching legs disgusted her. Fear nearly choked her now, and she wanted to vomit. What if she didn't find Billy in time?

It was wrong to interrupt a wedding ceremony. She'd grown up knowing the rules at church, respecting those who attended even though she'd walked away from religion this past year. Too confining. Too quick to condemn, those good Christians back home. And her mother, the organist, was the leader of the pack who'd heaped guilt and shame upon her at every turn. She needed Jesus more than ever now, but everyone else in her life made churchgoing unthinkable, made it clear her condition would offend the Lord, as it obviously offended them.

But that was behind her.

Before her, the simple church beckoned. Eve walked faster, aware of her ungainly sway and the ridicule she was inviting by coming here. No doubt her condition would embarrass Billy—not to mention his bride. Why would he have any use for her, the daughter of the man who'd foreclosed on his home? He'd probably torn up her letter rather than bothering to respond.

But he was all she had. The thinnest thread of hope hung on her belief that Billy Bristol would understand her predicament. That he would right the wrongs of his wayward twin brother.

Eve stopped with her hand on the door. Organ music swelled, making her frown at the memory of her mother's playing.

Was she too late? Had the couple been pronounced man and wife?

She gripped the door handle as another powerful wave of pain crested in her belly. She'd waited too long—had no time to waste if she wanted to see Billy while he was still single and she was able to make coherent conversation.

She wanted to kill Wes for heaping this humiliation on her!

And then the music from inside washed over her, a progression of triplets she would have recognized anywhere, from the familiar Bach tune her mother had played for dozens of weddings.

Jesu, Joy of man's desiring,
Holy wisdom, love most bright.
Drawn by Thee, our souls aspiring,
Soar to uncreated light.

For a blissful moment Eve forgot her misery. The singer sounded very young, but what a voice! She sang with utter trust and conviction—

And you've left those things behind, remember?

Eve hefted the heavy door, hoping its creak didn't disturb those in the back pews. Every nerve within her jangled, telling her this was wrong—this was holy ground she was treading! God might strike her down with a lightning bolt for the way she'd behaved nine months ago, and for her motives now.

But she stepped inside, daring the Lord to interrupt a wedding with His punishment for her.

She let the door close slowly. The church was larger

than she'd expected from its plain exterior, and the pews were crammed. Billy had a lot of friends in Abilene. And he'd obviously found a woman to share his life with.

But that little inconvenience couldn't stand in her way, could it? He would probably toss her out—every thundering beat of her heart told her so. But for the sake of the baby kicking her rib cage, she had to take her chances.

Eve clutched herself to keep from crying out with another pain. The girl on the chancel steps wore a gown of shimmering pink, and long blond ringlets framed her lovely face. She looked toward Heaven as she began the second verse.

Through the way where hope is guiding,
Hark, what peaceful music rings!
Where the flock in thee confiding,
Drink of joy from deathless springs.

The irony of those words helped her focus her thoughts again. It was all well and good for these people to hear such lofty phrases, sung by a young lady in pink frills, whom they obviously adored. Eve was about to shoot down their ideas about God's providence—just as those Border Ruffians had shot Billy and Wes's father and started the decline of that fine family . . . and her own.

Folks in the congregation nodded, holding their breath as the girl's voice soared to the high ceiling. She sang like an angel, with a God-given confidence and sense of purpose Eve envied.

A collective sigh filled the church as the solo's last note lingered like a blessing in the warm, still air. Eve stood absolutely still. She swallowed hard, torn between speaking out and walking away. What right did she have to barge in on this sacred ceremony? What had Billy done to deserve the burden she was about to thrust upon him?

The preacher opened his book and intoned the familiar words that made her heart clench.

"Dearly beloved, we are gathered here in God's house to witness the sacrament of holy matrimony, to join together this man, William Henry Bristol and this woman, Emma Jane Clark."

Eve's throat tightened. She felt ugly and fat and tainted. She had no right to intrude on the bride's special day; no right to expect her childhood friend to come to her rescue, as he had when they were young. It wasn't Billy's fault his brother still couldn't tell the truth or honor his promises.

She swallowed again, battling the urge to collapse with exhaustion or vomit from agitation—or both.

"If there be anyone present who believes this man and this woman should not unite as one, let him speak now or forever hold his peace."

A spasm ripped through her abdomen and Eve cried out. Her knees buckled. As her body slid down the back wall, she saw a multitude of faces turn toward her in horror, and Billy's eyes widening in disbelief.

"My word, she's passed clean out—"

"Who in tarnation would come into a church during—"

"You can't tell me she was invited! Look at her! Obviously a harlot—"

"Step aside, please!" Malloy ordered. His voice was quiet, but commanding enough that everyone got out of his way. Mercy moved around him and knelt to cradle the young woman's head in her lap.

"Poor girl's going to deliver her baby any minute—"

"No! She can't do that here!" Emma cried, gripping her bouquet. She stood on the chancel steps, scowling behind her veil. "Of all the—"

Amid the chaos and outrageous remarks, Billy made his way down the aisle clogged with his friends and family. He'd turned in time to realize a young woman had walked in, and that she was very much in the family way, but then everyone had rushed to the back when she hit the floor.

"Who is it?" he asked, breaking through the last row of people. "Asa! Better fetch some water from the restaurant!"

"Yessir, Mr. Billy!" The wiry Negro headed for the door as fast as his stiff legs would allow. "I'll get us some tablecloths and linens, too. 'Less I miss my guess, we'll be needin' 'em real soon."

When Billy got a good look at the young woman sprawled across Mercy's lap, his eyes widened. She resembled an undernourished mare who'd been ridden hard and put away wet: her baggy dress smelled of sweat and dust, and her mane of chestnut hair had come undone. She clutched her huge belly even though she was out cold, as though she was used to defending herself and protecting that baby.

His heart lurched. He recalled delivering Mercy's firstborn during a blizzard and the hot autumn afternoon when Temple Gates bore a stillborn child despite the power of the angels in that room. Another such situation was at hand, and these crises never came at a convenient time.

Maybe this is God stepping in, a voice inside him whispered. *Maybe this unlikely angel has come to steer you down the path He wants you to follow.*

He heard Emma fussing as she came down the crowded aisle, but the other voices faded as he knelt beside Mike and Mercy.

"She's gonna birth that baby any minute now," he breathed, brushing away the damp hair that clung to the girl's face. "Where can we move her?"

"Damn right we'll move her!" Emma's face was

flushed as she broke through the murmuring onlookers to glare at the stranger's big, shifting belly. "Anybody who'd barge in on a wedding—in *her* condition—is up to no good!"

Billy closed his eyes against the sharpness of that voice. Though Emma had endured her share of grief and pain, she didn't understand the torment their uninvited guest was going through.

Asa returned then, wheezing as he came through the door with a jar that sloshed water.

"Here—give her a sip of this," Michael said quietly.

Billy took the jar and then steadied the girl's head. Beneath her damp coating of dust, she was pretty; fine-boned with a graceful, slender neck and skin the color of cream.

He fought a surge of emotion. Why did she seem familiar to him? He knew just about everyone in Abilene, and this young woman would certainly have caught his eye.

"Easy now," he murmured, placing the jar's cool rim to her lips. "You better open your eyes, hear me? Don't want this water runnin' down your chin, or chokin' you."

She shuddered. Her eyes flew open, but she couldn't focus. "I—where—"

"Never mind about that," Billy said. "Take a minute and get yourself together. You're gonna be all right."

How he knew that was beyond him. This sweaty, shaking young girl looked anything but—

Those eyes—where had he seen them? Intensely green, like the windbreak of evergreens back home, with a distinctive ring of gold around the pupils. She was looking full at him. As if she *knew* him.

When she clasped his hand, Billy felt her quivering pulse. She gulped the water greedily.

Gently he pulled the jar away. "Easy there. Don't want you to—"

"Billy," she breathed. "Please—please hear me out."

A murmur surged through the crowd, while Billy's pulse galloped. How could she possibly know him? And why had she shown up *now*?

"If I know you, you're gonna have to help me out." His voice sounded high and thin. Emma's gaze scorched the back of his neck.

"Stay calm," Mercy soothed the girl when she began to struggle. "You're scared. Maybe not in your right mind, with the baby coming so—"

"I know exactly where I am," she replied tightly. "I've come to Abilene to find Billy Bristol. Wrote you a letter last spring, and . . . you never wrote back."

Billy's jaw dropped. Things were spinning out of control way too fast. "I—sorry, but I never got a letter—"

"In my pocket," she rasped. Then her distended body arched with another contraction.

"Hang on," Mercy urged. "It'll pass better if you take deep breaths."

Billy set aside the water and gingerly reached into the girl's gritty pocket. Never had he imagined his wedding being halted for a birthing—by a stranger who knew him and said she was looking for him.

When he unfolded the limp, yellowed paper, a short laugh escaped him. "Been a day or two since we saw *this*," he said, showing the faded article to those around him. "It's the piece that reporter wrote up after I stopped Reuben and Sedalia's runaway mule. What's it been—five, six years ago?"

"At least that," Michael agreed. He was studying the girl in his wife's lap with a curious compassion that made his hazel eyes shine. "So who are you, honey? Why have you come here?"

The girl's eyes softened with gratitude, and after her contraction passed, she drew a shuddering breath. Billy was ready to burst, but he nipped back his anxious questions.

"Eve Massena," she whispered. "I wrote earlier—because—because I hoped Billy would see me through this situation—"

"Billy did not *cause* your—your *situation*," Emma blurted. "So if you'll just move along to someplace else—"

"I'm truly sorry." Eve braced for another pain, her eyes wide. "But Wesley pulled another of his quick getaways, and Billy's my last hope—"

"Last hope for what?" Emma demanded shrilly.

Eve doubled over with another contraction, her face contorting.

Wes is alive! Those Border Ruffians didn't kill him!

Billy sat back hard on the church floor, his breath escaping in a rush. The confused expressions around him were nothing, compared to the wild way his thoughts were racing. Could it really be Eve Massena, from back home? Should he believe what she'd said about his brother?

This brought Mama out of the crowd, with Carlton right behind her. "Did somebody say my boy's name?" she rasped. The feather on her hat quivered crazily as she stared at the girl on the floor.

"Somebody's got a lot of explaining to do!" Emma replied hotly.

Billy's stomach bunched. Bad enough that his bride-to-be had gotten her plans waylaid. Now Mama was in the thick of things, at the hint her long-lost son was alive. Another plague of grasshoppers—topped by a tornado—would seem calm and controlled compared to the way *this* storm was whirling.

Chapter Three

Emma clutched her bouquet so hard, its stems cut into the hot flesh of her hand. She felt light-headed and lost, as she had when they'd lowered her mother's casket into the ground. Felt the same claustrophobic fear, as though *she* had been dropped into a grave and buried alive.

If she let this conversation go any further, her nightmare would only get worse. Who could have guessed Eve Massena would show up? And why on God's earth had she appeared *today*?

Emma recalled accounts of how Billy had helped with Solace's birthing; how he'd doted on Mercy when she grew huge with baby Grace. He had a big soft spot in his heart for women in the family way, and for their kids.

But this was terribly wrong! And so unfair!

"Billy, why do you believe a word this stranger's saying?" she demanded, not caring that Miss Massena could hear her, too. "She kept that newspaper clipping as a reminder of old times, and she's taking advantage of your trusting nature! You have no proof her baby is your brother's!"

Billy blinked. "Emma, Eve's a friend, from when Christine and I lived—"

"Well, she's obviously got no manners! Or morals! Only a *harlot* would allow—" Emma's vision blurred with anger. "Didn't this girl's daddy foreclose on your home? And besides, we're getting *married* today, Billy! What about all the months of preparation that've gone into this wedding? How can you let this intruder change our plans? Our *lives*?"

His deep blue eyes watched her, but anyone could see Billy Bristol was a man adrift. His mind was in Missouri, and somebody had to talk some sense into him, because Mike and Mercy Malloy would remain neutral. They had a reputation for allowing their children to make their own mistakes and choices.

Well, this wouldn't be one of them!

"Billy, please! *Do* something," she pleaded, widening her eyes at him. "All these people are staring at her, wondering about the wedding—"

"Don't you dare imply that my Wesley is the father of your misbegotten baby!" Billy's mama had suddenly come out of her shock, and she planted her fists on her hips. The feather on her stylish green hat fluttered like a wild bird's wing. "Even as a girl, you tried to lure my sons into—"

Virgilia Bristol Harte looked as startled—yet as excited—as Emma had ever seen her. And *she* had traveled the country posing as a land office agent, selling cheap Bibles, and pretending to be a medium. *Nothing* bothered her! Yet now she was dabbing at her eyes, disregarding her husband's attempts to settle her. Such quicksilver mood changes had always irked Emma, and this was no time for Virgilia's theatrics!

"How *is* he? Wesley, I mean?" Billy's mother breathed. She clutched her hanky, searching for words. "After all this time, not knowing whether he was dead or alive, I can't believe I'm hearing—where does he live? What does he *do*?"

"Your precious Wesley promised to marry me, and

then left me in this—*unseemly* predicament!" Eve muttered. Her jaw clenched with contractions that were coming much closer together now, and she looked extremely uncomfortable. "I should've known better than to trust an outlaw! But I thought I loved him."

Oh, this wasn't sounding good at all! Emma caught the murmurs running through the curious crowd and tried to take the reins again.

"Billy," she whispered tersely, "you've got to do something! This girl can't just have her baby in church—during our wedding! We need to—"

Something flashed in Billy's blue eyes, like the spark when an icicle snaps in the sunlight. He nodded; looked again at Mercy Malloy, who cradled the girl from his boyhood, and then at Michael, who wore the same wise concern on his handsome face Emma had seen in every time of crisis.

"Whatever you think, son, we're with you," Malloy said softly. "This is a tough call, but you'll do the right thing."

Billy drew a deep breath. He stood up, gazing at the anxious guests around them.

"Folks, this isn't convenient, but I'm askin' you to leave now, so we can deliver Eve's baby," he said. "We'll let you know when to come back for the ceremony."

"*What?*"

Somehow Emma refrained from slapping him with the bouquet that grew limper each time she squeezed it. He'd just called a halt to their *wedding*! Didn't he realize the gossip this would cause?

Emma stood taller, watching the chattering crowd that was now heading for the door. By God, if Billy could make such a decision—without even asking her—she'd show him who would *not* be the doormat of their new home!

"Come back next Saturday," she called after them,

not meeting his eyes—or his mother's. "Same time in the afternoon. And thank you for coming today."

Fueled by the keen disappointment Billy had just caused her—the *humiliation* of having to come to church a second time—she reached behind her to gather the beautiful silk train of her wedding gown. She would show Billy, and everyone here, what she was made of! She would speak her mind and then take action. No bride with any sense would behave differently!

"We'll talk about this later, Billy," she muttered, "when I'm not feeling so embarrassed and rejected by the man I've loved for half my life."

She turned and searched the sanctuary. Her father, looking old and worn out in the suit he'd borrowed, slumped against the end of the rear pew.

"Come on, Daddy, we're going home. Billy has important matters to tend to—without me."

A lump rose in Billy's throat, lodging so tightly he couldn't speak. He watched Emma Clark, decked out in her beautiful wedding dress—for him—stride out the church door as though she never wanted to see him again.

He understood that. No man in his right mind chose another woman's predicament over his bride.

What bothered him most, however, was that Emma refused to believe Eve Massena's wounds went far deeper than her own. While it was an embarrassment to walk away unmarried—something folks around Abilene would cluck over for years—the young woman writhing on Mercy's lap had been stripped of her dignity, her self-respect, and any chance at social acceptability.

And it was all because his twin was up to his old tricks: causing a big stir and then ducking out, so his victim bore the burden of guilt and shame. Lord knows he'd felt the sting often enough when *he'd* been left to explain Wesley's shenanigans.

But a baby . . . a woman left alone to bear it in disgrace. Eve Massena still had several questions to answer about her situation—like why her parents had allowed her to leave home in her condition. Right now, though, they had a baby to deliver.

"Let's go, Virgilia," Carlton Harte said, taking Mama's elbow.

"But that's my grandchild. Wesley's own—"

"And you'll love it even more after it's cleaned up." The detective's expression suggested he knew more about this whole thing than he was letting on, but Billy was just relieved to see them go.

"I'd better look after Emma," Gabe suggested, warily watching Eve squirm in her agony. "Unless you want me to stay and—"

"No, somebody needs to be with her."

Like me, his conscience jeered.

But Eve Massena needed him more right now, and she had too many answers he needed to hear. When Temple Gates and Aunt Agatha escorted the children next door for pie, the sanctuary echoed with the laboring woman's insistent moans and the soothing remarks Mercy and Mike made.

Let this go right, God, he prayed fervently. *And let everybody live to tell about it.*

Eve wanted to die. Or at the very least, have the floor open up to swallow her. Never in her most desperate dreams had she imagined her reunion with Billy Bristol happening this way!

But ever since Mother had cast her out, her life had been spiraling downward. No place to stay, no one to turn to. She'd come to Kansas on the slim chance of finding Billy—or someone who'd put her up until this brat was born—but the horse had spooked during a storm. She'd started out in fairly good condition, clean and hopeful and determined. But that rain had drenched her and ruined her hair; the rutted road had rattled her bones the whole way here. Cinders from a passing train had nearly caught her borrowed dress on fire. And then she'd had her own private flood when sticky fluid gushed from her body and soaked her skirt, a few miles outside of Abilene.

Was it supposed to happen that way? Or was her body taking revenge for the way she'd given herself to Wes Bristol in a weak moment?

Mama had never discussed such personal matters, so Eve had worried she was about to die, right there in the wagon, out on the street. Somehow, she hadn't believed things could get worse.

Yet here she was surrounded by strangers—in a church, of all places—unable to help herself. Unable to present herself as a reasonable young woman wanting a big favor from the twin of the man who'd put her in this predicament.

How she *hated* feeling beholden! Being laid low by misfortune, and at the whim of her traitorous body and the baby she'd despised from the moment she knew it lived within her.

And now these do-gooders were about to deepen her degradation.

"I can—if you'll just leave me here to see to this—I'm truly sorry I interrupted—"

"Nonsense," the sandy-haired man beside her replied. She liked his eyes, and the compassionate smile that didn't judge her.

"Sometimes God works things out in ways we can't understand," he went on, "but He always, always has our best interests at heart. He answers our prayers and sends us help, even when we're too far gone to ask for it."

"Amen to that!" came a cheerful voice from the door. The old colored man who'd gone for tablecloths had returned with a tall stack of them, plus a bucket of steaming water that probably outweighed his skinny body.

"You's in the right place, child," he went on, his coffee-colored face creasing in a hundred places. "Why, Billy and me and Michael here—we's brought a lot of little babies into this world. The doctor, he's outta town. Healthy as you look, though, I's bettin' we won't even need him."

"Let's spread these linens on the floor," suggested the woman who held her, "and Billy, you'd probably better take off that new suit coat. Wouldn't do to have blood on it next Saturday."

Billy nodded, slipping the deep blue jacket from his arms.

Eve studied him through her haze of pain. He wasn't as burly as Wes, nor as tall, but he displayed a graceful strength: muscled arms and hands that looked capable and work-worn. His skin was burnished by the sun, which made those twinkling blue eyes even more gorgeous and set off his thicket of auburn hair. He layered the tablecloths on the floor nearby, and then gave her a purposeful look.

"Let's shift her this way, Mercy, so we'll have a clean surface for the baby."

"You're *not* going to watch while I—"

"Nope," he said, returning her gaze as he rolled up his shirtsleeves. "I'm gonna be right here helping that baby out. It's either me, or Michael, or Asa—but it's more my place, since Wesley apparently—"

"Lord, *no*! You're not going to—I'm fat and ugly and—"

"No, you're not." He flashed her a grin that took her back a few years. "You're not gettin' things your way, and you're peevish about it. Just like when we were kids. Just like my sister Christine."

"I am *not* peevish! It's just so embarrassing! To have a man—"

"Honey, you'll soon find out that your definitions differ from the way men see it," Mercy Malloy said with a low laugh. "Billy's helped dozens of mares when they foaled. And he delivered my daughter Solace during a blizzard, when he was only eleven. Whether you know it or not, God guided you to the right place."

Eve was too overcome by another grueling spasm to reply. Could her body withstand any more of this awful pain? She clenched her eyes shut as the contraction ripped through her belly. Despite her protests, they shifted her over to a folded tablecloth. And when Billy gently raised her skirts, she thought she'd absolutely die.

Billy tried not to gape at her long, slender legs. Her creamy skin felt so soft as he lowered her soggy drawers.

"Here's the head already," he murmured reverently. "Won't be much longer now, Eve. Ride out your pains, and give a big push when you're ready."

How could he sound so calm about this? Her belly felt ready to split in two with the awful pressure. The next contraction hit her right on the tail of the previous one, and she cried out for mercy.

"Scream all you want," the old colored man said, "but save a part of your mind for that little baby, so's you can help it into this world. Seems to me a fine thing, to be born in a church. A sign from God and his angels that you's done the right thing, a-comin' here."

Eve blinked. How could he make such a pronouncement—as though he had powers to know about God's presence, and about angels?

She gasped at the lightning strike of another pain. "If this baby doesn't come out soon, I'm likely to die of the—oh, Lord—"

"You're doing fine, Eve," Michael encouraged, while Mercy held her shoulders.

"Head's out!" Billy whispered. He felt utter wonderment, even though he'd caught more than his share of slippery little bodies coming from their mothers.

But this was Wes's child! And this young woman bringing it into the world was unlike any mother he'd ever tended—even if her father *had* betrayed them years ago.

"One more good push. Come on, Eve, you can do this," he coaxed her.

When Mother Nature and Eve worked together, a tiny, blood-covered baby slithered into his waiting hands.

The awe he'd felt at previous births returned in a rush. With hushed voices, Asa and Michael tended to the baby on clean cloths and wiped its squirming body. Its eyes were pinched shut but that little mouth opened, and what began as a timid hiccup became a wail that echoed through the sanctuary.

"You's got a daughter!" Asa crowed. "She looks fine and dandy, too. Almost as pretty as her mama!"

Eve was too spent to respond. Emotions rose from deep within her: relief, yet despair. Victory, yet sharp misgivings. These people obviously had a lofty opinion of babies, but this wasn't the time to say they could *have* the damn kid if they were so overjoyed! How could *she* possibly give it a home?

She'd only carried it all these months because she'd had no choice. Too late she'd realized she had misplaced her trust when she gave herself to Wesley Bristol in a daring flash of passion.

And now she was a mother. She had a little girl.

For a few fleeting moments, Eve Massena's tired mind found sanctuary in the memories of her own early childhood, when Daddy and Mother had adored her. They'd dressed her like a fine china doll, and taught her all she needed to find the right man someday, and to run his household. He would be well-to-do and worthy of her—

But that was claptrap, wasn't it? She was used goods now. Damaged goods, down deep. Was there a man alive who could overlook her flaws?

Chapter Four

Eve's eyes flew open. She was still half-sitting in Mercy Malloy's lap, still dazed with pain, and being offered a bundle swaddled in a white towel. She made a callous remark about what they could do with this squirming—*scary!*—little package, but the look on Billy Bristol's face took her breath away.

So like his brother's face, but leaner, it was. Bronzed by the sun, which was unusual for a man with red hair. Alight with a special quality she couldn't put a name to yet.

Her heart told her Wesley Bristol had never felt the overwhelming love she saw blazing in Billy's fiery blue eyes.

"I—I don't know what to—"

"Just take her, Eve," he murmured. And then he gave the baby a look she envied—a look she longed to see on a man's face when he gazed at *her*. "She's just a few minutes old, but already she needs her mama. Doesn't matter to her how she got here, or how you feel about it. She's hungry for *you*."

He pressed the baby into her arms. Was she so

exhausted she was beginning to believe the wonder that lit up his striking face? Was this child really the miracle he made her out to be?

Eve peered down at the wrinkled, red face and went breathless—not because the baby inspired any maternal stirrings, but because it was so *ugly*! Why, it barely had facial features or hair! Those miniature hands were flailing at her, fueling her own frustration, for she had no idea what to do.

And now the kid was crying! Screwing up that tiny face until her eyes were slits and her mouth was a hole where a huge wail came out. Eve laid it in her lap with a horrified gasp.

"I don't—I can't—"

"It's all right, dear," Mercy murmured. "Nothing really prepares us for mothering."

"Nobody told me *anything*! Mother was so outraged, she didn't speak to me for a week after she found out! She forced me to stay indoors all those months, out of sight, and when I said I was coming here to—"

Billy scooped the baby into his arms. He'd walked the floor with many a fussy child, and he'd forgotten how helpless newborns were . . . how they protested the sudden shift from their mother's womb once daylight hit their new eyes. He began the slow, rhythmic walk that was second nature to him.

"You're gonna be fine, little girl," he whispered. "We'll take good care of you and your mama, so don't you worry about a single thing, hear me? Hush-a-by . . . don't you cry. . . ."

The baby quieted. Her little hands landed on the towel, and he stroked them with his finger. Then Michael was standing beside him, and Asa, touching her cheeks in silent awe.

"I don't b'lieve I'll ever tire of seein' these fine little angel faces," the old Negro hand whispered. "I so recall holdin' your babies this-a way, Miss Mercy. Just like they's my own."

"There've been days I'd let you *have* them, too!" Mercy said with a chuckle. Then she smiled at Eve. "Asa named my daughter Solace while he was singing 'What a Friend We Have in Jesus' to her. I was so exhausted—so out of my mind, grieving her dead daddy—that Solace would've shriveled away from neglect, if it hadn't been for these three men."

Eve took a scrap of comfort from Mercy's admission that she hadn't been a perfect new mother.

"I've never seen grown men so . . . wrapped up in a baby," she agreed. That, too, was a comfort, since she herself might leave, knowing her child would have a better home here than she could ever give it. "They make it look so easy . . . so natural. I don't know a thing about—about *any* of this!"

To her horror, tears streamed down her face. She was sobbing and shuddering, further disgracing herself in front of these strangers, as though she hadn't already disrupted their day enough. Where had *this* come from? A moment ago she was plotting her escape, and now she was weak and quivering. So overwhelmed, she just wanted to sleep and shut everything out forever.

"Sounds to me like you've endured quite a lot, Eve. What with being turned out of your home, and the long ride here, and the effort of giving birth, you have every right to cry."

It was Michael speaking this time. Through her tears, Eve saw his patient smile and felt worse instead of better, because this man had no reason to accept her so unconditionally. Why, if he *knew* how she'd behaved—how she'd allowed Wes his way for the defiant thrill of it— he'd be casting her out just as Mother had.

"Let's make a stretcher out of these heavy tablecloths,"

he said to Billy and the old Negro. "She can lie across the carriage seat, out of the sun."

"When we get her home, we'll put the bassinet in the yellow room Christine stayed in. It's cooler there, and quiet," Mercy added.

Eve heard this conversation, yet felt herself drifting . . . slipping into a pain-induced stupor. It sounded as if they were talking on the other side of a wall she was holding a glass to. As they made their plans for her, she floated off.

She wanted to cry over the concern on their faces and the compassion they'd shown her. She felt she'd been beaten and left for dead on the road, like in the Bible story, and this whole tribe of Good Samaritans had wrapped her in the cloak of their unconditional love.

Eve smiled weakly, letting herself drowse. . . .

She was vaguely aware of being lifted from the sanctuary floor, on tablecloths that let her body sag as her stretcher-bearers carried her outside. She squinted in the bright sunlight. Glancing back, she saw Billy gripping the sheet behind her head, while Michael led the way, carrying her feetfirst.

Michael carefully stepped into the carriage, then held her level as he gave Billy room to enter as well. He smiled at her. "We'll have you home and in a better bed soon, honey. Asa can brew you some tea for your pain. You'll feel lots better when you wake up."

After they laid her along the leather seat, the Negro entered the carriage with the baby, whose squawking rang so sharply, Eve cringed.

"Please! Take her! I don't have the strength to—"

"She wants what only her mama can give her, Miss Eve," the Negro explained. He had to be as old as Moses, with all those wrinkles and springy hair that had gone white. "Our girl's hungry, after that hard job of bein' born. She's awaitin' for her dinner—and a name, too. Whatcha gonna call this pretty girl-child?"

Eve gaped at him. She'd been so intent on ridding herself of this burden, she hadn't considered a name for it.

When Asa stepped down the carriage stairs, Mercy Malloy came in. With a glance at Billy, she knelt beside the carriage seat where Eve sprawled.

"Turn a little. Hold the baby in the crook of your arm," she instructed softy. "She can suckle that way, and you won't have to sit up during this bumpy ride."

Eve's gaze flickered to Billy, who showed no sign of leaving. Matter of fact, he shut the carriage door and sat down across from her, as though he were settling in for the show.

Did he think she was going to expose a breast while he watched? Her cheeks tingled with embarrassment; this, coupled with her ignorance of how feeding worked, upset her so much, Eve feared no milk would come out, no matter how badly she wanted to stifle the baby's cries.

Mercy was unbuttoning her bodice, oblivious to her anguish. This total stranger had the audacity to fondle her breast and guide the baby's mouth to it! As though she hadn't suffered humiliation enough during the birth!

Then Mercy draped the tablecloth over Eve's shoulder. "If nature isn't taking its course in a few moments, I'll help you, dear," she said. "I've fed two daughters, and they were as different as spring and fall."

Eve held herself stiffly, unsure of what to do about the wet mouth fitted over her nipple. Mother had told her nothing of these mysteries. How would she even know if she was doing it wrong—

The baby sucked, feebly at first, but then with more determination. A new sensation surged through Eve: it was finally quiet in the carriage, because this baby, only minutes old, was drinking from her breast. Taking care of her own needs, even though Eve hadn't known how to meet them.

It was a humbling thought. How frightening, the way this alien, wiggling *thing* depended on her, when she had no idea what to do with it. Eve remained absolutely still so she wouldn't disturb the unnerving process.

How often would she have to feed it? What if she were busy, or out of the room, when the baby got hungry again?

Would it starve if she left it?

Eve felt the weight of Billy's gaze from across the carriage, but she couldn't look at him. She owed him her thanks—an apology for interrupting his wedding. But she kept her eyes closed and concentrated on the pull of milk between little lips she didn't want to look at, either. No sense in getting attached.

"Can't tell you how my heart started poundin' when you said Wesley was still alive," Billy said in a husky voice. "No matter what the situation is between you and him, I can't thank you enough for makin' the trip here, Eve."

Her eyes flew open. Billy's gaze was blazing with that blue fire again, and startling emotions danced over his lean, masculine face. Gratitude. Surprise. Curiosity—lots of that—sharpened by questions he was biting back so the baby wouldn't cry again.

Why didn't he seem upset? His bride had stomped off, and he was certainly going to pay for the way he'd spoiled Emma's big day. Had *she* been the jilted, set-aside bride, Billy wouldn't be able to walk right now.

Yet he sat relaxed, slightly slouched, with his legs extended toward her. This was the kid who'd been turned out of his home by her father's conniving, yet Billy Bristol had set aside his anger—had sent his mother away!—when she'd collapsed in the sanctuary. He'd shown no signs of impatience or anger or disbelief when she'd said the baby was his twin's.

Billy—and the Malloys who'd taken him in—seemed

too good to be true. Best to beware their ulterior motives—

Eve slowly lowered her eyelids so she could watch him through the filmy haze of her exhaustion without engaging in conversation. If she said too much, she'd break the spell he'd woven. His awed expression was truly a sight, even if it wasn't aimed at *her*.

"Don't worry about explaining right now," he said softly. "Plenty of time for that when you've rested. We're almost home."

Home? The confident way he said that, as though he hadn't left his bride in the lurch, made her wonder again what this redheaded sweet-talker was made of. He'd lost his home after the war, same as she'd lost hers last month. Even though his mother had returned from her galavanting and law-breaking days in the West, Billy still considered himself part of the Malloy family.

This was beyond her right now. Eve let herself drift, because the baby had finally nodded off. The bumpy road kept her from sleeping, yet the deep sense of devotion she felt in this carriage made her believe she could share in this wonderful sense of family.

She hadn't felt that way since long before Daddy killed himself.

The carriage stopped. Outside, dogs were barking a welcome and the scents of freshly cut grass, livestock, and heat came in when the door opened. Once again Asa entered, smiling as he scooped the baby into his arms. Once again she swayed on the tablecloths Michael and Billy carried her on, past a sandy-haired boy about Billy's size last time she'd seen him, with features like Mike Malloy's.

Into a white frame house they went, and Eve drank in the impressions of light, airy rooms filled with homey furniture. Aromas of ham and apple pie teased at her. They passed a young Negro woman, who greeted her with another of those kind, accepting smiles. They passed through a parlor, where that blond songbird in pink grinned at her from beside a younger, dark-haired girl who had an arm slung around a third child.

Lord, how many children did these Malloys have? And what about that young black woman? Did they still keep slaves in these parts? Or was she related to that crinkly-eyed old man who'd taken the baby?

So many things to find out. So many people she'd have to keep track of, when she was ready to break away. But Eve kept her mouth shut about that, of course.

Mercy and the young Negro woman—who had the oddest name of Temple Gates—gave her a sponge bath and a fresh nightgown, which felt heavenly soft against her skin. She gazed around the pretty bedroom, painted a soft yellow that soothed her like morning sunshine. When she sank into the bed—a real feather mattress!— Eve thought she'd died and somehow slipped past St. Peter's inquisitions, into Heaven.

"Here's Asa's tea!" a perky voice cut through her exhaustion. "Drink it all down, and don't worry a thing about your baby, Miss Eve. We're going to spoil her to pieces while you get your rest."

Surely an angel had said that! Eve recognized the young girl in pink who'd been singing "Jesu, Joy of Man's Desiring," smiling prettily as she offered a steaming cup.

Eve gulped it, eager for the release it promised. The liquid left a path of warmth down her throat and into her uneasy stomach, and she felt her entire body relax for the first time in weeks.

Moments later, she was deeply asleep.

Chapter Five

Piano music woke her, drifting through her window from the parlor below. Eve kept herself in that comforting place between dreaming and reality.

Rescue the perishing, care for the dying,
Snatch them in pity from sin and the grave.
Weep o'er the erring one, lift up the fallen
Tell them of Jesus, the mighty to save!

Eve let her mind float with the familiar hymn's rhythm. Whoever played that piano had a wonderful touch: The song flowed like rippling silk with flourishes only an accomplished musician could add to the bare-bones notes in the hymnal.

And the voices! Why, it must be an angel choir singing that four-part harmony so clearly! The choir back home had sung skillfully, but these people—why, maybe she *had* died and ascended to the Pearly Gates!

Down in the human heart, Crushed by the tempter,
Feelings lie buried that grace can restore:

Touched by a loving heart, wakened by kindness
Chords that are broken will vibrate once more!

She frowned, her mind rising toward wakefulness. That wasn't the heavenly band singing—it was the Malloy family! They sang with fervor and delight, those lines about sinners and the power of grace to save—

Which meant she'd been taken in by a bunch of do-gooders who sang not for the joy of the music, but to sway her toward their own purposes. They were girding their spiritual loins to battle Satan, who dwelled within her!

Rescue the perishing, Duty demands it
Strength for thy labor the Lord will provide.
Back to the narrow way patiently win them,
Tell the poor wandr'er a Savior has died!

Eve sat up, fighting the dizzy spin of her head. Of all the uplifting songs they could have chosen, the Malloy family instead sang a rousing, righteous chorus before reclaiming her lost soul! Well, she would have none of it.

She sat up to dangle her legs over the edge of the bed. The bassinet was empty, which made her escape a lot easier.

And now, the family was having a devotional session. Had she slept an entire day? Or was it still the Saturday she'd come to Abilene? Her head felt fuzzy from that tea; confused from waking up in a strange place.

"For our Scripture this evening, we'll read from the teachings of Jesus as recorded in Matthew's twenty-fifth chapter," a sonorous male voice began. "We're near the end of Jesus's life and ministry, when He was imparting all the spiritual knowledge He could to His disciples, for He knew He was soon to die. Listen to His words, which seem particularly meaningful today.

"When the Son of Man comes in his glory, and all the holy angels with Him, He'll sit on His throne, and before Him shall be gathered all the nations. He'll separate them, like a shepherd divides his sheep from the goats, and He'll put the sheep on His right hand, but the goats on the left."

Eve noticed how Michael Malloy delivered the Scripture in a down-to-earth way, simplifying the King James version's archaic language. After years of enduring Reverend Searcy's stilted readings, this was a pleasant change. It made the Bible feel more personal; more meaningful even to the young children she pictured in that sunny room downstairs.

"And the King shall say to those at His right, 'Come ye blessed of my Father, inherit the kingdom prepared for you from the foundation of the world. For I was hungry and you fed me, thirsty and you gave me a drink; I was a stranger and you took me in; naked and you clothed me. I was sick and in prison, and you visited me.'

"Then the righteous shall answer, saying, 'Lord, when did we see you hungry or thirsty and gave you food and drink? When did we see you a stranger and take you in, or naked and clothe you? When did we see you sick and in prison, and visit you?'

"And the King shall answer, 'I say to you that if you've done it to one of the least of these my brethren, you've done it to me.'"

Eve's feet twitched with the need to escape. It was no accident that Malloy had chosen this passage—and was reading it near the open window, for *her* benefit. They were patting themselves on the back for taking her in. They were so proud of themselves for rescuing her from her sinful situation, and would now prod her back onto the straight and narrow!

But how could she believe in this religious claptrap

now? Her mother, a pillar of the church, had cast her out with only the clothes she could carry, when she'd needed help the most.

She had to be on her way, before they brought their Bible thumping and soul saving up to this room.

"And then He'll say to those on his left, 'Depart from me, you cursed, into the everlasting fire prepared for the devil and his angels: For I was hungry and thirsty, naked and a stranger, sick and in prison, and you didn't help me. You ignored me!'" Malloy continued below her.

"Then they shall also answer Him, saying, 'Lord, when did we see you hungry or thirsty, or a stranger or naked, or sick and in prison and didn't help you?'

"Then He shall answer them, 'Since you did not help one of the least of these, you didn't help me.' And these shall go away into everlasting punishment, but the righteous into eternal life."

Scooting to the edge of the bed, Eve glowered. Now he'd warn his family not to follow the path *she* had taken—not to become the naked stranger, but to do their duty and care for her and her ill-begotten baby. To lead her back to the Upward Way for her sake and theirs, too.

No more of this. She would slip down the stairs and out the back hall, while they remained in the parlor with their songs and Scripture. She hadn't come here for sermons about her wayward inclinations. Nor would she accept help that came with such a humiliating price tag.

Eve scooted forward until her feet found the cool wooden floor. Steadying herself against the bed, she saw her dress draped over a chair. It had a dark stain in the back and was badly wrinkled, but it would have to do. Taking a clean one from the armoire would make her even more beholden to these people.

Stepping toward the dress, she teetered. Her head

did a lazy spin and her knees shook like jelly. Eve gulped air, forcing herself to remain upright.

With the next step, she wobbled. And with the third, she fell to the floor with a sharp cry.

Tears sprang to her eyes and she curled into a pitiful ball. She felt so helpless—how she hated that!—and her knees throbbed from landing on the floor. Her stomach lurched, and she feared she might retch on the pretty rag rug Mercy Malloy had probably made.

There was a pause before the pianist struck up another familiar tune, then quick footsteps on the stairs.

Eve looked up and cringed. Billy had come to check on her . . . to rescue the perishing. He'd slung the baby in the crook of his arm, as though he handled such foreign creatures all the time.

She flushed, humiliated. What could she do but accept the arm that guided her up from the floor? He'd caught her trying to leave. What could she possibly say?

And indeed, when Billy Bristol steadied her against his sturdy body, Eve forgot to chide him for becoming a two-faced Christian sheep determined to save her—a goat—so he'd look good to God. She could only blink away her tears and lean on him.

"You got up too soon," he said gently. He was smiling. Looking at her stringy hair and pale face as though she were a debutante at a ball they might've attended, had his family stayed in Richmond. "Let's get you back to bed. When you've caught your breath, you'll want to hold this little doll baby. Mama says she looks just like Wesley and me when we were born."

His mother was downstairs? Joining in with all that religion? Eve could hardly believe it, considering the articles she'd seen about Virgilia Bristol's spectacular life of crime—while living with a man she hadn't married.

She glanced at the baby, who was nuzzling at Billy's twill shirt. The down on her head shone a carroty red in the light from the window, and for a fleeting moment she imagined *this* man was the baby's father—so different from his twin. Billy was gentle and strong and kind; not likely to belittle or taunt her, the way Wes had. Wesley Bristol would have dropped this baby and run the minute she showed it to him.

And as the baby curled a tiny hand around Billy's strong, bronzed finger, Eve's heart ached for what she'd so foolishly given away—and for what she could never have.

A good man like Billy Bristol was more than she had a right to hope for.

Emma Clark wrapped her arms around the white porch post and sobbed. Would she ever live in this pretty little house that smelled of new lumber and fresh paint? Was she a fool to believe Billy Bristol was still her man?

The sunrise blazed across the eastern sky, painting the horizon with shades of flame and deep pink: the colors of her anger when she thought about how Billy had humiliated her—and how her father said she was getting paid back for the way she'd manipulated this wedding.

But what did *he* know? Heartless and cruel her daddy was, not caring that Billy's rejection had torn her in two. She'd gotten so mad she'd flung herself on her mare and ridden here straightaway, to spend the night alone—to convince herself she still belonged here, and that Billy would come back to her and make everything right again.

You saw the way he looked at that girl. He still likes her, even if her father foreclosed on his family. He's a fool to listen to her lies!

But why was she surprised? The Billy she knew had always stood by the less fortunate and stood up for those who'd been taken advantage of.

But the Billy I love delivered Eve's baby. On my wedding day. Instead of marrying me.

With another sad sigh, Emma sank against the wooden pillar. Her border collie, Boots, nuzzled her hand, whimpering in sympathy. But it wasn't enough.

No sense in spending all day here; it would only be harder to face her father—and her fiancé—if she wallowed in her misery. Better to return to her room in that dreary log house, where her wedding dress hung beside her only photograph of Mama.

Lost. Everything she'd ever loved and hoped for was gone.

Boots pricked up his ears and strained forward. Were those hoofbeats coming their way?

Emma peered around her pillar. Surely Daddy hadn't come after her—but if he had, it was to scold her for leaving him without a decent meal since yesterday. She wiped her eyes, ready to return his glare.

When she saw the glint of Gabriel's eyeglasses, however—and Hattie, the black-and-white dog who never left his side—she relaxed. He slowed his painted pony as he neared the house, and Emma realized how much taller he'd grown lately, and how—even if he was her cousin—Gabe Getty had become a fine-looking young man. At seventeen, he'd graduated from school long ago and then worked for Roger Beecham, a lawyer who'd made his name during Abilene's cattle drives.

Hard to believe he was leaving them, bound for St. Louis with Agatha Vanderbilt, who'd arranged an apprenticeship with a prominent lawyer there while Gabe continued his schooling. Just thinking about all that book work gave Emma a headache, but Gabe was perfectly suited to the scholarly life.

"Finished pouting yet?" he teased, halting his horse in front of her. His dog immediately sat down beside Boots, where they both followed the conversation intently.

"You have no idea—" She swatted at him, but he backed his horse a couple steps, still grinning.

"I asked because your behavior surprises me," he continued, arching an eyebrow. "The Emma Clark I know would've kicked Billy's butt to Kingdom Come when he postponed the wedding. It's not like you to wander off by yourself, when you could be making your displeasure known."

She blinked. Sometimes Gabe used such high-and-mighty phrases, in such an eloquent tone of voice, she wasn't sure when he was insulting her.

"I like it here at the house. *Our* house," she replied. "No point in staying there with Daddy, when he'd constantly remind me of my sorry state of—"

"For him, cuz, everything's in a sorry state. I doubt he'll ever recover from your mother's death, and I'm sorry he takes out his frustrations on you."

Gabe studied her, his brown eyes missing nothing from behind those spectacles. "But you can't hide forever. I'm going to the Triple M now, so Billy can drive Miss Vanderbilt and me to the train station. I was hoping you'd go with me, since—well, we've been like brother and sister for half our lives. I'm excited about going to St. Louis, but I'll miss you, Emma."

His raw emotion caught her by surprise. Her hand fluttered to her mouth, and she swallowed hard to prevent a whole new crying fit. He'd been scared mute— only eight years old—when he'd witnessed the Indian attack that claimed his family. It was Billy Bristol who'd coaxed little Gabe out of his silence by giving them the border collie pups who were still their constant companions.

To keep from blubbering, Emma sat on the top step to stroke his dog's soft black coat. "Hattie and I'll miss you, too, Gabe. We'll look after each other till you get home again."

Those words stuck in her throat: could be, after he got

a taste of life in St. Louis, Gabriel Getty wouldn't return to these Kansas plains. In her excitement and preparations for the wedding, that thought had escaped her.

Gabe's brave smile didn't fool her, either, but she didn't have the heart to tease him about getting homesick. Now that Mama was gone, and Billy had stood her up, and Gabe was leaving for greener pastures, it seemed the two dogs were the only friends she'd have as she faced certain spinsterhood.

Boots nudged her sharply. Those keen brown eyes looked into hers as he let out a *woof*, as though the border collie knew something she didn't.

"I think the dogs want to go with us," Gabe translated. "When I told Hattie I was going away, she acted like she might grab her blanket from the barn and come along. Maybe you'd better accompany us, to be sure these two don't follow me into town."

Emma saw a challenge in his expression that had nothing to do with the dogs—a shine in his eyes and a tilt to his chin, which meant he was thinking way ahead of her. As usual.

"Why would I want to go to the Malloys'? That girl and her baby are probably the center of attention—"

"How do you know they haven't left by now? How do you know Billy's mother hasn't shooed them off?"

There was a thought. Virgilia Bristol Harte manipulated every situation to be sure things worked out for the best where her boy was concerned. Surely she'd seen through Eve Massena's story. Surely she'd recalled the wrong Eve's daddy had done her family, and wanted nothing to do with that wanton young woman. Why, Eve's own mother had put her out! There had to be things the pretty, educated brunette wasn't telling them—parts of the story she'd left out to make herself look better in Billy's eyes.

"Seems to me," Gabe went on, "that Billy will interpret your absence as a sign you don't care that he put off the wedding. If you stay here pouting, you might as well let *Eve* wear that pretty wedding dress, after she coaxes Billy—"

"Oh, all right!" Emma stood up so suddenly the two dogs sprang away from the steps. "I'll go so I can give you a proper send-off. And *maybe,* seeing's how Billy'll be sorry you're leaving us, I'll take him aside for a little chat."

"Catch him in a weak moment, then lay him low!" Gabe's sorrel curls quivered as he nodded emphatically. "That's more like it! You can't let that other girl and her baby steal him away, Emma. I suspect you painted Billy into a corner, as far as persuading him to marry you, but he's known your feelings for years. You didn't take him by surprise."

Emma glared, planting a hand on her hip. Maybe it *was* time for her know-it-all cousin to make himself scarce, if he was only going to poke fun at her.

"That's between Billy and me," she snapped, stepping off the porch to fetch her horse. "I guarantee you that when you come home for a visit, it'll be *my* baby Billy's showing off. Eve Massena will be long gone!"

Chapter Six

Billy's throat tightened when he saw his two best friends approaching on the road. Bad enough that the skinny little kid with the big spectacles had shot past them all in school and was now moving to St. Louis: Gabe Getty's absence meant Emma would have only *him* to cluck at now . . . and boss. Her blond hair caught the morning sunlight, but he didn't mistake its glow for a halo.

Her grim smile told him she had a piece of her mind all primed for him, too. Not that he didn't deserve it, after asking everyone to leave their wedding.

Shifting the baby higher on his shoulder, he turned to the delicate, brown-haired girl in the porch swing. "You might want to go inside, Eve. Looks like Emma's decided to see Gabe off, and I doubt she'll stop at that."

Eve Massena stood slowly, steadying her knees beneath the calico dress Temple Gates had loaned her. The young Negress had also washed her hair and arranged it in a simple upsweep. Her bulk had already subsided to the point she felt civilized again. Almost pretty.

"You think I can't handle a betrayed bride?" she

asked, her green eyes flashing. "Considering what I went through with Mother and your twin, this'll be a cakewalk, Billy."

He sighed, kissing the baby's velvet cheek. "Why do I get the feelin' you're the only girl who's not gonna claw me to pieces today?" he whispered against that tiny ear.

A little arm went around his neck and Billy's heart swelled six sizes: she was an angel, no matter how she'd come to be born, and the joy this baby brought him—partly because she was a sure sign Wes was alive—made him stand taller. No matter what happened here today, he felt responsible for this little girl. Even if Eve Massena went away.

And he thought she might—but not until she'd served Emma some piss-and-vinegar punch, to go with the wedding cake Asa had stored in the spring house. Eve Massena was a woman to be reckoned with. And this would be his day of reckoning.

He tried to swallow the hard lump in his throat: Eve stood beside him on the porch now, slipping her slender hand into his bent elbow as her baby nuzzled his cheek. And Emma, watching from the wagon that stopped a few feet in front of them, looked ready to nail him to the porch pillar.

"Emma. Gabe," he said, nodding at each of them. "Miss Vanderbilt's just about finished her packing. I'll drive you to—"

"This has nothing to do with Miss Vanderbilt, and you know it!" Emma spat. Her gaze cut so sharply, his clothes should have been shredded. "Tell this—this *hussy* to take her brat inside. We need to talk, Billy."

Eve sucked in her breath. "I will *not* have my daughter Olivia slighted in such a way! Apologize this minute!"

"Olivia?" Billy breathed, instinctively holding the baby closer.

"This is Olivia Bristol," Miss Massena continued, narrowing her feline eyes at Emma, "and she has every right to remain on her Uncle Billy's shoulder. I must ask you not to offend her again."

Emma's eyes clouded into a dull blue, a storm warning Billy recognized.

"You said yourself that Wesley ran out before he married you! That makes your baby a bastard in my book—"

"This is not about Olivia," Billy chimed in, wishing he could savor the taste of that pretty name instead of bickering. He looked toward Gabe for help, but his best friend simply observed this brewing cat fight from the wagon seat. His long fingers fiddled with the reins.

Somehow, that helped Billy keep a more patient perspective. He realized then how much he'd miss Gabe in the coming months. Gabriel Getty had the look of a wise man—the ways of a saint—and Billy frowned when he thought about how long it might be before he saw his best friend again.

"I'll miss ya, Gabe," he murmured, and then, below his rolled-up shirtsleeve, he saw the scar like a lightning streak. "Blood brothers since we met, and blood brothers to the end! Bound to avenge the wrongs done to our families after the war."

Gabe bared his forearm, too, raising it proudly in that gesture Emma was sick to death of. "Blood brothers to the—"

"Beggin' your pardon, boys," she jeered, "but this seems a mighty odd time to be talkin' about things from ten years ago, when the *real* problem is standin' right here in our midst. Seems to me any banker's daughter who can paint pictures and—"

"And how do *you* know that, Miss Clark?"

Emma's eyes widened into steely blue plates, but she recovered quickly. "Why—Billy told me, of course!"

He blinked. First Eve had made up a name for her

baby, and now Emma was spouting off about things he had *not* told her—things he hadn't thought about for years. Which meant—

"You saw my letter!" Eve accused, looking from Billy to Emma. Her face flamed and her fingers cut his arm to the bone. "You told me you never received my letter with the painting of your home place, Billy! But now it's obvious—"

"I'm tellin' ya, I never got no letter!" Even to his prairie ears, the return to his childish grammar sounded crude. "And I *sure* never got no paintin' of my home in Richmond, or it'd be framed and hangin'—"

Emma's flaming cheeks made his jaw clamp shut. Maybe he hadn't seen that painting, but only a blind man could miss the guilt that colored Emma Clark's face.

"What'd you do with Billy's letter?" Gabe asked her quietly. "Don't tell me you—"

"Nothin'!" Emma squeaked. "I have no idea what letter she's talkin' about!"

Eve exhaled with a hiss akin to a snake's. "It was a letter I sent last spring, asking Billy if I could come and tell him about Wesley," she replied in a tight voice. "The envelope also contained a watercolor painting of the Bristol home before the war—before it sank into ruin when Wesley and his gang made it their hideout."

Billy's insides clenched, but this was no time to question what Eve had said about Wes.

"So instead, you just showed up!" Emma concluded. She stood in the wagon, pointing at Eve. "Somehow you knew Billy and I were getting married—from sticking your nose where it didn't belong, no doubt! So then you barged in to—to foist that *brat* on him, and coax him away with talk of his long-lost brother! Oh, I know your tricks, missy!"

"And I know yours!" Eve crowed.

The air around them got as still as the plains before a tornado blew up.

The baby hiccuped and shifted on his shoulder, upset by these escalating voices. Olivia wasn't the only one who wanted to cry, however. The ache in his heart confirmed what Eve was saying: there had been a letter, with a painting. And Emma had somehow kept it from him.

His blond bride-to-be was no coward, but this morning he saw abject terror on her face. Those red-rimmed eyes might've been crying over a ruined wedding day, but now that Emma Clark had seen pretty Eve Massena, after reading a letter that would've been perfectly penned and included a painting of a home worth far more than the Malloys'—far more than the Clarks' log house—she was scared spitless.

Afraid of losing *him*.

When the baby clung to his neck, he felt Olivia's birdlike pulse racing against his cheek.

Suffer the little children to come unto me . . . for of such is the Kingdom of Heaven.

Billy blinked. Had anyone else heard that? The voice resembled Mike Malloy's—or Judd Monroe's, from Heaven. Yet when he turned, no one was looking out at them from the doorway.

It was a sign. And he knew what he must do.

With a sigh, he gazed at Emma, recalling the stalwart tomboy who'd first welcomed him when he came to Kansas. She'd declared herself his friend from the beginning—and had made no secret of her feelings for him as they grew up. She didn't deserve what he was about to do to her.

But Lord, what he wouldn't give to see that painting of his home before the war—before his daddy was shot dead and his brother was abducted and his mama took off with a huckster.

Did he deserve Emma's betrayal?

Did little Olivia deserve to be a pawn in this nasty predicament?

At her first cry, he swayed with her, praying for the right words—knowing there were none.

"I'm sorry, Emma," he said, his eyes stinging, "but I'm goin' back to Richmond to find my brother—Olivia's father. I don't know how long I'll be gone."

Her mouth puckered into a little O that opened with dismay. "But you can't—we've told everyone the wedding's on Saturday."

"The wedding's off," he said quietly.

Billy pivoted on his heel, freeing himself from Eve's grip to retreat into the house with a wailing Miss Olivia.

Chapter Seven

"Billy, don't you *dare* run off! That's my granddaughter you've got!"

Billy froze in the open doorway. His mother's voice and the rumble of wagon wheels told him there was no way out: *Three* females were vying for his attention, and not one of them would leave him be until she had her way!

A glance into the front parlor made him smile, however: Miss Agatha Vanderbilt, Mercy's aunt and the headmistress of the Academy for Young Ladies, was standing at the bottom of the stairs beside her steamer trunk. As always, her snowy white hair was pulled into a neat twist, and she was immaculately dressed in a dove-gray traveling suit. Her warm smile fixed a lot of what was wrong right now.

"I couldn't help overhearing your confrontation through my window, dear," she said in a low voice. "Though I'm not surprised you have two pretty young ladies trying to claim you, I believe you've chosen the right one."

She nodded toward Olivia, who was now snuggling

against Billy's shoulder. The infant's cries became coos as he rocked her side to side.

"I've always envied your way with babies, Billy. Why, Solace, Lily, and Grace took to you as soon as they laid eyes on you!" she continued with a chuckle. "And Olivia needs you even more than they do. She's lucky to have you."

While these words warmed him, Billy closed his eyes against the baby's dewy-soft cheek. "But I broke my promise to Emma," he rasped. "Worse yet, I broke her heart. That's just not my way—"

"Between you and me," Aunt Agatha said in a low voice, "you deserve better than Emma Clark. She's been your friend for years, that's true, but I've never sensed a—a *passion* between you. Not like the passion you have for your horses, or for little children."

As her piercing eyes held his, Billy realized Gabe Getty would have to be *very* careful while he roomed in the academy's guest quarters: Miss Vanderbilt had legendary powers of observation. But then, Gabe had never given anyone a lick of trouble. It was *he* who found so many ways to upset women.

"Thank you," he murmured, "but Mama and Carlton just pulled in, so I'll ask Michael to drive you into town."

"If I don't get to speak with you again, please accept my best wishes as you reunite with your brother and visit your former home." Her brown eyes grew pensive then. "Remember that both of them may have changed as much as you have in the past ten years, Billy. Perhaps not for the better."

When she held out her arms, Billy slipped the warm, sweet bundle of baby to her and then trotted through the house and out the kitchen door.

A loud howl followed him. Thank goodness the three girls had gone out to greet Emma and the Hartes: they could soothe the baby while he took a few moments alone with Mike Malloy.

Billy slowed to a walk as he approached the corrals. The Triple M's yearling Morgans nickered, watching young Joel with wide, wary eyes as he worked at getting a halter on each of them. Malloy stood with a foot on the bottom white rail, murmuring encouragement to keep his eleven-year-old son on task.

"How's he doin'?" Billy noticed Joel's improved skills: He'd learned to let the horses come to him, rather than approaching with the halter and expecting them to stand still.

"He'll never be the horseman you are, Billy," Michael replied with a knowing smile. "But he's giving it a shot."

"Well, I—" He nearly choked on the words, but he couldn't let this man hear his decisions secondhand. Malloy had seen potential in a skinny, abandoned kid, and had eventually put him in charge of the horses' training.

When Michael focused those shining hazel eyes on him, Billy knew he'd be leaving a lot behind. Disappointing another important person in his life.

"I'm goin' home, Mike," he rasped. His heart pounded as though he were confessing some awful crime. "I—I just have to see my brother Wesley."

"And I've known you'd go eventually, ever since Mercy and Judd took you in," Michael replied. "It's what God's had planned for you all along, son."

"But that leaves you to tend all the horses, and do the plantin' and—"

"Which means Reuben Gates will pull more weight until I can hire another hand," he said with a shrug. "Joel and Solace will take on more of the chores, and so will I. That was always part of the deal, Billy."

Billy choked. He gazed toward the river, where the

green cottonwoods swayed in the breeze. "But I—I feel like I'm lettin' you down, almost as bad as I've hurt Emma."

"If your marriage is meant to be, it'll happen. If it's love, it'll survive this separation and you'll both be stronger for it."

"What if I don't come back?"

The thought took him by surprise, like a sob from the bottom of his tormented heart. Malloy's warm hand landed on his shoulder, but it didn't help much. Just reminded Billy once again what he was leaving behind.

"Maybe this little shake-up is what you and Emma needed," Malloy mused aloud. "Maybe someday you'll see it was for the best that Miss Massena interrupted the wedding. God works in mysterious ways, and he sometimes sends the most unlikely angels to carry out his work."

"Yeah, well, when I left the porch it wasn't *angels* carryin' on that cat fight! And then Mama and Harte drove in!" he added. "I'd figured on driving Gabe and Miss Vanderbilt into town, but—"

"But you want to collect a few claw marks, eh?" Malloy's eyes sparkled with mischief that brought back the ornery kid he'd probably been.

"Nobody can accuse you of taking the easy way out, son," he went on in that patient way Billy knew so well—the voice of reason he would miss more than anything else. "Your brother's done damage on a lot of levels, yet you're defending Eve's honor. Looking after her baby's future. That little girl's got a hard row to hoe, and someday you'll have to explain why you tried to help her. Just like I'll be telling Joel about his ma and how she loved him.

"Never assume marriage and children are easy," Mike went on in a lower voice. "And never figure you'll get far before your deeds—good or bad—come back around to you, Billy. A few moments of careless pleasure gave me that little man who's struggling to follow in your footsteps. I have a lot of explaining to do someday, because I didn't honor his mother."

"He'd be nowhere without you and Mercy."

Malloy flashed a lopsided grin, "We all know Joel's like a May beetle with his wings pulled off—not quite whole, since he watched his ma die. No sense of where he's going, or what he's supposed to do with himself."

Michael glanced back at the house as the baby's wail drifted on the breeze. "Guess I'd better hitch up the carriage, so Gabe and Aunt Ag don't miss their train. I've got the easy part, considering the guests you'll be entertaining while I'm away."

Michael's smile bespoke a love Billy had never known from anyone else.

"Good to hear a baby again," he murmured. "Not sure why, but Mercy and I can't seem to make another one. Not that we don't have enough chicks in our nest already."

"Olivia," Billy whispered, letting the name linger in his mouth. "Eve named her Olivia—just to annoy Emma, I suspect."

"She chose well! Olivia . . ." Malloy repeated tenderly. "We'll take good care of her while you're gone, son. She'll be so spoiled, Mercy might not turn her loose."

Billy smiled as the woman in question stepped outside to wave him in. Even from a distance, her compassion glowed like the summer sun.

"Somethin' tells me that between Eve, Emma, and my mother, the conversation has gotten way too interesting," Billy said with a laugh. "Thanks for taking Gabe and Miss Vanderbilt. And thanks for, well—*everything*.

"All these years, you've made me feel like I *belonged* here. And now you're lettin' me go without complainin' about the extra work it'll mean," Billy went on in a voice that threatened to crack. "I'll do my dangdest to repay—"

"You're welcome, Billy. And you're stalling," Malloy said with a grin. "Time to let the voice of reason resound above the mewing and hissing. Lucky man."

Billy heard their voices coming from the parlor now, and saw Temple Gates carrying in a tray of lemonade and cookies. His gaze followed the young Negress in, but something told him to remain unseen—get the drift of the conversation, which had taken a more urgent turn now that Mama and Carlton Harte had arrived.

"Tell me about my Wesley!" his mother insisted. She was holding the baby, studying Olivia's features as avidly as any doting grandmother would. "No matter what you want to believe, Emma, this child is a Bristol through and through. The spitting image of my red-headed sons and daughter when they were born."

Emma turned up her nose and looked away; took a cookie from the tray Temple offered, and then jammed it into her mouth.

Eve didn't look any more comfortable about the direction the conversation had taken, but she straightened in her chair and held her head high, the way his sister Christine used to do. It made her neck look endlessly inviting, so Billy closed his eyes and tried to fill in the gaps he might have missed in this story.

"What can I say?" the brunette replied brusquely. "Wesley always took what he wanted, regardless of who got hurt, so—"

"But he's well?" Mama demanded. "Hasn't been shot up by any of those Missouri gunslingers? I can't believe he's become one himself. You must be—"

"No, ma'am, your son's a sly one," Eve countered. "You've probably read in the papers about the James boys and the Youngers causing such a stir, but Wesley has evaded the Pinkertons. Which, considering how they've bungled their attempts to capture Frank and Jesse, doesn't take much."

Billy saw Carleton leaning closer, listening intently. The quiet, mustachioed man now worked as a telegraph operator in Topeka. They'd moved east, to that larger town, when Mama married him. He'd done a multitude of things to prove his love, at Virgilia Bristol's whim, yet Billy sensed his mother's new husband still kept a few professional secrets—maybe some about Mama's other son.

What Eve Massena didn't know was that Harte had served as a Pinkerton operative himself. It was only natural for the quiet, unassuming man's eyes to burn a little brighter when Wesley's rejected lover mentioned outlaw activity.

"The way I hear it, the James boys garnered a lot of local sympathy when an explosion went awry and cost their mother an arm—and a younger boy," Carlton remarked. "Notoriety like that always spawns imitators, too."

"Yes, sir," Eve replied, "Wesley Bristol's got his own band of marauders now, similar to the Border Ruffians who kidnapped him. But he knows how *not* be seen when the lawmen come too close."

"And how would he know that?" Mama asked.

"Well, you recall how it was after the war!" Eve exclaimed, raising her hands in graceful agitation. "Frank and Jesse have been crowned as kings for getting back at those damn Union sympathizers and politicians who ruined us! So when the Pinkertons move in, or Governor Woodson cracks down, those outlaws lay low with neighbors, or in the caves and woods.

"Then they pull off another outrageous bank heist or train robbery, and write a letter of denial to the newspaper editor," she went on in a strident voice. "Everybody knows who did it! They're just rubbing the governor's nose in it—baiting all those operatives who can't catch them."

Billy observed the faces in that room: Emma sat with

her arms crossed, peeved because she could no longer badger Miss Massena; Mama cooed at Olivia, while Carleton's bushy mustache concealed his interested grin. Temple Gates had chosen a chair near the girls, who sat on the floor: Solace, Lily and Grace were politely sipping their lemonade under their teacher's watchful eye, their crossed legs covered by their skirts.

"So why would my son risk his safety to see *you*?" Mama asked pointedly. "I can't believe he'd associate with the family who foreclosed on his home! He had to know about that, even if he was kidnapped."

Billy's heart skipped a beat. A muscle in Eve's rosy cheek twitched, but those deep green eyes didn't flicker.

"I may have been reduced to earning my keep as a school marm, Mrs. Harte," she said in a cool voice, "but your son has a legendary eye for the ladies."

"And why should I believe Leland Massena's daughter took up *teaching*?" Mama huffed. "You were no more inclined to earn a living than any of us in—"

"Teaching's a damn sight more respectable than forging land office sales, or organizing fake lotteries to—"

"I'll thank you to watch your language, Miss Massena," Temple Gates cut in sharply. "We have impressionable young ears in this room."

Mama arched a triumphant eyebrow at Eve, without a hint of remorse for the wayward life she'd once led.

Eve, however, lifted her chin with a feline grace Billy recognized immediately: She had a conversational ace up her sleeve, and was now itching to play it.

"Your darling boy Wesley *used* me, Virgilia—as though what he did to Daddy weren't enough!" she whispered bitterly. "Daddy was paying him handsomely to scare landowners off their ranches so he could seize them for nonpayment of their mortgages and resell them. Though I'm not proud of how my father operated, he did not deserve the way Wesley and his gang members blackmailed him. Mother wouldn't be giving piano lessons, living in only two rooms of our house, if he were still alive!"

The parlor rang with a tense silence. Billy blinked, realizing just how difficult things had been for the Massenas—how the tangled web Leland had wove had caught his entire family. Was it really Wesley's fault, or was Eve playing on everyone's sympathy?

"I'm sorry for your loss," Carleton murmured, as though to defuse the escalating tempers in the room. "May I ask how your daddy died?"

"He hanged himself in the barn!" Eve rasped. "I found him myself. I only responded to Wesley's advances to get my revenge, but he turned the tables—left me with a bun in the oven, after promising to marry me!"

"So you're not only a whore, you're a fool!" Emma crowed.

"Miss Emma!" Temple Gates stood up, glowering at the blonde as she gestured for the girls to precede her out of the parlor. "Please excuse us, but I'll not expose these young ladies to any more of this vile, upsetting conversation!"

As the three girls in their flounced dresses caught sight of him in the hall, they grinned knowingly. Billy rumpled Solace's thick sorrel waves and squeezed Grace's little shoulder, giving Lily his best smile.

Temple Gates had a good point, though, and it was time to make his own. He entered the parlor, taking the chair Temple had vacated. The sparkle in Emma's blue eyes told him she was glad to see him—but not because she'd forgiven his change of mind and priorities.

"Billy!" she began, "we've been hearing how Wesley's caused all sorts of commotion—and how he blackmailed Eve's daddy, and—well, your hometown must be a den of robbers now! And Eve has admitted to being his fallen woman! What do you say to *that*?"

Miss Massena's dragonlike scowl prompted him to speak up while he still had a chance. Each of these ladies seemed intent on outgossiping her adversary, and he had more important things to discuss.

"Emma, do you recall that story in the gospel where the Pharisees bring Jesus a woman who was caught in adultery?" he asked quietly. "They were set on stoning her to death, till Jesus said 'Let him who has no sin cast the first stone.' And by golly, they all walked away, didn't they?"

Emma's face reddened. "And just what do you mean by that? What gives you the right to go quotin' Jesus, as though—as though—"

"As though you didn't rip up that letter and the painting I sent him?" Eve demanded. "If you hadn't meddled in Billy's mail—"

"Hush now! Both of you!" To make his point—and to make an escape before these cats clawed him to pieces—Billy stood up. The parlor was so quiet, so tense, that the clock on the mantel sounded like a warning from God himself when it chimed ten o'clock.

"I'm goin' back to Missouri to find my brother—the father of that little girl right there," he said, nodding toward the baby asleep on Mama's lap. "But I'm goin' back for my own reasons, too. And nothin' you ladies can say is gonna change that."

Emma jumped to her feet. "I get the picture!" she whispered tersely. "You're usin' this as a chance to back out of our marriage, like a coward with his tail between his legs. Well, go on then! Go to Missouri and get yourself shot! I'm liable to shoot you myself if you stay around, after the way you betrayed me!"

Her tears made his own cheeks sizzle with the pain he'd caused her. *Was* he a coward? Had he seized upon this opportunity not to marry her? Hunting his outlaw twin sounded like a happier risk than spending his life with the Emma Clark he'd seen these past few days! Or was that a dishonorable way to look at this situation?

She stumbled from the parlor, not caring that everyone saw her tears and felt the heat of her shame—probably hoping he'd follow, to comfort her, as he had after her mother died.

But Billy stood firm. The eyes in that room watched every flicker of his eyelashes as he considered his options.

"So, you're going to Richmond for Olivia—to see Wesley—rather than to give me the help I asked for?" Eve demanded.

She rose slowly, widening her eyes at him. "And what will that accomplish, Billy? Your home's in such a state it'll break your heart—and your twin's farther gone than that. He *will* shoot you down, Billy. Or he'll find a way to use you for his own devious purposes."

Billy sighed. Her words rang with truth, but also with a wheedling need for him to take her part.

"Maybe I'm like Doubting Thomas, touching the nail holes and the wound in Christ's side," Billy murmured. "Have to see things for myself—"

"The last thing I need is a do-gooder spouting Bible stories!" she cried. "Mother did enough of that when she kicked me out! I need a hero, Billy—somebody who'll make my world right again. I can see it won't be you."

With a toss of her pretty head, Eve Massena strode from the room. Despite her exhaustion and the plain calico dress Temple Gates had loaned her, she held herself like a queen—at least until he could no longer see her.

Billy admired that. It reminded him of his sister Christine's manipulations when they were kids.

But he let Miss Massena go, too. This trip to Missouri was for his own peace of mind, and on the behalf of

Olivia, although he couldn't believe Wesley would act anything like a daddy to her.

The time and opportunity have arrived. They might be God's way of telling you it's time to go home.

Billy blinked, and then looked at the expectant expressions of Mama and Carleton. Relief washed over him when he saw the serene acceptance on Mercy Malloy's face. At least these three wouldn't hound him about his decision.

"Guess I'll get my gear together," he said quietly. "Might as well head out first thing tomorrow."

Adult responsibility weighed heavily on him as he crossed the glossy hardwood floor, in a room that glowed with light shining through the beveled window. He saw the same glow on three little faces when he reached the kitchen, where the girls sat at the table with Temple, counting out forks, knives and spoons for the meal Asa would serve everyone in a couple hours. He would miss their sweetness . . . their innocence.

"Is it true, Billy? Are you really leavin'?" Solace blurted. Her dark eyes shone with concern, and she looked so much like her father, Judd Monroe, Billy had to swallow hard.

"Yep. Goin' to see the brother I haven't laid eyes on for more than ten years," he replied. "And I'm goin' because Olivia needs a chance at a daddy—just like you girls have had."

"Are *you* gonna be a daddy, Billy?" Gracie piped up.

He smiled, swinging her up from her chair to his shoulder. At six, she was a wisp of a thing in her ruffled dresses, and she spread sunshine with the same exuberance she'd scattered flower petals at his wedding yesterday.

"Well, it would help if I'd get married," he confessed, gazing into those tawny eyes so like Michael's, "but sometimes life surprises us. Sometimes things happen out of the blue—like when Temple and Reuben and

Sedalia came to stay with us. Now things go a whole lot better, don't they?"

He returned the young colored woman's smile, for Mercy Malloy relied on her assistance as much as Temple had needed the home they'd provided.

"Amen to that, Billy," she replied, gazing fondly at her charges. "And we need to pray for Miss Emma in her time of trial, and for Miss Eve—because just like her, I was betrayed by a man who used me for his own selfish purposes."

"Pray for me, too," Billy added. His voice hitched because he was leaving this family who'd loved him when his own could not. "Ask God to keep me safe so I can come back—and so I can be a daddy and have girls just like you."

It was Lily's tight smile he saw then. As the oldest of this trio, she clucked over Solace and Grace, because Joel would have none of her mothering. Now, however, she looked troubled.

"And what about my father?" she asked quietly. "Michael's our daddy, but Solace and I aren't his true children—"

"You're his girls in every way that counts," Billy assured her quickly. "Your mama can give you a better account of that than I can. But I recall when we found you on the porch in a big basket tied up with pink ribbons, after we came home from Solace's baptizin' that Easter. You were the best present we ever had, Lily. Whoever your daddy was, God convinced him to leave you with this family."

"I can see it's time to talk about that story, tonight after devotions." Mercy stood in the kitchen doorway, drinking in the sight of her daughters. She smiled at Billy, and then wrapped her arms around his shoulders.

"I haven't hugged you for the longest time," she said as she squeezed him, "because you got too big and embarrassed by such things. But our love goes with you to

Missouri, Billy. You'll be in our hearts and prayers until we see you again, and we'll ask the angels to keep you safe. All right?"

As his arms encircled Mercy's slender waist and he inhaled her clean scent, he suddenly wanted to cry on this angel's shoulder—as he'd done when he was a little boy hurting from life's bumps and bruises. This woman had loved him when he doubted his own mama did, and the wetness in his eyes was sheer gratitude for all she'd given him.

"I can't thank you enough," he murmured awkwardly, "so I'll just have to stay safe and come back, soon as I can. I—I'd better get my things together now."

Why did doing the right thing make some people mad at him and other people worry more than he was worth? Billy couldn't figure that out. But Missouri beckoned him as surely as he knew the trip would *cost* him. Maybe more than he could afford to give, or to lose.

But when he glanced back at the faces in the kitchen, he knew for sure he was loved.

And that counted for everything, didn't it?

Chapter Eight

Eve dozed on the small bed by her window, where a breeze came in from the river. Keeping up a good front had exhausted her, but she'd sent that Clark girl packing, hadn't she? And she'd scored points with Billy's mother by letting her hold the baby, which was certainly no sacrifice! Lord, but that little girl was wearing her out—more now than before she was born. How could she be expected to tote her around, and feed her, and look after her constantly?

She slipped into slumber, relieved because Olivia was sleeping, too. In her mind she saw a handsome redheaded man, tall and strong and smiling at her—telling her she was pretty without having to say the words.

She smiled and settled deeper into the feather mattress. Was it Billy or Wes? Those blue eyes belonged to a Bristol, that was for sure! In her fantasy, Eve didn't really care who the young man was. He was complimenting her: He would see to her needs—sweep her off her feet—because she was fiery and alive, not because she had a baby. In her dream, she could forget she had a child. She smiled invitingly at the young man, luring him in for the kiss that tickled her lips with anticipation.

A loud howl made her jump. Just when the man of her fantasy was holding her close, that damn kid started to cry! Eve stayed still on the bed, determined that this child would *not* dictate her every move or get attention at every little turn!

Get used to it, Olivia, she silently advised the bawling baby. *Life can bring you pain and heartache at every turn.*

Still the baby howled, an amazing racket considering how tiny and delicate everyone said she was. With a disgusted sigh, Eve turned her back to the infant, determined to have her way.

On and on the infant squalled, while Eve clenched her eyes shut, cursing this baby who'd turned her life upside down.

She heard footsteps on the stairs and then someone bustled into the bedroom. "Come here, sugar pie," a low voice murmured. Then came more endearments and a quiet lullaby. Still the baby wailed.

Eve didn't move. The melodious voice belonged to Temple Gates, and if it hadn't been for Olivia's hissy fit, it would've lulled Eve back to sleep.

Then the crying was directly behind her. She felt the weight of a glare.

"Miss Eve, you're not sleeping," Temple stated. "Your baby won't stop crying until you feed her. Only a mother who doesn't love her child would let it keep crying."

"No darkie's going to tell me what's best for me or my baby!" Eve retorted. She twisted around to glare at the young woman with the chocolate skin and eyes with a shine like hot coffee. "So you'd best resume your rightful place as—"

"It doesn't work that way in this home, Miss Eve." Temple's gaze didn't waver. "The Malloys have put me in charge of everyone who's not an adult. If you count yourself among that number, you won't get far in this household, because—"

"I really don't give a damn, Temple! I didn't *ask* for your charity!" she said tiredly. "Michael, Asa, and Billy brought me here. I am a *guest*, and I insist you treat me like one!"

"You are the mother of this angel sent to you by God—"

"Enough of that holier-than-thou claptrap, too! *Take* that baby if you like her so much, just as the Malloys have taken in the others! I have no—"

Temple swayed from side to side to quiet Olivia, but her eyes took on a determined look. "I was younger than you, missy, when a white overseer on a Georgia plantation had his way with me," she began, and her expression warned Eve not to interrupt.

"He nearly killed me taking his pleasure. Said if I told anyone about it, my brother and his wife would be turned out—or shot while I watched. Whichever he was of a mind to do.

"So I kept my mouth shut. I *know* what you've suffered at the hands of a man who used you, Miss Eve," Temple continued in a tight voice. "But I also know the pain of having my baby taken from me, stillborn after all those months of carrying. I nearly died along with it, from an infection, and I owe Asa, and Mercy and Mike Malloy my life. It was Christine's mother-in-law who called in the angels to save me, and—"

"Christine's married?" Finally, information she could latch onto!

"Yes, ma'am. She and Tucker live out in San Francisco now, so we don't see nearly enough of her twins, Rachel and Rebecca." Temple sighed, smiling. "She's carrying again, too, or she'd have come for her brother's wedding. But that's neither here nor there. And this is *your* baby. Feed her!"

When Temple thrust the infant at Eve, the wailing

became unbearable again. Gritting her teeth against another retort—for what recourse did she have in this house full of do-gooders?—Eve unbuttoned the loose, faded calico dress.

Temple Gates had the nerve to stand there watching, as though she longed to feed the baby. Probably she was thinking of her own child. But that sad story wasn't going to soften her, not Eve Massena who had a life to live and vengeance to wreak upon the man who'd ruined it!

The tug of milk through her breast still astounded her, but the baby's stillness was her real reward.

"Go on now," she muttered. "You've told me what to do. You've gotten your way. Maybe you think I should be grateful for this ugly dress and your uninvited advice, but I am not! Go tend your other sheep, Temple. Leave me be!"

Half an hour later, Olivia lay in her bassinet, smacking her little lips. The Harte wagon had pulled away. Male voices and barking dogs told Eve the horses were being tended. Delectable scents of baked ham and biscuits drifted up to her room.

Eve's stomach rumbled traitorously. The cookie she'd eaten in the parlor was long gone, and though she hated being beholden to these people—didn't want to spar with Billy anymore—her hunger won out.

Down the stairs she went, quietly, so as not to startle the baby. On the landing, she checked to be sure her dress was properly buttoned, smoothed her hair, and widened her eyes in pretended penitence. No doubt Temple had reported her unmotherly attitude, and these Malloys didn't seem to know that mere *servants* had no right to irritate houseguests! Best to remain cordial, regain her strength, and plan from there. . . .

But in the dining room sat Mercy Malloy with an open box on the table in front of her. The blond girl who'd sung in the church and the dark-eyed daughter with the tousled curls sat on either side of her. The hush in that room—the shining eyes of the girls— warned Eve not to enter. She stood silently, peeking in at them.

"Here's a picture of your daddy, Solace," Mercy was saying to the younger, darker one. "I want you to have this for your room. His name was Judd Monroe, and he was so excited that you were going to be born."

"So where *is* he?" the girl asked. She gazed at the photograph, gripping it between her sturdy hands.

"He died in an Indian attack, over on the other homestead," Mercy replied with a hitch in her voice. "Someday soon we'll visit his grave. He would have loved the tiger lilies blooming along the back fence, so we'll take him some."

"He looks like . . . *me*," came the awed reply.

"Yes, he does, honey. Not a day goes by that I don't think of Judd, when I look at you. You have the shape of his brows, and his thick, wavy hair, and his dark eyes and skin tone—"

"May I see him?" the blonde whispered.

Solace solemnly handed over the picture, pleased yet pensive about the face it framed.

"He looks like a really nice daddy," Lily remarked wistfully.

"He was. He took Billy and Christine in without batting an eye, when Michael stopped the stagecoach at our house, looking for their mother."

"The Mrs. Harte who was here?"

"She was Mrs. Bristol then," Mercy clarified, "and she . . . well, she was very sad and upset after the war. Not thinking straight—like I wasn't after I lost Judd— and she did some unfortunate things."

"But now she's crazy for little Olivia!" Lily said. Her face lit up and so did her sister's, but as she handed back Solace's picture she cleared her throat.

"So what about *my* daddy?" she asked hesitantly.

"Billy says you found me in a basket, on the stoop, and nobody knows who left me there."

"It was a mystery," Mercy agreed, reaching over to stroke the girl's golden ringlets, "but we knew right away that you were a blessing! Prettiest little thing—like a baby doll all dressed in pink, with a sweetness about you that made everyone want to spoil you."

Lily giggled in spite of her concerns, watching Mercy take a folded paper from the box on the table. Her dress, a confection of rose taffeta, still gave her the air of a fragile china doll, Eve noted from the door. And though she was clearly the queen of this young brood, she wasn't at all bratty about it.

"This note was pinned to your little dress, honey. You should have it now," her mama said softly. "None of us understood why anyone would abandon you—and we don't know why your father's never returned—but we hope God has eased his pain. We thank him every day for the joy you've blessed our lives with, Miss Lily. We've always loved you, and you'll always be our daughter, and a child of God."

Eve wiped away a stray tear. What she wouldn't give to have someone speak to her so tenderly! She couldn't recall Mother making time for her, or telling her she was special, or loved, even when she was little. She'd secretly wondered if she was really Florence and Leland Massena's natural-born child, for it often seemed her parents had resented her presence.

Just like you detest being tied down by Olivia!

The voice in her head struck like thunder and Eve covered her gasp. Her heart beat wildly and her knees quaked beneath the calico dress.

She sucked in air, focusing again on the scene at the table to calm herself. Lily was gazing raptly at the note, as though trying to know her absentee father by his penmanship and turn of phrase.

"What's it say?" Solace demanded eagerly. "Read it to me, Lily!"

The willowy blonde smiled at her sturdy sibling as though she were accustomed to these outbursts. "It says, 'My name is Lily, and I am eight months old,'" she began in a low voice. "'My mama has died, and my papa can't take me where he needs to go. He has visited you before, and he believes you are an angel of mercy who will care for me until he can return. He's a man of great wealth and influence, and will repay you a thousandfold for your kindness. God bless you for opening your heart and home to me.'"

Eve blinked. What an odd note for a father to pin to a baby girl! Judging by Lily's size and behavior, she had to be at least ten or eleven. Why hadn't that presumptuous man returned, as he'd promised?

Solace and Lily also wore confused expressions as they pondered the message. Mercy Malloy, seated between them and taking each girl's hand, waited patiently for their questions. The glow from the sunset, reflected in the window, caught the shine of her upswept sorrel hair, almost like a halo.

Don't go thinking that way! Eve's thoughts warned her. Nobody can be as saintly as that note lets on! The man was desperate and—

"So did he leave you a lot of money in the basket, too?" Solace piped up. "If he's rich, will Lily ride away in a fine carriage someday, to live in his mansion?"

"Has he been here?" Lily quizzed without missing a beat. "If he knew who you were—that you would care for me without question—it must true that he'd met you before!"

Mercy put on the careful smile of a mother who wasn't sure how to respond. "We had those same questions, sweetheart," she replied, as though she was going back in time, trying to solve the riddle that day had brought them. "You see, when the stagecoaches came through several times a week, Judd provided fresh teams of Morgan horses—"

"Just like we raise now!" Solace chirped.

"Yes, dear, it was your father who started that business, at the other house, when we first came to Kansas as homesteaders," Mercy confirmed. "We had strangers at our door—and at our table—from all over the country, because I cooked meals when the stagecoaches arrived. Passengers crowded into the little front room of that log house and ate in such a hurry, to keep their schedule, that we barely got a good look at them before they were gone."

Mercy smiled at this recollection, reaching for Lily's hand. "And as the cattle drives began, we attracted buyers for Judd's fine horses. We don't know which one might've been your father, Lily, but we were so grateful that he entrusted you to us. Billy and Christine were here by then, and Aunt Agatha had come for Solace's baptism, and Michael—"

A flush colored her face, and Mercy glowed like a young girl. "Well, Michael was trying very hard to get me to marry him. But I'd just lost Judd the September before, and I wasn't ready for that."

Solace stared into space, and then blinked. "So you had four children, but no father for any of them?"

"That's how it worked out, yes—although Christine was going to Aunt Agatha's academy by then. So it was just Billy and Asa and me, to tend the horses and meals for stage passengers—and *you* two!"

She tweaked their noses to bring this serious conversation to a close, as footsteps and voices were coming through the kitchen door. "If you need to talk about these things—if you have questions—be sure to ask your daddy or me anything that's on your minds. I know it gets confusing, wondering who Lily's father is, or what your father was like, Solace."

The girls nodded, each holding their treasures. As they stood up, Lily licked her lips thoughtfully. "So you met Michael when he was driving stagecoaches, and he wanted to marry you because you had the two of us girls?"

"Nah!" Solace teased. "It's because Mama was so pretty—and she cooked good!"

Mercy's laughter filled the room like the light from the window. "You girls were a big draw, because he was crazy about you both—love at first sight, it was. And by then Joel's mother had been shot, too. Michael felt we'd all be happier if we were a family. So he kept asking me to marry him."

"Did he kiss you a lot?" Solace teased.

"Every chance I got, little girl!" Michael Malloy swooped in with a grin on his face, grabbing a giggly Solace with one arm and slipping the other around Mercy's waist. "And you know what? She *still* makes me kiss her lot! Just like this!"

Eve's heart throbbed at the sight: that handsome man, somewhat younger than Mercy, pressing his lips to hers with an eager affection she returned. Their eyes closed and they hid nothing of their love for each other—it was more than she could watch. It was what she'd longed to share with Wesley Bristol, but that relationship was never going to work out like the pretty scenes she saw in her mind . . . or the scene she'd witnessed here. Her parents had *never* kissed, as far as she knew.

Eve turned toward the stairway, not wanting to be caught eavesdropping. She'd seen enough to know she couldn't possibly stay here: She couldn't stand so much happiness. People who praised each other and loved so openly—why, they would drive her crazy with their displays of joy and affection! And Eve knew life really wasn't that way.

"Please come back! We're ready to have some supper now!"

She froze with her foot on the first step. Etiquette demanded she acknowledge Mercy's invitation—and the fact that she'd been spying.

Pasting on a smile, Eve gripped the newel post to steady herself. "I—I thought I heard Olivia crying. I'll be down with her in a little while. Please, don't hold up your meal on my account."

Mercy's deep brown eyes took her in; saw right through her little ruse, yet she nodded. "Take your time with her, dear. You're welcome to whatever you need, whenever you're hungry. Ask and you shall receive!"

That settled it! Eve smiled sweetly, but once out of sight, she scowled. "Sanctimonious do-gooders," she muttered as she entered her room. "Can't even invite you to eat without tacking a Bible verse on it!"

The invitation wasn't wasted, however.

Late that night, when the house was silent, Eve slipped down the stairs barefoot and into the kitchen. Ravenous, she tore into the last quarter of a cherry pie, wrapped in a clean towel on the table. Then she folded the towel around the half loaf of bread in the bread box, and rifled quietly through the kitchen cabinets. After snagging cookies from the jar and some soda crackers, she spied a small box with money it.

Enough to get a few things at the mercantile, she reasoned. And to reclaim the poor old horse and buckboard that had brought her here from Richmond.

She sniffed wistfully at the lingering scent of bacon. With a last look around the big kitchen, homey and peaceful in the shadows, Eve Massena put on her shoes. Best to be down the road before that baby woke everyone up.

Chapter Nine

Billy set out early the next morning, shaking his head as he mounted his gelding, Pete. Why did girls think they could just take off, alone? Unaware of the dangers and distance they faced.

At least when his sister had pulled this stunt— twice!—she'd stolen a reliable horse. Eve Massena was on foot, and he had no trouble imagining how he'd find her: sprawled on the side of the road, bawling over blisters from walking in borrowed shoes. Or worse yet, passed out from not eating enough. He knew she was still weak from birthing the baby she'd abandoned.

Sure enough, there she was up ahead. Temple's calico dress hung like a sack on Eve's slender body; her hair was hanging loose, drifting with the breeze. She carried a small packet under one arm and was already favoring her left foot. Limping along with only her stubbornness to keep her going.

As he caught up to her, Billy reminded himself about how girls lashed out when folks questioned their actions—or, God forbid, suggested a better way. Eve and Christine were birds of a feather: peacocks mostly, born to strut and show off their plumage. His sister had become a high-class dress designer and snagged a good husband, however. And now she was the mother of two redheaded twins who'd captured Uncle Billy's heart at first sight.

Did Eve have gumption enough to improve her life, too? It was time to find out.

He held his tongue, hearing her breath coming in angry bursts as she hobbled along the rutted road. Not yet a mile away from the Malloy ranch, and she was already wearing thin—not that he would mention this. She was walking taller now. Knew someone was behind her, but Miss Massena would *not* turn around to ask for help.

"How 'bout if I let you ride my horse, Eve? No sense in being weak *and* crippled."

She whirled around, her green eyes full of venom. "You are *not* taking me back to that house! I've had enough of—"

"Oh, I know better than to try that, Peaches. I'm just offerin' you a ride, while we talk."

"—those *perfect* people and their—who're you calling Peaches?"

Billy grinned. Their cook Beulah Mae had caught them eating peaches she'd set aside for pies, when they were maybe eight. He'd called Eve that name now and again to remind her of the switching they got—because of *her* idea.

Behind her scowl, though, Billy saw frustration and fear, mostly. He witnessed such wariness in horses that had suffered heavy-handed owners who'd brought them to the Triple M, hoping Billy could "set them straight." Train them to trust again.

Like those skittish Morgans, Eve Massena was perfectly capable of behaving well. She was just out of her element here, after so many bad things had happened these past few months. Her emotional wounds hadn't healed.

"I'm sorry you feel that way. The Malloys have been nothin' but wonderful to me," he went on, gazing down at her from his horse. "You musta trusted 'em with Olivia, though, or you wouldn't have left without her."

One eyebrow arched in annoyance. "What use do I have for that baby? Where I'm going—"

"And where might that be?" Billy swung down from his mount, his movements slow and easy so he wouldn't spook her. "Sounds like you've got nothin' to go back to in Richmond."

"But it's a nothing I *know*! At least there are places I might get a job, or a friend of the family who might take pity and—"

"You don't need pity any more than I do."

He held the reins with one hand and slowly offered her his other one, as though she were a skittish mare needing the reassurance of his scent. Her own sweetness teased at him on the morning breeze. Billy reminded himself that kissing her wouldn't get him anywhere except in trouble—as it had when they'd gotten caught sneaking those peaches.

Eve scowled at his extended hand. "If you're trying to drag me back—"

"That would never work," he confirmed. "You came to Abilene lookin' for me, and didn't get things your way. So now you're walkin' off in a hissy fit to get my attention again. Well, you've got it."

When those green eyes widened, he swallowed hard. He knew all about young women who batted their lashes and stomped their feet—and he might fall for this one anyway. After all, she'd come here believing he'd help her. That was bait he had trouble resisting.

"If this is a trick—if you're just making fun of me—"

"No tricks. I'm givin' you a ride to town, and you can either board the train for Missouri with me, or you'll go back to Mercy and Mike's," he said, watching her reaction. "Or, take your chances out here on the road. Just a matter of time before those blisters lay you low—and *then* where will you be?"

Her scowl told him he was right but she didn't appreciate it one bit. So why did that put a tickle down in his belly, as if butterflies were trying to break loose?

Billy laced his fingers into a toe-hold for her and stood beside his horse, waiting.

"That's no choice at all!" she protested. "There'll be hell to pay whether I go back to face Mother or answer to the Malloys, so—"

Billy stood silently beside his horse, still stooped over. Her voice was more musical now than when they'd been kids, and he liked the way she'd filled out since then, too.

"—don't think for a minute I'm going to—Billy, you're not listening to a thing I've said!"

Your actions are speaking so loud, I can't make out the words. But he couldn't tell her how shaking her head made her shiny brown hair catch the sunlight, or how that calico dress clung to the curve of her hips when she scolded him. He just held his hands in position, meeting her green eyes with a gaze that didn't waver.

"Well, if you must know," she finally blustered, "I was heading for town because that horse and buckboard I drove is at the livery stable, waiting for me to—"

"Nope. Mike brought 'em back to the ranch when he took Gabe and Miss Vanderbilt to the train. So you might as well climb onto Pete."

Her exasperation made him chuckle. With a huff and a curse word, Eve placed her foot in his hand. She would have kicked him—accidentally, of course—if he hadn't ducked his head.

He swung up behind her, taking the reins again. "Now maybe we'll get somewhere."

Eve sat stiffly, as though leaning on him was beneath her. For half a mile, he felt the waves of her frustration and bitterness, yet he had no idea how to help her. Sure, he'd gotten her off the road and out of danger, but *now* what would he do with her? The last thing he needed while he was tracking Wesley was a sickly female to slow him down—and this particular female would arouse his twin's anger and suspicion about him, as well. Eve Massena might vow she'd stay at her mother's, but he knew better.

So it was time to find out why, exactly, she was now sitting in front of him, with the scent of her loose hair teasing his nose like the lilacs that bloomed in Mama's garden, back by the gate.

That memory stabbed at him. While Mama's lilac bush was the least of his concerns, he was anxious about the Bristol homestead. He didn't want anyone with him when he looked it over, after ten years of being away. So it was time for some tough talk.

"I have been listening to what you've told me," he began in the low, steady voice he used to coax a contrary horse, "but tell me the *real* reason you're at loose ends now. The real reason you came to Kansas."

She whipped around so fast the horse spooked. Billy had to grab her and rein in Pete at the same time.

"What don't you understand?" she demanded. "For you it was different after the war—you've found yourself a whole new life! But I'm only nineteen, and my life is *over!*"

Her pain resurrected his own, from deep down and long ago. Billy kept his arm around her, against his better judgment: Eve felt poised to turn around and slap him—and then they'd make even slower progress toward that train he wanted to catch.

"Surely you recall the horror of losing your father—but I found mine hanging from his belt in the barn, Billy!" she rasped. "And when it got out about *why* he hanged himself—how he'd been paying outlaws to bring on foreclosures—my reputation was shattered! And now I've had a baby out of wedlock. What decent man will marry me?"

Her eyes looked huge and wet, and Billy wished he'd picked a better time to start this conversation. Eve turned sideways, so she was sitting across his lap with her legs to one side now.

"Imagine my humiliation, having to support a mother who was no more able to earn her keep than I was!" she continued in a distressed voice. "I only got a position because so many of our male teachers had gone to war. I *detested* having to discipline those horrid children and clean that schoolhouse like somebody's slave! These are the hands of an artist—not a maid!"

To emphasize her point, she held out her hands. They were reddened and chapped. Not at all the creamy, flawless hands of one raised to be a lady.

"I'm sorry about all this, Eve," Billy murmured. "I saw my daddy shot down, so I know how awful it is to—"

"But you're a man, Billy. You can set your own course," she blurted. "I was such a fish out of water—never enjoyed ciphering or geography or spelling—but I had to pretend I knew what I was doing. I was so desperate—so beside myself at the prospect of being an old maid school marm—I *believed* your brother when he said he'd marry me! With so many of our men lost to the war, Wesley seemed my only hope."

Billy got caught up in the shining eyes only inches from his own. Eve's cheeks were flushed and she was trembling so hard he had to wonder what sort of a beast his brother had become.

Or was this all an act to play on his sympathies? Billy listened intently, separating his sentiments from the bleak picture she painted with her words.

"When I lost my—my innocence—to him and his pretty lies, I soon found out the consequences," she continued nervously. "The bigger I got, the harder it was to hide my condition. The school board dismissed me for being an immoral example to the children—and then Mother got so mortified, she kicked me out! Said I was a disgrace to her and to the church.

"That's when I lost all faith in religion, Billy," Eve whispered solemnly. "Lost all confidence in myself, as well. My need to have a man ruined what was left of my sorry life."

"Have you asked God to forgive you?"

The question was out of his mouth before he thought about it, and her quick scowl told him he was treading on swampy ground.

"Why would I do that?" she asked with an unlady-like snort. "I'm sick to death of Mother's preaching about how I've sinned and been her ruination!"

"Ah, but that's *religion* you're railin' against," he re-marked softly. "That's not the same as havin' *faith*. Askin' God to forgive you—and then believin' He *has*—leads to forgivin' yourself, Peaches. You need to let go of—"

"Stop calling me that childish name!"

"—your mistakes and start from where you are—havin' Olivia—and go forward again."

Her exasperation slapped him. "Billy! I've just told you I have *nothing* to go back to, and certainly no way to progress beyond—"

"Instead of thinkin' about what you've lost, let's con-centrate on what you *have*, Eve," he countered. He was in up to his neck, so he might as well state his case—let her know the sort of man she'd be dealing with if she returned to Missouri. "The way I see it, you're still the prettiest girl ever to live in Richmond. But don't tell my sister that."

Eve blinked. Stared at him like a doe frozen at the sound of gunfire. Her lips tried to deny a grin. "You're just saying that to—"

"And while you don't count it as a blessing yet, you

have Olivia," he continued earnestly. "Most men value a woman who can be a mother—like Michael Malloy loves Mercy.

"And you saw how my mama took to that grand-child?" he went on in a more exuberant voice. "I bet your mother will, too, Eve. One look at that carrot-haired angel, and she'll see how her life would be a whole lot happier if you two were home. She'd be the sort of help you need raisin' a baby, too."

Eve glanced away, toward fields of cornrows that stretched into forever. "I'm not so sure about that, be-cause—"

"And you have your painting, too. Nobody can take that talent away from you, Eve." He gazed at the smooth line of her jaw until she faced him again. "Plenty of folks around Ray County would love a like-ness of their homes—and they'd pay you for them! I know I would."

Eve sighed sadly. "Honest to God, Billy, I sent you one. I hope you believe—"

He placed a finger on her lips. His heart was beating so hard, his chest hurt. They'd be in town shortly, and he needed to know something before they arrived.

"I do believe you sent it, honey, but I'm not so sure *why*. Why'd you come all the way to Kansas, lookin' for *me*?"

She went so still, he nearly pinched her to make her breathe again.

"Why'd you call off your wedding, Billy?" she whis-pered. "You've been asking me all these questions, making me talk. It's time you revealed yourself, as well."

The words were soft, with a breathy quality that lured him where he shouldn't go just yet. But they cer-tainly got to the crux of the matter.

He stopped the horse in the middle of the road. Why

had he walked away from Emma and the life they'd been preparing for together?

"Fair enough," he hedged, praying he didn't say something stupid—or something he'd regret the rest of his life. "I'm not a man who backs out on a promise. I feel as low as an earthworm for what I did to Emma."

She nodded, drinking in his face as he made his confession.

"Partly I latched on to the possibility of seein' Wesley, after all these years. And I want to go home again—even though I realize things won't ever be the same there. But—"

Billy let out a long, slow sigh, carefully considering his words.

"It seemed like you went to a lot of trouble—took a huge chance—comin' out to find me. And maybe God was tryin' one last time to steer me away from a path I wasn't meant to take," he said softly. "I'm not sayin' I'll marry you to make up for the trouble my brother's caused, but I feel responsible for Olivia—for seein' she's got a home. Am I makin' any sense?"

He looked into her eyes, wondering if she saw hope and strength—or the world's biggest fool—as she returned his gaze.

"Dang it, Eve, I wasn't expectin' to ever see you again, and—and I can't leave you hangin' the way Wes did. Got to get you on your feet again."

"That's a tall order," she murmured.

"If you believe it can happen, I want to help."

Chapter Ten

Billy Bristol wasn't the most romantic man she'd ever met, but he wasn't full of bluster like his brother, either. Eve remained sideways on the horse the rest of the way into Abilene, relishing the closeness of his body, the way he closed his eyes and inhaled the scent of her hair when he thought she wasn't watching.

He'd be easy to fool. He was so engrossed in doing the right thing by her and the baby, she could make all sorts of promises and he'd see the best in them. He'd give her the benefit of the doubt, despite the way she'd disrupted his wedding—his whole *future*.

Sitting this close to him, Eve was aware of how much shorter and smaller Billy was than Wes, yet he radiated a confidence, an inner strength, that didn't need physical might to make things right. His body looked lean and compact in his simple clothes of denim and chambray. His dark auburn hair was thick and neatly trimmed—and he didn't sport that thicket of a beard his brother Wesley wore.

She'd done the right thing, betting on Billy. And as the flat crop land and farmsteads gave way to the shops and buildings of Abilene, Eve sensed she'd better speak

up. She had no intention of returning to the Triple M—
ever—so she'd have to convince Billy she would make
amends with her mother.

Once she was back in Missouri, she'd get even with
Wesley—and what could Billy do to her? He'd delivered her baby without a qualm and rescued her from
the road, so he wouldn't let her become his wicked
twin's target. He'd protect her to the death, although
she hoped it wouldn't come to that.

When they arrived at the train station, Billy gave her
a pointed look, with blue eyes that seemed to see
through her secret plans.

"Here's how it's gonna be," he said as he helped her
dismount. "You can go back to your mother's—mend
fences and get your strength back—while I find my
brother. Or I can have somebody drive you back to
Mike and Mercy's."

His eyes softened. Or was she imagining that?

"Either way," he went on, "I'm glad we had time to
talk things out. And I'm glad I got to see you again,
Peaches. It brings back happier times."

Was that all he had to say? Eve reminded herself that
although Billy meant well, he didn't blow on and on
with flowery phrases.

"You're absolutely right about my needing more faith
in myself," she said softly—even though she'd been in
command the whole time they rode. "And now, while
Olivia's being spoiled by her grandmother and Mercy, I
can regain my strength and figure out what comes next
for my daughter and me."

She kept her gaze fixed on his. "I—I hate to be beholden to you for train fare, Billy, because Mother
won't have the means to repay—"

"I've socked away my pay from managin' those
horses at the Triple M. This is a good way to spend some
of it."

He grinned at her, looking besotted. When he reached

for her hand, Eve knew he'd be her willing victim. "It'll be good to have company on the ride back home," he said. "I can't figure out how you came the whole way in that rickety wagon, close as you were to birthin' your baby."

Eve shrugged, glancing toward the mercantile, watching the women walk by in their plain but respectable dresses. "It's what I could afford. I—I wish I didn't look so frumpy, though, Billy. People will wonder why you're so neat and clean, while I'm—and Lord, if Mother sees me in this dress—"

"She'll be too excited to notice what you're wearin'," he replied pointedly. "You're nearly back to the size you were before the baby came, so you'll have clothes at home. Your mother surely won't have emptied out your room."

When he turned to enter the train station, Eve made a nasty face at his back. She'd hoped to rub Wesley Bristol's nose in the fact that she'd not only latched onto his brother, but Billy was taking care of her. Treating her like the lady she was! It wouldn't be a convincing conversation if she were dressed in cast-offs, would it? She had *no* intention of going home for clothes.

When Billy came back outside, however, Eve smiled sweetly at him. She took his arm as he led his horse to the last stock car of the eastbound train, where Pete would ride while they sat in a passenger car. There would be plenty of time to plan her revenge—and what she'd wear for that occasion—during their ride back to Richmond.

At least she wouldn't be seeing anyone she knew.

"Good to be back in Missouri," Billy murmured as they stepped down onto the platform at the Lexington train station. "Good to see trees and hills again."

Eve slipped her slender hand into his, and Billy held it as they walked the length of the train to fetch Pete.

From here it was about an hour's ride to the house, but after ten years away, he felt so dang close he *tingled*! And the feeling had nothing to do with sitting next to Eve on the train, sharing stories of their childhood as she smiled and batted her eyes.

The uniformed station attendant stopped unloading mailbags to stare at him. Without a word, the man went inside. He had the look of a man getting a lynch mob together.

Billy frowned. "Now why do you suppose—I don't even know that fella, but he's actin' like—"

"You look a lot like Wesley. Maybe that man was wondering if you're here to pull a robbery," she replied quietly. Her voice had an edge of excitement to it, though, as if she enjoyed being seen with an outlaw. Her head was tilted, and that sparkle in her eyes made him smile. Eve Massena was making the most of his twin's notoriety, even if it was at his expense.

He understood: his brother had caused more problems for Eve than he was worth—and the most compelling "problem" had remained behind, in Abilene. Here, free and unencumbered, Eve Massena could feel like her old self again, at least in her imagination.

During their train ride, as she recounted goings-on since he'd left, Billy sensed this young woman was good at talking her way out of tight spots—or talking others into doing whatever she wanted. Although that might not be the most admirable trait a young lady could have, it showed a brave heart that could rise above life's little injuries. And frankly, Billy was tired of women who got their feelings hurt over every little thing.

Not that forsaking Emma Clark was a little thing.

He sighed, pushing her image away for now. He'd come to accomplish a monumental task, for himself and for Mama, and it'd be best if he didn't get side-tracked by regrets or misgivings. He smiled politely at the railway agents who watched closely as he entered the car to reclaim his horse and tack.

"Hey there, Pete," he crooned. "You ready to see where I was born?"

The Morgan bobbed his head and whickered, happy to walk out of the rolling, rumbling boxcar. A few minutes later Billy had him saddled.

"Let's mount up," he said, making his hands into a step stool for Eve, "and we'll be on our way. I appreciate your tellin' me about the places Wesley's been hidin'. I know it has to bother you—"

Before he knew what hit him, Eve cupped his jaw and kissed him!

It was a light, feathery brush of her lips that took him by storm. Billy sucked air, feeling heat in his cheeks. "Now don't you go thinkin' that just because—"

"Sometimes you talk too much," she teased. "I'd tell you what you want to know a whole lot faster if you'd pay me a little attention. Like this."

His breath left him again as she moved in for another kiss—right here on the railroad platform, where the agents and everyone else could see them! This time she leaned into him as her lips opened his.

Billy's pulse thundered and he kissed her back. Then, somehow, he found the strength to put his hands at her waist and step away from her.

"Enough of that," he gasped.

But Eve didn't believe him. He was showing all the signs of being a love-struck fool.

This is how Wesley got suckered into her web, Billy thought fleetingly.

But he knew her tricks. He'd had a sister, after all: Christine had flirted mercilessly with men when she wanted something. And though Emma Clark's moves weren't as smooth as Eve's, she was insistent about getting her share of kissing. Girls liked that part, he'd heard. More than what came after—more than what his brother had done to Eve—whether or not she'd lured him into it.

He had no trouble understanding why Wesley had wanted Miss Massena. He wanted her himself. Billy inhaled and let his breath out forcefully, to get his mind back on his original mission.

"You gonna ride?" he asked, cupping his hands beside the horse again, "or you gonna stand there moonin' at me like a coyote on a summer night?"

"Billy, really!" Daintily, Eve lifted her foot, swinging herself up to sit sideways again.

Billy landed behind her, well aware that when she fixed those shining green eyes on him, he was at her mercy.

Or you'd better make her think so, anyway.

Experience had taught Billy that if he showed sincere interest in a lady of any age, he could have what *he* wanted, too. Which could be the best way to set Eve straight without her knowing it.

"Giddap," he murmured, gathering up the reigns.

They took the road toward Richmond at a good clip, and then slowed Pete's pace as they got closer to home. Billy's heart was pounding. His gaze lingered on the familiar farms as he recalled the names of the childhood friends who'd lived there.

"The Mayhew place looks awfully run down," he remarked as they passed a farmhouse that needed some paint. The rose bushes had overgrown their trellises and dead tree branches littered the yard.

"I hear Jared's still around, but once Jewel took off with a Union officer, and after their brother Curtis died for the Confederacy, the family just sank into sadness," Eve remarked. "Some of these things were going on when you still lived here, Billy, but we were too young to understand them. And since you lived a little farther from town than I did—"

"Yeah, we didn't know what happened to some of

these folks unless we heard about it at church. And after Daddy got shot, well—we had our own worries about keepin' body and soul together."

Eve slung her arm around his shoulders, partly to keep her balance but mostly to make another point with those green, green eyes. "I hope you know I was *mortified* when Daddy foreclosed on you, Billy. He said it was just business—that the bank had to cut its losses to stay afloat.

"I pitched a fit when I found out about it!" she went on, her face alight with the memory. "Told Daddy your family deserved more time—at least until you could sell your hay—"

"You were only nine," Billy reminded her. "I'm sure your daddy wasn't inclined to pay attention to his little girl's business opinions."

But he was pleased Eve remembered these details. And he believed her indignation was sincere.

"Yes, he told Mother I was behaving like a temperamental little princess. Insisted my tutor find a new avenue for my outspoken ways—the old 'children are to be seen and not heard' idea."

She shook her head, which made her hair quiver around her shoulders, glimmering in the sunlight. It tickled his cheek when the breeze blew those long, soft strands into his face. To keep from being distracted again, Billy looked at the landmark trees and houses along this road: only a few more intersections, and he'd have her where he wanted her.

"So that's when Mr. Buckhurst—you remember him? The man who looked like Ichabod Crane from the Sleepy Hollow story?"

Billy laughed, nodding.

"Well, he showed Mother and me his studio. She was so taken by his paintings, she signed me on for private lessons and commissioned him to do all our portraits, plus several large Biblical murals for the church."

Eve's expression grew pensive then. "I never attained the level Mr. Buckhurst expected of me—I was more interested in dancing lessons than landscapes, you know—but I took comfort in painting my childhood memories in those dark days after Daddy died."

Billy found himself watching her rose-colored lips form the words and the gold rings shining in her emerald eyes as she recalled these things. "I wish you'd paint me another picture of our place," he said softly. "I—I don't know what got into Emma, but she must have destroyed the one you sent along with your letter."

"She was afraid of losing you, Billy. Afraid you'd come back here—without her."

He swallowed hard, unable to release her gaze for several seconds. This young woman got right to the point—so different from the way Emma's flushed cheeks and lame protests told the tale she denied with her words.

It was scary, how fear made so many decisions, even for folks who believed God was working his purpose out in their lives.

He eased the horse down a side street with the slightest tug on the reins. If he could keep Eve talking, reliving the times that had branded them as surely as those hot irons he applied to the haunches of Malloy's cattle, he could have his way with her. But in an entirely different sense than Wesley had.

"Do you still have your paints?"

Her brow puckered. "Of course, I do, but they're at Mother's, and—"

"You should get 'em out again. The school board relieved you of your teachin' post, but nobody can fire you when you're makin' your own way!" he said urgently. "You're not the weak-kneed kind of woman who sits with her hands folded and starves to death, just because folks don't approve of her. And I like that. A *lot*."

Her slow smile made something flicker in his belly. "Thank you for recognizing that, Billy. You realize, of course, that I could never stay with Mother again to—"

"No reason you couldn't use a room at our place to—"

The words caught him up short; made him realize just how far gone he was. "But then, if Wesley's usin' the house as a—"

"Far as I know, he's a squatter," she said with a winsome grin. "I believe the bank still holds the deed, because the locals were so incensed that Daddy foreclosed, why—nobody would buy it. It was your friends' way of standing by your family, even after your mama took you away."

The thought lit a tiny flicker of hope within him.

For now, though, Billy watched for the next lane while he kept Eve talking, and looking at him. His quick glance at the stately brick house told him the lace curtains and the double-globed lamp still graced the picture window in the front parlor. The old maple tree at the side still cast its cool shadow across the roof, too—over the spot where he'd peeked into Eve's upstairs window one time, on Wes's double-dog dare.

He hadn't realized just how much he and his brother had competed for Eve Massena's attention, even as boys. Back then, they were just sneaking peeks, seeing what they could get away with. The stakes were a whole lot higher now that they'd grown up.

Billy prayed quickly for the right words as they approached the house. And when Eve scowled, opening her mouth to protest, he grabbed her by the arms to keep her from spooking Pete—or worse yet, falling off in her struggle.

"Billy Bristol, you conniving, underhanded—"

"Hear me out, now!" he said, in what he hoped was a reasonable tone of voice.

"But I *told* you I wouldn't come crawling back to Mother's—"

"And you haven't. I brought you here—and for good reason." He held her gaze again, noting from the corner of his eye that the front door was opening. "I'm leavin' you here while I look for Wesley, so he won't hurt you again."

The door slammed.

In the time it took Eve to twist around toward the porch, a pale, slender woman had stepped outside—and she held a gun. Billy saw how the pistol quivered as she pointed it, but he could take no chances: even if Mrs. Massena couldn't aim accurately, she could do plenty of damage if she pulled the trigger.

"I've brought your daughter home, so she can be safe—and so she can tell you about Olivia, your new granddaughter!" Billy piped up. He smiled at the woman, still holding on to Eve even though she'd gone stiff in front of him.

"How *dare* you show your face here!" the woman retorted, but her voice had a hitch in it. "So help me, I'll shoot first and proudly tell the sheriff I laid you low, Mr. Bristol! Lord knows I could put the reward money to good use! Turn loose of my girl before—"

"Mother, this is Billy—not Wes!" Eve cried. "Put that gun down before you shoot somebody. Especially *me*!"

"I've had all I can take of *your* shenanigans, too, young lady! Get down off that horse and come inside, before the neighbors see you!"

Questions spun in Billy's mind, but he didn't doubt that Eve's mother would rather shoot him than look at him. Still, it couldn't hurt to explain.

"Mrs. Massena, it feels so good to be home—and I promise you I've come to talk some sense into Wesley," he offered. "I'm gonna dismount now, so I can help Eve off my horse, and then I'll be on my way. Just don't do anything rash, all right?"

Florence Massena looked ready to cry and swear—and yes, fire that gun—as she stood her ground. Billy slowly swung his leg over the horse, hoping his smile reflected his honorable intent.

Eve, however, was glaring at him as though smoke would come from her nostrils. He had to give her dress a good tug to get her down. She slipped into his arms and landed with a little gasp, but her flirtatious ways had been replaced by wrath. "You conniving, underhanded—"

"You've already said that, Peaches," Billy reminded her. He couldn't resist brushing her hair back from her flaming face—and then felt the sting of her slap. "You're gonna stay here while I get some answers from my brother. And when I come back, we'll go fetch Olivia. Maybe your mother'll want to come along," he added, watching for the woman's face to soften.

"That's Satan speaking, Mr. Bristol. Your sweet talk doesn't fool me one bit. Now turn loose of my daughter."

He did as he was told. Billy wanted to reassure Eve—no, he really wanted to kiss the indignation from her pretty face. But she'd be safe here. That was what mattered right now.

He mounted his horse and rode toward the street. When he reached the end of the Massena's overgrown lane, he turned to see them standing apart, a mother and daughter whose stories didn't seem to match up. He waved, not surprised that neither of them waved back.

Then Billy urged Pete into a canter down the tree-lined street, feeling the gazes of curious neighbors from behind their curtains. But he was too intent on his mission to care what they thought.

He was *home*. He'd go to the house tomorrow, when he was rested—ready to meet his twin again after ten long years.

Chapter Ten

Billy slowed his horse at the end of the long drive, feeling as if the overgrown bushes and untrimmed trees hid the house from him on purpose—as though they covered its shame and disgrace so he wouldn't feel it, too. He noticed how unearthly the silence was: not a bird call to be heard, not even the whisper of the summer breeze. The Bristol home seemed to be waiting, holding its breath. Warning him of things he'd wish he'd never seen.

Maybe he should have stayed at the hotel longer, asking some questions and planning his strategy.

But perhaps his feeling was just caused by his own jumpiness. His reaction to Eve's warnings about what sort of shape the place was in. Some deterioration was to be expected, if no one had lived here for the ten years since he and Christine and Mama had left.

Were the furnishings still in place? Were his left-behind clothes still in the chiffonier, and the dishes still in Mama's china cabinet with the glass doors? If Wesley and his outlaw band had been using the place as their hideout, he really couldn't expect the remnants of his childhood to be intact.

Yet he hoped. He dreamed of walking inside, seeing the dining room table and chairs that had once formed an imaginary fort; sniffing for a hint of Beulah Mae's pies in the kitchen. He gazed at the tall white house with its massive pillars along the front porch, and looked at the window of the room he and Wes had shared. Billy took a deep breath.

The glass was broken. Only a jagged bottom half remained.

"Giddap, Pete," he murmured. "Let's see what we're gonna see and get on with findin' Wes. Might be long gone, if he or his outlaw cohorts got wind of me bein' here."

The horse nickered, his ears pricked forward. The maple trees along the drive had grown so tall they formed a canopy over him, shading his eyes so he could drink in the details of the house as he grew closer to it, step by purposeful step. From what he'd heard, he might get shot at, and he wasn't armed. He'd learned to shoot, of course—Michael wanted him to protect himself and the family from wolves and Indians and other intruders.

But he'd never bought a gun. Didn't feel it was his place to take another life. He believed God would be his strength and shield until he was called away from this earth.

Slowly he rode forward, watchful when a rabbit jumped out from under the overgrown forsythia bushes. The lawn was choked with weeds; piles of horse manure suggested the men who stayed here let their mounts graze while they were inside. A sudden creak made his head snap up—

But it was only a dusty black shutter, waving at him from one hinge as it bumped against the house. Those windows had always seemed like eyes on the face of this place, and now they stared at him vacantly, dull with dirt.

Trumpet vines had taken over the front steps, and their bright orange flowers reminded him of the angel Gabriel's horn—warning him away from the house, maybe?

Billy stopped, sighing sadly. Mama's heart would break in two if she saw this. Their fine home and horse ranch, once the pride of Ray County, was now an eyesore. The rolling pastures were colored more with wildflowers and weeds than the fine grass their thoroughbreds had feasted on when he was a kid. There wasn't a horse to be seen. Just acres of untended grassland, spotted with volunteer oak trees. The white fence had rotted in places and railings were down; all the hours he'd spent whitewashing those planks as a kid kicked him in the gut.

He was about to swing down from his horse when the click of a pistol froze him to the saddle.

"Well, well, well! If it ain't the illustrious Billy Bristol, come back home for a visit. Like what you see, Beaner?"

The nickname scraped like a dull razor: only Wesley had ever called him Beaner, referring to his skinniness as a kid. He swallowed hard.

"Cat got your tongue, little brother?" that familiar voice goaded. "Or has that whore of a banker's daughter been bendin' your ear? Either way, you may as well clear out, Billy. This ain't your place anymore."

His pulse pounded in his ears. The voice came from inside the house, upstairs, but Wes wasn't showing himself.

"Fine way to treat your brother, after ten years of bein' apart!" Billy countered. His voice sounded shrill, but he had some things to say before this situation got nasty. "Christine and Mama and I figured you might be dead, after not hearing from you for—"

"Too bad Eve had to shoot off her mouth. It *was* Eve, wasn't it?" his twin demanded. "Showin' up with her belly stickin' out and blamin' it all on me."

"No doubt in my mind—or Mama's—that the baby's yours, Wes," Billy retorted. He squinted beneath the hand shading his brow, wishing he could see his brother, the notorious outlaw. "Would it be such a horrible thing to own up? To take care of the girl you ruined, and the baby—"

"Still stupid, ain'tcha?" came the retort, followed by a low, hard laugh. "Still takin' up for the one who whimpers loudest. Don't tell me you *believed* everything that traitor's daughter said!"

Billy bit back a retort. For all he knew, other members of Wes's gang were using this conversation as a cover, while they encircled him from behind the trees. Or watched him from downstairs, with their guns against the window sills, waiting for Wes's order to shoot him down.

"All I know is what I've seen," he replied carefully. The shifting of his horse confirmed his suspicion that all was not right. It would be typical of Wes to fire just to scare the bejesus out of him. His twin had always delighted in catching him off-guard, and now that they were adults, his shenanigans would be a lot more dangerous.

"Why don'tcha put down that pistol?" Billy suggested. "We had our differences as kids, but you've surely wondered what Christine and I—and Mama— have been doing with ourselves."

"Oh—Mama! Now *she's* a fine piece of work!" Wesley blurted. "Last I heard, she and that Wyndham fella were writin' up phony deeds for homesteads. Saw in the paper where she was holdin' a lottery out in California to fund some asinine school for spiritualism."

His laughter sounded out of kilter. "Guess Mama's been way too busy to worry about the boy the Border Ruffians snatched away from her."

Billy was about to tell him Mama had reformed and remarried, but such information might be an ace up his sleeve for later. His outlaw brother didn't need to know that her new husband was a Pinkerton operative, either.

"You're not the least bit interested in that baby, are ya?" he asked, his anger rising. "You have a sweet little girl named Olivia, Wesley. She needs a daddy, and Eve Massena—"

"Eve Massena can go straight to hell! Nothin' but a tease who bats those eyelashes and flashes her assets," Wes jeered. "And then what's she do but bemoan the consequences, after I gave her exactly what she asked for?

"No thanks!" he went on with another sarcastic laugh. "I've had all of that slut I can stomach. Got what she deserved, findin' her daddy strung up in the barn."

"No one deserves that!" Billy cried.

A shot rang out, making Pete dance and toss his head.

"Worthless! That's what those Massenas are!" Wes hollered. "Whatever bad happens to 'em, they got it comin', after the way Leland foreclosed on Mama."

Billy clenched his jaw; he couldn't let his brother see how agitated this talk was making him.

"So you're sayin' this was all Leland's fault?" Billy ventured. If he could keep the conversation going, maybe he could talk Wesley out of the house.

"Nope. None of this—*none* of it—woulda happened, if Daddy had just given them Border Ruffians the horses they came for."

His twin paused, to be sure Billy got the point. "It was that simple, Beaner. Daddy was tryin' to be the hero, standin' up for his rich man's principles, but we lost *everything* that night, didn't we?"

Billy's mind froze. No one had ever blamed their misfortune on his father. Owen Bristol was protecting his family and his prime breeding stock when the Border Ruffians galloped in, brandishing their guns and demanding fresh mounts. If Wesley believed for one minute that those no-account bandits deserved their horses—or deserved to live when their daddy didn't—

But his brother had run with the outlaws so long, apparently he thought they were right to take whatever they wanted.

"You can't really believe—"

"Doesn't matter what I believe, Billy boy!" came the retort. "Fact of the matter is, you're trespassin'! You're on my property, and I didn't invite you here. And maybe I'll defend it a whole lot better than our daddy did."

Billy paused, stalling. Did he detect movements from the sides of his eyes, or was fear spooking him?

"What do you mean, it's your property?" he called out. "When Leland Massena—"

"Leland and I became partners, Beaner. He deeded the place back to me as payment for some of the *business* I did for him."

"And what sort of business would that be?" Billy didn't really want to know, but he needed to find out if Wes's story matched up with Eve's.

"Let's call it cullin' out the bad apples," his twin answered with a nasty laugh. "Folks who weren't keepin' up with their payments, or other bankers competin' against Massena's bank. Real easy to shoot the man of the family—like the Border Ruffians did—and then scare the widows and kids into movin' out, so the bank could take over their land."

Billy's jaw dropped. "That's the most underhanded—"

"Aw, what do *you* care?" Wes taunted. "When I saw that piece in the Kansas City paper, about you bein' the big hero in Abilene, I figgered you weren't gonna reclaim the place. So at least I kept it in the family," he scoffed. "Soon as I saw my brother had rescued a family of niggers, there was no use in askin' you to come home. You'd obviously forgotten your *place*."

Billy bit back a remark, his mind spinning. Had Mama been here, she'd have fallen over in a faint and—

No, she'd be rushin' inside to box that boy's ears, came his mind's reply.

And why wasn't he doing that? What kept him from going into the house where he'd grown up—where it was his birthright to be, same as Wesley's?

The breeze stirred the trees around him—a breeze that caressed his sweaty face and whispered in his ear like a guardian angel.

Have you not known? Have you not heard? The Lord—the Everlasting God—tires not, nor grows faint! He gives power and strength to the weak, and His understanding is unsearchable!

Billy inhaled deeply, trying to sort this out: the verses from Isaiah were running through his mind as though Mike Malloy were reading them during devotions. It was clearly a sign from God. And though Billy wasn't used to receiving such direct messages from the Almighty, he knew better than to ignore them.

Those who wait on the Lord shall renew their strength! that confident voice continued. *They shall mount up with wings like eagles! They shall run and not be weary! They shall walk and not faint!*

But then it was his brother's voice taunting him again. "Are ya tongue-tied, Billy boy? Or are ya settin' there wettin' your pants?"

Billy nudged his horse forward. He'd come all this way to see the place—to find his long-lost brother and demand respect for the woman and child Wesley had abandoned. He wasn't going to tolerate this confrontational talk any longer! God had led him here today for a reason, and—

A shot whined, striking the ground not ten feet away from him. Billy gripped Pete with his knees to keep from being tossed off.

"Don't come another inch!" Wesley warned. "Like I told ya, this here's my land and you're trespassin'! You got a home, you got a job on that Kansas ranch, and you got a family, Billy. You don't belong here no more."

His heart thudded in his chest. Why would his

brother shoot at him? That was envy he heard in Wes's words, but what could he have done differently all those years ago? He hadn't *asked* Mama to abandon him!

Lord, watch over me. I don't know what might happen next! came his frightened prayer.

And then, over the sound of his galloping heart, he heard hoofbeats behind him. Another shot whistled past his head, followed by a female shriek.

"Well, looky here!" his twin crowed. "If it ain't that purty little Massena gal! She comin' to save you, Billy? My God, Beaner—you hung behind Mama's skirts when we was kids, and now you've got Eve watchin' out for ya!"

"You have no idea what—"

"Get outta here, sissy-boy!" his twin cried. Billy saw his shadowy form in the window, aiming the rifle. "After all the trouble Eve's daddy caused us, I'd just as soon shoot her as look at her! Get outta here! You'll be nothin' but sorry if ya stay here runnin' your mouth!"

Billy glanced back and yes, it was Eve. She looked as terrified as he felt. The image of her red-haired infant flashed through his mind—a baby who couldn't help it that her daddy had gone bad—and he wheeled his horse around. Surely his brother wouldn't shoot him in the back—

But then, this show of bravado—these words hurled at him from inside the house—were the acts of a far bigger coward than he. Any man who'd threaten a woman wasn't worth dealing with: Wesley would behave even more recklessly if he didn't get Eve out of here.

Chapter Eleven

"Billy, what's happened?" Eve cried. "He's gone crazy!"

"And what would you know about *crazy*?" Wes retorted from the window. "You had it easy all your life! You never lost your home or got kidnapped. You're crooked just like your daddy, blamin' *me* for that baby! I hear tell it coulda belonged to any one of a dozen—"

Billy grabbed the reins of Eve's mount and wheeled it around. "Hang on!" he whispered hoarsely. "We've gotta ride beyond the range of their rifles. There might be men in the bushes around the house, too."

Billy cantered back down the tree-lined lane as fast as he dared, recalling that Eve had never been much of a rider. The peace and security he'd felt here as a kid was shattered—yet a sudden surge of power was shoving them out of harm's way.

They shall mount up with wings like eagles . . . they shall run and not be weary . . .

Behind them, more shots rang out, ricocheting against the tree trunks. His heart thudded hard in his chest. What would he tell Mama? What could he do now? It wasn't safe to return—and his twin could track him down when he went back to Abilene.

He suspected Wes wasn't finished with him: His twin had always been the type to pick at scabs and re-open wounds—a kid who'd delighted in wringing the necks of the chickens Beulah Mae cleaned for their Sunday dinners. Wes didn't let his prey limp away and lick its wounds. He demanded total victory.

"Whoa, Pete," he breathed as they reached the road. "Let's go a little farther, to be sure they aren't follow-in' us."

He caught the shine of frightened tears on Eve's face. She looked away, determined he wouldn't see them, so he gave her a moment to compose herself. He, too, needed to collect his thoughts after that unexpected showdown with his long-lost brother.

Why have you led me into this trouble, Lord? Will we be like Cain and Abel? Brother against brother, like happened so much during the war? I can't believe Wesley's gone so rotten he won't listen to—

"You should've shot him when you had the chance," Eve sputtered. Her voice sounded tight and high, as if she was still frightened.

"I've got no gun," he said, wishing he sounded more heroic. "Never dreamed I'd have to defend myself—much less *you!*"

His emotions boiled over then, more fear than anger. "What in tarnation were you doin', comin' out here, if you knew Wesley would—"

"I was checking on *you*, dammit! If he shot you down, I'd never know what happened to you!" she cried. "The countryside's littered with unmarked graves where Wes and his men have dumped their victims. Af-ter all you've done for me and Olivia, I—I couldn't stand it if you were one of them."

Billy watched her gush all this, in a voice that wasn't shaking just from riding hard and being shot at. Eve's eyes shone like huge green moons. She couldn't stop looking at him—as though it really would matter if he hadn't made it off the place alive.

"I didn't mean to scare you, honey. Should've listened to your warnings, but I didn't want to believe my own twin had gone from bad to so much worse." He stroked a tear from her blotchy face. "And what would I have done if *you'd* gotten shot?"

His insides clenched—and not just for the baby who'd be without her mama. "I left you at your mother's for a reason, Eve."

The worry in her eyes blazed into bitterness.

"And I'm sick of her telling me how evil I am!" she spat. "You'd think she'd be glad to have me, after living alone in that gloomy old house! But no, she says my presence upsets her—and that my baby is the spawn of the devil."

Her face was contorted with such anguish that Billy had to believe she was sincere—and that Wes was lying about her wayward inclinations. He squeezed her slender shoulder. "Did you love him, Eve?"

She sniffled, looking away. "I—I thought I could make a home for him. Change him into a decent man again," she whimpered. "He was so different in the beginning; so considerate and caring after Daddy hanged himself. I've known you Bristol boys all my life, so I wanted to believe he was the same old Wesley—ornery, yes, but not cruel. I was a fool to get caught up in the web he was spinning, wasn't I?"

Billy's lips twisted in a rueful grin. He knew just how cunning his brother could be, after being blamed for Wesley's stunts when they were younger. "So when he asked you to marry him, you thought he meant it? I'm really sorry, Eve," he whispered. "You don't deserve that."

How difficult it must have been for her facing her father's suicide, being the one to find his lifeless body.

Enduring the local gossip about it—and then learning of her daddy's misdeeds with other people's property. Taking a job she'd never prepared herself for, to keep food on the table.

A girl like Eve Massena, reduced to such circumstances after reigning over a childhood even more privileged than his own, would fall for things she'd have turned her nose up at before. It had to hurt that she'd not only lost her father but had become one of Wesley Bristol's living victims. The dead ones were actually much better off.

Eve shook all over, trying not to bawl or fall off her mother's sorry old mare. She had no explanation for the unseen force that had swept them ahead of the gunfire. Had Billy gotten himself killed, it would have been her fault. If she hadn't let him come here—if she hadn't run from Mother's hellfire-and-damnation sermon this morning and then chased him down—

—*if you hadn't thought you could outsmart Wesley Bristol*—

—none of this would have happened. She'd still be teaching school, eking out a living with—

She looked down in horror. Two dark, wet spots were spreading across the bodice of her threadbare dress. Her breasts were so achy and swollen, she wanted to cry about that, too.

What was happening to her? She was wet in the eyes and wet on her dress and unable to control *anything* anymore! She'd always been so self-assured, believing she could have whatever she set her heart on, and now nothing was going her way. Wesley Bristol had cast a huge shadow over her life, and she wondered if she'd be cursed forever.

She turned away so Billy wouldn't see her predicament.

"You all right, Peaches?" he asked. Then, despite his

sun-bronzed complexion, he flushed. "What a stupid question! You've just been shot at, so of course you're upset about—"

When his gaze moved lower, she wanted to die. He quickly looked into her eyes again, but he'd seen those horrid, telltale spots on her bodice.

"Eve, you didn't get shot in—? If one of those bullets hit you—" He nudged his horse close to hers so he could put his arm around her shoulders. Eve was torn between swatting him away and craving the comfort of his touch, until the wail of a baby made them both stare down the road, toward an approaching wagon.

The woman driving it wore a stylish purple suit with a matching plumed hat. Her red hair blazed like fire in the sunlight.

"Mama!" Billy cried. "Mama, what on earth possessed you to—"

"Well, first of all, Olivia needs her mother," Virgilia Harte replied with a sly smile. "And if you thought for one minute I could stay away, knowing my Wesley was using our home as his hideout, you've sadly underestimated your mama, Billy."

Eve's heart thudded. She had no choice but to take the bundle of wiggling, wailing baby Billy's mother thrust at her. Always a woman who took the direct approach, Mrs. Harte focused on Eve's wet bodice.

"I see you're needing Olivia as much as she needs you. Let's find you a place to—"

"Mama, it's not safe here!" Billy insisted. "We nearly got ourselves killed when Wesley turned peevish, talkin' to me. I can't let you—"

"That's ridiculous! Your brother might be ornery, but he would never shoot his own—"

"Please believe him," Eve pleaded as she rocked her fussy daughter. "I tried to tell Billy his brother has changed for the worse, but he wouldn't listen."

"Well, he'll listen to *me*!" The woman sat taller,

arching her neck like a swan in regal purple plumage. "Feed my granddaughter, so he won't ride out here to shut her up. I'm going to the house to—"

"Mama!" Billy turned his horse to block the one hitched to her wagon. "You can't go up there. The house looks awful, and Wesley—"

"Will hear what his mother has to say about this whole deplorable situation." She gave him a look Eve couldn't interpret.

Billy scowled, still blocking the wagon. "What's goin' on here? You can't tell me you came all this way alone."

Virgilia widened her eyes pointedly. "Of course I didn't travel alone. I had Olivia with me, and some bait to bring your brother to his senses. So if you'll excuse me"—she continued gazing at him, as though sending a message only the two of them would understand— "I'll drive up to the house now. Your mother knows what she's doing, Billy. Just as surely as she knows her own sons."

Confused and wary, Eve unbuttoned the front of her dress to relieve Olivia's misery as well as her own. At the first full glance of her baby's face, she paused—felt the wonderment of those little lips sipping her milk, and then noticed those blue, blue eyes watching her. Could it be Olivia *knew* her and had really missed her? Eve was suddenly awash with an inexplicable love for this child. Unspeakably sorry she'd abandoned her.

But she smelled a rat, too. Virgilia Bristol Harte was fearless to the point of being brazen, but she wouldn't rush in where angels—incredible, yet the only plausible explanation—had swept them out ahead of Wesley's onslaught.

"Please, Virgilia, my baby needs a grandma!" she pleaded. But where had that sentiment come from? Was she losing control of her mind as well as her body now?

"If I have my way about things, Miss Olivia will have both her grandmothers vying for her attention before the day's out. My advice to you, young lady, is to go back home with her. Florence will forget her priggishness when she lays eyes on this precious child."

With that, Virgilia raised an eyebrow at Billy. "Excuse me, son. We have fences to mend, and I'm just the woman for this job."

Chapter Twelve

As Billy watched the wagon lumber down the over-grown lane, terror shot through his body. If Wesley fired at her—if he lost his mama to that overgrown bully whose power came from a gun—Billy would never forgive himself.

Yet when he looked at Eve, he felt pulled in an entirely different direction. What a fetching sight, this pretty young mother suckling her infant—like a Madonna and child in a church painting. He gazed at Olivia's puckery little face; smiled at the contented sucking noises she made. He blew Eve a kiss.

"Stay out of the sun, out of sight, while I cover Mama." He gestured toward an old bench nearly hidden by forsythia bushes, where Christine had watched the wagons passing by when they were kids.

"But you don't have a gun."

"I can't let her ride in there alone, Eve. Wesley's done enough damage."

With that, he cantered along the unpaved side road, skirting the row of overgrown lilacs that marked the edge of Bristol property. Farther down, he broke through the bushes to ride in the dense shade of the catalpa trees so he could slip behind the house. He hoped Wes would still be at the front window watching for him—and that he'd hold his fire when he spotted Mama in her special dress, smiling up at him.

The back of the house looked even more bedraggled than its entry, but Billy couldn't let this sad decay distract him. He dismounted and wrapped Pete's reins on a nearby tree. Then he eased through the back service door, where he and Wes had escaped Beulah Mae's broom as boys.

In the center of the kitchen, he let out a sad sigh. How he wished that old colored cook would turn to him from the pans on the cookstove, flashing that grin she'd always favored him with.

But it was a filthy old bucket on the burner now, and the cast iron sides were coated with dust and the debris of misuse. The aromas of frying chicken and baking pies had been replaced by the heavy scent of grime and dead mice. The larder door hung open, but he didn't have the heart to look inside.

Billy held his breath. Crossing the plank floor, he went back into his ten-year-old mind to recall which boards creaked, and how the stiff parlor door had always announced their comings and goings. If Wesley was still upstairs in their old bedroom, he could move around down here without being detected.

The front parlor window had a hole broken out, probably where some outlaw had stuck his rifle. As Billy entered the room, the ivory settee and chairs appeared ghostly in the shadows. Then Mama started talking.

"Wesley! Wesley Owen Bristol," she cried. "Come here and talk to your mama now!"

Billy hurried over to follow the exchange from behind the tall, tattered curtains. Above him, a solid weight shifted by the window. The silence and a sense of over-whelming emptiness told him his brother was here alone.

"Wesley!" Mama called out again. "Wesley, I've come to see you, honey, and I've brought one of Beulah Mae's pies! It's rhubarb custard. Your favorite."

Billy's eyes flew open. Sure enough, she was reaching beneath the driver's seat, picking up something covered in a white kitchen towel. She held it high as evidence of her intentions.

How on God's earth had she gotten a pie from their old cook? Was she lying through her teeth, expecting Wesley to fall for her sentimental offering?

"Go 'way, Mama. You're too late," his brother replied gruffly.

"Nonsense! You're here, and I'm here, and we've got lots to talk about," she insisted. "But I'm not coming inside that house. Too many memories, and they're all behind me now."

"Why should I believe Beulah Mae is still alive, when—"

"Think again, Wesley. She seemed old to you where you were boys, but she's got her own bakery in town now. Doing quite well at it, too." Mama focused on the upstairs window, raising the pie higher. "Better come on down here and have a piece. While it's still warm."

Danged if Mama didn't pull a knife from beneath the white towel after she removed it. As she made a show of slicing the pie, Billy's mouth watered so much, he almost dashed outside to grab it himself—even though his personal favorite had been Beulah Mae's pumpkin pie.

He assessed the situation: Wes—if he took Mama's bait—would come down the front stairs. It pained Billy to see scuff marks and muddy footprints on the carpet runner, for this had been one of Richmond's most glorious stairways, with glossy oak balustrades he and Wes dusted with the seats of their britches.

But those memories no longer served him, did they? Billy slipped through the vestibule and into the back hall, where the service stairway went up the rear wall of the house. He stepped over loose boards and places that had always creaked, figuring he'd get in position to grab his brother from behind—or wrestle the gun from him—before he shot Mama.

"Don't know what you're tryin' to prove, Mama, but I ain't fallin' for it."

Was it his imagination, or did his twin's voice waver? Billy reached the top of the narrow, uncarpeted stairway and paused, catching his breath. With so many windows broken, Mama's voice carried clearly—just as it had when they were boys, pretending they didn't hear her calling.

"You and I have nothing to prove, son," she replied in a steady, steely tone. "I've spent the last ten years not knowing if you were dead or alive—"

"From what I've heard, you were too busy carousin' with that Wyndham fella to *care* whether I lived or died. Never even came lookin' for me, did ya?"

Billy cringed. His brother had made a valid, if brutal point.

"I've committed my share of sins, Wesley," Mama replied in that same unwavering voice. "I won't excuse my behavior—just like I won't accept a trumped-up story about why you're robbing banks and killing people.

"But what you don't know," she challenged, "is that Wyndham left me for dead in a San Francisco alley. If Christine hadn't been hardheaded enough to follow me—I'd be long gone."

"That's a heart-warmin' story, Mama, but I ain't buyin'—"

"I'm not asking you to do a single thing!" she shot back. "Just come down here and have a piece of pie with your mother. You have my word that I'm alone.

You're still my boy, and I still love you, and I want the best for you before somebody leaves you for dead, too. Humor me, Wesley! I don't have all day, and I'm not getting any younger."

Billy smiled in spite of the awful scenarios he could imagine. The old tone had slipped into Mama's voice—the one that said she'd cut a willow switch, or otherwise take matters into her own, deceptively powerful hands, if her boys didn't obey her right this minute.

Lo and behold, he heard footfalls crossing their old bedroom! Hidden in the unlit alcove at the top of the service stairway, Billy pressed himself against the wall.

Please, Lord, don't let him do anything to Mama! Wrap Your protection around her, even though we know dang well she's got something up her pretty purple sleeve.

Saying his silent prayer like a litany, Billy held himself absolutely still as he watched a big shadow approach and heard his twin's uneven footfalls.

It was all he could do to keep quiet when Wesley filled the doorway.

The brother he hadn't seen for ten years looked tall and stocky; his belly hung over his belt. He wore wrinkled denim pants and a chambray shirt that had seen better days. In the shadows, Wesley's beard bristled like a thicket and his hair stunk out in uneven clumps.

Billy held his breath so he wouldn't cry out—or gasp from the stench of Wes's body. His twin looked totally disreputable.

Even so, his arms ached to grab this brother in a hug. Billy swallowed hard, his eyes fixed on Wesley's side.

His twin's right arm dangled limp. That shuffle came from his left boot dragging slightly behind as Wesley entered the upstairs hallway, inching toward the top of the main stairs.

Billy's throat stung from a silent sob. All the bluster about Wesley Bristol and his cutthroat band of bank robbers—all the threats and shots fired around him and Eve—came from a man only twenty years old, the same age as he was. Yet Wes was maimed and gimpy. Downright pathetic.

Billy watched the ungainly way his brother descended the stairs. Mama would have a fit. Probably drop that pie to crush his brother in a weeping, wailing outburst of love for the son she'd not seen all this time.

After that, of course, she'd start in on him. How had he been so horribly wounded? Why did he continue in a life of crime, when it had taken such a toll on him? *Why hadn't he tried to contact his mama?*

Billy snickered. She'd put on a little scene then, complete with a disgusted grimace, pinching her offended nose.

And yet, as Wesley approached the front door, his heavy boots clumping across the vestibule floor, a bigger question puzzled Billy: Why had fine, feisty Eve Massena fallen for his brother?

Even in her impoverished desperation—even if so many local men hadn't survived the war—Billy couldn't imagine Eve giving Wesley a second glance, much less an invitation to know her in the most intimate way.

He swallowed so hard his throat hurt. Had Eve played with fire and gotten burned? Or had Wes driven Leland Massena to hang himself and then taken his pleasure—and made false promises to Eve—to destroy the entire Massena family?

Billy started quietly down the stairs. If his twin had sunk so low, he couldn't be trusted alone with Mama, even though she had pie—and a knife.

Outside, he heard her anguished cry. Footsteps pattered rapidly across the driveway. "Wesley! Wesley, come here to your—oh my Lord, you're hurt!"

Her rising voice was met with a loud grunt. Billy got

to the window as Mama threw herself against Wesley's bulk. Her arms barely went around his waist—

And then she backed away, wary as a trapped fox. She gazed up at the son who now stood head and shoulders taller than she did.

"Wesley Owen Bristol," she gasped, "you come away from here and let me take care of you! We'll have a doctor look at that arm and—"

"That's enough, Mama."

Wesley's low retort was so devoid of affection, it hurt Billy to watch from behind the rotted curtain at the front parlor window. There they stood, his grubby brother and Mama in her purple suit, staring each other down as they'd done years ago. He knew that expression on Mama's face—that fierce determination to have her say and have her way. Yet Billy detected a quiver in her chin; the tightening around eyes that had seen their share of misery and shame.

"I'm your mother, Wesley. I will always need to take care of—"

"Don't want your fussin'. Don't need your pity." Wesley's arms hung at his sides; his bearded face showed no expression. "You brought me a pie, and that was nice. But I'm not invitin' you in, 'cause we won't be eatin' off the china or sittin' all polite and proper around the table."

"I—I wasn't expecting to—"

"Good. Don't expect *nothin'* from me, Mama!" His gaze went to the seat of the wagon, and then he hobbled over to pick up the pie. "This won't be no purty reunion scene, 'cause you're leavin' now, Mama. Don't come back, understand me?"

The purple plume on her hat began to dance with her agitation, but Mama held her ground. And her tears.

"And tell my fine, upstandin' twin not to show his face here again, neither," Wes grunted. "I got no use for

Eve Massena, nor that brat she was carryin', so don't try to reform me, Mama. Things ain't like they used to be."

"Wesley, listen!" Mama planted a white-gloved fist on her purple hip, glaring. "You can't go on this way! The law's going to catch up to you—"

"Only if you or Billy shoot off your mouths!" he retorted. He looked haggard and hard and old. "Give me your word that won't happen, Mama.

"Son, if you'll only—"

"Promise you'll keep your mouths *shut*, Mama! Or I'll have to keep usin' Billy and Eve for target practice. Understand me?"

How *dare* Wesley talk to Mama that way? Make her promise not to betray him, and then threaten her family? He was deranged—more dangerous than they'd anticipated—if he expected them all to keep quiet!

Billy gripped the limp, dusty curtain. Should he remain here undetected, or rush up with something—the fireplace poker, maybe—to silence his cruel, callous brother? Instinct made him turn toward the hearth— and then his jaw dropped.

Carlton Harte stood there, his finger across his lips. His other hand rested on a pistol protruding from his holster.

"Go on now, Mama!" Wesley taunted outside. "Don't make me hurt nobody else. You can't smooth it all over no more. Can't make the past disappear!"

Harte gestured toward the kitchen. Walking quickly and quietly, they slipped out the back door so Wes wouldn't catch them. Silently they grabbed the reins of their waiting horses, hurried through the thicket of lilac bushes, and then mounted up on the other side of the leafy barricade.

"I'll explain it all later," Carleton muttered as they rode toward the front road. "It was your mother's idea. She doesn't know I followed her here."

Billy's gut clenched. He grabbed Carlton's sleeve. "What do you mean, this was Mama's idea?" he rasped. "And you let her come here? You can't tell me you didn't know—"

The detective's ominous wave silenced him. He waited until the clatter of Mama's wagon wheels had passed their hiding spot before he replied. "You saw her when Eve showed up at your wedding, saying the baby was Wesley's! You knew she'd come to see him for herself—and that no one could stop her!"

"But why'd she bring Olivia? They could've both been shot!"

Harte let out an exasperated sigh. "Virgilia believes the baby belongs with her mother. And she saw Olivia as a bargaining point."

As Carlton peered through the overgrown foliage, Billy reminded himself to simmer down—to trust this Pinkerton operative's instincts. After all, Harte had rescued his mother from Richard Wyndham's chicanery in San Francisco. And in his quiet way, he doted on Mama like no other man had.

"Maybe you'd better tell me what you know, Carlton. No sense in our workin' at cross purposes, or Mama will feel caught in the middle," Billy reasoned. "She might do somethin' even more reckless than takin' that dang pie to Wesley's door!"

"My point exactly. And it looks like she's talked Eve into going home. They'll be safely out of Wesley's way now."

Billy bit back the rest of his questions. He watched Eve hand the baby up to Mama and then clamber onto the buckboard seat. Miss Massena didn't look entirely happy, but at least she'd reclaimed her child. Mama must've worked some maternal magic—or simply informed Eve she was going to cooperate!

Harte's shoulders relaxed. "Well, for several months now, I've followed the activities of Frank and Jesse

James and the Younger brothers, through an exchange of coded telegrams from operatives around Richmond and Lexington." Carlton urged his horse forward at a walk, and Billy did the same.

"My trips from Topeka to Missouri have been covert assignments to keep track of their whereabouts and follow up on their robberies—which isn't too difficult, considering Jesse's yen for writing up his adventures and sending them to the *Kansas City Times*."

"Writin' his own alibis and lies, the way I hear it," Billy murmured.

"Precisely. And your brother has played on the same local antigovernment sympathies to hide in neighbors' root cellars and outbuildings while he was doing Leland Massena's dirty work."

Carlton slowed their pace so Mama wouldn't spot them when they entered a clear intersection.

"Unfortunately, your twin isn't as sharp as Jesse," he continued quietly. "When he got your ranch back as payment for assisting Massena, two of his cohorts— Jared Mayhew and Slick Searcy—"

"The preacher's son?" Billy's eyes widened.

"—got perturbed because they received no equivalent pay. Mayhew got drunk and mad a couple months ago—shot Wes in the foot, and then Wes's horse threw him," the detective explained. "He landed on his arm. Refused medical help because any doc with a conscience would turn him in."

"So now he's meaner than a stirred-up snake," Billy murmured. They were walking the horses now, far enough behind Mama that she wouldn't sense their presence.

"Which was why I already had my men surrounding the grounds, not knowing *you'd* show up before Virgilia did," Harte continued. "And that's why I slipped inside to cover her at close range while she was sweet-talking Wesley."

"He sure wasn't sweet-talkin' her back." Billy's grip tightened on his reins as he recalled his twin's malicious threats. From their vantage point behind some trees, he saw Mama's wagon stop just before the Massena place.

"That's why we'd better wait at the hotel. Virgilia's putting on a good act for Eve, but she'll be upset once she's alone."

Billy nodded, pondering what he'd heard just now— piecing it together with Eve's stories in Abilene. "I don't understand how Mama got here so fast, though— and with Olivia," he mused, watching the sunlight glisten in Eve's upswept hair. "After all, she had to go back to Abilene to fetch the baby, and—"

The detective's low laugh riffled his mustache. "Never underestimate your mother," he said proudly. "Her keen intelligence was what first attracted me to her. The way she puzzled things out faster than anyone else.

"I wasn't surprised when Virgilia insisted on going straight to Richmond, instead of home from the Malloys', but I did *not* expect to see several telegrams she'd decoded. Telegrams about Wesley's dealings with Leland Massena."

Billy considered this carefully. "So she already knew my brother was holed up at home."

"But knew better than to go there alone," Carlton confirmed. "And when we saw you and Eve at the Abilene train station without the baby—"

"Mama went back for her."

"And we were on the next eastbound train. She'd threatened to blow my cover—to inform Wesley we were on his trail—so I had no choice but to swear I'd stay back in town."

A grin twitched at Billy's lips. "Sounds like Mama, all right. I don't know what they're doin' in the back of that wagon," he added, nodding toward the two women, "but Eve and her mother don't stand any more of a chance against Mama than you do."

Carlton turned his horse down a side street. "Might as well get some dinner uptown and then wait for her. She's sly and she's strong, but Virgilia's got a chink in her armor when it comes to her boys. Might take us both to smooth her ruffled feathers—and dry her tears."

Chapter Thirteen

Eve climbed carefully over the back of the buckboard seat, envying Virgilia Harte's agility. The woman in purple might be dressed in her Sunday best, looking like the prosperous rancher's wife she had been years ago, but Eve sensed Billy's mother always hid a proverbial ace or two up her stylish sleeve.

"I thought we were taking Olivia to see my mother."

"And we are," Mrs. Harte replied as she took the lid from a large box in the back of the wagon. "But no girl should meet her grandma without being properly dressed for the occasion."

With a flourish, Virgilia lifted layers of tissue paper to reveal a collection of little dresses—some plain, and some frilly, and trimmed with lace. She took out a calico dress with a yellow rose design, and then her eyes widened in delight. "This lavender satin one is *so* gorgeous! Where on earth—?"

"Mercy Malloy wants you to have them," came the pleased reply. "Her little girls outgrew these long ago, but they're still serviceable."

"Serviceable? They look new!" Eve blinked back

tears, riffling carefully through the box, which contained more than twenty dresses.

"Mercy and Temple sewed most of them, and Agatha Vanderbilt tatted the lace accents you see." Virgilia looked up with the fondest smile Eve had ever seen—but of course, it was really for the baby in the basket.

With a girlish giggle, Mrs. Harte lifted Olivia to her shoulder and then pointed to the box of clothes. "You choose, Livvy! So many pretty dresses you have now. Some to grow into, but several are just right, aren't they? Show your mama what you want to wear, sweetheart!"

As Eve held the colorful dresses up before her, Olivia gurgled happily. She was secretly pleased that her little girl let out a loud "Aah!" for the lavender satin dress. Who knew if she was choosing or just making new noises? But it was enough to satisfy her and her grandma.

As Virgilia laid the baby on the blanket from her basket, changed Olivia's diaper, and then slipped her chubby arms into the lace-trimmed sleeves, Eve once more envied the ease with which the redheaded woman handled her grandchild. Her own mothering skills lagged so far behind. . . .

But when Virgilia held the baby up to show her off, Eve's joy wiped away her misgivings. "What a pretty girl!" she cooed, holding out her hands. "Mama's little angel! And you're growing so big, so fast!"

When Olivia flapped her arms as though she had wings to fly, Eve's heart rose into her throat. What an amazing feeling, to see this child so excited about *her*! Wanting *her*—even though she'd left Olivia behind for a trumped-up mission. Why had she wasted a single moment trying to get even with Wesley, when this precious little girl needed her so much more?

Precious. Now there was a word that seldom popped into her mind!

Something shifted inside Eve. As she took Olivia to her shoulder, she wanted to laugh and cry and rock her daughter and tell her so many things—

But first they must see Mother.

Eve sighed—although the sound was more content, more confident than before. "Thank you, Virgilia," she breathed, nuzzling Olivia's downy head. "I can't thank you enough for bringing my little girl to me."

"Well, I had to coax her away from Mercy and Temple Gates," Billy's mother admitted with a grin. "The Malloys just dote on children. Goodness knows I owe them a tremendous debt for the way they took Billy and Christine in when I—when I did some very unmotherly things myself. We all make our mistakes, Eve. There's just no getting around that."

Eve nodded, swaying with the baby. She hadn't always liked this woman when she was Mrs. Bristol. But then, maybe that was because her own mother had felt Virgilia acted uppity and superior back before the war.

That was a long time ago. Right now, as she gazed toward her mother's more modest home, Eve realized that she, too, had some fences to mend—and if her mother rejected Olivia, she would make a new home for this baby somehow. When it came right down to it, she was the only person on the face of this earth in whom little Olivia could put her innocent trust.

What an unexpected revelation. And as Eve climbed down from the wagon, taking her little girl from Virgilia's firm, gloved hands, she felt the weight of that responsibility in a deep, deep way.

Virgilia stepped to the ground, smoothed her hat, and squared her shoulders. With a resolute smile, she strode toward the front door. "No time like the present," she murmured. "And no present like a grandchild."

How did she do it? Eve dared not lag behind this woman who, an hour ago, had withstood a malicious rejection from the son she'd thought she'd lost. Somehow Mrs. Harte had endured the ultimate disappointment while Wesley pelted her with his pointed, poisoned words.

Yet here she was, rapping smartly on the tarnished knocker while radiating an aura of confidence and the supreme belief that her mission with Olivia could not fail.

From the front parlor came strains of piano music, and her mother's clear, high soprano:

> *There were ninety and nine that safely lay*
> *In the shelter of the fold,*
> *But one was out on the hills far away,*
> *Far off from the gates of gold.*

Eve sighed at the words of the familiar song, noting how that voice didn't sound quite as strong these days. Had Mother heard their knock? Or was she ignoring it? Eve hoped she would cooperate, because Florence Massena could load up her temper and shoot off angry words like ammunition—words that would never completely lose their sting.

> *But all through the mountains, thunder riven,*
> *And up from the rocky steep,*
> *There arose a glad cry to the gate of heaven,*
> *"Rejoice! I have found my sheep!"*
> *And the angels echoed around the throne,*
> *"Rejoice for the Lord brings back His own!*
> *Rejoice for the Lord brings back His own."*

Virgilia knocked again, more insistently. The music stopped.

Behind the door they heard quiet footsteps. They stood taller, smiles fixed on their faces. When Olivia let out a wail, Eve realized how tightly she was holding the poor child.

Mother opened the door. For a few painfully silent moments, she glared at them.

"Miss Olivia has requested the honor of making her Grandmother Massena's acquaintance," Mrs. Harte began boldly. "Have you ever seen such a princess? She—"

"I don't know what you're up to, Virgilia," Eve's mother replied tightly, "but from I've heard about your *adventures*, you and Eve—and Wesley!—are three of a kind. I won't have you contaminating my home!"

"Don't be a fool, Flo!" Virgilia shot back, grabbing the door before the other woman could slam it. "This baby—and the daughter you've denied—*need* you. More than you know!"

Tears prickled in her eyes, but somehow Eve stood firm, rocking Olivia. She'd anticipated such humiliating words from her mother, but she was nonetheless hurt by them. Yet beside her, Billy's mother held herself regally erect; proud, but not haughty.

"Why do you want to live alone, in a house haunted by a painful past," she asked quietly, "when you could welcome a whole new life? For yourself, as well as for Eve and your grandchild."

Florence tossed her head, her nose aimed at the ceiling. "Is that what *you* were doing—welcoming a new life?—when you abandoned your children so you could run wild with that—that rapacious Englishman?"

Virgilia Harte cleared her throat, her gaze still fixed on the woman standing before them. Mother showed no signs of letting them in, so Eve held her baby close, as much to protect Olivia from such ugliness as to draw comfort from her solid, warm body.

"I admit that I wasn't thinking clearly after my husband was killed," Billy's mama replied. Her words were measured, chosen so Mother couldn't miss the parallels. "I made some outrageous mistakes after I lost my home, Flo—all in the name of enjoying myself and the attentions of a handsome man."

Her mother started to protest, but Virgilia held up a slender, gloved hand with the bearing of a queen.

"I realize now that Leland foreclosed on our home because of political pressure and the unfortunate financial effects of the war," she went on. "I've let that go, Flo. Tried to put it behind me, that one of our family's closest friends betrayed us so grievously."

Virgilia held Mother's gaze, ever the mistress of the purposeful pause. "And because I, too, have lost a husband—the mainstay of my family at that time—I'm sincerely sorry for your loss, Florence," she said softly. "We flounder beneath such a heavy burden, and your disowning Eve is every bit as wrong as my galavanting around the West after deserting Billy and Christine."

Were those tears shining in Mother's eyes? Eve, too, felt like crying at Mrs. Harte's touching confession, but she clenched her jaw. She stood taller, facing Olivia out, so she could see her grandmother's face and hear her voice. Just in case she never met this thin, weary woman again.

"I will also admit that while I chided Christine for chasing after me, demanding the reasons for my behavior, it was the daughter I'd abandoned who *saved my life*." She paused again, letting her words soak in. "You see, Flo, had Christine not searched so persistently for me, I'd have rotted in a Chinatown alley. That high-toned—*rapacious*—Englishman left me for dead when I no longer met his nefarious needs."

The pale face before them lifted in surprise, but Mother kept her hand on the door as though she might slam it anyway. "Why are you telling me this?" she rasped. "Why would I care what happened to you, after—"

"Because you're doing yourself and your family a horrible disservice, Flo!" Virgilia cried. "Perhaps my son and your daughter have done wrong in your eyes, but it's a far greater mistake to widen this rift when Olivia needs a family! The Florence Massena I know held her standards higher than most, but she was not self-righteous to the point of being cruel. She put her family first. She was the mortar that held her home together."

When a little sob escaped her mother, Eve stepped forward to slip an arm around her. But Mother stiffened. When her expression changed from sorrow to disdain, Eve let go.

"How can you expect me to welcome a child who looks exactly like the beast who ruined my daughter?"

Eve's mouth fell open. And as though little Olivia had understood every word, she began to squirm.

"Mother, I can't believe—how can you blame Olivia for her looks?" she demanded. "Didn't you always dote on the way I so closely resembled my father? Do you think you're the only one who's been wounded by his betrayals?"

Her pulse was pounding, but for a different reason now. She'd had that commandment—*honor your father and your mother*—drilled into her from her earliest days. She knew the consequences of disobeying it, even if her father was gone now. But she could take no more of this!

"Do you think I like it that Daddy committed such heinous crimes against our friends and then killed himself, rather than face his shame?" Eve cried. It tore at her heart to say these things, but they must be heard. "You can sing your hymns about lost sheep, but it's another thing entirely to welcome one home, isn't it?"

Never had she dared to condemn her mother in such a tone, with such pointed accusations. But the time for prim-and-proper behavior was long gone. Her child deserved a future that matched her sunny disposition and sky blue eyes. Not the shadows of this family's past.

Eve stood taller. The proud look on Virgilia's face bolstered her courage. It felt good to express her anger,

and to ask the questions her mother had always refused to answer.

But if this was to be the last time she stood in this
doorway, Eve had a few other things to say, as well.
Olivia was squealing now, so she turned the baby to her
shoulder, swaying side to side.

"I'm sorry for the way I disgraced this family,
Mother," she breathed, although she felt sure she'd suf-
focate any minute. "And I'm sorry for my mistakes in
judgment, and for falling prey to my need for attention
and—and for what I thought might be love."

Eve looked away, blinking rapidly. Determined to
finish what she'd started, she rocked Olivia faster, even
though it only upset her child more.

"Turns out I was just as full of myself as Wesley was,
and I'm paying for it now," she confessed above the
baby's wails. "But I will *not* subject this innocent child
to your judgment, Mother. If you can't accept my
apology—and meet your granddaughter—well, I won't
bother you again. I'll find a way to make a life for the
two of us without you."

"Don't you worry about a thing, dear," Billy's mother
said, slipping an arm around her. "Carlton and I are returning to Richmond. You and Olivia have a place with
us as long as you need one."

Eve's mouth fell open. She searched Virgilia's face—
was she saying this to goad Mother into accepting her
and the baby? Surely this woman wasn't returning
here thinking she could reclaim her outlaw son! The
parts of their conversation she'd overheard had not
sounded promising.

Yet Eve saw determination in those deep green
eyes—determination mixed with pride and joy, and
maybe even love.

Eve blinked, holding Olivia closer. What had she
done to deserve such acceptance? She fully realized

what she'd lost today, but somehow she'd gained, as well. Just like that sheep in the song, who'd been reclaimed by one who went looking for a soul gone astray.

Maybe Mother's hymns had some relevance, after all. Who could have guessed Billy's brazen mother would be her personal shepherd?

Virgilia Harte opened her arms, and Eve handed her the squalling baby. The red-haired woman began to coo and kiss and cuddle her granddaughter as though she had no mission in this world other than Olivia's happiness.

Didn't everyone need such a guardian angel?

"Thank you," Eve breathed, smiling at Billy's mama through her tears. In the length of a sentence, she'd been offered a place to stay: hope for her future, and her child's.

"Quite all right, dear," Virgilia replied, smiling at the baby all the while. "We should be getting back so Miss Olivia can nap. Poor thing! Any girl would be fussy after traveling so far, only to be the subject of such unfortunate conversation."

Without another glance at Mother, Mrs. Harte swung around, swooping Olivia up and down as she headed toward the wagon. Etiquette dictated that Eve should at least say good-bye to her mother, but she could think of nothing more to say.

They were halfway to the wagon when a quavering voice stopped them.

"Eve! Virgilia, I—why don't you come inside?" Florence called out. "The house is cool and quiet. Olivia can nap while we catch up on a few things."

"Well, now!" Virgilia whispered smugly. She glanced back toward the doorway, and then, of all things, she *winked* at Eve. "Let's go in, before she changes her mind."

Chapter Fourteen

Billy stood at the registration desk of the Richmond Hotel, gazing at the fancy wallpaper and ornate chandelier that hung in the dining room. Carlton rang the desk bell, which brought a slender cleaning girl around the corner with her broom and dustpan.

When she saw Billy, her eyes widened. "Why, Wesley Bristol, look at *you*! After what we've heard lately, I never figgered on—mighty fine to see you up and walkin'—and comin' *here*—"

"Beggin' your pardon," Billy muttered, "but I'm the other Bristol. Wes's twin brother."

She gawked at him. "Sorry, sir. I coulda swore you was—"

"Maisie, have you finished your sweeping?" an imperious voice demanded from behind them. "If the places aren't set for dinner in five minutes, you'll be departing without your pay. This is your third warning, girl."

The maid hurried away, but stole another glance at him over her shoulder. And when the tall, reedy man who'd reprimanded Maisie took his place behind the desk, Billy felt another set of eyes studying him closely.

"How may I help you gentlemen?" he inquired.

"I'm sure you recall that my wife and I checked in earlier," Carlton replied. "We'll be needing another room near ours, please, for Mr. Bristol."

"I—oh, yes, of course, Mr. Harte!" The man couldn't smile widely enough as he flipped through the hotel's register. "Might I suggest that Mr. Bristol would be more comfortable in the suite at the end of your hall? Compliments of the management, of course."

Billy blinked. "Why do I deserve special treatment?"

"Why?" The man behind the desk laughed so hard he banged the edge of the counter. "Mr. Bristol, your modesty! Why, you've systematically rid us of so many Northern sympathizers! Their choke hold on our economy has nearly ruined—"

"Like I was tellin' Maisie," he interrupted quietly, "I'm not Wesley Bristol. I'm his brother Billy, come in from Abilene. I'd like to pay for just a plain ole room, thank you. How much'll that be for tonight?"

He took a roll of greenbacks from his back pocket, once again stunned that people mistook him for his notorious twin. Surely he looked cleaner and more reputable than Wes. And surely Wesley had made as many enemies as admirers while he'd eliminated those local families. Might be a lot of lawmen gunning for him when word got around that "Wesley" had come out of hiding.

The man took his money, a flush riding his cheeks. "Thank you, Mr. Bristol," he said stiffly. "I'll put you next to the Hartes, in room twenty-two. Enjoy your stay."

Now *there* was a challenge. With a sigh, Billy looked at the man beside him. Harte's crow's feet and the dark circles beneath his eyes made him look older than he had only a few days ago.

"Let me know when Mama gets in," he murmured,

heading for the staircase with his saddlebag. "I've got some things to think about."

Once inside his room, Billy considered his encounters at the desk. The single bunk and nightstand were over by the window, where the afternoon light was fading behind the buildings on this side of the street. He let his saddlebag drop, poured cool water into the washbowl to rinse his face, and then caught his reflection in the small gilt-framed mirror.

Did he really look like Wes? Or were folks just expecting to see his infamous twin? As Billy blotted his face with the towel, he recalled his brother's scraggly beard, dirty hair, and the air of malevolence that hung around him like a storm cloud.

Lord, help me not to be like him! he prayed. *Thank you for Your protection today—for gettin' Eve and me out of the line of fire, and for keepin' Mama safe when Wes came out of the house . . . picked up that pie knife—*

What would he have done if Wes had lifted a hand against Mama?

I'd have killed him, came the quick reply. I'd have had no choice!

Had he sunk so low that he'd take his brother's life without a second thought? The idea twitched within him, like the tail of a nervous cat. Yet he'd hidden himself in the house to be sure Mama wasn't shot. It was God's doing entirely that Carlton Harte and his men had already surrounded the place.

Because they see Wes for the dangerous, hunted animal he's become. And they intend to bring him in. Or bring him down.

That, too, made him flinch. Billy longed to stretch out on the bed after this long, complicated day, yet he lingered by the window. The light soothed him. He wished he could detain the twilight until he knew Mama, Eve and Olivia were accounted for, because although the street below bustled with activity and economic progress, Richmond no longer felt like his hometown.

He felt silly about it, but Billy wondered if any of them would be safe in their beds tonight. While he trusted the Lord implicitly, he had serious doubts about his twin. And he wasn't prepared to feel these low-down, snake-in-the-belly suspicions about his own brother.

Out in the hall, purposeful female footsteps passed by his door, pausing a little way beyond it. Billy had no desire to listen in on Mama's conversation with her husband, but the walls of the hotel were pretty thin.

"Virgilia!" Carlton's footsteps approached the door in the next room. "Did you convince Mrs. Massena to see Eve?"

"Well, I had to do a *lot* of talking!" Mama responded briskly. "Time has not been kind to Florence, nor to her attitude. It was all I could do to keep my hands to myself when she started in on Wesley and his—his—"

Billy closed his eyes. His mother's voice sounded angry. He could envision her removing that proud purple hat before yanking at each finger of her gloves in her frustration.

"Carlton, can you—believe that boy—wouldn't even—look me in the eye?" she said with each tug. "He smelled—to high heaven—and yet absolutely *refused* to sit by me and—and—"

Billy walked out his door and knocked quietly on the next one before twisting the knob. His mother gasped at his intrusion, but from over her head Harte gave him a grateful smile.

"Billy! Of all the—"

"Mama, I'm sorry for what Wesley said and did—"

"But how did you—"

He crushed his mother in a hug, absorbing the first of her sobs. She felt so fragile—so much more vulnerable than the mother who'd disciplined her boys with a strong hand and a willow switch. As he held her close, Billy realized he'd let the cat out of the bag: Mama didn't know he'd been watching from the house. She'd give him an earful about that.

"Mama," he whispered, "I couldn't let you face Wes alone. Not after he shot at Eve and me."

"But he's your brother! He'd never—"

"Everything's changed," he murmured, closing his eyes against that harsh reality. "When I saw how dirty he looked. How he'd lost the use of his right arm and walked with a limp—"

"He needs our help, Billy!"

Mama's outburst rang in the small room as she glared up at him, and at Carlton, who stood at her other side. "You two hard-hearted schemers see him as an outlaw and a—"

"Hired gun," Billy murmured sadly.

"—but I'm his mother! He needs me more than ever!"

"Virgilia." Carlton's weathered hand followed the curve of her back. "Honey, I know how you poured all your hopes and dreams into seeing your boy again, but he's grown up cold. *Cruel.* And I won't let him hurt you."

His mother's red-rimmed eyes were running over now. Billy suspected she'd been crying during her ride from Eve's house and had composed herself to come into the hotel, but her bravado didn't fool him. Her slender body trembled uncontrollably.

"You won't tell *me* how to—"

"He's right, Mama. Just like Eve was," Billy countered quietly. "Much as I hate to say it, I can't deny all the horrible things my brother's done to folks in these parts—folks who were behind on their payments, just like we were after Daddy got shot. Folks whose only fault was their poverty, or the loss of the family bread-winner. Which Wesley also had a hand in."

"That is the most—the most—"

Her efforts to defend Wesley got drowned out then: She realized her boy was bad to the core, and that she'd arrived too late to mend his ways. Billy held her, rocking her as though she were a child, letting her cry out her anguish and fear. Carlton kept a hand on her back, trying his best to soothe her, too.

When she stopped crying, Mama focused her watery green eyes on him. "You surely believe, from your years of living with the Malloys," she whispered, "that we must do more than pray for those who would do us wrong, Billy. I'm no Bible-thumper, but I believe we were led here because Wesley needs us in his darkest hour."

Billy sighed. "Mama, he's been taking the men away from their ranches—arranging 'accidents'—so he could scare their families off the land. Just like Leland Massena did to us."

"But you took right up with his pretty daughter, didn't you?" his mother challenged. Her eyes shone like green daggers. "You loved that baby, knowing her mother would take to you because—"

"Partly because Wes left her destitute, and partly—"

"She's back with her mother now. Thanks to me!" Mama crowed.

"—because God was wakin' me up to the mistake I'd be makin' if I married Emma," he finished in a tight voice. This wasn't the easiest conversation to have with his mother, because she'd likely change tactics as it suited her. Use his own words to win her argument.

"And who's to say God's not leading *me* here? I firmly believe, after seeing the state Wesley's fallen into, that it's my responsibility to take him in." She turned to Carlton then, her green eyes burning with purpose.

"And I believe we should live here in Richmond," she stated in a steadier voice. "Could be we're intended to buy that boarded-up hotel across the square from—"

"Absolutely *not*."

Harte didn't stand much taller than Mama, but he took her by the shoulders so she looked square at him. His face was taut. He had a way of sparring with his wife until he won, although he remained calm and kept his voice low so no one else would be in on their business.

"First of all, I was in the house same as Billy was—to protect *you*!" he said firmly. "I'm convinced Wes Bristol is even more dangerous now that he's wounded and forced to lay low. He'd get word if you moved back, and he'd be on you like a duck on a bug, honey."

Mama planted her hands on her hips. "Carlton Harte, you're using your position with the Pinkertons to—"

"It *would* be stupid to jeopardize my cover by living here," the detective confirmed, "but I assure you, my love, that *your* welfare—and the welfare of Olivia and Billy and Eve—are my highest priorities."

Billy held his breath. He could feel the heat and frustration rolling off his mother's small body: She didn't like being challenged or told what to do. But he agreed with Harte. Wesley and his cohorts would get mighty suspicious if Mama moved here. She'd be an easy mark, trying to nurture her boy back to respectability again.

And respectability wasn't high on Wes's list of priorities. By all appearances, his twin just wanted to be left alone to regain his strength, so he could go back to "cleaning up" for whomever bought his bullets.

His mother, meanwhile, was pointing a finger at her husband. "If I've told you once, Carlton, I've told you a hundred times, you'll not be making my decisions! Or telling what I can or cannot—"

"Fine." Harte's eyebrows rose but his voice did not, and Billy could see how he talked his way around hardened criminals. "There's a place for sale in Excelsior Springs, a few miles down the road from here. We can move to Missouri if you insist, Virgilia. But it won't be to Richmond, where so many folks know you."

"Mr. Pinkerton arranged this, didn't he? Because he needs your help with the lawlessness in these parts."

Harte had the good sense to shrug and slip his hands into his pockets. "Isn't that convenient? You can move closer to your son—"

"And *you* will vow not to lay a hand on him!"

Carlton shifted, but he didn't drop his gaze. "If he threatens you, sweetheart—if he retaliates against any member of our family—I'll have no choice but to defend you."

Billy's pulse thrummed in his ears. Though he'd never doubted his father's love for his mother, Daddy had never dared cross Mama this way. He'd agreed with her to her face, and then quietly worked around her.

But then, Daddy had never dealt with a son like Wesley. Owen Bristol hadn't seen or felt the emotional arrows Wes shot, or the way he'd used Mama for target practice.

He sighed, sensing Harte needed some time alone with Mama.

"I'm goin' to fetch Eve and Olivia," he said quietly, "and I'm takin' 'em back to Abilene tomorrow. So they'll be safe while I figure out what to do next.

"I'm sorry things worked out this way, Mama," he added with a rueful smile. "I had my dreams of comin' home, too. Buyin' our ranch back from the bank and raisin' horses there again. But it's not worth losin' more lives to have my way about it."

Before his mother could protest or call him a coward, Billy left the room. As he stepped out of the hotel into the twilight, he prayed his brother wasn't poised to pounce on him between here and the Massena place.

Chapter Fifteen

As Billy slipped past rooms where the children still slept, and then down the stairs toward the aromas of bacon and biscuits, the deep peace of early morning settled over him. He paused at the foot of the stairs, entered the front parlor to marvel for the hundredth time at how, when the sunrise beamed at the beveled picture window, a rainbow colored the wall.

The rainbow—God's promise that he would never again destroy the earth with a flood.

And yet even as he gazed at this symbol, where comfortable chairs and Mercy's new piano and a dozen other homey, familiar things proclaimed this the Malloys' favorite room, Billy's gut rumbled. And it had nothing to do with hunger for Asa's breakfast.

He entered the kitchen, inhaling deeply, grateful to be sharing this morning meal with the two men he loved most in this world. The men who'd given him a home and a faith to grow up in so long ago.

The old Negro flashed him a grin as he forked sizzling strips of bacon onto a platter. "Mornin', Mister Billy! These old eyes is mighty glad to see ya. My prayers has been answered, havin' you here safe and sound again."

"Mine,too," Billy breathed, taking a plate of steaming, golden biscuits to the table. He sat across from Mike Malloy, nodding his greeting. "For a few minutes there, I wasn't sure I'd make it back. At least not in one piece."

Malloy's brows arched over hazel eyes that reminded Billy of an old hound dog's: devoted and always happy to see him, yet wise to the ways of the world. The owner of the Triple M had his share of concerns, managing so much crop land, and raising Morgan horses and four children: Billy noticed a few silvery hairs catching the light from the window. Michael was a year or two beyond thirty, prosperous despite the hardships of this homesteading Kansas life. Yet he never seemed to doubt. His faith never wavered.

As he drizzled sorghum over his split biscuits, Malloy revealed the worry he'd kept from the younger children last night, when Billy had arrived with Eve and Olivia.

"So you met up with your brother? And you saw your old home place?" he asked quietly. It was his way to lead with questions and allow his kids to answer—even though Michael instinctively knew when they weren't telling the whole story.

Billy sensed he might as well spill out his heartache and distress, because if Michael didn't coax it out of him with those wise eyes and that patient, mustachioed smile, Asa would peck at him like a sly old rooster, going after every last kernel.

"Yessir, I rode down that long tree-lined lane, bracin' myself for the deterioration Eve had warned me about," he mused aloud. "But nobody coulda prepared me for meetin' up with Wesley again. Or havin' him shoot at me from our bedroom window."

"Lord a-mercy, he *shot* atcha?" Asa grasped his arm,

looking him over for wounds. "Now what woulda possessed him to—"

"He's earned that bad reputation Eve came here cryin' about," Billy said with a sigh. "And he got the home place as payment for some dirty work he did for that banker who turned us out after Daddy died. The way Wesley saw it, I was trespassin'. Showed no inclination to talk with me, let alone come away from his outlaw life."

Michael's fork was poised over his plate and his expression made Billy's heart ache. "I'm so sorry, son," he murmured. "I suspected things got nasty, the way you didn't want to elaborate last night with the girls all over you, but I never dreamed your own brother would fire at you."

"And you wasn't carryin' no gun, were ya?" Asa cut into his biscuit, shaking his white-sprigged head. "Musta been the Good Lord hisself got you outta harm's way, Mister Billy. That was entirely uncalled for!"

"Yeah, well Wes seems to have a different view of right and wrong these days." He bit into a thick slice of bacon, savoring its salty goodness. "As you say, I felt a force—like a strong wind or the beating of angels' wings—pushin' Eve and me ahead of those bullets."

"Eve was there, too? And he still fired?" Michael rasped.

"Yessir. And those same angels who got us outta there were watchin' over Mama, too," Billy replied. "I no more'n got out to the main road when here she comes, drivin' a wagon, hellbent on seein' her boy. Takin' him a pie, no less, to win him over to her side. Or just to lure him out, so she could lay eyes on him again, after all these years of not knowin' if he was even alive."

The two men shifted in their chairs as they shared an uncomfortable glance. "Is she all right, son? I mean, other than getting her heart broken?"

Billy smiled ruefully. "Well, she performed her own kind of miracle, findin' a pie from a shop where our old cook, Beulah Mae, bakes now—'cause Wesley did take her bait. But he wouldn't stay by the wagon long enough to eat a piece and talk to her. Just snatched it up and told her to get outta there, or he'd come gunnin' for the rest of us. Meanin' Eve and Olivia. And me."

Billy thought for a moment, and then realized he'd better share his darker suspicions now, while it was just the three of them.

"I want you to be real careful for a while. Watch the trees by the river, and check inside the stables before you tend the horses. My brother's got a bum leg and his shootin' hand's danglin' useless, but he's a mean one. And he knows I've been livin' in Abilene, after seein' that article years ago in the Kansas City paper. He doesn't think it's fair that I have a home and a family and a good job these days."

"Sounds like his heart's gone darker than the devil's," Asa muttered. "Mighty long trip fer 'im, just to carry out his orneriness."

Billy swallowed another bite of biscuit, recalling Wes's childhood tricks—wishing such orneriness was all that would happen if his twin came looking for him.

"Yeah, well, he wants nothin' to do with that baby, and he's callin' Eve a whore who brought her situation on herself," he answered sadly. "Then he accused me of hidin' behind her, like I used to hang behind Mama's skirts when I was little. I wanted to punch him so bad, my whole body shook with it. But I got outta there when I realized how hard things'd be for Eve if I got hurt playin' the hero.

"Could be Wes called it right," he added in a small voice. "Could be I'm too lily-livered for my own—"

"You did exactly the right thing, son," Michael insisted, reaching across the table to grasp Billy's arm. "Nothing wrong with getting yourself out of harm's way, especially since he was armed and you weren't. No shame in that, Billy."

"No, sir, no shame fer certain," Asa echoed with a decisive nod. "You was takin' responsibility, protectin' what the Good Lord's given you. You seen that situation for the trap it was, and you knew nothin' good was gonna come of gettin' yourself shot fulla holes."

"Amen to that!" came a voice from the doorway.

Billy turned to see Mercy, dressed in her everyday calico with her chestnut hair tied back at her neck. Billy felt such a warmth radiating from her that he dropped his fork and shoved his chair back. She opened her arms and he hugged her fiercely. It was a deep sweetness Mercy Malloy inspired in him: the sense that he mattered more than anything in this world to her, even though she had her own young children. Even though he now stood taller than she did, and held her against his chest instead of being held.

He felt her sigh with love and relief, and the long breath she let out warmed his neck.

"Tell us what you need, Billy," she stated quietly. "You have to make your own way, and you're facing some tough situations. But we're your family and we'll always love you. Always help you."

Where would he be without Mike and Mercy Malloy's unconditional love? What would have happened to that lost ten-year-old boy in the patched pants who stepped off the stagecoach and into their home, had they turned him away?

You mighta gone just as wrong as Wesley. There, but for the grace of God and these kindhearted folks. . . .

He hugged her again, and then followed Michael and Asa outside for the morning chores. Snowy and Spot circled him immediately, their eyes still bright despite their age. Billy knelt to accept their licks and grab each dog in turn.

"These two ole pups was beside theirselves after you

left, Mr. Billy," the old Negro said with a cackle. "Just no consolin' 'em, when I told 'em you might not be comin' back fer a while."

He indulged in their excited kisses for a moment, realizing how much he'd missed them, and how quiet life would be in Richmond if he didn't have these faithful border collies sharing his days. "Unless you've got something more urgent, I thought I'd ride the fence line along the west boundary today," he suggested.

The other two men were kind enough not to quiz him about riding past the unfinished house in the northwest corner of the homestead. Billy gathered his tools, filled his canteens, and saddled Pete, glad for some time to think things through. Way too much had happened these past few days, and he sensed he was at an important crossroads. A day in the blazing Kansas sun, repairing the barbed-wire boundary with only the dust-muffled hoofbeats of his horse and the company of his dogs, would set his mind straight again.

He stopped briefly at the old log house where Mercy and her first husband, Judd, had staked their original claim. Sedalia Gates was hanging out dresses and overalls, while in the nearest field, her husband Reuben walked behind a plow.

"You folks doin' all right?" he called to the colored woman.

"Yessir, Mister Billy, we's gettin' along just fine!" she replied brightly. She was barely bigger around than a handful of cornstalks, yet Sedalia gave him the distinct impression she could handle anything—or anyone— who crossed her.

"Reckon you's goin' to see Miss Emma, aint'cha?" she asked with a glint in her deep brown eyes.

He had to smile: this field hand's wife missed nothing, and never hesitated to ask straightforward questions. "I'm mending fence today, but I thought I'd stop by there, yes. Have you seen much of her this week?"

Sedalia shook a wet dress so hard it snapped like a firecracker. "Miss Emma was never one to come aroun' here, even 'fore her mama died, so I cain't tellya how she and her daddy's gettin' on. But it ain't a happy household," she added, shaking her head. "No sir, them grasshoppers ate more'n the crops and the clothes last summer. They ate big ole holes where that man's heart was—and his daughter's, too."

Billy nodded, wishing he didn't feel responsible for some of that heartache. "Tell Reuben I said hello—and tell him his sister's even more of a godsend now that Eve and Olivia have come back with me. Temple's a saint, the way she keeps all those kids corralled!"

"You tell her we send our love."

With a nod, Billy nudged Pete into a trot and continued over to the far side of the Malloys' combined homesteads. He rode north then, along the fence of barbed wire and wooden posts that followed the property line farther than his eye could see. This boundary had been a joint effort between the Clarks and the Triple M Ranch, to prevent herds of cattle from trampling their fields of corn and wheat. Nowadays, the big drives from Texas were only a memory—outlawed by the people of Abilene, who'd despised the damage done by drunken cowboys and the spread of disease from their tick-infested longhorns.

Billy dismounted and deftly patched a bottom strand of the wire, under the close supervision of his two dogs. He recalled how he and Gabe and their four border collies—hardly more than pups then—had ridden hellbent-for-leather to prevent a massive herd from stampeding through one of their summer Sunday gatherings of neighbors.

He blinked hard. In his mind, Billy could still hear the heavy plodding of those longhorns' hooves and see the sleek black-and-white dogs dodging and nipping to escort the herd down the road. Judd and Nathaniel, a fine Negro hand, had been alive then . . . he and Gabe had been inseparable . . . and Emma had been so impressed with his cowboy competence, she'd kissed him soundly on the cheek for the first time, that day.

So much had changed.

So much more change loomed ahead of him, and Billy wished he felt better about it. He remounted, his eye on the horizon as a modest house came into view. The walls were solid and the roof was on. They'd hung the doors and put plate glass in the windows, too, but otherwise the little house sat unfinished—a stark reminder of how things stood between him and Emma Clark.

He intended to speak to her, but he half hoped she'd be back at her daddy's house. After all, what was here for her? Just rooms that echoed when she walked the plank floors, and an emptiness that bespoke broken promises. He hoped Emma had gathered her inner strength—like the tomboy he'd known as a kid—and was figuring out a new purpose for herself.

But no, a lone figure stood on the front stoop, staring out across the prairie. There was no way around greeting her.

Some fences need mending, and I'm just the one for the job.

Mama's voice ran through his mind. And she'd been right, as far as making things work—on the surface, at least—between Eve and her mother. When Emma turned toward the sound of Pete's hoofbeats, gripping her broom handle, Billy sensed he wouldn't be nearly as effective as his mother. Or as lucky.

"Mornin', Emma." He halted the horse a few feet in front of her, praying he'd say the right things, while his panting dogs joined her two in the shade beside the house. "Didn't figure you'd be here. Not much reason to stay."

The blue eyes that had once adored him looked dull. "Yeah, thanks to you that's about right," she replied in a tight voice. "I s'pose that fine Miss Massena and her baby are still the light of everyone's lives—including yours?"

Billy winced. She was in no frame of mind to hear how they'd narrowly escaped his brother's gunfire. "They returned from Missouri with me, yes. Eve sorta fixed things up with her mother. Brought back her paints so she could—"

"How lovely for her." Emma looked into the distance, as though she'd rather not talk to him. She wore a faded blue gingham dress and her straw-blond hair hung limply around her shoulders—a far cry from the fetching sight she'd made as a bride.

Billy's pulse throbbed in his temples. He reminded himself that sharp words—or suggestions that she find someone else to love—would only make her more bitter. More brittle. And he owed her better than that.

But why has Eve accepted her mistakes with Wesley and moved on?

He didn't have an answer. Some girls could wallow in their misery and hold a grudge until Kingdom Come, but he'd never, before this summer, suspected Emma Clark would be one of them.

Billy sighed, knowing that whatever he said would be wrong. Might as well get this over with so he could get on with his fence work.

"Emma, I'm sorry for the way I—"

"You broke my heart, Billy Bristol! You ruined my life!" she cried. "So why are you sittin' here tormentin' me about it?" Emma's face grew red and two tears dribbled down it.

"I—I came to apologize," he faltered, "and seein's how you like to spend time here—I thought I'd offer to paint the rooms and—"

"And what good will that do?" she retorted. "I'll feel beholden to you then—obligated to bring your meals and tolerate your presence while you work. And then

I'll have to pretend I'm grateful and have some sort of a life, just because you finished this house before you left me for good!"

His throat tightened around a large lump. Not so much from what she said, for he deserved every hurtful word she was hurling at him, but because she sounded helpless. Hopeless. Stuck here. Forever.

"Emma, you're a fine woman, and you'll make some man a—"

"How can you say that?" she shrieked. Her face contorted and she gripped her broom, ready to swing it at him. "*You*, who left me for that—that floozy and her misbegotten daughter! *You*, who left me to wither up and die!"

Hattie and Boots trotted around the house at the plaintive rise of her voice, and Spot and Snowy came along. Four black-and-white bodies tensed and four sets of eyes followed Emma's broom as she stirred up the dust on the stoop, sweeping with a vengeance. Pete whickered, shifting restlessly, so Billy let the gelding retreat a step or two.

"That's it! Back away—just get out of my sight!" Emma whined. "It'd suit me fine if I never laid eyes on you again, Billy!"

His heart bottomed out. He was at a total loss for words, or for ways to ease Emma's bleak outlook.

"Stop gawking at me that way, dammit! Just *go*!" With a flourish of her broom she came at him, and Billy didn't hold his horse back.

"I'm sorry this happened, Emma," he said from a few yards away. He gripped the reins tight, so he could finish what he had to say. "And I'm sorry you tore up that letter Eve wrote last spring—'cause maybe if I'd seen it, things would've gone different when she showed up at the wedding. But we'll never know that, will we?"

Chapter Sixteen

After enduring the hot July sun and the words of a woman who'd grown as sharp as fence barbs, Billy was glad to be back at the Triple M that afternoon.

"Whoa, Pete," he murmured when Spot and Snowy shot ahead of him. A big grin overtook his face: Solace was riding his former horse, Mr. Lincoln, around the training corral, and danged if she wasn't bracing herself—adjusting her rhythm to his—so she could stand up on his back! Like the trick riders they'd seen at the Centennial Circus a couple months ago.

Thank goodness the other kids were in the house: one raised voice or distraction might send the seven-year-old daredevil flying backward off her mount. For a few glorious moments, Solace rode with her bare feet on either side of Mr. Lincoln's spine. What a picture she made, with her arms extended for balance, her denim pants flapping around her spare body, and her rich brown waves blowing back in the breeze.

Her triumphant, terrified smile was something Billy would remember forever.

She caught sight of him then, and thank goodness

she knew to fall forward and grab the sturdy gelding's neck. Solace crooned her praise into the horse's ear as he continued to canter around the ring. She was riding him so effortlessly, she could have been an extension of the small Morgan she'd inherited when Billy had received Pete for his last birthday.

Spot and Snowy had settled themselves inside the fence to watch her, ready to race over if she took a tumble. The two dogs adored that girl, and for Solace, it went far beyond the mere love of pets: ever since she'd been big enough to frolic with the collies and sit in Billy's lap when he rode, she'd shown an intuitive talent with animals. A gift from her father Judd Monroe, no doubt.

"You're dang lucky your mother wasn't watchin' that!" he said as he stopped Pete beside the corral.

Solace grinned, her tanned face lighting up like the sun. "Mama doesn't scare *me*! Didn't I tell you, after we watched those circus riders in town, that I was gonna try it, too?"

Billy couldn't help returning her grin. "And didn't I tell you that was a good way to get your neck broke, if you didn't plant your feet right?"

"But I did! I told Mr. Lincoln to keep it steady, around and around the corral, so's I could feel his rhythm and balance with it!" she explained, as though it were a perfectly normal thing for any seven-year-old to do.

"I know better'n to tell you to quit," Billy admitted, "but come get me when you wanna practice, all right? I know a few things about horses myself, so—"

"Oh, Billy, you are *so* fulla bluster sometimes!"

"—maybe I'll convince Mr. Lincoln to learn some tricks with you," he continued in a conspiratorial voice. "If you get good enough that your daddy doesn't string me up for helpin' ya—and your mama doesn't lock the stable on us—I'll pick you out a yearling we can train from scratch. He'll be all yours, Solace. He can grow up with you, and perform in whatever exhibitions you set your sights on."

Her mouth dropped open. "You promise, Billy?"

Lord, but he loved those big brown eyes and that toothy grin with the gaps in it! He had to be careful, or this little tomboy would talk him into things he knew better than to allow.

"You got my word on it, sweetie." Glancing around the yard, he realized no one else was in sight, which was unusual in a family this big. "So how come your sisters aren't out here—"

"Screechin' like scaredy cats and tattlin' on me?" She rolled her eyes. "They're inside playin' with Olivia. Watchin' Eve paint a picture."

"And Joel is—"

"Muckin' out the stalls. He back-talked Mama this mornin', so now he's all mad at Daddy for comin' down on him."

Billy nodded at this familiar pattern. "I'll put Pete in the pasture for a bit then, so's not to interrupt Joel's chores. And after I go inside, I do *not* wanna see you flyin' butt-over-teakettle off the back of this horse. You hear me?"

Solace's cheeks dimpled with a wry grin. "Loud and clear, Billy. Just like I heard you say you'd help me with my trick ridin'—and sharp shootin', too! Just like the guy—"

"No guns for you, little girl!" he objected, ruffling her loose hair. "Your folks'd tan my hide for sure if I agreed to that! So don't start on me!"

Before she could talk him into anything else, Billy led Pete through the gate that opened to pastureland and the shade of the cottonwoods along the Smoky Hill River. When he'd put his tack and blanket by the stable door, he saw that Solace had taken Mr. Lincoln out of the ring, as well.

He moseyed toward the house then, taking in the way the late afternoon sun blazed against its white frame walls, a sharp contrast to the leafy green lilac bushes Mercy had planted along one side. The scent of honeysuckle tickled his nose as he stepped onto the back porch, and when he opened the door into the kitchen, he closed his eyes in ecstasy: Asa had baked pies for Sunday dinner. Aromas of cinnamon-sugared apples and tart cherries made his mouth water.

The steam was still rising from the lattice-top crusts, or Billy might've been tempted to sample a slice. It was hardly fair that Wes had hobbled off with an entire pie for himself—a pie made by none other than their Beulah Mae. But voices in the dining room warned him he'd get caught, sure as sin, if he snitched anything.

So he stood in the doorway, his heart swelling at the sight: Lily sat in a chair by the window, where the light made her face and blond ringlets glow, holding *very* still while Eve sketched her. The ginger cat sat in Lily's lap, while Gracie watched the pencil lines take shape on the paper from beside Olivia's basket.

And from what Billy could see, Grace had every reason to be enthralled: Miss Massena was deftly roughing in Lily's hair . . . her puffy, ruffled sleeves . . . the arch of the cat's fuzzy back as it nuzzled her chin. A few strokes more, and he saw the pinafore with its edge of lace, and individual fingers appeared at the front and back of the cat.

But it was Eve his eyes lingered on. With her hair pulled up into a topknot, wearing a dress from Mercy's wardrobe, the girl from his childhood appeared as she must have looked before the war—and Wesley— brought her privileged life to an end. Her hands flew gracefully, and her neck arched just so as she gazed at Lily before adding facial details.

When the little blonde brightened at the sight of him, Eve turned.

"Billy!" she said, her voice lilting in his ears. "You look like you've had a hard, hot day."

"And you look like you were born to be doin' that. Not just drawin' Lily's likeness, but showin' Gracie how it's done."

Where had that come from? He was treading cautiously with Eve; didn't want to lead another young woman on, only to disappoint her. But it was true. He'd seen the way Eve Massena studied her subject while that pencil kept moving over the paper, as though it were a magic wand that reproduced what her eyes were observing.

She shrugged prettily. "We girls had some time before dinner, so I thought I'd see if I remembered how."

"Let *me* see!" Lily wheedled, inching to the edge of her chair.

"All right, dear. I've sketched enough so that for our next lesson, I'll mix my paints on a palette and start the actual portrait."

Billy chuckled when Princess Lily hurried over to lean on Eve, her eyes bright as her hand slipped around the young woman's arm. "You drew all *that* in just a few minutes?"

"Will you paint *my* portrait, too?" little Grace piped up. "And Olivia's?"

"All in good time," Eve assured them, her face alight with affection. "We need to clear away our art supplies and help Temple set the table for dinner."

All in good time . . . a time for every purpose under Heaven, Billy mused. He watched them as long as he dared, aware of how the little girls had taken to Eve and her baby, not to mention how settled Miss Massena seemed, here among folks who loved her. As a kid, he'd thought she was a little snooty—and way too well-behaved in church, sitting there as though she were actually *listening* to Reverend Searcy's sermons!

Billy now realized that he, too, felt calm and in control when he was doing what he loved—what he was meant to do: horses had always been his passion, and he was a natural trainer. It was only when he strayed from that path—like when he'd gone looking for Wesley, expecting to be welcomed back—that things went wrong.

Which explains why Emma's so peevish, doesn't it? All she ever lived for was to be your wife.

He went outside to wash up in the basin beside the barn. Splashing the cool water over his dusty, wind-burned face made him feel better on the outside, but he wasn't sure what would help him heal on the inside. He'd made such a mess of things for the woman who'd been his friend practically forever.

It helped that the Malloy family was following the patterns he'd known since he was Joel's age: The girls had set the table and were carrying out plates of fried chicken and bowls of string beans they'd picked this morning. Temple's dark face beamed as she helped them, listening to Grace's excited account of her first drawing lesson. Asa was scrubbing a few pans while the others made their way to the table.

And then it was Michael's calm, reverent voice as he prayed over the food, and Mercy urging the children to eat a little bit of everything—this aimed at Joel, who scowled at anything from the garden. Billy passed the food and ate, and felt the contentment of this happy home. The others talked about the picnic after church tomorrow.

"I think you should take a big bowl of your corn pudding, Mama!" Gracie suggested with shining eyes.

"Nah—biscuits!" Joel crowed, drizzling honey over the one he'd split on his plate. "I want a *pile* of biscuits! And apple fritters! And Asa's shoofly pie!"

"Nuh-uh!" Solace chimed in. "We gotta take fried apples—and Asa's *cherry* pie! Right, Billy?"

Billy smiled at her over a forkful of green beans. "Back about the time you were born, little girl, Asa was makin' me the thickest, sweetest punkin pies, weren't ya?"

"*Pump*kin," Lily said quietly, patting his wrist to soften the correction

"Well, whatever ya wanna call it, Mister Billy could do a punkin pie justice like nobody I ever seen!" the old colored man said with a laugh. "That's what we made fer 'is birthdays, 'stead of cake, you see. He thought it was a fine thing, that you could lift a slice outta the pan and not need a fork to eat it."

Billy chuckled at this memory, and then felt Eve looking at him from across the table. Her face was alight with what she was learning about everyone's tastes in food, as well as a secretive something that glimmered in those green eyes.

"I recall a Sunday when Billy's bottom was so sore he could hardly sit through church," she offered with a lilt in her voice.

The younger faces around the table lit up with anticipation.

"What'd he do? Get a lickin'?" Solace asked with a gleeful giggle.

Eve grinned at the recollection of it, while Billy's cheeks flushed.

"The Bristols had a cook named Beulah Mae," she told her eager listeners, "and on the day before they had the preacher and his wife over for Sunday dinner, she made two fine pumpkin pies. As I recall it, Billy's twin brother bet him he couldn't eat a whole one by himself."

"So didja?" Gracie nipped her lip, which showed how she'd lost a front tooth last week.

Billy chortled. "I gave it my best shot—but that doesn't mean it stayed down. Worse yet, Wesley bolted for the barn when he heard Beulah Mae squawkin' about those pies bein' gone. I was still bein' sick outside the kitchen door, so *I* caught the switch, and had to explain to the preacher about why we didn't have pie the next day."

Joel, in his offhand way, squinted as he considered this. "This the same brother who was shootin' atcha couple days ago?"

A collective sigh went around the table, and Billy nodded. "Yep. Only brother I've got."

"So how come you didn't turn out like him? How come you always get caught and gotta take the blame?"

The room went quiet, except for the pulse pounding in Billy's ears. He focused on Joel, with his rumpled brown hair and slender face, and those dark eyes that never quite met anyone else's.

"That's how I was made, I guess," he replied after he thought about it. "Never could seem to run from trouble, maybe because I wasn't as big or as fast or as ornery as Wes—"

"And maybe because you wanted to please your mama," Eve remarked.

"And maybe because you wanted to be like Jesus," Temple Gates cut in. While the young colored woman didn't belabor her faith, she made the most of examples from real life for the benefit of her young charges. "He always caught opposition and ended up dying to pay the price for all the times we don't do the right thing, didn't he? I've always believed Billy to be a lot like that."

The burn crept higher in his face, but he flashed her a grateful grin. He wished he could live up to Temple's high opinion of him—especially lately, when he seemed to stir up nothing but trouble with Emma. And Wes.

Michael, meanwhile, was rising from his place at the head of the table to take the large Bible from the sideboard. "Seems a good time to share our reading for the day," he said as he riffled through its pages. "It's Jere-

miah who tells us . . . yes, here it is—the words of an
Old Testament prophet who spoke to this subject long
before Jesus taught about it."

His eyes met everyone's in turn, until he was sure
even the youngest at his table was paying proper attention. "I'll read from the seventeenth chapter, about
what befalls those who don't follow the Lord's ways,
and those who do. This was a favorite way for my own
ma to point up that God was watching, and would reward me according to my behavior."

Mercy smiled at him from her end of the table, an
example to her children about how to listen when it
mattered.

" 'Thus says the Lord: Cursed are those who trust in
mere men and make flesh their strength, whose hearts
turn away from the Lord,' " he began. Then he looked
up, to continue in his own words. "They shall be like a
shrub in the desert, and they won't see when the rain
comes . . . they'll live in parched places of the wilder-
ness, in an uninhabited salt land."

"Kind of like Kansas in the summer," Solace remarked.

Billy laid a hand on her arm, smiling to himself. She
was a pistol, this tomboy, but at least she was listening.
And thinking.

Michael smiled and went on. "But *blessed* are those
who trust in the Lord," he paraphrased in a more hopeful tone, "whose trust is in the Lord and whose trust *is*
the Lord. They shall be like a tree planted by water,
sending out its roots by the stream. It won't be afraid
when the drought comes, and its leaves will stay green.
It does not cease to bear fruit.

"And here's the whole crux of it," he said, laying the
large book on the table to address them. "The heart is
devious above all things. It is wicked and perverse—
who can understand it? I, the Lord, test the mind and
search the heart, to give to all my people according to
their ways—according to the fruit of their doing."

"That is so true," old Asa said. "Ain't nothin' the Lord don't know about every single one of us. We gotta be doin' *good*, while we's still got the chance!"

"And I think we need to pray on it while it's fresh in our minds," Mercy said, reaching for the hands on either side of her.

Billy took hold of Lily's slender fingers on his right and felt Asa's bony ones gripping his left. As he bowed his head, he sat in awe of the power in this simple ritual: the way ten people ceased to be separate beings when they joined together in these devotional moments. Even Eve, across from him, held onto Grace and Temple despite the way she'd railed at her mother's religious zeal. She made him think of a pretty, slender tree who'd sent roots into the wellspring of this family and was flourishing because of it.

Emma's image flashed in his mind, and Billy grimaced. She was so alone; as dry and brittle as that bush withering in the desert.

Hold her in your hand, Lord, he prayed before Mercy began. *I tried my best, but you're right—I can't understand her heart. And I can't heal it the way you can.*

"Precious Lord, we thank You for being present in our home and in our hearts," Mercy said in a quiet, melodious voice. "We ask Your blessing on the reading of this lesson, just as we require Your grace to live the way we were created to—in Your image. Watch over us this day, and cradle us through the night, that we may rise with the sun to praise Your name all our lives long."

"Amen," echoed around the table.

Amen, resounded in Billy's heart.

He wasn't sure why, but as they rose from the table he looked at each of the people he loved so dearly—yes, even Eve—and hoped Mercy's prayer held true for all of them.

Chapter Seventeen

Billy went out early to do the morning's chores before church. He nodded to Asa, who was stirring up batter for fritters to go with the rasher of bacon waiting to be fried. When he stepped outside, the stillness of the July dawn warned him it would be a hot day with no rain or relief in sight.

The leaves of the cottonwoods along the river seemed to hold their breath—but they were still green, while the grass around the house and in the pasture was looking dry. It brought to mind Michael's message from last night, about how those who loved the Lord were like the trees who sent their roots into the stream and flourished.

Was he faithful enough? He'd spent a fitful night, wondering if he could have said something different to Emma. Wondering if his feelings for Eve and Olivia were the beginnings of a lifetime of love the Lord had sent him, or just his sense of duty kicking in. Once more Wesley had made a mess of things and he, Billy, the responsible twin, was making things right.

He stopped at the barn to gaze back at the white house in the shimmer of the sunrise. Feelings welled up within him, for this had been his home—and yet it really wasn't. The Malloys had taken him in and loved him like family, but he was a Bristol. And that would never change.

He turned his face from the sun as warring emotions punched him in the gut. Much as he loved Michael and Mercy and the family they'd pieced together, he wanted to go *home*. Here in the summer sun's unflinching light, he realized he had no desire to finish that little house at the corner of the homestead—whether Emma decided to live there or not. He wanted that place in Richmond with the white pillared porch and the lilacs, even if the fences were falling down and the windows were broken.

A sigh escaped him, and bitterness rose up in his throat like bile. Best to feed and water the horses like always: Obadiah Jones had sent word yesterday that he'd be coming for his horses this week. They figured he'd show up today for Sunday dinner, as he always did.

Billy swiveled to go inside the barn, but then gasped. Michael was standing there, watching him. His hair was still mussed from sleep. His golden brown eyes were as devoted as an old hound dog's.

"Mighty serious thoughts, Billy," he observed. "If something's on your mind—and it's been that kind of a summer—I hope you'll tell me about it. It'll go no farther, you know."

Billy's eyes smarted with unshed tears. He suddenly felt like that ten-year-old waif this compassionate man had taken up onto the seat of his stagecoach, after he'd been abandoned and his sister Christine became such a pill.

"You always know when I'm stewin' on somethin'," he breathed, "so tell me this, Michael: why can't I think of nothin' but going back to that house in Richmond? Why do I feel so—so *mad* at Wesley, because he got the place by bein' devious and underhanded?"

Billy stopped, amazed at how his heart was racing. *Years* it had been since he'd felt so upset—so cheated. And it didn't feel good.

"Anyone could understand your anger, Billy. Only natural to champ at the bit when your brother throws you off the place as a trespasser," he replied, slinging an arm around Billy's shoulders.

Billy nodded, still blinking. It felt odd to have this man comfort him now that he was twenty, but he didn't shrug out from under Malloy's hug.

"Am I bein' ungrateful, wantin' to leave here?" he rasped. "Is it childish to want the Bristol place just because Wesley took it—just like when we were kids?"

Michael smiled with the infinite patience Billy had always admired. His face took on that same ethereal glow artists painted on the face of Jesus—a real comfort when a crisis crowded out that still, small voice he should be listening for.

"You've heard me tell this, but when I was your age, Billy, I'd already fought in the war, and came home to find my ma had just died. Then I went out with a couple of friends, to see the young lady who became Joel's ma as a result of my selfish behavior," he recounted quietly.

Malloy's brow furrowed with his recollections. "It's natural for a young man to leave his home—to see something of the world and find his own place in it. Yet in your disappointment and anger, I don't see you lashing out like I did. I don't see you taking out your grief and frustration on Emma—or Eve. You've always had a good head on your shoulders, and you heart's in the right place, Billy."

"Oh, I got Emma good and riled up, to the point she never wants to see me again."

"But she's been a party to that problem, hasn't she?" Michael pointed out. "Though we all feel bad about her situation—and understand her need for love and her desire to marry you—we've wondered if she wasn't forcing your hand a bit. Emma's shown a different side during this crisis, and it's not a very flattering picture, is it?"

A grateful grin curved his lips. "I thought maybe I was the only one who saw it that way."

"Nope." Michael's smile hit him like a little jolt of lightning. "You're our boy, Billy, and we want what's best for you—what God has in his plan. And we always hoped you'd look farther than Emma."

Billy felt his load lift. He stood taller and found his smile again. "Guess I shoulda followed my gut instead of—"

"And you did, when you tended Eve at the church and then announced the wedding was off," Michael insisted. "Although you certainly waited until the last minute to tell Emma how you really felt!"

Michael's soft chuckle made Billy feel better. But his situation hadn't really gotten any easier.

"So now I've gotta think about Eve and Olivia," he murmured. "But I still don't know whether that's the right path to follow, or if I'm just so used to fixin' what Wesley's messed up, I'm actin' out of habit."

"Time will tell, son. At least now Eve has some options, and she's mothering that baby like she ought to. She can behave as she normally would, instead of running scared. We'll gladly help her for as long as she needs it."

"Yeah," Billy said with a nod, "you've always been Good Samaritans, that's for dang sure."

"I have a soft spot for girls in her predicament, same as I did for Joel's ma," Mike replied wistfully. "You might've been too young to realize it, but my helping Lucy Greene with grocery money—and the way little Joel flung himself at me when we came out of church one day—nearly turned Mercy away from me. It was easy to see what sort of woman Lucy'd become."

Billy smiled as he recalled that Sunday morning.

Easter, it was; the day Solace was christened. "Good thing we got home to find Lily on the porch, or you'd have caught the cold shoulder a whole lot faster!"

He nodded, smiling. "And when Lucy was killed, and I took Joel as my own, it strained our romance even more. But Mercy and I look back now and see it as God's hand guiding our lives."

"So what sorta woman *was* my mama? Did she get shot down 'cause you were bein' such a do-gooder?"

They both whirled around to see Joel standing behind them with a pitchfork. Wiry as he was, with his hair still in clumps from sleeping, he didn't look big enough to be handling horse chores—nor did he ever look happy about it. His sullen eyes were throwing darts at Michael Malloy.

"Son, don't misunderstand me when I say—"

"Am I *really* your boy? Or did ya tell that story so's it would sound good to the neighbors?" he demanded shrilly. "Was I just a way to make Mercy feel sorry for ya after Ma got shot? I remember that like it was yesterday—and I still ain't figured out why you didn't *stop* those guys with the guns!"

Billy swallowed hard. How would Michael answer these questions, fired at him like the bullets that had killed Joel's mother? Was there a way to help this man who'd saved him from more difficult situations than he could count?

"Yes, you are my son, Joel. Although I know you haven't always felt you belonged in this family. It didn't come as easily for you as it did for Lily and Solace," Michael said. His voice was low, more cautious than usual. He took a step toward the boy, his arms open.

Joel backed up, still gripping the pitchfork. "You talk like my mother was a *whore*!"

Billy let his breath out slowly. Should he be concerned about the bile rising in that boy while Joel held a potential weapon?

Michael stood his ground. He let out a weary sigh and said, "Better not go calling any woman by that name unless you know what it means, young man."

"She had a lot of men comin' and goin'—*that* much I recall! You were only one of 'em, and—"

"And I knew my carelessness helped set your mother on that path. Just like I knew you were mine, the first time I saw you." Malloy seemed to age in the dim light inside the barn, but he went on, quietly resolute. "That's why, when she moved to Abilene, I often gave her money to care for you and—"

"You coulda married her! Insteada Mercy!"

"I can see why you'd think that," the man went on in a tight voice. "But God had already led me to help the Monroe family, and—"

"Let's leave God outta this!" Joel blurted. "He wasn't there to save my ma, was he?"

Billy sucked in his breath and stepped forward. "You mind your mouth, mister! I wasn't there to see how it happened, but those men who were shootin' weren't listenin' to what God wanted! They were fightin' mad, and stupid enough to draw—"

"And your mother stepped outside right then, holding you tightly by the hand, because you could squirm away and escape faster than anybody I ever knew."

Malloy sagged. A tear ran down his cheek. "When you caught sight of me, you hollered 'Papa!' and bolted across the street—and your mother, naturally, followed you. I suspect you startled a couple of those men, and their guns went off. Your ma was in the wrong place at the wrong time, Joel. Nobody's sorrier about that than I am."

The boy's face remained a mask of anger. "You coulda stopped 'em! You coulda hollered at 'em to—"

"I walked into that situation at the same time your mother did, Joel. I was trying not to attract your attention, knowing how you'd—"

"So you're sayin' it's all *my* fault? Hell, I was only—"

Billy shot forward at the same time Michael did. Somehow he yanked the pitchfork from Joel's hands while Malloy scooped the kid up as if he was going to give his backside the blistering it deserved.

But Joel had never been one to accept punishment, and when he kicked and swatted at his father's face, Malloy struggled to keep hold of him. He wasn't a large man, but he was deceptively powerful—and Billy couldn't recall *ever* seeing Michael this wound up. With a quick pivot, he tossed Joel—a skinny bundle of flying arms and legs—onto a hay pile, and then landed on him to pin his limbs down.

Malloy was panting, struggling to maintain control of the fury that had festered in his son's mind a long, long time. When he leaned into the boy, Billy recognized his frustration and fear and—

A love so fierce he could hardly stand to watch. Michael swallowed hard, holding his emotions in check as he searched for the right words.

Billy wondered if there *were* any. He stood by, feeling helpless, yet sensing he might need to step in again.

"Don't—you—*ever* doubt that your mother was doing the best she could, and that she was keeping you alive when she died," Malloy rasped. "I won't hear of you disrespecting her. You understand me, son?"

Joel nodded, wide-eyed. He looked as pale as the hay.

"And while we're at it, I'll remind you that in this house, we do *not* 'leave God outta this'—or otherwise go on like He doesn't know what He's doing," Michael continued.

It hurt Billy to listen to this. He himself had provoked Michael's lectures over the years, but he'd never been one to challenge authority, let alone question God!

Malloy let go of his son and struggled to stand up. "I'm sorry our discussion went in this direction, Joel. You have every right to ask about your mother, and to know how you came to be a part of this family.

"And I can understand that you'll challenge me from time to time—and maybe you won't like me much," he went on, wiping sweat from his brow. "One of these days you'll be too big to take a switch to. You'll make your own decisions—make your own way in the world. But you'll never outgrow your need for love and your family. Just like your family—and I, as your father—will never stop loving you, Joel. Do you understand that?"

"Y-yessir."

"Do you *believe* it—that I love you?"

A long moment went by before Joel nodded.

Michael's sigh filled the silent barn. He cleared his throat, casting a glance at Billy.

"Yessir, I believe it, too," Billy murmured. It wasn't what Malloy expected of him, but he said it as much for the man's benefit as the boy's. "Nobody could love his children more than you do, Mike. If anybody could make the hard parts of life any easier, you'd be doin' it."

Those hound dog eyes flickered with gratitude. "Guess we'd better leave the rest of these chores and get dressed for church," he said quietly. "If anybody's standing in the need of prayer right now, it's me."

Chapter Eighteen

As though the whole family had witnessed the squabble between Joel and his father—and because they were skipping the picnic to meet with one of their buyers—the ride to church was unusually quiet. Joel sulked between Asa and Temple, while at the end of the pew, Michael wore a strained expression Billy hadn't seen since—well, since his sister Christine had run off, in defiance of the Malloys' faith and family values.

"What on earth happened?" Eve whispered, keeping her voice beneath the organ's prelude.

Billy wiggled his finger at Olivia, who was cradled in her mama's arms, looking cherubic in a sky blue dress Solace had long since outgrown. "Michael and Joel got into it while we were chorin' this mornin'. Things went farther than either of 'em figured on."

"They came to blows?"

"Close enough. Michael had some tricky back-trackin' to do, when Joel challenged him about his real mother." His heart rose into his throat when the baby gripped his finger and focused those Bristol blue eyes on him. "Lucy Greene's parents sent her away when they realized she was carryin'. Turns out it was Michael's baby—"

"No!"

"—and when she showed up in Abilene, he felt responsible for her, even though Mercy was the woman he was meant to marry." Billy cleared his throat, aware that on the other side of him, Lily and Grace were listening closely to the details of their daddy's bad mood.

"And she died? How awful."

"Walked into crossfire outside a saloon, when Joel broke away from her," he replied with a sad smile. "Which explains why he's never felt at home with the rest of us. No easy way to tell a kid his mama was a prostitute, gettin' by the only way she knew how."

Eve rocked Olivia more intently, looking away as this story soaked in. Fear furrowed between her forest-green eyes, tightening a face that had looked pretty and carefree a moment before.

"Before that misunderstandin', Michael told me how *glad* they were to be helpin' you with the baby," he said gently. "So don't compare yourself to Joel's mama, worryin' you'll suffer the same fate, honey. Nobody's gonna let that happen. Even if you don't move back with your mother."

"I hope she stays with us!" Lily said in a loud whisper. She leaned across Billy to tickle the sole of Olivia's tiny foot.

"Me, too!" Grace chimed in.

Temple shushed them as the preacher stood up to start the service.

Although Reverend Larsen's sermon was about Jonah, who ran from the Lord's assignment and got swallowed by a giant fish so he'd see things God's way, Billy's mind wandered. He loved peeking at Olivia as she dozed on Eve's shoulder, yet he saw Wesley stamped all over her impish face. Couldn't get those images out of his mind . . . how the shots rang out, and how his brother had snatched that pie from Mama . . .

the loose shutter and broken windows; the air of utter desolation in a house that was no longer a home.

Yet when he looked down the row of fresh Sunday dresses to where Joel sat with his arms tightly crossed, he didn't like what he saw there, either. That stormy face bespoke plans being made, or retorts composed. Ways to lash out because the truth about his mama was too painful to face.

While Joel was exactly the sort of boy today's sermon was aimed at—those who heard God's call but ran the other way—he wasn't listening. Nor would he like it if his father illustrated that same story during devotions tonight, to make the points on a more personal level.

It was a relief to see Mama and Carlton waiting outside by the carriage after church, just off the train. At the sight of Olivia, his mother brightened and reached for the baby. "I just couldn't stay away from this girl!" she cooed as Eve handed over her granddaughter.

"We certainly hope you'll join us for dinner," Mercy said as the kids piled into the carriage.

"Stay as long as you care to!" Michael added, as though he, too, were glad for a distraction from the strain of their morning.

Billy suspected, from the look on Carlton's face, that this surprise visit was mostly to keep Mama out of harm's way—or to keep her from going back to talk some sense into Wesley. He was grateful that the Malloys were so generous and accommodating toward his mother, especially now that things were more difficult in Missouri.

When they got to the Triple M, Billy finished the horse chores while Mercy, Asa, and the girls prepared their midday meal. As everyone gathered around the table, now extended with two leaves, Joel refused to sit in his spot between Temple and his daddy, which caused a disruption until Eve graciously traded places with him.

Ordinarily Michael wouldn't tolerate such a show of defiance—or was it fear? Billy suspected the man didn't have it in him to challenge his son again. Not when it meant the little girls might ask questions he didn't want to answer during dinner, in front of guests who weren't close family.

"Father, we thank You for this summer day and for the bounty You've once again spread on our table," he prayed when all the platters and bowls had been set down. "We ask Your guidance as we face difficult situations. We submit to Your wisdom as You show how we should follow Christ's example in our thoughts, words and deeds. Bless us all, that we may be reflections of Your love and light. Amen."

"Amen," echoed around the table.

As the platter of ham and bowls of boiled cabbage and potatoes were passed, Billy sensed Michael was about to apologize to his boy—so everyone would know Joel was still loved, and so Malloy could get it off his mind. He saw the words forming—and reforming—as the slender man cut his meat and slathered butter on potatoes he'd smashed with his fork. Mike glanced toward Joel time and again, while Lily and Solace were talking about whom they'd seen in church and politely making conversation with Mama and Carlton.

Michael was opening his mouth, ready to pronounce his forgiveness, when someone pounded loudly on the back door. "If you folks are eating dinner, I'll just wait outside," a voice called from the kitchen.

Mercy tossed her napkin aside while Michael rose, as well.

"Come in, Obadiah!" he called. "We've been expecting you, but we didn't know when."

"I'll set you a place," Mercy added. "No trouble at all."

When Eve glanced at the already crowded table and flashed him a questioning look, Billy lifted an eyebrow.

"Happens every time," he murmured, shifting Solace's plate and chair closer to his own. "Mr. Jones buys Morgans from us each summer, and he's smart enough to come for the week's best meal."

A portly man swaggered through the doorway to survey the crowded dining room, pausing for those who made him a place. Even in the heat, he wore a fine serge suit with a brocaded vest and a white shirt. A gold watch chain jiggled across his middle, and as Obadiah approached, a diamond stick pin winked at them.

"Afternoon, Mr. Jones!" Billy said. "Got your telegram a few weeks ago—and yesterday's, too. We've raised some mighty fine three- and four-year-olds for you to choose from. Ready to ride, of course."

"Always a pleasure doin' business with you folks," Jones drawled. "Been buyin' my horses here for what? Nearly nine years now?"

"Yessir, it's comin' close to that."

"And I have yet to take one that didn't exceed my expectations for strength and performance, as well as trainin'."

"Thank you, sir," Billy replied proudly.

The bulky man settled into the chair Asa carried out, squeezing between Michael and Solace, so he could converse with the two men he did his business with. When he'd fluttered his napkin over his lap, he grinned down at the little girl beside him.

"And you're the one with the pretty name and all that dark, wavy hair," he said. "Solace, isn't it?"

"Yessir! But don't you go takin' Mr. Lincoln away!" she spouted. "He's *mine*, 'cause Billy gave him to me!"

Jones laughed, helping himself to a slab of ham. "You've got a fine mount, then, and I wouldn't dream of takin' him. Now that little girl down there by your mama—could that possibly be Gracie? Why, she was knee-high to a grasshopper last time I was here!"

The girls giggled, taken in by this guest's overblown bluster.

"And I remember your sister Lily, too," he said with a nod, "and your brother Joel's certainly grown tall, hasn't he? But I don't believe I've met the pretty lady beside Temple."

"This is Eve Massena," Billy jumped in. "She comes from my hometown in Missouri. And that's her little girl, Olivia, and my mama, Virgilia Harte, and her husband, Carlton. This is Obadiah Jones. He raises cattle in Texas."

"That's *one* of my enterprises, yes." Jones held a spoonful of potatoes over the bowl to gaze across the table, which brought a flush to Eve's cheeks. Then he studied the baby, who snoozed in her basket on the floor. "Unless I miss my guess, Miss Eve's got her eye on *you*, Billy! And my, oh my—that baby's your spittin' image!"

The man's sanctimonious tone made Billy stiffen, but he knew better than to back down. "Yessir, you're right. Olivia's my twin brother's little girl. We're proud to have her here, because—as you know—the Malloys love every child who comes their way."

Jones coughed as though he'd gotten ham caught in his throat. And there was no missing the way Mama challenged him with one arched eyebrow. Nobody speculated about *her* grandchild!

"Why, you wouldn't be a-buyin' them horses from Mr. Billy if these fine folks hadn't took 'im in when he was just Joel's age!" Asa pointed out cheerfully. "Ain't a soul a-sittin' at this table who don't owe a mighty huge favor to Mr. Michael and Miss Mercy."

"Yessir! Amen!" Temple Gates said with a nod.

"Indeed we do," Eve replied, looking Obadiah straight in the face.

The cattleman blotted his brow with a snowy-white handkerchief. "And I count myself among them, for your hospitality over all these years. If no one else wants that last slice of ham—"

Billy passed him the platter: Jones wasn't used to being talked to that way by colored folks—or eating at the same table with them—but he knew when he'd been cornered. And Eve was sitting tall; not the least bit cowed by this Texan's insinuations.

Temple rose then, gracefully stacking the dirty plates and signaling with her eyes that Lily and Solace were to help. "We'll clear these dishes and be back with pie and coffee," she said in her melodious voice. "I know you gentlemen want to get down to your business."

Eve and Mama rose to help, as well, and with the pleasant clatter of plates and bowls filling the room, Billy collected his thoughts. He and Michael had discussed raising the prices on their Morgans this season, for the first time since the Triple M had begun its business. And from all appearances, Jones would have no trouble paying more.

Joel whispered something to Mercy. She felt his forehead and nodded. As he slipped from the room, the sorrel-haired hostess smiled at their guest. "And how are Elizabeth and the children? It seems like a lifetime ago when they were living up the road from us."

Jones guffawed. "Fine and dandy! Those little towheads who went to Texas with me after their daddy died are grown now. Got families of their own."

Michael smiled and stood up. "Excuse me, but I see my boy's not feeling well. You and Billy enjoy your dessert, and I'll catch up with you by the time you're ready to go to the stables."

Billy followed Michael with his gaze—and his heart—but kept up the table talk. He said a quick prayer that father and son would set things right between them before this day was done.

"You musta known Asa was makin' these pies for today, Mr. Jones," he teased. Mercy stood at her end of the table, cutting the pie, while Lily and Solace carried the pieces around to everyone.

"And as pretty as this slice of cherry pie, looks," Jones remarked, "the little lady bringing it to me outshines every star in the sky, doesn't she? You've got the face of an angel, honey."

Lily's smile wavered as the big, blustery rancher closed his hand over hers. "Th-thank you, sir," she murmured. She blinked, and her blond ringlets began to quiver.

Billy almost sprang up to snatch the girl's hand from Obadiah's, thinking he must be squeezing awfully hard. Across the table, Temple stiffened, her brown hands gripping the last stack of dinner plates. It wasn't like Lily to stammer when folks paid her compliments—which happened every time someone saw her.

Jones let her go as though nothing were amiss. He smiled widely as Lily set his plate in front of him. "Thank you, sweetheart," he crooned. "You'll make somebody a fine little wife someday."

Mercy, who'd been watching this exchange, resumed her pie slicing. "Let's not rush that, Mr. Jones. My girls have plenty of time to discover who they are, and who they're meant to marry."

Then she looked at him pointedly. "And by that time, I hope they'll know they don't *need* a man who expects them to wait on him hand and foot! Lily, Solace and Grace are much too remarkable to be caught in that trap."

"You are *so* right!" Mama chimed in, "and I applaud the way you're raising your daughters. Encouraging their education and talents—just the way you did for my daughter Christine!"

Jones stuffed a large bite of pie into his mouth, sensing he was outnumbered by outspoken females. Billy felt a surge of admiration for Mercy Malloy: She would never have survived the hardships of her earlier life, had she been dependent on a man. Nor would Judd

Monroe or Michael Malloy have loved her so much if she'd been biddable and complacent.

Billy smiled at her, drinking in her modest summer dress of yellow and a face that radiated compassion. He'd be a different man today were it not for the example Mercy had set, about the qualities of a good wife who kept her home in harmony.

He suspected Obadiah Jones wouldn't give a woman like Mercy a second look; wouldn't tolerate her opinions or methods of managing a household. Which was just as well. As Michael came back downstairs, brushing his wife's cheek with a kiss, Billy felt order had been restored: God was in his heaven and all felt right with the world.

"Shall we take a look at those horses?" Malloy said when they'd finished their pie. "I'm sure you'll feel they're worth the higher price we're charging now. Mr. Bristol's the backbone of my Morgan operation, so I pay him what he's worth to keep him here."

"You get what you pay for—in horses and help," Jones agreed, clapping Billy on the back. "Since the government's paying me to supply Army outposts all over Kansas and Oklahoma now, I hope you'll sell me a lot of Morgans for a lot of money, son. You'll be doing your part to protect our settlers from those shiftless, warmongering Injuns. Know what I mean?"

From his window above the dining room, Joel stared out at the corrals of horses, and the barnyard where chickens scratched, and the barns where milk cows swatted flies with their tails. *Manure.* Those animals were all about manure, and he was damn tired of shoveling it.

Gripping the windowsill, he listened to that Jones fellow brag about paying top dollar for Triple M horses. That Texas twang rang with a devilish aura of power:

painted pictures of cattle herds on vast acres of pastureland. Manure landed there, too, but he mostly heard
the jingling of coins. Jones swaggered in here every
summer, and the grandiose life he spoke of called to
Joel's lonely heart.

In Texas, a kid didn't have to step and fetch. There
was hard work, yes, but he wasn't afraid of that. He'd
been chained to it all his life.

In Texas, only the whisper of the wind, the pounding
of horses' hooves, and the jangling of the cook's trian-
gle would dictate how he spent his days.

No more sermons on Sundays, or evening devotions.

No more lessons from a school marm who preached
about how much better he could do at his lessons.

No more putting up with three sisters who could do
no wrong.

And no more obeying a lofty father and a substitute
mother who spouted Bible verses at every wayward
thought that popped into anyone's head.

And yet, for all their righteous ways, Mike and
Mercy Malloy had *cheated* him, hadn't they? They
minced words, in pinched voices, about the kind of
woman his mother was—implying he might be tainted,
too. Constantly watching over his soul, hinting it was
time he committed himself to Christ this summer, so he
wouldn't follow in Lucy Greene's soiled footsteps, no
doubt.

But he would make his own decisions now. And as he
watched the dandified Texan swaying between the
leaner figures of his father and that redheaded Bristol
he hated so, Joel's heart beat faster and harder.

Surely a man with spreads in Texas and ranches
sprawling all the way between here and the Rio Grande
could use another set of hands.

Surely Obadiah Jones would put him up in a bunk-
house and let him become a man on his own terms.
Anybody could see the Texan took instruction from no

one. He was a self-made man, unhampered by the constraints of faith; a man who gave the orders and rewarded those who carried them out.

He was down there at the corral now, viewing the Morgans Billy paraded before him. He signaled with a nod, scribbling notes on a tablet, as the minutes and the horses went by.

It was now or never.

Joel spread a shirt on his bed. He tossed some clothes on it, and then tucked in the top and bottom, tying the long sleeves to form a bundle. With a last glance at the room he'd grown up in, he slipped quietly along the hallway to his parents' bedroom. As he'd done on dozens of fine summer nights, when the moon called to him and the coyotes, Joel deftly hoisted himself over the railing of their widow's walk to scoot across the roof. Then he shinnied the length of the downspout.

Quickly, while the girls were in the kitchen doing dishes, he sprinted across the yard to the glossy black carriage parked in the shade. The matched team of blacks eyed him as he opened its door. Plenty of room inside the bin beneath the back bench seat, and as Joel climbed into it, he grinned.

This time tomorrow, he'd be far, far away!

This time next week, he'd have a whole new life!

Chapter Nineteen

"Well, son, for a day that started out on the rough side, it turned out all right!" Michael said, looking ready to whoop. "We were concerned about Jones paying the higher rate, and he took two dozen horses! More than ever before!"

"You's to be congratulated," Asa agreed. "Goes to show how hard work makes its own reward, and how the Good Lord looks after his own."

As Malloy handed him the large envelope of money, Billy glowed with satisfaction. They'd taken the Morgans into Abilene by tethering them to the backs of three wagons pulled by the largest of Jones's new horses. So now, with the twenty-four fine animals corralled for the night, they were heading back to the Triple M in one wagon with the others hitched on behind them.

Tomorrow Jones would escort his new mounts south and west on the train, to Fort Wallace, Fort Hays, and army outposts in Oklahoma before heading back to his spread in Texas. He always rode in fine first-class style, parking his carriage in a private boxcar that connected to his personal Pullman car—a palace on wheels with a

colored butler and a custom-painted design on the outside for all to marvel at. Never let it be said that Obadiah Jones spared any expense when it came to his own
comfort.

And now that he'd earned himself and the Triple M a
good profit from this transaction, Billy relaxed on the
wagon seat. "Thanks for helpin' out," he said, wrapping
an arm around the men on either side of him. "Say all
you want about me trainin' those Morgans, but I'd never
have gotten very far in this world without you two."

Asa slapped his thigh fondly. "You'd've done just
fine, Mister Billy. You's just made that-a way. Never
gave nobody a lick of trouble!"

Michael's chuckle sounded wistful as the evening
breeze riffled his sandy hair. "Too bad Joel's done
everything in his power not to follow your example."

"Was he all right when you went to check on him?"

Malloy's mustache twitched around his dimples.
"He was stewing in his own juice, too stubborn to talk
about his mother any more. Nor did he really accept my
apology for the way things went this morning. But I felt
better for making the effort."

"Mister Joel's not an easy nut to crack," Asa observed. "Been livin' his life under a dark cloud so long,
he don't recognize it when you offers 'im a way into the
light. Needs our prayers, that boy does."

"Especially since Mercy's determined to see him
baptized—which, at his age, calls for a public profes-
sion of faith." Michael grunted softly. "Should've seen
to that when he first came to us. Could've had him
christened with Lily or Grace."

"He's the kinda boy who needs to say those words of
his own free will," the old Negro said. "You's done
right by him, Mister Michael. Ain't nothin' more that
boy coulda asked for—even if he don't see it that way.
In the end, we all has to speak for ourselves and own
up for all we's done."

Billy reflected on this for the next few miles. Ahead of them, the twilight sky was fading into azure and a few fluffy clouds caught the last rays of the sunset. A full moon was on the rise, and all around them the nightly chorus of cicadas sang.

It was his favorite sight, right here along the Smoky Hill River, where the Triple M first came into view. He recalled the prairie grass and the rutted stagecoach road that cut through it when he was a kid first coming here. He got quivery with pride, seeing the white two-story house near the road, with two stables and a barn arranged around the corrals behind it. And then, as far as the eye could see, the corn crop stood tall and proud on one side of the road while the Turkey Red wheat resembled a lush green lawn.

It gave him a sense of pride and belonging, knowing he'd helped build the Malloys' dream into this fine spread that glistened in the sun's final brilliance.

Was it wrong to go home to Richmond? To start up his own place there, raising horses like his daddy had? Knowing how Mike Malloy depended on him here—how well the family had treated him—made the choice a tough one.

Billy sighed, and then sat straighter. "What do you s'pose that smoke's from? Way over yonder, where the Clark land borders ours?"

"Good-sized fire," Asa remarked. "You don't think a spark from the train set the pasture ablaze?"

With a clap of the reins, Michael urged the horses into a canter. "Better ride over that way to find out. Dry as it's been, a prairie fire'll spread faster than we can control it."

An odd tightness clenched in Billy's gut. What if it wasn't a train? What if Emma had done something careless, like forgetting to douse an outside fire she'd cooked with? Or what if she'd set the house aflame to spite him?

Surely she knew better! He was allowing his imagination to run amok when he should be thinking of ways to prevent a disaster to their homes and crops.

They barreled into the driveway at full speed, halting the horses near the first stable. "Asa, I want you to get buckets ready and warn the ladies to change into old clothes," Michael said as they clambered from the wagon. "Might need to form a brigade from the river, if the wind kicks up."

"Yessir, I'll do that!"

"And Billy, you ride on over to the Clark place," Malloy continued. "Let's hope George didn't set the house afire trying to fry up some dinner. I'll have Reuben and Sedalia round up their hands to carry water as soon as we find out what's burning."

"See you later! Be careful!" Billy called over his shoulder. Within minutes he'd saddled Pete and was headed down the road at a full gallop.

He clung with his knees, riding easy yet swallowing back panic. Bad enough that George Clark had never really recovered from his wife's death last summer: if the Clarks lost their crop again this year, they wouldn't survive the winter here. And Emma would find a way to blame it on *him,* for backing out on her.

As darkness fell around him, he prayed for safe travel—for all who would ride mounts over gopher holes and in the presence of fire. Billy prayed for guidance, too, because his years on the prairie had taught him how precarious life became when people made mistakes and Mother Nature magnified them.

When he arrived at George Clark's, however, the homestead's original log house sat intact. The front window was so dirty he could barely make out the flame of a candle inside.

"George! Emma!" he called as he dismounted. "Everybody all right here?"

No response.

Billy yanked open the door, ready to yell again, when he saw Clark slumped in a kitchen chair. An empty bottle sat on the table in front of him. The place smelled of cooking grease and unwashed clothing, which littered the floor near the curtain that marked off the old man's sleeping area.

"George! Wake up, dang it! *Fire!*"

"Uhn?" Clark shuddered before slowly lifting his head.

"Where's Emma? She out back—or over at the other house?"

Even in the dimness, Billy saw George Clark's unshaven face curdle in a scowl. "Dunno," he slurred. "She ain't here, takin' care of me, that's fer damn sure."

Sensing that George would be no help, Billy quickly ladled water from the bucket near the table. "Drink this! Shake yourself awake!" he cried. "You'll need to head for the river with your livestock if the fields catch fire. I'm goin' to find Emma."

Behind him he heard the *thunk* of George's head hitting the tabletop, but he couldn't worry about the old man: that pillar of smoke must be coming from the unfinished house at the corner of the two homesteads. And Emma must be there!

Urging Pete along the darkening trail, Billy prayed to God that he'd find her safe. As he rode closer, he saw that angry red-orange flames had engulfed the roof—smelled the tang of new wood and squinted at the intense light from the fire. Pete was starting to spook, so Billy hopped down and wrapped the reins around a fence post. He tried not to think about their plans for a chicken yard and a garden in this spot.

"Emma! Emma, you here?" he cried.

The roof beams made a gut-wrenching groan as they collapsed, pulling the top of the house into the inferno with them. No sign of her on the front stoop, thank goodness, because tongues of flame were licking at it now.

Frantic, Billy dashed around to the back. If she was inside—if she'd gotten hurt somehow and couldn't move—or God forbid, if she'd seen this as a way to end her misery—

But he had to keep his thoughts logical. It wasn't like Emma to give herself over to a disaster. Not after she'd remained the sane, competent family member who'd seen to her mother's burial and then found the pluck to propose to him. When her dogs began to bark, he looked in their direction.

"Emma! Emma, can you hear—"

"Don't you come a step closer, Billy Bristol!"

The air rushed from his lungs as he peered through the darkness toward her voice—although it sounded like she might be aiming a rifle at him. When his prickly eyes focused on the two walnut trees—the place they'd planned to hang a swing—he saw the top of her blond head behind the trunk on the left.

And yes, she was pointing something at him.

"Emma, what in tarnation—"

"I said *halt*, before I fill you fulla holes, Billy!" Her voice wavered, but her wrath came through loud and clear. "Tried to burn me out, didn't ya? Thought you'd be rid of me once and for all, but—"

"What're you *sayin'*?" He inched closer, wishing the smoke didn't obscure Emma's eyes. She was talking crazy, scared out of her mind. As though *he* had set this place aflame!

"Seen you with my own eyes!" she cried over the crackling of the fire and her frantic collies' barking. "Ridin' past here a couple times, to be sure I was watchin' when you tossed your torch through the front window!"

"Emma, I would never—"

"Don't gimme that, Billy!" she screamed. "Ain't nobody else in these parts with red hair like yours! I'd've known your voice anywhere, when you said I was gettin' the hellfire I deserved! I didn't do *nothin'* to you, Billy! Nothin' that deserves—"

Billy's gut bottomed out. He had *not* thrown a torch through the window or hurled such words at this woman, but he suddenly knew who had.

And if Wesley had wreaked his vengeance *here,* nobody in Dickinson County was safe.

Chapter Twenty

Billy wanted to grab Emma by the shoulders and shake some sense into her. The "weapon" she was pointing was probably a broom handle. By the time he could convince her his malicious twin was responsible for this disaster, however, the nearest field of corn would be aflame.

"I'm goin' for help, Emma!" he hollered as he headed toward Pete. "It doesn't much matter who started this fire, if it wipes out all your crops while you stew about it!"

He rode hellbent toward the little log home where Mercy and Judd Monroe had taken him in, where Reuben and Sedalia Gates now managed the crops and horses on the original homestead. Again he prayed for God's protection as Pete galloped across the familiar but potentially dangerous terrain in the moonlight.

Now that his eyes had adjusted to the countryside, enveloped in evening's deceptive cloak of serenity, he could make out a wagon coming down the road toward him. Familiar voices were speaking urgently.

"Over here!" he yelled. "Can you help me with this fire?"

"We's on our way Billy! Go on back to keep Miss Emma safe!"

The familiar rasp of Reuben's voice steadied him, and Billy wheeled Pete around to follow the Negro's suggestion. This sort of prairie disaster had been a factor in choosing the site for their new home: it was close enough to the Smoky Hill to draw water—both for everyday use and to quench the flames that ravaged the plains during every summer's dry spell.

He was pleased to see Emma returning from the shoreline with buckets in each hand. It struck him how very small and defenseless she looked in the glare from the fire, one woman battling an inferno that involved far more than beams and rafters and lost belongings. Hattie and Boots panted beside her, protecting her but knowing to stay out of her way as she trotted along. Instinctively they kept their distance when Emma got near enough to the fire to throw water on it.

Billy grimaced at the hopes and dreams they'd built on this spot, and tied Pete to a fence post farther away this time. He ran to grab a sloshing bucket from her hand.

"Reuben's on the way with more help," he rasped. Together they doused the nearest edge of the fire and hurried back toward the river. "This is no time to argue my point, Emma, but I hope you'll figure out that the man who did this was bigger than me, and he rode a different horse—"

"It's partly my fault," she replied tightly. "Coulda doused the fire inside with my dish water, but I was feelin' mighty low about how things've—"

She stared at him as they stooped to refill their buckets. "If it wasn't you, then who?"

"Looks like my twin brother, Wesley, has come to take his vengeance. I made the mistake of showin' up at our old home place in Richmond, and then along came Eve with the baby—and then Mama—and we really set him off."

Billy hoisted his bucket, and then snatched the one Emma had filled, so they could run faster. "Seems I'm settin' off a lot of folks lately, but dang! I never dreamed it'd come to this."

By the time they arrived with their buckets, Reuben and his wife, Sedalia, were hopping down from their wagon with Will Smedley, their hired hand, and Michael. The tall colored man grabbed a spade, as did Will, while Malloy and Sedalia trotted toward the river with more buckets.

"Let's form a relay and pass these along," Mike suggested. "Emma, if you ladies will keep filling buckets, Billy and I can do the running."

It was the best plan, even though he secretly wondered if there was much left worth saving. A few grasshoppers had already shown up this week, probably hatched from eggs laid during last summer's second plague of them, so if the crops burned, maybe those pests would have nothing to eat.

But he shook those thoughts from his mind. Told himself not to count the hours and dollars he'd invested in labor and lumber here. Tried not to be angry with Emma for letting the fire spread for what seemed like a weak, selfish reason. He just hurried toward the flaming house with bucket after bucket of water from the river. Little was left except the main beams now, which resembled pillars of hellfire. Reuben and Will were gallantly digging a ditch around the place, their faces and arms glistening with sweat from the blaze's intensity.

"Shore wish it'd rain," the big hand huffed. "If we ever needed us a miracle, it'd be now."

"Not a cloud in the sky, though," Will returned. He stepped out of Billy's path, swiping his damp hair from his eyes. He watched the water land and the steam that rose from it. "We've about got this licked, though. It won't spread beyond this ditch."

It wasn't a jubilant thought, but it turned Billy's mind in a more positive direction. As he and Michael ran with more buckets, he had the sense that once this fire was put out, things between him and Emma would be finished once and for all. Though it hurt to lose his labor of love—all the time, money, and sweat Mike Malloy had invested, too—there would be no false hopes to mislead her now. No way but forward for both of them to go.

About an hour later, the six of them sat on the moonlit riverbank to catch their breath. Will and Reuben each drank deeply from a bucket and then poured the rest over their heads. Michael and Billy shared a bucket, too, allowing the two collies to drink after they did.

The poor dogs were winded and confused, still on edge as they looked at the wisps of smoke rising from the rubble and then trotted back to their mistress. As he cooled himself, Billy thought it was a shame how Emma stood apart from Sedalia. Scrawny but tough, like a prairie chicken, Reuben's wife had survived her share of hardships and would have given the Clarks far more than her physical assistance on this awful night, if they'd accept it.

But that had always been Emma's way, hadn't it? The Malloys' cherished colored help had remained outside her sphere of acceptance—even though, over the years, they'd been nothing but nice to the blond tomboy he'd grown up with. He felt bad for her: what choice did Emma have left now, but to live in that smelly, dark house with a father who was as lost to her as her dead mother was?

Wiping his face with his damp sleeve, Billy walked over. He put his arm loosely around her shoulders. "I'm sorry, Emma," he whispered. "If you and your daddy need us to—"

"Thanks for your help," she interrupted coldly, "but

what we need is none of your concern now. Please just go home. Leave us alone."

Malloy opened his mouth, and then shut it. With a heavy sigh, he turned to the others. "We couldn't have stopped this fire without you, folks, and we thank you for all your help. Let's go on back now. See if we can get some sleep."

Nodding, they moved tiredly toward the wagon. Billy kept step with Michael, lowering his voice. "I'm pretty sure Wesley set this fire," he murmured. "And if he knew about this place being mine and Emma's, he'll be watchin' the Triple M for the best time to strike there, too."

Michael's eyes shone urgently in the moonlight. "You don't think he'd go after Eve and the baby—"

"From what I've seen, I can't put anything past him." Billy's heart ached as these words lingered between them. "Folks in town would've filled him in on Eve's whereabouts—maybe even seen Mama and Carlton come in on the train. He could've found out how much livestock and property you have, too. Those stables fulla horses will be a real temptation—a whole lotta ways to show me how much trouble he can scare up."

"And if he started on this end of the property, waiting for us men to rush over and douse this house—"

"No tellin' what he's got in mind for the Triple M while we're gone."

They both looked east, scanning the horizon for signs of fire.

"Let's go!" Malloy grunted, loping toward the wagon. "Billy, I know you'd rather ride hellbent for the ranch, but I'd feel a whole lot better if you stuck close to us. No sense giving your brother any more advantage than he already has."

Everything within Billy longed to gallop ahead, to spare his loved ones, who'd be sleeping by now, unaware there was a dangerous man lurking in the darkness. As he mounted, however, Billy sensed the wisdom of Malloy's wishes: Wesley wanted *him* to suffer. So it made sense that his twin would await his return.

As he steered Pete toward the rumbling wagon, he turned for a last look at Emma. Common sense—just good manners—told him he should at least offer her a ride back to the house.

But she and the dogs were already gone. Only smoke and the dull glow of a few remaining embers marked the catastrophe he'd witnessed here tonight.

Malloy hopped off the wagon at the old Monroe place and saddled up quickly. Will, Reuben and Sedalia waved them off, their movements slow with fatigue and the midsummer heat.

"You're sure Emma didn't set that fire?" he asked as he and Billy loped toward the road.

Billy cleared his throat, hoarse from all the smoke and shouting. "She admitted she coulda put it out sooner," he rasped, "but she was accusin' *me* of tossin' a torch inside. That's how I know Wesley's behind it."

Malloy sighed with disgust. How was it Billy Bristol was drawing fire from nearly everyone he knew this summer? Hard enough to end an engagement gone wrong, but to have his own brother gunning for him. . . .

Michael scanned the sky as they rode carefully along the dark road home.

Lord, I thank you that I see no flames, he prayed, *and I ask Your help and guidance fighting fires only our hearts can feel. Keep us safe, Lord. Protect the women and children who depend on us. Help us all to do the right thing at the right time.*

And hold Billy and his brother, Wes, in Your healing hand, he added sadly. *Help us forgive him, Lord, for he knows not. . . .*

Michael inhaled the night air, careful not to assume

too much by praying for the wrong thing. By all accounts, Wes Bristol knew exactly what he was doing—
and how to fight with more than physical fire.

Help us forgive him tonight, Lord, he added, *because I'm
betting things will be drastically different by tomorrow.*

Chapter Twenty-one

Shortly after midnight, just as his wife and household finally got settled back in their beds, Malloy saw the first flames licking at the stable farthest away.

"There he is," he muttered, elbowing Billy, who dozed in the chair beside his on the back porch. "Must've hidden himself by the river after he came from Emma's. Been there long enough that the livestock's used to his scent and the dogs don't suspect his presence."

With a whimper, as though they knew they'd missed something important, Snowy and Spot sat upright. They sniffed the air and then loped across the yard, their bushy tails held high. Carlton Harte rose like a wary wolf who'd stalked this prey before. On the other side of him, Asa shook himself awake.

"Remember what's most important, men," Michael remarked as he gripped his Winchester. "We can build more barns and we can raise more horses—"

"But we cain't replace them folks a-sleepin' upstairs," Asa finished. "Lord a-mighty, I's sorry it's come to this. You's already tuckered out from fightin' that fire, and he durn well *knows*—"

" 'The Lord is my strength and my shield,' " Malloy

replied, gazing at each of them as they stepped from the porch into the moonlight. "'A present help in time of trouble.'"

"'And yea, though I walks through the valley of the shadow of death," the cook replied, "I will fear no evil. Thy rod and Thy staff, they comforts me.'"

Billy let out a tired sigh, his hand on the pistol that stuck out of his waistband. It was the Colt revolver Malloy had given him several years ago, when he became the Triple M's trainer. He'd practiced shooting tin cans with it behind the barn, in case he needed to defend himself while out among the horses, but so far he'd only had to use it on a few snakes.

"'If God be for us, who can be against us?'" he whispered, but his voice wavered. He knew too well who rose up against him in this darkest hour of the night.

The fact that Mama was upstairs in Christine's old room didn't help matters one bit.

Terrified whinnies rose from the stable now, along with the confused stomping of hooves. Spot and Snowy were barking insistently, circling the building. The door flew open and dozens of Morgans fled toward the river, sending the corral railings flying like toothpicks ahead of them. The dogs were on their heels, instinctively herding them away from danger.

"At least those horses are out of harm's way," Harte remarked. He cocked his Sharps with an ominous finality before he swung onto the ladder they'd placed against the roof of the porch. "Remember what we talked about, far as who's to cover what. And considering how many lives are at stake here, take careful aim—and shoot to kill. Miss him, and Wesley won't give you a second chance."

Billy blinked away a wetness he could have blamed on the smoke he'd inhaled earlier. But he had to face the truth. He had to assume this cruel craziness wouldn't end until either he or Wes was dead. How the squabble between them had escalated to this was beyond his—

You turn it over to God and hope for the best, son.

It was Judd Monroe's steadfast voice in his head, and Michael Malloy's hand squeezing his shoulder—and Mercy's face in the window when something told him to look back at the house. With all these strong, God-fearing people on his side, how could he fail?

You've got no options: it's win or die.

He couldn't second-guess. And he couldn't miss, if it came to that.

"He's comin' around the barns," Billy whispered, following the startled squeals from the hog pen. "Whippin' the sows into a ruckus to cover himself. I'm bettin' he'll hide inside."

"We'll split up now," Malloy replied, nodding to his left. "And when the smoke's cleared, I fully intend to see both of you on the other side."

Billy didn't ask for Michael's interpretation of that phrase. He didn't much like it that Asa felt compelled to be in the thick of the fighting, either: if forced to choose between saving Asa and going after Wes, he'd make the wrong tactical choice—even if it was for the right reason.

He swallowed hard, prepared himself to draw his brother from the shadows.

"You might as well come on outta there, Wesley," he called in the strongest voice he could muster. "We've got that barn and stable surrounded, so give it up! No need for any bloodshed between us, brother."

Manic laughter rang eerily in the rafters, drifting out through the loft vent. "If I fell for stupid lines like that, why I'd've been dead long ago, Beaner. Good thing you ain't a gunfighter!"

Billy watched Malloy slip behind the barn, a slender shadow skittering across its white, moonlit paint. Up ahead on his right, Asa crouched behind the watering trough in the corral, which was now empty and turned on its side as a shield. Through the stable's open door, he saw flames devouring the hay and was grateful those Morgans had broken down the door.

"This fight's between you and me—though I don't know what for," he continued, praying the right words would come and praying Malloy would get behind Wes to flush him out, without getting shot himself. "So far, you've scared the livin' daylights out of a defenseless woman—"

"Defenseless, hell! She *shot* at me!"

Billy fought a grin; that sounded like the tomboy Emma he'd known as a kid, except she'd thought she was firing at *him*. "She's a female all the same, Wes. Why not pick on somebody your own size?"

"'Cause she was *your* woman!" came the retort, followed by another laugh that sounded off-key. "But I hear tell you left her at the altar, Beaner! Now whose manners need some brushin' up? *Coward!* Mama taught you better than that!"

Billy inhaled deeply. He'd known his brother would bait him. His job now was to stay calm; to lure Wesley into plain view, and maybe get him to drop his gun. He suspected, by the sound of Wesley's disjointed laughter, that he'd been drinking—and he didn't know if the liquor was to his twin's advantage or his own.

"What'sa matter, Billy boy?" Wes taunted. "Mama ain't here now, and Eve's asleep, so you've got nobody's skirts to hide behind?"

"You're the one who's hidin', Wesley! You've got a useless arm and a bum leg, compliments of your *friends.* So what's your point?" he shot back.

"I can still ruin you, Beaner! And I can make these do-gooder Malloys sorry they ever saw your weasely face!" he hollered, his voice more belligerent now. "I seen a couple purty little girls in the window, puttin' on their nightgowns. Figure they might think it's excitin', to get kidnapped by a notorious outlaw!"

Before Billy could snap, the whine of a gunshot made Wesley curse. But he sounded surprised rather than hurt, which meant Malloy had made his displeasure and presence known. The dogs began to bark as though they were cornering a skunk, but smart enough to stay away from it.

Another shot was fired, probably by Carlton, as it loosened shingles on the barn's roof.

Then came a loud "HyAAAAAH!" and two more shots rang out. The cows, already bellowing, burst through the barn door then, stampeding across the barnyard in all directions, scared and bawling. The border collies rushed out behind them, still barking frantically.

Billy ducked behind a tree to stay out of their way. This stampede was his twin's idea: somehow, Wesley was mounted on his horse and had a sawed-off shotgun in his other hand. He stayed on the big buckskin horse as it came charging from the barn behind the frightened cattle. He looked like Satan himself, his smile a wicked grimace in the light of the full moon, which glinted off his gun barrel.

He yanked his horse to a dramatic halt, letting the bawling cattle flee across the yard. Behind him, flames engulfed the straw in some of the mangers.

"So you thought I'd never ride again, did ya?" Wes taunted. He gazed around the yard with exaggerated head movements, until he focused on Billy. "So *there* you are, you lily-livered kid! Hidin' behind that tree— with a *girl* coverin' ya, no less!"

The bottom dropped out of Billy's stomach. Was this a trick, or had one of the girls actually come outside? He couldn't take any chances, so he pivoted.

Solace was advancing across the yard, dressed in pants, with her hair tied back. She had a pistol aimed at Wes—had to hold it in both her hands to steady it, but Billy suddenly knew why those tin cans he used for target practice sported more holes than he'd ever shot through them.

"Solace! You get back out of—"

"Solace, is it?" Wes fired back. "If you think for one minute you're scarin' me, little darlin'—"

"I think you're the picture of meanness, to be botherin' Billy this way!" she blurted. "You've got no call to destroy our property! Nor to scare our animals, neither! And since you set my horse loose along with the others, you'd better know I'm not gonna stand for it!"

Wes sat atop his buckskin, which stomped and skittered in agitation—perhaps because his rider kept him under a tight rein, and perhaps because the two dogs had come back to defend Solace. They dodged and nipped, crouching and snarling. The outlaw smirked down at the dark-haired tomboy, still gripping his shotgun.

Billy held his breath: the weapon's shorter barrel meant it could do more damage at short range. It would be just like Wes to scare the bejesus out of the girl standing before him or shoot the dogs for spite. And if he was drunk on top of being mean—

"Well, if he's any kind of a horse, he'll come back to ya," his twin taunted. "And seein's how you're a whole lot braver than my pip-squeak brother, why—I've half a mind to take ya with me! Even though you're just pretendin' you can shoot that pistol, you'd make me a—"

"Don't you even *think* about it!" Billy sprang from behind the tree, drawing his own gun. "Like I said, Wes, this fight's between you and me."

"So let's get to it, Billy boy! Nothin' like a good fight to clear the air!" Wes spurred his horse forward, his maniacal laugh ringing around the yard along with the dogs' protests. He covered the distance between them in the blink of an eye, while out of sheer instinct Billy dodged as he fired. He saw Solace squeeze her trigger, too. He lunged, hoping to roll her out of harm's way.

Wes's horse reared up, its eyes flashing wide and white with pain as it screamed. Time seemed to stop, and Billy experienced every event as though it were in slow motion, even though things were happening way too fast.

From the ground he saw those flailing hooves: his life and Solace's would end in an instant if the terrified animal landed on top of them. Wes's gun went off and he lurched crazily, as though unable to jump away from his hysterical horse. Billy heard two more gunshots—was too busy rolling Solace out of the line of fire to determine where they came from. But he saw with sickening certainty that his brother had let go of his gun and was being whipped around like a rag doll.

Wesley hit the ground with a bone-shattering *whump* just before his horse landed on top of him.

An eery silence filled the moonlit yard. Billy lay with Solace trembling in his arms, refusing to let her go. It was God's grace that had saved this fearless girl—and him—yet already a keening welled up from deep down inside him. Neither Wes nor the horse was struggling. Snowy and Spot were circling them cautiously, growling low in their throats.

Suddenly the yard was swarming with people.

"Billy! Solace! Are you all right?" It was Mercy's voice, and as he sat up, he saw her running toward him, with Lily and Grace close behind.

"Right here," he rasped. It was hard to draw air into his lungs, he was still so shocked.

"Solace! Billy!" This time it was Michael, rushing across the yard, half crazy with fear. "Thank God you're safe, and—but where'd you get that gun, young lady? I thought it was Carlton firing! Nearly lost my mind when I saw you—"

Solace sighed impatiently, brushing grass from her pants. "What's the all-fired problem? I've been shootin' target practice since—"

"She hit her mark, too."

It was Carlton speaking now, as he leaned over Wes's big buckskin. "Here's the hole where she shot the horse's heart—and here's where I plugged Bristol. I—I had to shoot him, Billy. Couldn't sacrifice you and Solace to his mindless brutality." He rose quickly when Mama dashed from the house in her nightgown, muffling her cries in a handkerchief.

"I can't believe you—why would Wesley charge at his own brother? My God, what do we do now? What do we *doooooo*?"

Harte pulled Virgilia into a tight embrace, as much to control her raw anger as to comfort her. Ten years crept over the detective's face as he rocked Mama in the moonlight, closing his eyes against the horror that had just happened here.

Solace was now bawling, too, her arms around the dogs, with Lily and Grace crying behind her. Mama howled against Carlton's shoulder. Mercy stood shaking her head, her hand to her mouth as she surveyed the damage. Just outside this immediate circle of shock, Billy saw Eve standing apart. She held Olivia to her shoulder, staring wide-eyed at Wes's motionless form.

Michael straightened to his full height. "It was my shot that flushed him out—and then Wes fired twice to scare the cattle through the doors," he reasoned aloud, pointing as he spoke. "From behind him I saw Billy shoot, and then Solace. Wes's shotgun went off when he was thrown—but where's Asa?"

Mercy sucked in her breath. "Don't tell me he was out here—"

"We couldn't keep him away," Michael cried over his shoulder. He was running toward the corral, where the old cook was to cover them from behind the water trough.

Billy dashed after him, nearly blind with fear. If Wes's stray shots had hit the beloved old man—if Asa had been hurt, or, God forbid, killed by—

"Asa! Asa, you still duckin' behind that trough?" he called ahead.

The flames whispered from the stable.

He and Malloy raced into the trampled corral, to see the collapsed form that was curled into a tight ball, so close to the trough it was barely visible in the darkness.

"Asa! Asa, you gotta—" Billy grabbed the bony shoulders to pull the old man into the moonlight, sobbing frantically. He fell to his knees in the dust, pulling that withered body against his, uncurling it so he could look for signs of life or . . . bullet holes.

Asa's eyes remained closed. "Is it over yet?" he wheezed.

"Over?" Billy gripped those spindly arms, holding onto his sanity. "Dang it all, you had me thinkin'—"

Asa's body felt tight and wiry like a coil, but slowly his dark eyes opened. "You can stop this foolishness any time, Mister Billy."

"We thought you shot! We thought—"

"It was close, I'm a-tellin' ya that," the old man breathed. "Somethin' tole me to duck. Hands I couldn't see was pushing me to the ground, outta the way. I—I guess I's all right, after all. Not tryin' to scare anybody, you see."

Michael exhaled with relief. "You rest here as long as you want. Now that the commotion's over, though, we've got another fire to put out."

Would this night—this nightmare—never end? Billy trotted toward the shed for buckets, while behind him the rest of the family rallied to the cause.

Once again he carried water as fast as he could from those passing it hand-to-hand from the river. Exhaustion threatened to drop him on the spot, but somehow he found the strength to grab just one more bucket . . . trot toward the stable . . . throw the water onto the flames . . . dodge Michael and Carlton and go back for just one more bucket. . . .

When the flames were doused and the burned-out buildings sent up only sad wisps of smoke in the moonlight, their task still wasn't over. Once again they drank deeply from the rain barrel and poured cool water over their scorched clothes and sweaty heads. Then they faced the inevitable task of handling Wesley's body.

When she saw them approaching, Eve laid her hand on Mama's hunched shoulder and spoke softly. The wraithlike woman in the flowing white nightgown rose slowly from beside the slain horse and rider, her head still bowed, supported by the younger woman.

"It just can't have happened," she rasped. Her faraway voice told Billy she'd been repeating this litany mindlessly while they fought the fire. "My boys argued, but it was with words! They would never draw guns, or— Wesley was loud and brash and cocky, but he never would've—"

"Mama, I—I'm so sorry," Billy whispered, slipping his arms around her. She felt small and frail in his grasp. "I had to keep him from chargin' at Solace—or snatchin' her up—just like those Border Ruffians grabbed him after they shot Daddy," he added as that ironic thought struck him.

"He was riding right at you, son," Carlton confirmed with a sigh. "We assumed a useless arm and bad leg would keep him from sitting a horse, but we were desperately wrong."

Billy made himself look at the part of Wes that lay visible beneath the broad body of his buckskin. He was twisted at an unnatural angle, and his bloody shirt had ridden up under his chin. His hat had flown off, and except for the beard and the unkempt hair plastered to Wes's neck, Billy could have been looking at his own corpse. "I still don't know how he—"

Without a word, Malloy and Harte bent to the grizzly business of moving the man from beneath his mount. They grunted, shoving with the last of their strength, and finally freed Wes.

"Had the reins wrapped around his bad arm so he could handle his gun," Michael murmured.

"Must've held it against himself so he could cock it and shoot," the detective added. "Tied his bad leg to the saddle fender with a . . . a suspender, to hold himself on. So damned determined to get back at Billy—but how'd he fasten himself on that way if his hand—?"

"Musta had help," Billy breathed. "But if anybody could find a way, it was Wesley."

They looked cautiously around the yard, studying the shadows cast by the moonlit buildings. Carlton frowned at the short figure approaching them from the house. "Solace, honey, this is nothing you should be looking at."

"I—I came back out to hunt for Mr. Lincoln," she stammered.

Michael rose to slip an arm around her shoulders, as much to comfort her as to confine her. "Honey, he knows his way home. I'm sure the horses'll be back," he said in a choked voice. "I need to know where you learned to shoot—"

"Been practicin'. Ever since we saw that sharpshooter at the circus," she admitted in a thin voice. "*Never* intended to shoot a horse, but anybody could see that man was gonna kill—"

"Don't change the subject!" Malloy raked a grimy hand through his hair, struggling with his frustration.

"How'd you practice? You were doing lessons with Temple, or helping your mother, and *they* certainly never knew you were shooting!"

Her sooty face sobered; so full of love and bravado Billy hated to see her catching this lecture. But it was serious business, firing a gun—more deadly than she realized. Marksmanship was a skill she saw as a new challenge. "Slipped out at night. To that cave down by the river."

"By yourself? What if the gun had backfired? Or what if you'd shot yourself in the foot and—"

"But I didn't!" she protested, her face crumpling. "I might be a girl, but someday I wanna ride in the circus ring, just like at the—"

"Solace, where'd you get that pistol?"

She bit back a whimper and then sucked in a noisy breath. Her wide brown eyes suggested there was something besides a hiding place at stake. "Joel f-found it in the shed—and the bullets, too. Hadn't ever seen anybody usin' it, so—"

Malloy's gaze met Billy's in the darkness. It was the pistol they kept out there in case snakes or coyotes got in with the livestock.

"—he kept it in a—a shirt wadded under his mattress—'cept when Temple was cleanin'."

"Joel!" Malloy straightened, gazing quickly around the yard. "In all the fracas, I haven't seen—he wouldn't have stayed in his room once he heard—"

"He wasn't *in* his room!" Solace whimpered. "I—I couldn't take time to look for him, once I heard Billy and his brother out here fightin'."

Her daddy's head snapped back and he lifted her chin. "There's something else you need to tell me, isn't there?"

The girl's lip quivered and she let out a tearful sigh. She nodded, scrunching her eyes shut.

"Something about Joel." Michael's voice had the rasp of sandpaper, and the hand holding Solace shook slightly.

"He . . . he wadded up some clothes," she gasped, shuddering with sobs of realization. "Stuck 'em under his covers, to make it look like he was in bed."

Mike scowled. "But when I looked in on him after dinner—"

"He was real unhappy, Daddy. Mutterin' to himself all day, like he was stewin' over things that bothered him *bad*."

Malloy's eyes closed. He let out an exhausted sigh. "I had to tell him some things about his mother—and myself—that weren't very—complimentary. And—like anybody would—Joel took exception to them."

Billy glanced up at the window of the room he and Joel shared, recalling how his sister had pulled such a bed-stuffing stunt when she was younger. Why hadn't he guessed the kid was hiding a pistol? Or sneaking out at night? He sighed, too, because he'd shown Solace and Joel that cave by the river years ago—the cave Emma Clark took him to the very first day they met.

"Joel always had a knack for gettin' away—runnin' off at the least little problem," he pointed out tiredly. "He could've slipped out while we were fightin' that fire at Emma's. Or even while we were takin' Jones's horses to town. How long do you s'pose he's been gone, sweetie?"

Solace's lip quivered. Her dark eyes shone with tears she was determined not to shed. "Could've shinnied down a drainpipe any time. We were cleanin' up the dishes while you were out with Mr. Jones. And then Temple had us girls play our latest piano pieces for your mama, while she and Mercy and Eve sat with the baby."

Billy envisioned that picture of domestic tranquility, and Joel using the piano music in the parlor to mask his escape. "With all the horses on the loose, there's no way to tell if he rode Hickok, or walked, or—"

"No doubt in my mind he's getting as far away from me as he can." Malloy looked as whipped as Billy had ever seen him. "He didn't like hearing that I was responsible for his mother's—"

"But you made up for that!" Billy protested. "You've raised him since—"

"When you're a kid, you don't see it that way. You look for somebody to blame, and then you hold those grudges until you can't believe anything else." Carlton clapped Malloy on the back, his face a mask of compassion. "Joel's a smart boy, Mike. I'm betting he'll ride out all that resentment, and when he's out of luck and money, he'll head back. It's still a worry, I know, but he's old enough to take care of himself on the road. Better than you might think."

"Tell that to Mercy," Malloy mumbled. "She hasn't noticed he's missing, with everything else that's happened. She'll be upset with herself about that."

Billy listened intently, trying to piece together Joel's day. "He's never been one to miss supper, though. I seem to remember he went upstairs when we were cuttin' the pie, after dinner."

Michael perked up. "Was he here then, honey? Did your mama take up a tray, or—"

"She sent Gracie upstairs to check on him," Solace said, thinking back as she spoke. "And about that time, you drove in, hollerin' about that fire—and Asa told us to change into old clothes—"

Sighing, the slender man glanced toward the house and then at the dead horse and rider, as though he didn't have the energy to deal with either situation right now. "Billy, it might be best if you take Solace inside and talk this out with Mercy—"

"And see how your mother's doing," Harte added

quietly. "We'll put your brother in the root cellar, until she decides where she wants him buried."

"Yessir," Billy replied heavily. As he walked toward the house, his legs felt like lead weights and his head pounded. His clothes were damp and clingy, and they reeked of smoke and sweat.

"Not one of our better days," he said sadly.

"Nope," Solace replied with a sigh. "And it's not over yet."

Chapter Twenty-two

Ordinarily the parlor shone with a welcoming glow when the lamps were lit, but it was a somber scene in these wee hours: Mercy was on the settee beside Mama, holding her as she wept, while Lily and Grace leaned into Temple on the striped sofa across from them. Their faces looked pale with exhaustion and shock.

Billy was glad Eve had gone upstairs with the baby, because she, too, had plenty to think about. He lingered in the doorway, hat in hand, wondering how to best comfort his stricken mother—and how to mention Joel's escape. This hardly seemed the time to lay yet another burden on Mercy—

"Mama, Joel's run off!" Solace's urgent voice drew the attention of everyone in the room.

Mercy's brow furrowed. "Honey, whatever can you mean? He was asleep when Gracie went upstairs."

"Right when Daddy was hollerin' about the fire!" Solace explained. "He rolled his clothes in the bed so it'd *look* like he was asleep!"

The alarm on her mother's face told Solace she'd timed this topic poorly, but there was no getting away from it now. "I—I thought it was odd that he slept through supper," she went on, 'cause Joel *never* gets sick. But when I was headed outside to—to challenge Wesley Bristol, I knew he'd outfoxed us. Joel wouldn't have missed the fires—or the gunfight—for anything!

"Sorry, Mrs. Harte," she added in a voice that cracked. "I—I only shot his horse so he couldn't massacre—"

Billy grabbed the girl and pressed her face against him. At her age, she didn't understand how such sentiments might tear out a mother's heart. Solace didn't have a mean bone in her body, but her earnest attempt at the truth was a little hard on him, as well.

Mercy's dark eyes widened further and she stood up. Her hands fisted at her sides until Billy thought she must be puncturing her palms with her fingernails.

"Yes, young lady, you and I will have a long talk about tonight's gunslinging episode," she rasped. "And if you know *anything* you're not telling me about Joel—"

"N-no, ma'am!"

"—it'll be a long, *long* time before you ride Mr. Lincoln—"

"He's gone, too, Mama!" Solace slumped against Billy then, blotting her tears as she tried to explain. "I—I feel just awful that I never even noticed Joel was gone, during all the—the fires and—"

Mercy's face crumpled. Although she stood tall, she balled her fist against her mouth to compose herself. "That's the crux of it, isn't it?" she murmured. "Nobody even noticed he was gone. I was playing with the baby, and then keeping you girls out of harm's way and—"

"Don't blame yourself, Miss Mercy," Temple put in. Her eyes looked huge in her dark face. "That boy's *my* responsibility. I should've known he was upset enough—defiant enough—to pull a stunt like this!"

Mercy lifted her head. "He told me his dinner wasn't setting right—"

"Because he was so mad at his daddy. He ran off,

rather than facing the hard facts." Temple leaned forward, clutching Lily and Grace to her sides. "That boy has always run from trouble. Turns a deaf ear during devotions, because he sees no need for religion—"

"Wasn't any too keen on bein' baptized, that's for sure," Billy put in.

"—so while I beg your forgiveness for my negligence, Miss Mercy, I see this as a lesson in life Mister Joel needs to learn the hard way."

Temple's exasperation had forced her to face some facts herself. "He's not stupid. That boy's hiding somewhere, safe and sound. *Proud* of himself for putting us in an uproar! He won't feel so high and mighty when he comes back to find out other matters—matters of life and death—have held our attention."

"He won't feel too good when I take a switch to his backside for deceiving me, either," Mercy muttered. But she was wiping fresh tears away. "That goes for you, too, Solace. First thing tomorrow, we'll discuss your sneaking around and shooting at things."

Solace stiffened against him, but Billy knew her mother wouldn't let her off without punishment for what she'd done tonight. And though Temple's words had taken him by surprise, this teacher had a sixth sense for seeing beneath the surface—for looking past Joel's attitude and pranks. He admired her forthright response.

"I think Temple makes a good point—"

"And I think we'll all see things more clearly after we've gotten our rest." Temple stood up then, bringing the two girls with her and gazing purposefully at Solace. "Let's go upstairs, ladies. We'll get ready for bed again and say our prayers—again—because all we can do with a night like this is turn it over to God."

Like a shepherdess, the young woman followed her flock from the parlor. She turned in the doorway, though, smiling sadly.

"I'll say a special prayer for God's grace on that boy," she said. "I'll ask guardian angels to surround him and guide him back to us, Miss Mercy. I'll ask them to surround you with their love and light, too, Mrs. Harte. I'm so sorry for what's happened to you—and to you, too, Mister Billy."

The way she gracefully extended her hand, her expression keen with grief, made his throat close over a lump. His attempt to clear it came out as a cough that turned into a sob. How was it he could face Emma's rejection, and fight fires all night, and look death squarely in the face, yet one word of whispered sympathy could wring him inside out?

"Oh, Mama," he rasped. "Mama, I can't believe Wesley—I'm sorry I had to—"

She rose from the couch and opened her arms. Fresh tears streamed from her red-rimmed eyes and she looked ten years older than she had at dinner. Her arms closed around Billy as though she were holding on to life itself.

"I've lost my boy," she wailed, her body shaking. "Years went by while I could only wonder if Wesley was even alive—and then we shared a few brief words together—just enough to get my hopes up. But tonight he's been snatched away from me! *Forever!*"

Billy closed his eyes but it didn't stop his tears. Now that the fires were out and the dangers were behind them, he had to face what had really happened. "Mama, I didn't think he'd come after the Malloys, or—or Emma! What'd she ever do to—"

"You should've left him alone, Billy," Mama rasped. "You went back to Richmond with the best intentions, but if *I* could've talked to him first—just time alone with my troubled, wounded son—I could've coaxed him home with me. I could've taken care of him—persuaded him to change his ways and—"

"Mama, I was watchin' his every move to be sure he didn't use that pie knife on *you*. And Carlton was, too!"

She had curled in against herself, but Mama stepped back to glare at him. "I don't believe that for a minute! I'm his *mother!*"

Mercy came to them, placing a hand on each of their shoulders. "Virgilia, I understand how devastated you must feel—"

"You have no idea!" Mama spat. "My son is *dead*! My heart has a hole in it that will never be filled! *My life is over!*"

Billy's breath left him in a rush. He backed away, stunned.

Even though he'd seen his mother pitch many a fit and play the martyr like no other woman he knew, her barbed remarks pierced his soul. Hadn't Christine once said Mama favored *him* so much that she and Wesley might as well not have existed? Now he felt she was blaming him for his brother's death. As though he felt no loss himself.

He noticed then that Michael and Carlton had come inside. They were watching all this from the doorway when the detective said, "Virgilia, you're distraught and—"

"Damn right I am! You people have no idea—"

Harte entered the parlor quickly, to embrace her. "If you're going to point a finger, blame me. It was my bullet that took him down," he said in a ragged whisper. "It was the last thing I wanted to do, Virgilia. I'll regret it forever. But Wesley was like a mad bull—"

"Wesley only wanted what Billy had! A good job—a home—a woman who loved him!" his wife cried. She struggled to escape his grasp, but Harte held her fast. "If we'd given him a chance at those things, he might have left his outlaw life behind!"

Billy blinked, noting the wariness on the Malloys' faces, because they, too, realized Mama was at the end of her tether. Mercy gazed at him with a tenderness that made him ache, while Carlton Harte was murmuring more words to quiet his mother.

Asa, thank goodness, entered the parlor just then with a tray of tea and cookies. He set them on the table, and, knowing this white woman would be incensed by his touch, he folded his hands.

"Miz Harte, I's seen a lot of trouble and sorrow, but I *aches* for you," he murmured. "That was your boy, and you's gonna feel this loss the rest of your days. This special tea won't fix what's broke, but it'll make you sleep, so's you don't feel the pain for a while."

"Thank you, Asa." Carlton led his trembling wife to the settee, keeping his arm firmly around her waist. "You're going to drink this now, and then I'll take you upstairs to get some sleep, sweetheart. We'll all—"

"What if he's trying to poison me?" she demanded, glaring at the cook. "It's not *natural* to allow—he's trying to shut me up because I'm causing a—"

"I'll drink a cup of it myself," Harte insisted. He reached for the large ceramic teapot, but Mercy grabbed it first and began pouring.

"I'll have a cup, too," she murmured pointedly. "Asa's herbal potion is exactly what I need tonight."

"Pour me one while you're at it," Michael said, "and Billy's no stranger to pain, so he'll be wanting some, too."

Mama blinked, watching them with her lips pressed into a thin, ungiving line. "Don't you dare patronize me! This is all a ploy to—"

"Believe what you want, Virgilia, but I intend to get some rest tonight so I can think straight tomorrow."

Carleton raised his cup in a sad salute to the others, and they returned the solemn gesture. Everyone sipped deeply, savoring the tea's sweetness and warmth.

"As you can see," the detective continued, sounding tired but sly, "we're all sipping Asa's tonic, and we'll soon be at peace with what's happened tonight—at least until morning. Which means you'll have no one but yourself to blame if you're confined to bed tomorrow with exhaustion. And no one to listen to you any more tonight."

Billy pressed the rim of his cup against a grin. Already the warm liquid was settling him, and it did his heart good to see, once again, how Mama had met her match in Carlton Harte. She sat stiffly, looking mightily peeved at them for downing Asa's tea, but she finally took a swallow.

Setting his empty cup on the tray, Billy sighed. "It's time I turned in," he said sadly. "I've had all of this day I can handle."

Joel jerked upright. Had someone called his name? His head spun with hunger and the stifling heat, and then he remembered: He wasn't in his room. He sat on the floor of Obadiah Jones's carriage, wrapped in darkness as thick as a blanket.

Closing his eyes against the heat, he listened for voices—or the sound of saloon pianos, or trains whistling in the distance. He sat up straighter, ready to spring away if Jones opened the door. It was hotter than blazes in this closed-up carriage, and the scent of the leather seats reminded him of saddles taken off horses after they'd worked up a lather—and how much farther away he could be right now if he'd ridden Hickok instead of stowing away with Jones.

But that wouldn't have worked, of course: Solace would have noticed right off that his horse was gone. She was pretty good at keeping his secrets—and taking his double-dog dares—but she would have sounded the alarm as soon as she realized he was gone.

He'd miss her some. But not enough to stay. Not enough to put up with Temple's lectures and all that re-

ligious malarkey his father and Mercy tried to drill into
him. Especially since he now knew Michael Malloy
wasn't as spotless as he'd made himself out to be.

His stomach rumbled, and he needed to relieve himself, but Joel sat tight. He'd be collared if anyone caught
him slipping out of the carriage: The do-gooders in this
town knew he was a Malloy. They'd see to it that he
walked the straight and narrow back to the ranch—

"Enough of *that*," he muttered, and reached up to un-
latch the door.

Cool air that smelled of horses teased his face; quiet
nickerings told him those Morgans Jones had corralled
near the rail head were still here, waiting for their train,
while Obadiah spent the evening with one of Abilene's
fallen angels. "Mattie Silks" was the name he recalled
from the cattle baron's overblown conversation with
the station clerk. From the tone of their talk, Joel gathered Miss Silks ran a fine house with high-class ladies.
Served only champagne to her clients, he said.

Curiosity had egged him to follow the fat, swagger-
ing Texan, to learn more about night life and liquor and
women—women like his mother must have been. He
needed to know about such things—to understand the
ladies polite folks only whispered about with self-righteous shakes of their heads. Didn't he have that right?

There it was again—like somebody was calling his
name.

But when he poked his head outside—saw the full
moon fading off in the distance as a thin ribbon of light
appeared on the horizon—Joel realized the train station
would soon be coming to life. Obadiah Jones had left
orders for his new horses to be herded into straw-
strewn livestock cars, and this carriage hauled into his
private boxcar for the trip across Kansas, which was not
where *he* intended to hole up. Not if Jones would ride
in the plush Pullman car he used for his cross-country
business dealings.

Nope, Jones was a high roller—whatever that was. Joel figured he could impress the Texan with his ranching experience and land himself a job working with those horses at Army outposts—or better yet, head to Texas and bunk with cowboys who used to drive cattle into Abilene and shoot the place up—and had probably visited his ma! It sounded like a much more rewarding life than he'd ever know at home.

"Passengers traveling to points west, on the express run to Omaha, Ogden, and San Francisco, should proceed to the platform, please!" a station agent called out. "All aboard for California!"

No one would spot him in the shuffle of luggage and travelers, so Joel slipped out of the carriage with his bundle of clothes. He stretched, looking out across the rows of railroad tracks and side spurs, among dozens of boxcars, to find that fancy Pullman car. How hard would it be to hide himself in it until the train was rolling? A man like Obadiah Jones would admire his pluck; his desire to work hard at such an early age.

Sure enough, there it was! The private parlor car—with a porch!—and the sleeper car hitched to it were painted a royal blue with black and silver trim. The ornate initials "O.J." proclaimed these cars his ride into a bright future, so Joel ducked through the crowd. He stepped onto the Pullman's porch wearing a big grin.

He was reaching for the door handle when a voice stopped him.

"You there! Boy who's up to no good! Back away, or I'll have to shoot!"

Joel froze. Should he hit the floor, duck inside, or do as the man said?

"Th—it's just me!" he replied, wheeling around with his finest smile. "I'm workin' for Mr. Jones, and I was told to—"

"Nice try, kid." A man in a black broad-brimmed hat

strode toward him, with his jacket pulled back to reveal a holstered pistol. "*I* work for Mr. Jones, and he would never hire a scrawny, smart-mouthed—"

"Why not?" He'd branded himself and blown his story, but he kept trying. "I'm here to fetch—"

The door to the parlor car opened behind him, and Joel jumped a foot. Obadiah Jones, resembling a cross, crazy-haired Santa Claus in his red longjohns, scowled down at him. The scent of perfume drifted out around him, along with a honeyed female voice.

"Who is it, Obie? Why, have you had our breakfast delivered here before the trip, you sweet thing?"

The Texan's frown dissolved with his abrupt laugh. "No, darlin', it's just some no-account kid who—wait a minute! It's the Malloy boy! Does your daddy know where you're at? Your mama's gonna tan your hide for—"

Joel dodged the arm that shot toward him, to hit the ground running. Past the laughing watchman he sprinted, knowing he was done for: Jones would order his guard to catch him and take him home—or throw him in jail—or—

He could take no chances. Joel raced behind the train that was pulling away from the platform. Great white bursts of steam rolled around him as the cars eased into a clackety-clackety rhythm that seemed to call his name.

Jo-EL Mal-LOY, Jo-EL Mal-LOY—

He tossed his clothes, grabbed a railing, and swung onto the steps of the caboose. His heart was pounding so hard, it was all he could do to hang on and look back at the rail yard, where the train station—and Obadiah Jones—were growing smaller by the second.

Jo-EL Mal-LOY, Jo-EL Mal-LOY—

Did he remember right, that this was the express train to California? It hadn't been his original plan; but then, what kind of traveling man would he be if he couldn't take advantage of a change in plans? And a train ride across the West!

Maybe later he'd drop Solace a note and brag about his fine new life. But right now, he just wanted to sit on the back of the train and watch the countryside go by.

Chapter Twenty-three

Breakfast was later than usual and a somber meal: The girls sat sadly, picking at their fried mush and glancing at Joel's empty seat. Billy ate, but he had no appetite. He was thankful Asa's tea had settled Mama last night, and that she sat quietly now, staring at her food without seeing it.

Michael swallowed his last bite of bacon with a sigh. His eyes looked bloodshot from fighting the fires.

"Virgilia, this is a hard time for you, but I'm sure you understand that with the heat, we need to make decisions about Wesley's burial today," he said softly. "You're welcome to lay your boy to rest here on the ranch, or—"

"Wesley should be beside his daddy. In the family plot back home."

Mama's voice was expressionless, but at least she was thinking clearly. Billy closed his eyes, praying for the strength to be a good son—a son she would appreciate and love again.

Malloy nodded, encouraging her with his gaze. "The undertaker in Abilene has a selection of caskets, or I can build you a simple—"

"My Wesley deserves better than an ugly pine box," she said, her chest heaving with a sigh. "I—I just don't have the heart to choose a—"

"I'll go, Mama." Billy looked intently at her pale, haggard face, but she wouldn't meet his eyes. "I'll head into town first thing and get Wes a—a real nice one."

"And while they're gone, I'll clean him up and—"

"You'll do no such thing, Carlton."

Mama straightened then, her chin quivering but held high. "It was the last thing I could do for Owen when he was shot down, and you will *not* deprive me of this privilege. I know you're trying to protect me from how horrible he must look."

"I'll help you, dear," Mercy joined in. "We'll find some clean clothes and wash him as best we can—with Carlton's help."

Mama nodded, not wiping the tears streaming down her cheeks. "I—I don't know what to do about a preacher. I've not attended services in Richmond since—"

"Don't you worry about a thing, Virgilia," Michael replied. "I'll ask Reverend Larsen to speak, or I'd be happy to say a few words, or—"

"Maybe Mother would play—and Reverend Searcy would preach—if you had the funeral at church," Eve offered. She bounced Olivia on her lap to keep the baby from fussing during this conversation. The dark circles under her eyes bespoke a sleepless night. She had food on her plate, but she'd moved it around rather than eating it.

Mama found a small smile for her grandchild, and Billy sensed the little girl would be her salvation in the coming months.

"I don't want to impose on her, dear, since I know she didn't . . . approve of Wesley," Mama replied with a hitch in her voice. "Let's keep things as private as possible. A simple graveside service. No sense in inviting a lot of tongues that would ask questions and wag all over town later."

Carlton nodded beside her. "Probably best not to announce Wesley's death in the papers, either. We don't need trouble during the service, if his cohorts feel he owed them payment—and it'll be a way to watch the unsuspecting thugs who come to visit the house, not knowing he's been shot."

Resentment flashed in Mama's eyes. "Carlton, *must* you conduct business when I'm—"

"These are desperate times in Missouri, sweetheart. Your safety is my first concern." The detective took her hands in his. Then he looked around the table, his expression taut. "I must insist that you all keep silent about my position with the Pinkertons, of course. The welfare of everyone here might depend upon that."

"You have our word on it—and our thanks," Malloy said. He stood up then, smiling at Billy. "Let's you and I go to town for that casket. We can ask around about Joel—"

"B-before we leave for Wes's funeral, I'll be packing my things to—to take back home." Eve's voice wavered, and she sounded ready to cry. "I can't tell you how sorry I am for bringing on this trouble by coming here when—"

"Eve, that's not so!" Mercy rose to stand beside her.

Michael, too, went to her side, placing a gentle hand on her shaking shoulders. "We don't see it that way at all, honey. It wasn't your doing that Wesley came here to—"

"But if I hadn't interrupted the wedding, looking for Billy's help, none of this would've happened!" she wailed. She handed Olivia up to Mercy so she could blow her nose on a handkerchief that was already saturated. "If I hadn't come here, Billy would have a wife—and a new house! And—and your livestock wouldn't be wandering loose, and your stables—"

"It were Wesley's meanness that brought 'im here,

not you, child," Asa murmured. He began stacking their dirty dishes. "He was crazy mad at Mister Billy—drunk, I suspected—and he was strikin' out like a wounded animal.

"Beggin' your pardon, Miz Harte," the cook added with a sympathetic glance, " 'cause I knows this has to hurt your very soul to hear these things about your boy. But Miss Eve did nothin' to provoke those fires or the way he came a-ridin' in here with killin' on his mind."

"You and Olivia are welcome to stay here as long as you like," Mercy repeated.

"We love having you here," Michael joined in. "You've shared your little girl with us, and you've taught our daughters about drawing and painting. Please don't feel you've only taken, because you've given us so much more in return."

Billy felt tongue-tied. It wasn't his place to invite her to stay on with the Malloys, yet he wanted to encourage her—wondered if his galloping heartbeat forewarned how empty his days would feel, if Eve and Olivia weren't with him after he buried his brother.

Where had *that* thought come from?

Though he'd always been head-over-heels for red-haired Olivia—as he had been for Solace, Lily, and Grace when they were born—his heart bottomed out at the thought of not watching Eve tend her—of not peeking at Olivia as she slept so sweetly in her bassinet.

Or was he just aware that if Eve Massena went home, and Emma Clark refused to speak to him, he'd have too many reminders that two young women had left him behind? He'd have a good job and a roof over his head here at the Triple M, but now he'd know what he was missing.

He shouldn't say anything to Eve now, though, before he was *ready*. He'd never been the quickest to catch on about women and what they wanted—how they liked to be won over. But he'd never been one to lead them on, either.

"Are you sure your mother'll take you back?" he asked, mostly for something to say. "Last time you were there, she didn't seem willing—"

"You were right about Olivia being the key to her grandma's heart." Eve smiled at him from across the table, her green eyes shining. "When your mama took us back—with a huge boxful of baby dresses!—Mother and I made amends. It won't be as nice as staying here—because *you* won't be there. But it's the right thing to do."

"Yes, Florence finally realized she was only hurting herself by turning you out," Virgilia joined in. "But I'll miss having *my* turn to spoil that little girl!"

Eve sat taller now, managing a smile as she reached up for Olivia. "I appreciate all your reassurances," she said softly, taking in everyone with her gaze, "but I'm going home. It's time I took responsibility for my life and my child. Now that Wesley's gone, I can lay my mistakes to rest. Start fresh."

"Ever'body needs to do that now and again," Asa agreed.

"Lord knows I've been through that very Valley of the Shadow," Temple murmured, "and I thank Him every day that these fine people gave me a new life here. You'll do just fine, Miss Eve. But we'll miss you two, that's for sure!"

Something about these goingaway sentiments made his heart hammer. Billy burned to blurt out something romantic to change Eve's mind—convince her to give them more time together, here where love surrounded them on all sides. In these past few weeks he'd grown used to having her around—

But he had a brother to bury. And a mother who would need his attention—all the love he could muster—even if she talked as if Wesley was her only begotten son. Taking his cue from Michael's smile, he rose from the table.

"I s'pose we'd better be headin' to town, and lookin' for Joel," he said.

Malloy nodded. "Won't hurt to check with the neighbors about our horses and cows on the way in—"

"And look for Mr. Lincoln, Daddy! You've *got* to find him!" Solace piped up. She glanced at her mother then, withering at the thought of the switching to come.

Billy grinned at the girl's outburst. Her chestnut waves were escaping the ribbon she'd hastily tied them back with, and she wore a red calico dress without the lace and frills Lily insisted upon, yet he could see the striking woman she'd someday be. Not to mention the challenge she'd present to any man interested in her.

"He was my horse first, little girl," he reminded her, tweaking her nose. "Don't think for a minute I'd forget about him. But right now other things—like findin' Joel, and Wesley's funeral—have to come first."

"I had a dream about Joel last night."

Temple's whisper filled the room, piquing everyone's curiosity. With her hair braided close to her head, her face looked prominent and pretty, as serene as a twilight pool. Her dark eyes dilated as though she were reliving her vision.

"What'd you see?" Asa whispered. He'd stopped scraping plates to lean closer.

"Joel was in a dark place," she began quietly. She focused on a corner of the ceiling, as though the images were playing out there for her to watch again. "It felt very hot—"

"Did he have a pointy tail and a pitchfork?" Solace whispered, but then Lily glared at her.

And she shushed right up when Temple focused on her, although the teacher showed no irritation at Solace's remark. She seemed to be speaking from a faraway place inside herself.

"The full moon last night affected us all." Her tone sounded more academic now, yet still detached—as though some unseen angel might be using her as a mouthpiece. "I believe the moon was partly responsible for Wesley Bristol's rampage, and for your reaction to him, Miss Solace. Just as I believe the wily, wayward side of that moon spoke to something we haven't been able to reach inside Joel."

"Is he all right? What else did you see?" Mercy's brow was furrowed in concentration. Even Olivia stopped chattering to watch Temple's face.

"I sensed no danger or fear in him," she replied, again looking toward the high corner of the dining room. "He stepped out of the darkness this morning. But when a man in black tried to stop him—"

"Was this man human, you think? Or symbolic?" Michael, too, believed in Temple's visions—or at least respected that they came from a God-given source within her. "Did you see his face?"

"Nooooo," she murmured. "But I believe he was keeping Joel from trouble—perhaps trying to guide him home—"

"Like an angel?" Lily breathed. "A dark angel—"

"A guardian, yes—but we all know how Joel responds when folks steer him where he doesn't want to go."

Blinking, Temple looked at them as though she were back in charge of her thoughts again. "Joel ran from him. But I don't know where. I think he'll be a long time in coming back. He's happy with this choice, knowing we are not."

"That's Joel, all right," Billy murmured. "But it won't stop us from checkin' around when we get into—"

"What about Wesley and that full moon?" Mama sat ramrod straight now, her green eyes catlike as she studied Temple Gates from across the table. "Can you contact him? On the Other Side?"

Temple had a way of knowing more than she let on, and her innate sensibilities about his mother made Billy smile. "Mama, if you're wantin' to set up a séance, like when you were—"

"I want to know if my son is at rest. If those inner forces that controlled him will torture Wesley—and me—into eternity." Mama looked vulnerable yet surprisingly steady. "I may have staged a few special effects when I was living in Denver, working as a medium, but I truly believe in the power of the human soul to reach out—to communicate with those who have gone before, and to help them find their peace. So we may be at peace, as well."

"Amen to that," Asa murmured as he carried dishes into the kitchen.

"I understand what you're asking," Temple replied, reaching a hand toward Mama, "and we'll look into these mysteries in due time. In God's time. It's He who reveals everything, after all, when He feels we're ready to understand."

Mama gazed at the slender fingers so close her own. She didn't clasp that dark hand, but she nodded. "It would be too much right now. We—we all have our appointed tasks, don't we?"

"Are we ready?"

Mercy took Solace's hand, not because she thought her daughter would bolt, but because these disciplinary occasions were lessons in love—and because she could gauge the feelings in each of her children when she held them.

It pleased her that Solace, so much like Judd Monroe in looks and temperament, trembled a bit but didn't draw back. She took her punishment and owned up when she'd done wrong—and for this, Mercy was grateful. God—along with Michael and Judd—had given this rough-and-tumble daughter a strong sense of right and wrong, and a lot of love for others.

And then there's Joel, she mused, her heart clenching as

she wondered for the hundredth time where that boy was. And why. She was hoping Solace's answers might clear some of the painful haze that clouded her heart right now.

"You know why we're going to the river to cut a switch, don't you?" she asked calmly.

"Because I shot Wesley Bristol's horse? With Daddy's pistol?"

Mercy closed her eyes. This child had always seen several sides to each story—and Solace's behavior begged to be brought to light, so they could better understand last night's drama.

"Let's talk about shooting that horse first," she clarified. "While you think about your answer, choose your switch from this willow tree."

It seemed a shame to further burden an already difficult morning, but the shimmer of the sun on the river's surface calmed her—always set things in perspective, when it came to figuring out where each of them fit into God's creation.

"Daddy told me to."

Mercy's brow furrowed as she cut the slender branch Solace had selected. While she believed Temple Gates had the gift of second sight—and that it was God-given—her children had been known to imitate their teacher's mystical ways when it suited their purpose.

"How do you mean, your daddy told you to?" she asked carefully. "I can't believe either of your fathers would condone your—"

"My first daddy," the girl replied.

When Solace looked up into her eyes, Mercy saw Judd's love and integrity—his way of facing the most difficult situations head-on. She nipped her lip to keep tears from falling.

"Ever since you gave me his picture," Solace went on, "I look at his face sometimes, and I ask him about things—like, what would he do about Joel?"

"And what did he say about that?"

The sturdy little girl shrugged. "Didn't have an answer—but last night? When we heard all that hollerin' and stampedin'? And I looked out my window to see Mr. Harte climbin' onto the roof with his rifle?" she went on. "I asked Daddy what I should do."

Mercy let a tear dribble down her cheek unchecked. How could she deny this child such a source of wisdom: the opportunity to think about things from Judd's loving perspective?

"And he told you to grab that gun and—"

"He said Billy was in big trouble, because he always fought fair. Anybody could see that man on the big buckskin horse didn't *care* about fair!"

"So you went downstairs with that pistol, which belongs to Michael—"

"I had to get it from under Joel's bed," she elaborated, "which was when I saw he'd stuck those clothes under his covers. But Billy was in worse trouble than Joel was—so I ran outside."

Mercy considered this. "And how did you dress in your pants fast enough to get there in time?"

Solace grinned sheepishly. "Joel and I were plannin' on some target practice later."

"But he'd already left. So you were alone, facing an angry, armed man you'd never seen."

"I was a diversionary tactic," she explained matter-of-factly. "Billy and Daddy have taught us about that. I figured if I distracted that outlaw, it'd give Billy a chance to get out of his way. And since I was a girl, I didn't figure that big ole bully would shoot me—at least not 'til the element of surprise wore off."

Mercy gazed at her daughter's face, seeing nothing but the forthright telling of this tale.

"Did it bother you to pull that trigger?" she asked quietly. "Neither of your daddies believe it's right to kill."

"You must never aim a gun unless you intend to shoot it!" she insisted, pointing her finger for emphasis. "And you must only shoot to defend yourself—or somebody else who can't. *Never, never* because you're horsin' around!"

Solace said these last words with decisive nods of her head and the conviction she'd obviously learned from Michael. Or maybe Billy, which brought up another angle.

"Did Billy know you were taking a pistol out here for target practice?"

"No, ma'am! He nearly tanned my hide for it, too, once we both quit shakin' last night. Said I was too young to be messin' with a gun."

Mercy smiled at this. "But you *did*. Knowing that your daddy—both your daddies—and I would never allow you to come out here at night. That's sneaking—acting deceitful—because you knew we'd never give you our permission. Isn't it?"

"Yes, Mama," she admitted forlornly. "And we've talked about this before. About how I get caught doin' stuff, and how Lily is so much—"

"Let's don't bring your sister into this. She's another case altogether."

Solace sighed, blinking back tears. "Mama, you *know* I wouldn't shoot a horse—or any animal, or anybody—just because I felt like it. You don't believe I'm a hardened killer—like—like they say Billy's brother was. *Do* you?"

Mercy blinked. Solace wasn't asking insolent questions, but she was certainly turning things around, taking the role of interrogator. "No, you don't have that in you, dear," she admitted. "There was never any doubt about that part."

"And I don't guess I'll be slippin' out here in the night to practice, now that Joel's gone and Daddy's got the gun."

"Don't sass me, Solace. It'll only make things worse when—"

"So can we just get on with this whippin'?" Solace widened those brown eyes—the color of dark chocolate, with the sparkling intensity of Judd Monroe's when he'd challenged her, chuckling because he loved her so much.

Clearly Mercy needed to devise a different form of punishment for this girl who could turn her inside out just by looking at her. Or, at seven, did Solace already sense her power—the power she'd gotten from her father?

"Lean over. Grab that tree," Mercy murmured, but it was more from habit than because she wanted to swat her daughter. "This'll hurt me more than it will you, young lady."

"Oh, you always say that."

Before she lost her nerve, Mercy gave Solace's bare calves a halfhearted flick of the willow switch.

"That's for slipping out to practice with Michael's pistol, knowing you weren't supposed to. And for going along with Joel's idea to do it. You *know* he needs you to steer him straight."

Solace jerked a little, but remained in position. "I may be my brother's keeper, but there's just no keeping Joel."

Mercy stopped with the switch lifted, but then gave Solace another flick across her legs. "And that was for challenging my authority." *Even if you're usually right*, she added silently.

"And this," she said, grabbing her little girl from behind, "is because I love you, and because both of your daddies would hug you this way, if they ever had the strength to spank you in the first place."

"Spare the rod and spoil the child?" Solace quipped. "Just like in the Bible, where it says to honor your father and your mother."

"You are so right, Solace," Mercy replied, subtly blotting her tears against the girl's calico dress. "And you are so much my own child. And I'm thankful for that every single day."

Solace turned, reaching up to hug her neck. The strength in those sturdy, tanned arms stunned Mercy. When had her little girl grown so tall? Her dress pulled at the shoulders, too—and Solace would have no part of wearing Lily's delicate, ruffled cast offs.

"Shall we go back now?" Solace murmured. "I'll act like I've been properly whacked, and I'll do whatever you ask me to, Mama. 'Cause we're not nearly done with trouble yet, are we?"

Mercy let out a sad laugh, gazing toward the white house now shrouded by Wesley Bristol's death. "That's a pretty wise way to look at it, yes."

Chapter Twenty-four

Billy followed Michael out the kitchen door and across the back porch, already feeling the heat this day would bring. His gaze wandered to the place where Wes's horse had reared: matted grass and some dried blood brought back sensations that made him suck in his breath.

"You okay, Billy? This part's harder for you than it is for your mother."

Malloy's arm found his shoulder and Billy shook his head to clear his whirling thoughts. "The details I missed when Wes charged at me are all comin' back now—the hoofbeats, and his threats, and that big ole buckskin screamin' when it went over backward. . . ."

He blinked the mist from his eyes. "The way my brother's arm was wrapped in the reins, and his bad leg strapped to the saddle—why, he probably would've died anyway, when his horse landed on him."

"Or he'd *wish* he were dead, with injuries like that. Which would make things even harder, for all of us—not to imply that any of this is easy."

"Too bad Carlton had to be the one." Billy forced

himself to keep walking toward the stable. "Mama'll never completely forgive him, but you'd be buryin' *me* if he—and Solace—hadn't shot when they did. I was so stunned, my mind wasn't connectin' to my trigger finger. Might as well not've had the gun, the way my shot went wild."

"I'm not sure how to handle that situation," Mike admitted with a sigh. "Solace *was* protecting you—and everyone else. And she hit her mark! But I had no idea she and Joel were slipping out at night to practice with that pistol."

"Mornin' there, Malloy! Looks like you had some trouble last night!"

Clyde Fergus and his wife, Nell, were driving in, with several yearling Morgans tethered to their wagon. Another neighbor, Newt Billings, was riding behind some older horses to be sure they followed the others, which prompted Snowy and Spot to herd them into the yard, yipping happily.

"You're an answer to a prayer!" Michael called out. "Until we get the barn and the corrals fixed, we'll put them in this east stable."

Billy loped ahead to open the door, hearing some reservation in Malloy's voice. It was one thing to thank these friends for returning their horses—and he was glad to see Mr. Lincoln was among them. It was another matter entirely to explain why these buildings gave up ghostly wisps of smoke had burned to the ground.

"Sure hope we don't have a fire bug in the area," Nell remarked as she took in the damage. "Dry as it is, you're fortunate the house didn't catch, too! Is everyone all right?"

"Did I hear you say your little Solace had a *gun*?" Newt sat forward in his saddle, his hawklike features intent beneath the broad brim of his hat. He turned to watch Mercy as she walked her daughter back to the house.

Billy's heart ached for Michael. He was by the stable door, waving in horses eager to return to their feed and water. It was only a matter of time before the story got out.

"We had a surprise attack last night," Malloy replied, his eyes imploring these old friends—and this newer fellow—to understand his predicament. "Wesley Bristol from Missouri—"

"You mean the Bristol ridin' with Frank and Jesse James?" Clyde's eyes widened as he set the wagon's brake.

Michael closed his eyes for a moment. "Yes, and as he happens to be Billy's brother, I'm asking you to bear with us. He set the barn afire and got the livestock riled up enough that they broke loose, thank goodness.

"But then he charged right for Billy, aiming a sawed-off shotgun," Malloy continued in an ominous tone. "Lucky for us he gave us some warning, so we had a man on the roof in case things got out of hand. And yes, Solace astounded us all by plugging his mount when it reared up. She saved Billy's life, and probably more of us, too."

He let out another long sigh, gauging his listeners' reactions. "It was a long, hard night, my friends. Billy and I are going into town to fetch a casket, grateful it's not for *him*."

"My word, Mercy and the girls must be beside themselves!" Nell clambered down from the wagon, her blue gingham skirts swaying over her ample hips as she hurried to the house.

"Goes without saying you've got things we could do for you," Clyde remarked. "Newt and I could fix this corral fence, or—"

"If you wouldn't mind, we've got a horse to bury.

Dragged it behind the barn last night," he explained, pointing toward the building. "Spades are on the far wall of the shed. Billy and I need to see to Wesley's burial today, since his mother's here—and it's so hot."

The two men nodded, their expressions serious. "You go on to town, now, Malloy. We'll tend to things until you get back."

"Can't thank you enough, Clyde. You fellows are a godsend."

Once they had the wagon hitched up and were rolling toward the road, however, Michael shook his head somberly. "I couldn't make up a story, knowing the women'll tell their side like it happened, but sometimes the truth just doesn't look good. There was no way to spare you, son. I'm sorry about that part most of all."

"Folks had to hear about it sooner or later," Billy said with a sigh. "There's just no dressin' up what went on here—but I know what you're sayin'. Newt Billings looked like he's just itchin' to spread this around. 'Specially about Solace shootin' Wesley's horse."

"I hope her moment of bravery doesn't come back to bite her someday."

Billy's throat tightened: had Joel fired that pistol, he'd be hailed all over Abilene as a hero making good at an early age. Folks would go out of their way to congratulate him—compare him to his idol, Wild Bill Hickok. But it was unthinkable for a *girl* to fire a gun. Never mind that she was a crack shot.

The Malloys would be explaining this, and Joel's departure, for months to come. Even though time and again Michael and Mercy had proven themselves to be decent, generous people, other folks latched onto gossip and scandal like his dogs enjoyed gnawing on a fresh bone.

Along the road they stopped at each homestead, again putting the Malloy name on trial by asking if anyone had seen Joel. Their neighbors sounded concerned, of course. But Billy couldn't miss the rise of their eyebrows.

"Sorta like when your sister took out after that wild mother of hers," one old coot reminisced.

"Joel's a handful, ain't he?" another man teased. "Never could figger out why he's got such a chip on his shoulder."

Such remarks did nothing to brighten their day, and by the time they reached town, Billy was in no mood to pick out a casket. He glanced over toward the railroad station, where there seemed to be a lot of activity.

"Looks like Jones's hands are just now loadin' those horses." The sight of the old scar on his arm made him smile. "I like it that our Morgans are goin' to Army outposts. Sorta keeps my part of the bargain with Gabe, that we'd see justice done for the way Indians slaughtered his family and outlaws fractured mine."

That thought hit him hard, now that Wes was dead.

Michael's eyes softened. "I bet Gabe would like to hear about that. Doubt he sees much livestock, living at Miss Vanderbilt's and studying the law."

As Billy nodded, his smile felt a little crooked. "Lots of things I need to write to Gabe now. But that letter'll have to wait for when things slow down."

They stopped the wagon in front of Bedloe's Furniture and Undertaking. As they were climbing down, a loud, familiar voice hailed them.

"Malloy! And Billy Bristol! Have I got a story for *you!*"

They cringed, noting how folks bustling along the sidewalks turned. Of course, Obadiah Jones loved being the one who made everyone take notice, so the portly Texan was in his element as he swaggered toward the wagon. He wore a fashionable new hat, and his frock coat and trousers were set off by a red vest. His gold watch chain caught the sunlight as he sauntered up to them, a fat cigar in the crook of his fingers.

"Yessir!" he exclaimed, clapping Michael on the back, "I saw quite a sight this morning—you've saved me sending you a telegram. When my guard hollered at some kid trying to sneak into my parlor car, I never dreamed it'd be *your* boy, Malloy!"

Michael's face went pale. "Joel was here, in—?"

"Don't know how he got here—except I knew right off you weren't with him, and that he was, shall we say, looking for adventure?" The cattle baron guffawed loudly, and then sucked on his cigar. "Did the same thing at his age! Would've let him ride the rails a ways with me, too—and then put him on the train back home, of course!"

"Of course," Billy echoed, frustrated by all this bluster.

"Except, well, I had a lady friend along. Didn't think you'd want your boy seeing what she wasn't wearing!"

Malloy looked flummoxed, gazing toward the train station. "So what'd you do with—where'd he go? When we realized Joel was gone—"

"Oh, he's gone, all right." Obadiah smiled around his cigar as he studied Michael's worried face. "The kid's got speed, I'll give him that! Took out across the rail yard, passed the platform, and swung himself onto the daily express west as it was leaving. I reckon he'll be seeing the sights of San Francisco in a few days. Unless he gets off somewhere, of course."

"San Francisco? Why on earth would he—"

Obadiah shrugged. "That I can't tell you. But you know more about it than I do. Didn't have much for luggage, so I'm guessing he'll either be home soon—or he's just one of those boys who're here today and gone tomorrow, and travels light in between. Not a bad way to live sometimes, trust me."

He made a show of opening his gold pocket watch, his eyebrows flying up. "Where does the time go? Why, those horses should've been loaded by now and I've got a train to catch, gentlemen! See you next summer for more of those fine Morgans!"

They watched him swagger grandly down the street, shaking their heads. In a time when average folks were scraping by, after two grasshopper invasions and the fall of the cattle market had left them grateful for the simple things they had, Jones stood out as a monument to misbegotten wealth. Billy doubted anyone could prove the Texan cheated or dealt under the table, but he had his suspicions.

"Trust me," he mimicked under his breath. "Why would I do that, after he let Joel get away on the west-bound—"

"Joel was on his way out, no matter which direction he ended up going." Malloy looked sadder than Billy had ever seen him: his shoulders drooped and when he rubbed his mustache, it was a gesture of weariness and worry.

"Mercy won't accept this. She'll think it's her fault we couldn't win that boy over," he went on. "But I was restless—and reckless—at his age, too. I'll go send some telegrams along the rail lines, hoping my old stagecoaching friends are still working for the Union Pacific."

Mike sighed, still gazing toward the trains. "I guess we just give him over to God now, and trust that he'll know what to do with Joel."

Billy nodded. "Same as we did with Wesley after he got snatched, but let's not think about how my brother turned out," he added with a glum smile. "Let's get him buried, so's we can pick up the pieces and move forward. One of these days."

"All in good time, son. That's how we have to handle our lives, whether we want to or not." Malloy gripped his shoulder a little tighter than usual. "We'll see that Wes gets a funeral to make you and your ma feel better about the whole—"

"Will *you* do the service, Michael?" The request stung his throat, but it seemed like the right thing to say. "Mama might not care who—and you didn't even know Wesley—but it would mean a lot to me."

Those tawny eyes glowed at him, even though Malloy had his own burdens to bear. "I'd be proud to say a few words, Billy. It'll be my gift to your family—for letting me love you like a son all these years."

Chapter Twenty-five

"What are you going to sketch, Eve?"

"Can we watch?"

"Let me sit real close, so I can see!" Grace settled against Eve's side, near enough that she'd have a hard time drawing, while the young woman patiently opened her sketchbook. Lily and Solace squeezed into the same seat of the train, all of them smiling—eager to be entertained on this somber trip from Abilene to Richmond.

Billy watched them from across the aisle. Carlton and Mama sat facing the girls, cuddling a sleepy Olivia, while Mercy and Michael occupied the bench seat across from him. Asa looked out the window and Temple sat beside him, watching the girls, as well.

"It makes quite a picture, doesn't it?" the teacher murmured. "With the sun shining on all those different shades of hair, and those pretty dresses, and the light in their eyes, those girls radiate a beauty—a joy—no artist could capture on canvas."

"You've got that right," Billy replied, wishing he'd made the original comment.

But then, he was wishing he'd said a lot of things.

He just didn't know *what*. Didn't know why his mind seemed to be unraveling, just as he hadn't realized how much he'd taken Eve's presence for granted. Didn't she need him, now that Wesley was gone? Did she intend to raise Olivia alone, with just her mother's help?

Would she scoff—or laugh—if he asked her and that red-headed baby to be a permanent part of his life?

Billy set aside such thoughts, hoping an appropriate time would come to talk with her. For now, he watched the sunlight dance in Lily's blond ringlets, and Solace's thick, dark waves, and little Grace's wispy curls, which glistened like sunswept sand.

Soon these three angels would be all grown up—just as he and Eve had come into adulthood—and he wished he could protect them from the troubles that came with maturity. No doubt they'd have young men swarming around them, and only the most suitable would do! If anyone so much as tried to disgrace them, the way Wesley had taken advantage of Eve Massena, he'd personally—

Billy caught himself clenching his fists in his lap.

"You all right, Mister Billy?" Temple whispered. "I guess that's a ridiculous question, considering why we're on this train."

He smiled sadly at her. "Just thinkin' how different things would be if those Border Ruffians hadn't snatched Wes when we were ten. Hopin' our girls never know the heartache of havin' their lives turned upside-down that way."

"For now, let's enjoy these pleasant moments," Asa said with a wise smile. "We's got plenty of sadness to get through 'fore this day's over."

Nodding, Billy turned his attention to the girls again.

"Would you like to see what Billy's house looked like when he was your age?" Eve asked. Her pencil moved with rapid confidence, centering the vertical lines that set the house apart from the surrounding gardens.

"Did you go there a lot?" Solace piped up.

"Were you and Christine best friends?" Lily leaned closer, following Eve's swift motions—lines that defined the porch columns and the front door. "When I was little, Christine and I were like magnets! I wish she lived closer now, so we could talk—and I could see Rachel and Rebecca more often."

"Christine and I went to dancing classes together," Eve replied. Her eyes were on her paper, but her lips curved in a secretive smile. "Billy was little for his age—shorter than the girls. But he had to come to our lessons, too, because we didn't have enough boys."

"And he was not happy about it!" Mama chirped.

Then, realizing she sounded too cheerful for her state of mourning, she sighed. Two tears slid down her cheeks. "Even then, Wesley refused to behave himself. Had to stir up trouble with his brother and make Christine miserable. I—I always suspected he'd come to a bad end—if he wasn't the death of me first."

Billy felt the mood grow heavier around them, but when he tried to think of something to say, the rhythmic *clackety-clack* of the train drowned out his rational thought. Why was he so dumbstruck? Was this part of his grieving, or had he always lacked for the right words at the right time?

Mama smoothed the skirt of her purple traveling suit, clucking—just getting warmed up. "I was wearing this dress the last time I saw him," she said in a quavery voice. "But Carlton, I'll need to have my dresses and underthings dyed black now and—"

"Oh, it would be such a shame to change that suit!" Eve looked up from her sketching, her eyes filled with pain. "When I first saw it, I thought how splendid you looked, and how stylish, with that matching feathered hat! A sure sign you'd recovered from losing your home and—well, I was hoping to paint your portrait in it someday."

"Decorum demands black," Mama stated, shaking her head sadly. "This is the worst week of my life! So much more horrible than losing Owen when—"

"But think of how far you've come," Carlton reminded her gently. "You've put scandal behind you—started fresh, like Eve and Temple talked about yesterday. It would be such a shame to—"

"Veils. Black veils and gloves and—" She dabbed her eyes, sniffling loudly. "Why, I don't have one proper thing to wear to my son's funeral! We'll have to shop in Richmond before—"

"Yes, my dear, I hope you will. But consider this." Harte had turned in the seat and was holding both her shoulders as she cradled Olivia. His voice remained soft but he brooked no argument. "Since when have you been a slave to decorum, Virgilia? It was your brazen, outspoken originality that first attracted me to you, not to mention the way you dressed in bright, becoming colors.

"Appearance has always been so important to you," he went on "that you insisted I grow a mustache and dye my hair dark—and go by my alias—because you wanted me to be a dashing detective rather than a stodgy small-town sheriff. Isn't that right, my love?"

"Saw that myself," Billy remarked. "And Christine had some interesting things to say about how Carlton made himself over, just to suit you, Mama."

He enjoyed these conversations between his mother and her new husband, especially when he saw the circuitous path Carlton was taking to make his point.

"Do as you wish, Virgilia. I'll always love you. But I'm asking you to think carefully before you spoil the lovely wardrobe you've acquired."

Harte was smiling kindly, well aware of how his wife's heart was breaking, but determined to convince her.

"Black may be the *proper* thing to wear, but it will wither the roses in your cheeks and drain the delight from those lovely green eyes," he murmured as he looked into them. "Buy yourself a black dress and veil for the funeral, of course. But as an everyday thing— well, you'll look old before your time, Virgilia. And just as you don't want to associate with the stuffy little lawman I once was, I'd rather not be married to an *old* woman."

Billy stifled a snicker, and saw Eve nipping her lip, too. Mama's transformation was nothing short of miraculous: She looked ready to smack Carlton's face, but she glowed in the light of his affection. It was only a temporary repair—she'd feel the weight of her loss for a long, long time just as he would—but Billy sensed this man had diverted her from playing the martyr.

Mama was lucky to have gained another good husband before she'd lost a beloved son.

There's a lesson there. It was a voice inside his head, very similar to Michael's or maybe Judd Monroe's. And when Billy glanced at Eve—saw the heart-rending detail in her drawing of his boyhood home—he thought maybe God was trying to tell him something.

Will you listen, my son? Or will you fly blind like your brother did?

It was late afternoon when Michael and Asa pulled him from the grave he'd finished digging. Billy felt satisfaction in the throbbing of his arms and the blisters he'd worked on his palms. Hard work cured a lot of ills, and kept him from thinking maudlin thoughts—gave him something to accomplish before they gathered around Wesley's final resting place.

"Better drink up, son," Malloy said, handing him a

dipper of water from a bucket. "Soon as your mama and Carlton come back, we'll have our service. Can't think of a nicer place for it, either, here among these trees and honeysuckle bushes."

"Real peaceful," Asa agreed. He shaded his eyes to look out across the pastureland. "I can just picture them fine thoroughbreds your daddy used to raise, and feel his pride in the home and family he had here."

"The house has really deteriorated," Billy murmured, wincing when a loose shutter banged. "If Mama takes a notion to go inside, it's gonna be a long time before she gets over her shock."

"A home falls into disrepair when the love leaves it— just like a life does." Malloy walked around the over-grown hedgerow for a better look. "With some time and attention—lots of paint and pruning—this place could do somebody proud again. Have you considered coming back, now that Wes is gone?"

Billy's jaw dropped. How should he answer?

"There was a time I wanted nothin' more than—" he began, but once again his tongue didn't feel fully connected to his brain. "I've been real happy trainin' your Morgans! Beholden to you and Mercy for—"

Malloy shushed him with a firm finger. Those golden eyes softened with a love that made his heart hammer in his chest. "I couldn't have found a better ranch manager if I'd created you myself, Billy Bristol. But comes a time you want your own place—your own life—that's what I want for you, too."

Billy opened his mouth to protest, but the rise of Michael's eyebrows beat him to the punch.

"No arguments, young man! We've got serious business to attend, and I wanted to speak my mind, man-to-man. Keeps things simpler."

Billy nodded, wiping his sweaty face with his hand-kerchief. Girlish voices drifted through the honey-suckle hedge, so he parted the leafy limbs to enter the garden where Mama had planted her favorite flowers. They grew in wild abandon now, brown-eyed Susans and day lilies poking through the Queen Ann's lace and dandelions. But even the weeds made a pretty setting for the three girls as they sat around Eve again, entranced.

"Back when we were kids," she was saying, "the front porch of this place was surrounded by bright red poppies that waved like wildfire, and caladiums with pink streaks in the center—"

"Elephant ears," Solace clarified for little Grace.

"—and those maple trees lining the front drive dropped little seed spinners in the spring. We'd toss them up like whirligigs," she said wistfully, her brush moving as she spoke, "and in the fall, their red and orange leaves would catch the sun, well—almost like the fire in Billy's hair!"

He swallowed hard. Had she really noticed all those things about his home—about *him*—when they were kids? Her reminiscing made him ache for those days long ago, but that was foolish. Time marched on, and so had they. And they would continue until they were in a casket like Wes—

And what will you have to show for it? How will you spend the rest of your life?

Once again he swore Judd or Michael was talking to him, guiding him away from morbid thoughts. He kept walking until he was behind Eve, looking down on her picture.

His heart stopped. He didn't know much about art, except that she was painting with watercolors, and their muted, translucent hues gave his home a dreamlike quality that surpassed even his fondest memories of it.

"You . . . you recalled every little detail," he breathed, drinking in the subtle wash of color in the lilacs and the sweep of green lawn and those poppies that blazed in the afternoon shade. "Why, I could walk up those steps, between those white pillars, and swear the rooms inside would be just like they were back then, too. Just . . . perfect."

Eve smiled up at him, her eyes mirroring his nostalgic thoughts. "This was the prettiest place in town," she replied softly. "So cool and inviting, with all these trees, even on the hottest summer days. I must've painted it a dozen times since you went away, Billy. Even now, I see it like it was then."

Are you listening?

He blinked back tears, wishing some sort of miraculous magic could restore the house—and the simplicity of their childhood days.

But that was a silly thing to wish for. The truth stared him in the face as he looked across the sparse lawn and up the sunken, peeling front steps—and heard the incessant banging of that loose shutter.

"There's not a breath of air movin'," he rasped, "so why is that dang shutter makin' such a racket?"

The girls followed his gaze, and Lily giggled. "Could be an angel up there is trying to get your attention, Billy!" she replied. "An angel who won't let you rest until you do what you were born for."

He blinked. Once again the princess in pink spoke of higher realms as though she dwelled in them on an everyday basis, as though she knew his purpose on this earth—on this estate—better than he did.

"Or maybe it's Wesley's ghost, tryin' to scare you away!" Solace widened her big brown eyes at him as part of a very scary expression, until Temple Gates frowned at her.

"We should respect the dead, Miss Solace," she reminded the girl, "just as we should respect Mister Billy's feelings about his brother. Think how horribly upset you'd be if it were *your* sister or brother who—"

"It's all right, Temple." Billy smiled down at those

bright faces, at that painting, as Eve brushed in the pink of a sunrise across a cloud-dappled sky. "If Solace didn't tease me, I'd think she didn't like me anymore."

"Can we come and see you after you move back here, Billy?"

"Good idea! Can we stay the summer and help you fix the place up?"

Lily and Solace, bless their hearts, were looking at him with questions he hadn't considered since he'd learned Wes owned the place. But why did everyone assume he'd *want* to leave Abilene for this run-down house and acres of dried-up pastureland surrounded by broken fences? What was there in Richmond for him, except heartache and hard work?

You'll have those at the Triple M, too, you know.

He was working himself into a real quandary, over a situation that might not even be possible—and then Eve signed the painting with her fountain pen and handed it to him.

"It's not dry yet. Be careful how you hold it," she warned him. Her smile beamed up at him, open and warm. "I wanted you to have this, since you never got the one I mailed you last spring. And who knows how long it might be until . . . until I see you again?"

Her lips parted and that little furrow between her eyebrows made funny things wiggle in his stomach. Billy held the picture gingerly, around its edges, again at a loss for words.

"Thank you, Eve," he whispered. "I—I can't tell you how much I'll enjoy lookin' at this. And I truly hope things'll go well for you at your mother's."

As she hesitated over her reply, the clatter of wagon wheels and horses' hooves came down the long lane.

Billy glanced around, hoping everything looked all right—hoping Mama had found a dress that suited her—dreading the farewell that would take place in a matter of minutes. That was his twin in the casket beside the grave he'd dug, and no matter how surly Wes had become, Billy felt a deep sadness about losing him before they could have a proper reunion.

And maybe that never would have happened. He had to start facing a lot of facts head-on, didn't he?

"Better wash up and change my clothes," he murmured as the wagon pulled to a stop in in front of them. Mama was draped in black from her veiled hat to her gloves, to the dress that flared to reveal black petticoats as Carlton helped her to the ground. He was wearing a new black frock coat and trousers, no doubt to keep peace with Mama. Mercy, too, had found a simple, dark dress. Her expression told him the mood in the carriage had been bleak indeed.

But it was time for that. Billy fetched his better clothes, and then took Eve's painting through the back kitchen door with him. He brushed the debris from the table where Beulah Mae had made her pies, and laid his treasure there. Because he *did* treasure this picture.

And as he put on his dark pants and a clean white shirt, Billy let his mind wander . . . gazing at those red-orange poppies and shining white pillars . . . wondering about the way things were happening today. If he was hearing voices, and being summoned by angels— or Wesley's ghost—and getting questions he didn't have answers for, there surely had to be a reason.

"As we gather here to remember Wesley Bristol, we should remember that he was—and is—a child of God."

Michael Malloy's voice rang clear and calm in the shaded cemetery out behind the gardens. They stood inside the spiked iron fence that marked his daddy's resting place—a simple stone overlooking the pasture-land Owen Bristol had loved so much.

Billy stood with his hands clasped, staring at the gaping grave and the casket on the ground beside it. Beside him, Mama was crying into her handkerchief as

Carlton held her. The others were arranged around the grave with somber faces, the little girls in front of their mother, while Mercy—Mercy seemed to mourn the disappearance of Mama's son as if he were her own.

"It's perhaps the greatest comfort of our faith that God loves us even when we ignore him," Malloy went on. He spoke with his head slightly bowed, holding the Bible he'd brought from the sideboard at home. "It was for sinners like us he sent Jesus, who taught us that judgment is the Lord's task and not ours. While we feel sadness and disappointment over Wesley's life and the choices he made, and while we've wished things could've happened differently, we must remember that all things are in God's hands."

He looked up then, smiling sadly at Billy and his mother. "And even when we defy Him and behave in ways that God could never condone, He uses our lives to work out His purpose. It's a miraculous thing, to think the Lord can love us in our brokenness, and create order and wholeness from the messes we've made while we lived on His earth."

"Amen to that," Temple murmured.

"It pleases me that Lily helped me choose today's Scripture, and asked if she could read it." Michael opened the ponderous volume to a page marked with faded red ribbons. As Lily stepped to the head of the grave beside him, he held the Bible for her.

"I'm reading from the third chapter of Ecclesiastes," she announced, looking at each of them with solemn confidence. "Daddy and I thought it was a fitting passage, considering all the things that have happened this past week with Billy's brother, and before that, when Eve came to us. It makes me feel better about Joel's running away, too."

Billy's heart throbbed with pride. Not quite nine, Lily was a wonder—and as they often had, he speculated about whether she was older than her father's note had told them. She stood beside Michael in a spot where the sun shone through a gap in the trees, so much a part of that heavenly light that she resembled an angel herself.

" 'To everything there is a season, and a time to every purpose under heaven,' " she read. " 'A time to be born and a time to die; a time to plant and a time to pluck up that which is planted. A time to kill, and a time to heal; a time to break down and a time to build up.' "

Beside him, Mama shifted, but she was listening, as spellbound as everyone else in this circle their two families had become. Billy hoped she was finding comfort in these ancient words. With her, it was hard to tell.

" 'A time to weep and a time to laugh; a time to mourn and a time to dance,' " Lily read on. Her finger traced the words as she read. As he held the heavy Bible for her, Michael was crying.

" 'A time to cast away stones and a time to gather stones together; a time to embrace, and a time to refrain from embracing—' "

Billy's mind drifted with the rhythm of these familiar phrases—mostly so the finality of this funeral didn't make him burst into tears—tears Wesley had always made fun of when they were kids.

" '—a time to keep silence and a time to speak; a time to love and a time to hate—' "

He glanced up to find Eve gazing straight at him, as though trying to read his mind and figure out what came next. As though he knew! Her green eyes and pretty face stood out in sharp relief against her black bonnet, and it occurred to him that he could be gazing at that face for years to come, if he'd only *say* something—

But it was too soon. He'd felt that way about Emma once, too. Although he'd been wrong to go along with her proposal just because she was lost and lonely. As this passage said, there was a time for love and hate—a time to keep and a time to throw away—

" '—a time of war, and a time of peace.' "

Lily stepped aside so Michael could straighten to his full height. With the Bible in one arm and his other around Lily, the man with the sandy hair and heart of gold looked around the faces in their circle.

"We would do well to remember that life and death remain a mystery to us mortals—that we're not meant to understand why Wesley lived the way he did, or died like he did," he remarked quietly. "But I hope that as time heals us, we'll recall the better qualities this young man possessed. And we'll remember him as he was before the Border Ruffians turned him to their own way."

He opened the Bible again, to the New Testament this time, and then looked at the dark casket and the grave it would fill. "As we commit Wesley's body to the ground and his spirit back to God, I'll close with verses from Romans that have always reminded me that in life and in death, we belong to God."

He glanced down at the page, breathing deeply. " 'Who shall separate us from the love of Christ?" he asked—as though he expected each of them to have an answer. " 'Shall tribulation or distress? Or persecution or famine, or nakedness or peril—or sword?' "

Michael looked up, to close with words he'd committed to memory long ago. " 'For I am persuaded that neither death nor life . . . nor angels nor principalities nor powers . . . nor things present nor things to come . . . nor height nor depth nor any other creature, shall be able to separate us from the love of God, which is in Christ Jesus our Lord.'

"And Lord, we ask You to enfold us in Your love and hold us in Your hand as we mourn the passing of Your child Wesley," he prayed. "Give us light that we may see the way You would have us live now, so that his life was not in vain."

"Amen," Asa murmured in a shuddery voice.

"Amen," filled the little grove in a variety of subdued voices.

Numbly, Billy joined Michael and Carlton and Asa as they raised Wesley's casket by wide bands of leather the undertaker had provided, steadying the box over the grave and then lowering it. Mama and Eve and Mercy were crying openly now. Just as well, since he didn't want to hear that awful thump when Wesley hit bottom.

"You and Carlton should be with your mother now," Malloy whispered to him. "Asa and I will finish up here."

Billy nodded blindly, aware that each of the ladies was dropping a rose from the spindly bushes out front onto the casket before leaving the fenced enclosure. Mama lingered, quivering as she gazed into the grave. When Temple guided the girls out ahead of him, Billy threw himself into Michael's embrace. "Thank you, for—"

"It was the least I could do, son. I'm so sorry." Malloy's arms tightened, expressing a deep devotion that had grown like a wild prairie rose bush over the years: not always picture-perfect, but strong and beautiful all the same.

Had Wesley seen him hugging another man this way—

Despite the crude names that came to mind, spoken in his brother's coarse adult voice, Billy buried his head against his guardian angel's strong, warm shoulder. He sobbed like a kid who'd lost his—well, his twin brother; the boy he'd been so much like, yet so very different from since before he could first remember. He didn't understand the man Wesley had become, but he would always wish things had turned out differently.

As he stumbled past his daddy's tombstone and between the iron gate posts, Billy realized that from here on out, the way things turned out was largely up to him.

Chapter Twenty-six

The next day, Mama and Carlton arrived at Lexington's Union Pacific train station shortly after Billy and the Malloys did. Before his mother could see it, he took down a wanted poster of his brother, plastered alongside reward notices for the Younger brothers and Frank and Jesse James. He folded it and stuffed it into his back pocket before going over to greet them.

The detective looked drawn and tired. Billy had heard his low voice soothing Mama often during the night, through the wall between their hotel rooms. But Harte's eyes expressed an anticipation he wouldn't put into words.

"Your mother and I are staying in Richmond for a few days, to look into a couple of business opportunities. We're thinking of buying one of the hotels in town," he announced. "For her, it's a chance to live closer to Olivia, of course."

Billy had a hunch Carlton was also setting up a cover for his Pinkerton activities. "She'll like that," he agreed. "It'll help the days pass faster."

"She's never been terribly happy in Kansas," Harte

admitted. "But here, she can tend Wesley's grave when she wants to. That's important to her."

Billy nodded, noting how subdued Mama looked this morning. Recalling her weeping, wailing hysteria for months after Daddy died, he was relieved that she'd taken more control of herself since she'd married Carlton. Maybe those years of carrying out the illegal schemes of a con artist had taught Mama to appreciate a simpler life with a man who lived to please her.

Whatever allowed her to stand at the platform blotting tears instead of wailing in self-pity, Billy was glad for it. He took her in his arms, amazed at how small and delicate she felt. Mama laid her head on his shoulder and sighed like a lost little girl.

"I suppose, in time, we'll move beyond this horrible loss," she whimpered.

"You're stronger now, Mama," he replied quietly. "You have Carlton, and Olivia. And you'll always have me, too."

She sniffled. "I suppose you'll go on back to the Malloy ranch now? It—it's a wonderful thing, the way they've promoted you to—"

Over Mama's shoulder, he caught Carlton Harte's sly expression, as though the detective knew yet another secret he wasn't ready to reveal. "Who knows, sweetheart?" he said, rubbing his wife's shoulders. "Now that no one lives in your old home, maybe Billy'll move back there. It's still an ideal property for raising horses. And a family."

There it was again: the blatant hint that he should restore the house and business his daddy had built—and with a wife, too! Just as well Eve wasn't here to listen to this, or *she'd* start working on him.

Would that be so horrible? came that wise, patient voice in his head. *She's a wonderful mother now . . . you adore your niece. Malloy has given you his blessing. What more do you want?*

"I've got a lot to think about," Billy murmured.

As he eased away from his mother, he saw the Pinkterton operative's expression tighten, noted Harte's eyes narrowing as he watched a pair of men walking toward the same train they were about to board. Both fellows had an air of bravado about them. Although one was dark and stocky while his younger companion was slender and fair, it was easy to see they'd worked together for a long time.

"All aboard!" the station master cried, and the train at the platform let out a large, hissing cloud of steam. Mercy and Temple ushered the three girls ahead of them, while Michael extended his hand.

"Best of luck to you, Carlton," he said. "We hope to hear good things about whichever business you buy. And we wish you every blessing as you settle into Richmond."

"We can't thank you enough, Malloy—"

"Yes. Yes, it was a lovely service you and Lily gave," Mama replied with a tearful smile. "You and Mercy have been so kind to our family. Thank you—thank you so much for all you've provided Billy and Christine."

Malloy's smile crinkled around his eyes. Crows feet cut deeper into his face these days, yet they reflected a depth of character Billy believed in. With a final wave, he followed Michael toward the platform where the girls were now boarding—until Harte grabbed his arm.

"Be aware that Frank and Jesse James got on ahead of you," the detective murmured. "It's a good sign that they boarded like normal passengers, rather than holding up the train somewhere along the tracks."

He saw an eagerness in the detective's eyes, as though he'd love to go aboard and single-handedly capture those notorious outlaws. When Billy stepped into the passenger car, he realized he was going to walk right past the James brothers on the way to his seat. He looked them over from beneath the brim of his hat as he waited in the crowded aisle.

The younger one, Jesse, focused intense blue eyes on him. Stared for quite a lot longer than was polite.

He thinks you're Wesley—yet sees some differences. He'll keep an eye on you, because knowing who's around him has kept him alive this long.

Billy nodded to the pair as he followed the line of passengers past them, and they returned his silent greeting.

What was it that had made these ordinary-looking men go bad? Why did they feel their mission was to shoot and steal from innocent people, and then brag about it in the Kansas City paper? They—and the Youngers—had the governor and the Pinkertons so riled up, trying to bring them to justice, that their mother Zerelda had lost her youngest son and part of an arm during an attack on their home. A bungled raid that put a large scar on the Pinkertons' already ailing reputation.

Billy thanked God that he'd never had such notions, or the yen to rob the rich and repay the poor—when "the poor" mostly included the thugs in their notorious gang. He'd had enough troubles without stirring up more!

The train trip back to Abilene gave him time to ponder them. It was a quiet ride in the wake of Wesley's funeral; much less enjoyable because Eve wasn't entertaining the girls. It was pure joy to watch her create pictures with such quick, confident strokes of her pencil and paint brush. All the while, she'd been explaining a principle of depth perception or how to mix colors to an exact shade—skills he'd never had the knack for—to the three girls who watched and listened so eagerly.

He would forever treasure the painting Eve had given him. Because he missed the sound of her voice above the *clackety-clackety-clack* of the train, Billy pulled the small picture from his valise to study it.

Once again he felt the breeze those bright red poppies were waving in, and the coolness of the shade that invited him up to the gallery porch. He heard the contented creak of the swing and the warbling of mockingbirds; caught a whiff of lilacs and Mama's roses. It was almost as though he'd never been away. His eyes went wet.

"Miss Eve, she surely can bring a place to life, cain't she?"

Asa, sitting beside him, had phrased that very cleverly. Did all these folks know something they weren't telling him?

"She sees things the way she wants them to be," Billy replied. "The way they ought to be, in this case."

"Cryin' shame, the way your brother let that house go to ruin," Asa continued. "Didn't know the man, but I's awful glad it were *you* who showed up at Judd and Mercy's on that stagecoach, rather than Wesley. Lord only knows what mighta happened with him around!"

There it was again: that wistful "what if" that had pestered him ever since he'd seen his brother again. What if *he'd* been the boy the Border Ruffians had snatched?

"I'd've curled in on myself and died, if those horse thieves had taken me," he murmured. "Too much a scaredy-cat to—"

"Oh, Billy, you do go on so!" Solace teased matter-of-factly. She sat across the aisle, leaning forward to look around Grace. "You're not scared of a dang thing that I know of! Why, you taught me the meanin' of 'double-dog dare' and you made good on it every time! You didn't flinch an inch when Wesley Bristol rode right at you, neither! And we all know how he shot first and asked questions later."

His heart hitched. He gazed into that open face, so much tanner than the two around her, and was amazed at her view of him. Solace had been his girl since she was big enough to sit a horse in front of him—no, really

since the day he'd helped birth her—but he'd never realized how much she idolized him. Looked up to him
for every little thing.

And if this whippersnapper of a tomboy—a crack
shot and budding stunt rider at seven—considered him
big and brave, well—why should he doubt it? Why was
he so uneasy about the idea of moving back into his
boyhood home—perhaps with Eve and Olivia—and
other little redheaded children of his own someday?

Again his heart lurched. Or was that the train, slowing for a stop?

"I cain't see Miss Solace sayin' such things 'bout nobody else, Mister Billy," Asa murmured beside him.
"So you'd best b'lieve her. And live up to her opinion."

Ah, there was the rub! It seemed to Billy that lately,
Emma and Eve had certain visions—expectations of
him—and he'd fallen short. So why should he entertain
this notion of going back—

"But you *know*," Solace continued, planting her head
on her hand, "that if you move away from the Triple M,
you'll have to take *me*! And Snowy and Spot! 'Cause
we've never had to get along without you, Billy. And I
don't wanna start now."

Those dark eyes pierced his heart. Solace, with her
innocent bravado, had brought up an important point:
If he did return to Missouri, he'd have to say good-bye
to all he'd known and loved while growing up with
this patchwork family. He'd leave behind Asa's pies,
and Sunday dinners nobody else could cook the way
Mercy did—those Morgans he'd foaled and trained
from the day their feet first hit the ground—evening
devotions that had been the bedrock of his faith—not
to mention the man who'd invited him into this family
and then made him the mainstay of his ranch.

And it was Michael who addressed Solace now, with a
smile that twitched his mustache. "You know what, Solace? Someday you'll grow up and go away to school—"

Her nose crinkled in distaste.

"—or you'll get married and move into your own home—"

She rolled her eyes this time.

"—but even though we'll all miss you, that's part of growing up—finding your own way, and the place God intends for you to fill," he said emphatically. "Billy's hearing a lot of opinions right now about what he should do. And when he makes his decision—go or stay— we'll honor it. Billy's special, and he has a lot to accomplish for God in his lifetime—and for himself, as well."

"And even though we love him," Mercy added, her face showing a kaleidoscope of emotions, "we might have to let him go. It's a lesson we all learn several times in our lives."

His throat went dry at the looks on their faces. Every one of these folks held a special place in his heart, and there wasn't a one of them he wouldn't take along, if he left.

When they finally drove through the arched entry gate at the Triple M, and the two border collies raced out to greet their carriage, Billy saw another complication: sure, the dogs were his, but how could he take them away from Solace? Did he dare take one and not the other, thinking these constant companions of ten years would thrive apart? Spot's dark face now sported a muzzle gone gray, and Snowy showed signs of rheumatism in her haunches.

They followed him to sit on the river bank after the horse chores were done for the day. And with a panting dog leaning into him on either side, with the quiet burbling of the Smoky Hill River and the wind whispering in the cottonwood leaves, Billy tried to sort things out. He felt a distinct yearning—a clock ticking inside him, reminding him that time marched on in every life. When it came to raising horses, he made decisions without batting an eye. But *this*—this was a matter more far-reaching than training a dependable mount.

This was his life! His future was at hand, and the crossroads he found himself at felt crucial. It was the most important choice he'd had to consider since, well—since he felt the love in Judd and Mercy Monroe's smiles when they invited him into their home. They'd all known Christine would make her life elsewhere, but Billy had put down serious roots here.

"But you know, pups," he murmured, watching the first fiery rays of the sunset dance on the water, "Gabe's already moved to St. Louis to start his law job—and Christine's raisin' babies and designin' dresses in San Francisco—and Eve's decided to live with her mother, now that Wesley's gone.

"Not sure what Emma's gonna do, but she doesn't figure in anymore, does she?" he reasoned aloud. "I—I guess I've already made my choice there—even before she told me flat-out to leave. And like Lily read to us from the Scripture at Wes's service, there's a time for everything, every purpose under God's heaven. And maybe He's givin' me the boot."

Spot grunted, nudging his soft head beneath Billy's hand for a scratching. Snowy looked steadily at him, her pink tongue lolling out in the evening heat. Her eyes were clouding with age, yet she looked ever alert. He swore these dogs understood every word he said—and they'd certainly understood *him* all their lives.

He sat quietly then, listening to the summer insect songs, watching the blazing ball of sun disappear in the west, listening for whatever wisdom the wind whispered.

"We'd better go in and write a letter to Christine," he

murmured, shifting slowly so the dogs could get up first. "Maybe one to Gabe, too, since he'll want to know what's goin' on here. Pretty amazin', when you think how much has happened since he left."

Chapter Twenty-seven

Dear Christine,

There's no pretty way to say this, and maybe you've already heard from Mama. And you know me—I don't cotton to a lot of chitchat.

Wesley's dead, Sis.

Just got back from burying him beside Daddy, and my heart's heavy on a lot of counts. You see, the past few weeks have been pretty much one lightning strike after another—and it all started when Eve Massena had her baby in the back of the church while Emma and I were supposed to be getting married!

You know me and babies. This one looks exactly like Wesley and I did, Mama says, because, well—it's Wes's child. He went back on his promise to marry Eve, so she got kicked out of her home in disgrace. Her daddy hanged himself a while back, too, after some crooked dealings with Wes circled back to bite him. Eve came looking for me, thinking I'd help her out.

Well, something told me Eve got there when she did because I wasn't supposed to marry Emma in the first place. Of course, I caused a major upset by announcing this. Emma's had some pretty vile things to say to me ever since—except I found out she tore up a letter Eve had sent me last spring. And she tore up a picture of our home place in Richmond, which Eve had painted for me, too. I didn't think Emma could be that mean. She hasn't been the same since her mother died.

Anyway, I just had to see Wesley again, after all those years of not knowing if he was still alive—and of course, Mama had the same idea. Sad to say, he was holed up at our house and escorted Eve and me out of the yard by shooting at us. He at least came out and spoke to Mama when she brought him a pie Beulah Mae baked (in her own shop, I hear!) but then he threatened to come after Eve and me if Mama didn't leave him alone.

He made good on that threat anyway. Set fire to the unfinished house Emma and I were to live in, and then hit the Triple M, too. Scared the horses out of the stables and charged at me with his shotgun. In the blink of an eye, Solace had shot his horse, and Carlton, from the roof, shot Wes to keep me alive. It was a night I'll never forget.

We got Wes a nice casket and took him home to bury him. Carlton's looking for a business to buy in Richmond, so Mama can be close to her new granddaughter, Olivia, and Eve has made up with her mother.

I've all but decided to move back home, Sis. The house is in terrible shape, the pasture's a weed patch— it would mean nothing but hard work for a long time, to build the place up again. And, as you know, I owe Michael and Mercy for SO much. I'm their main man on the ranch. And the girls are squawking about how they don't want me to leave. And I don't know what to do about the dogs.

Sorry. Told you my news wasn't very pretty. But Mama's holding up pretty well, all things considered. I

*just thought you should know about Wesley. I hope life
out your way is much happier, and I bet Rachel and
Rebecca are more than a handful by now! Tell them
Uncle Billy says hey.*

Billy rubbed his eyes. His shoulders sagged from too
many long, painful days and restless nights, so he left
the letter on the floor beside his bed. With Joel gone,
the room they shared felt empty. Airless. Very sad, and
full of more questions than answers about the boy's
travels—and his own future path. Mike hadn't gotten
any telegrams back from the ones he'd sent along the
rail line, and didn't really expect to.

Billy put out the lamp and lay back on his narrow
bed. He realized that if he went back to Richmond, that
house—his old room—would feel just as forlorn as
when Wesley had first been snatched.

It would require a lot of money and attention to set
the place to rights. It would be a long, lonely job without the company of these people he'd spent the past ten
years with. And even though he'd socked away most of
his pay, Billy wasn't sure he'd have enough money to
start up his own horse business while making the
house livable again.

So many decisions . . . so many sides to this story . . .
so many opinions from everyone who loved him. He
drifted off, finally, but only after he'd made a mental
list of reasons to go, and reasons to stay—

Spot and Snowy were barking something fierce, and
when Billy rolled out of bed, he realized morning was
well under way. Squinting out the window, he saw *four*
border collies all circling to greet each other—and
then he saw why Gabe and Emma's dogs had joined
his own.

Billy swallowed hard. Emma was driving a wagon

piled high with furniture from their little log house, and her father slumped in the seat of the loaded buckboard he was driving behind her. Their faces were set in grim, determined expressions as they lumbered past the entry arch to the Triple M, into the glare of the sun.

They didn't even look toward the house.

Billy stepped into his pants and grabbed his shirt on the way to the stairs. By the time he'd sprinted through the house and across the front porch, Mercy and the girls were following him to see what the ruckus was about.

"Emma!" he called out. "Emma! George! Wait for me, will ya?"

The blonde he'd almost married barely glanced his way: only the presence of all the dogs in the road forced her to slow down. Billy ran alongside her wagon until he caught up, his heart pounding from more than his foot race in the heat.

"Where ya headed?" he panted. "Looks like—"

"That's none of your concern now, is it?" she replied. Her expression looked icy, but he saw the clench in her jaw, like she was trying not to cry. "After the way you made a fool of me in front of all our friends—and the way your brother burned down the house—what's left for me here? Daddy don't have the heart to farm this hard old ground anymore, after two seasons of losing our crop to the grasshoppers. So we're leavin'."

"And where will you go?" Mercy was still catching up, her apron flapping around her body. Solace and Grace trotted alongside her. "I—if you'd only asked, we could've helped you."

"What's done is done. It's been a downhill slide since my mother died, and . . . and we just haven't found a way to keep it goin'." She blinked rapidly, and tears left wet trails down her cheeks. "Daddy's got a sister livin' in Illinois. Reckon we'll go back to where there's family."

Billy's insides burned with guilt and remorse. He hopped up to the wagon seat. "But you've proved up on your place and—"

"Don't start now, Billy. You and I had fine plans, but I don't have those anymore," she said in a ragged whisper. "You know dang well Daddy can't farm the place anymore, and we can't afford a hired man. I decided we had to be gone before another winter here drove me insane. It's gotta be better somewhere else."

He gazed into her red-rimmed eyes—eyes a paler shade of blue than his, which had once sparkled and danced when Emma looked at him. Now he saw ice. Frigid, unrelenting ice.

"I'm sorry, Emma. I—"

Raking his fingers through his sleep-mussed hair, Billy looked at the four black-and-white dogs sitting in a half-circle, watching them intently. He recalled the day he'd let Emma and her mute cousin Gabriel choose their puppies from the litter in Judd's barn—the way Gabe came out of his deep, silent shock when a furball of a puppy started crawling all over him, licking his face.

Illinois. It was a long, long trek for four-legged friends when there was no room in the wagons.

"You think Hattie and Boots'll make it?" he murmured. "I mean, in this heat—and walkin' all that way. They're not the young dogs we used to herd Texas longhorns with, and—"

"You want 'em?"

Something in Emma's tone made him study her face—the sturdy set of it, with cheeks more weathered than a proper lady's would be. He saw the slightest quiver in those lips he'd kissed quite a bit this past year.

"I'd be pleased to keep 'em for ya," he said softly. "They're my friends, too—and maybe Gabe'll feel better, knowin' they're here with us. You—you told Gabe you were movin' yet?"

"He'll never be back, now that he's livin' high in St. Louis," came the tight reply. "Always thought he was a little better'n us, anyway."

Billy scowled, scooting back. "I'm sorry you feel that way—and more'n a little surprised at your attitude, Emma! Think how many days you'd've had nobody your age out there on that farm, if he hadn't needed a family!"

Her chin dropped to her chest then. She shook all over, looking defeated and pathetic in her worn blue dress. His first impulse was to reach for her, yet something about this whole episode sat wrong with him.

"I'm sorry," she sighed. "This is hard, and I didn't want to cry. Again."

He let out a long sigh. "Yeah, seems like nothin' much is easy these days. How 'bout if I tell Gabe you're leavin'? Gotta write him about Wesley anyway."

She nodded, mopping her eyes with her sleeve.

"And I meant what I said about keepin' the dogs."

Emma sniffled loudly. "I—I was hopin' you'd want 'em," she said forlornly. "It's a hard trip, like you said, and . . . and we don't have enough to feed 'em, or water to—"

"Don't you go another step, Emma." Mercy's face was a mixture of pain and determination as she looked from the girl back to her father. "I'll be right back, do you hear me? Come on, girls."

Billy watched three dresses fluttering around slim, strong bodies—the mother hen and her devoted chicks—and it occurred to him that they were the lucky ones, here on the Triple M. Somehow, despite drought and grasshoppers and a desperado twin setting fire to the stable, they'd thrived on the Kansas plains while neighbors hadn't been so lucky. Or so blessed.

"Don't s'pose you'll ever forgive me for lettin' you down," Billy murmured, "but I hope you'll—"

"We've been over this and over this, Billy. A blind woman could've seen how you wanted Eve and that baby, from the moment you laid eyes on 'em."

He blinked. Why was this attraction so obvious to everyone but him?

"You know how you keep sayin' God works things out his way?" she went on doggedly. "Well, for some reason you always end up with the sheep, and I'm just one of the goats, I guess. Maybe livin' someplace else'll change my luck."

"I—I hope that's true, Emma. I want you to be happy."

Her lips pursed around a tart reply, but then she looked over her shoulder. "Now what's this? I didn't come here for no charity—"

Billy turned, not a bit surprised to see Asa and Mercy carrying crates of tinned food from the cellar while the girls each grappled with lumpy sacks: more provisions, probably from the pantry. Behind them came Michael, pushing a wheelbarrow that held a barrel of rain water.

"George? Emma?" he rasped, walking as fast as he could without sloshing the water. "If I'd known you were packing up, we could've—"

The man on the buckboard behind them finally stirred, if only to raise his hand for silence. "Thank you kindly," he said in a resigned voice, "but we'll not be taking your—"

"Hand those sacks on up to Billy, girls," Mercy instructed firmly. "Asa, I think there's more room in that back wagon for these tins."

"Yes'm, I b'lieve you're right. You let me heft 'em up there, now."

Clark was having none of it. His eyes widened and he slid to the side of his seat as though he intended to start throwing punches. But Michael reached up with both hands to hold him, his expression full of regret.

"George, there's nobody sorrier than I am that things

didn't work out," he rasped. "It's been one misfortune after another for you two. But why just abandon your land? I don't have ready cash, but I'll certainly make you a fair offer for your place."

The man blinked, as though he hadn't considered this angle. Then he sank back down. "We're already on our way, all packed and headin'—"

"Stop in town, then. You're going through Abilene anyway," Malloy urged. "I'll follow you in and we'll make arrangements at the bank. If my offer doesn't suit you, you can at least let the land office know the place is for sale."

He wheeled the water barrel to the end of Emma's wagon, so he and Asa could load it.

"I tried to tell 'im that," Emma said under her breath, "but there's no talkin' to that man. Daddy wanted to slip on by without anybody knowin' we was gone—without sayin' good-bye, even."

Billy cleared his throat, nodding. "That's about the hardest word there is, Emma. You . . . you let us know where you're stayin'—"

"So we can tellya how Hattie and Boots're doin'," Solace piped up.

"So we can send news and—and we'll want to hear from you, too," Mercy added. Her smile wavered, now that this situation was settling in on her. "Travel safely. We'll keep you in our prayers, dear."

Billy heard his cue to climb down, but instead something propelled him forward to hug Emma, hard. For several moments, he pressed her against his chest, feeling her breathe—closing his eyes against nostalgic thoughts about things they'd done together as kids.

Then he sighed and released her. Though Emma hadn't pushed him away, she hadn't hugged him back, either. It was a message even a sheep like himself could understand.

"You've gotta get down now, Billy. We've got a lot of miles to cover."

With a glance back at her father, who sat up straighter, gripping the reins, she sighed. "Can't thank you enough for . . . for the water and supplies. It was nice knowin' you all. Mercy, you were my mother's best friend."

"I—I miss her, too, dear. Please write and let us know when you get to your aunt's."

The tight set of Emma's mouth told him it was time to get out of her wagon—out of her life. Forever. Billy had the fleeting urge to kiss her cheek one last time, but she'd swat him for it. So he squeezed her shoulder and climbed down.

"Spot and Snowy—come on over here," he called to the dogs. His voice sounded high and tight.

"Boots! Hattie girl," Solace joined in, opening her arms. "You're stayin' with us now!"

With a last look at them all, Emma clapped the reins and her horse started off.

"I'll be right behind you!" Michael called.

Billy stared after her, then at George as his buckboard rumbled by. Once again, a decade of his life was riding off to start over somewhere else—this time a scorned bride and a sorry old widower who took to the bottle when he had nowhere else to go for comfort.

Mercy slipped her arm around his waist, and he felt her trembling. Grace and Lily stood in front of her, and Solace had come around to his side, placing one hand in his and the other on Spot's head as they all watched the wagons disappear down the road. The Clark dogs whimpered, but they sat down when Solace called them back.

"That's about the saddest thing I ever saw," Mercy rasped.

Billy shook his head, knowing he should just look away—but he couldn't. "I guess it's all my fault. Guess I did the wrong thing by—"

"Billy."

The woman beside him pulled him close, as she'd done when he was a lonely little kid watching his sister ride off to Agatha Vanderbilt's academy. "You feel responsible, I know, but I just can't think she was the right wife for you. Emma—"

"She's a sourpuss, *that's* for dang sure!" Solace blurted.

He caught the hint of grin on Mercy's face, and felt better for it.

"Let's say she's poor in spirit," the woman amended, "and she's had a hard time of it since her mother passed on. We need to keep her and George in our prayers. And we need to thank God for showing Billy a better way. A happier way."

He wasn't so sure of that right now, but he felt relieved that Mercy Malloy had shared her feelings: Her vision had never been wrong. Even if he didn't have any notion of what to do with himself next, he trusted her judgment.

"Let's go, Solace," he said, turning toward the house. "We've left your daddy doin' the chores all morning. Time we earned our breakfast."

He wasn't much with fancy words, so that evening Billy dashed off a paragraph about the Clarks going back to Illinois before sealing his letter to Christine, and then said pretty much the same things in a letter to Gabe. How would Emma's cousin feel, hearing—from *him*—that his family had left their homestead? He doubted they'd stop to see him when they reached St. Louis.

And didn't that prove again what Mercy had said? It was sad to think about, but Emma was no longer the optimistic, capable young woman he'd once known.

And George Clark wasn't much more than a shell. Maybe Gabe realized this, and had jumped at Miss Vanderbilt's offer as his ticket out of a touchy situation.

They're all moving forward, making changes, Billy. How about you?

All day and into the evening, these questions made him restless. Should he go, or should he stay? It wasn't easy; he could see advantages on either side of his dilemma. Maybe he needed that last piece of Asa's cherry pie to put things in better perspective. . . .

He stopped at the bottom of the stairs, gazing at the familiar furnishings in the parlor. And then he saw it: the portrait Eve had painted of Lily sitting with her cat in her lap was now hanging above the fireplace. Michael must have made the frame and stained it, to match the mantel and the glossy plank flooring he'd put in this room.

Billy stepped closer. Voices drifted in from the front porch, where the others were talking over lemonade, so he took this chance to study the picture when the three little girls weren't all telling him about it at once.

In the glow from the lamp, Lily's blond ringlets shone like gold and her demure smile was so perfect he held his breath, expecting her to speak to him. The ginger kitty, sat proudly aloof in her lap, so lifelike he reached up to touch its soft fur.

His finger caressed the signature in the lower corner instead: *E. Massena.*

What's she doing right now? Olivia must be sleeping—

He shook those thoughts from his head—and when the light shone at just the right angle, he saw the little optical illusion she'd painted. Although the background of the portrait showed the wall of the dining room, with the Bible open on the sideboard, the brush strokes suggested the shapes of *wings*! As though their princess in pink was really an angel!

His breath left him. He walked slowly toward the

kitchen, his mind in a whirl as he passed through the dining room. Just like in the painting, the Bible lay open . . . and something drew him to it.

The lamp glowed, so it illuminated Psalm 37, where phrases had been underlined, which Michael often did when he found something noteworthy during his studies. Right now, though, Billy had the overwhelming sense that Malloy had intended for these verses to leap out at *him*; that he was seeing what he'd overlooked in the chaos of these past several days.

" 'Rest in the Lord and wait patiently for Him,' " Billy murmured. " 'Fret not because of . . . the man who bringeth wicked devices to pass . . . Cease from anger and forsake wrath; fret not thyself in any wise to do evil . . . for evildoers shall be cut off.' "

Billy closed his eyes—saw his brother charging toward him with that sawed-off shotgun. Wes had always accused him of being weak. A sissy. Yet these verses reminded him that anger and vengeance were never the right responses to wrongdoing.

" 'But those that wait upon the Lord shall inherit the earth,' " he continued in a thin voice. " 'The meek shall inherit the earth, and shall delight themselves in the abundance of peace.' "

The meek shall inherit . . . the abundance of peace. That pretty well spelled it out, didn't it? Maybe he'd mistaken his confusion and lack of direction—his meekness—for lack of faith, when he'd really been waiting for God to clear the proper path for him.

His pulse quickened at the thought. Stranger things had happened.

He continued into the kitchen—looking, as he always did, at Mercy's quilt of their patchwork family. It was a portrait showing all of them in front of Mercy's first house, right before she married Malloy—including himself and Christine. And they were being held, safe and secure, in Judd Monroe's large, loving hands.

Silently he lifted the pan with that last piece of cherry pie, and took it upstairs to his room. Then he sat on his bed, savoring every sweet, tangy mouthful, while looking at Eve's painting of his boyhood home.

The way suddenly seemed clear to him.

Chapter Twenty-eight

As Michael said grace over their breakfast the next morning, Billy knew he had to jump in feetfirst with his announcement, before he lost his nerve.

"—and we ask, Lord, that You hold Joel in Your mighty hand, and guide him safely home, if that be Your will. In Your son's name we pray, amen."

"Amen," went around the table—now less crowded and less lively, without Joel, Eve and Olivia. It occurred to Billy that his leaving would put another gap in this circle, where he'd had a place for half his life now. But he couldn't let that sentiment sway him.

Malloy passed him the biscuits, and Billy grasped Mike's work-toughened hands with the plate still in them. "I—I've decided to go on back home."

The room stilled. Everyone gazed intently at him, yet Michael's hazel eyes held a knowing look. His mustache flickered.

"Why am I not surprised?" he asked happily. "You have the look of a man who's made his peace and made his decision, as though both were divinely inspired."

"Nahhhh," Solace teased, grabbing a fistful of bacon.

"He's goin' back to take up with Eve and Olivia. He was just makin' us all *wonder*. And wait. Billy's real good at makin' folks wait."

He blinked. *Never thought about it that way, have you? What if you've made Eve wait too long—like you did Emma? What if—*

Temple beamed, while grasping Solace's wrist to remind the girl of her manners. "Congratulations, Mr. Billy! I knew God would guide you, and I think you've made the right choice. But we sure will miss you!"

Lily sat straight and still, focused on him from across the table. "It's meant to be," she pronounced quietly. "I knew it as soon as I saw that pretty stranger step into the back of the church. Desperation might've driven her there, but it was God's hand that held the reins."

Once again the room grew silent as the girl's profound ideas sank in.

"Well," Billy said, basking in the love on their faces, "I'm sure glad *you* all knew how everything would work out. Wish you would've just told me—"

"Oh, we tried," Gracie said, her wispy hair drifting as she nodded. "It was as plain as the nose on your face, Billy. We girls just know these things."

Coming from this pixie of six, it was about the funniest thing they'd ever heard.

Their warm laughter and good wishes made his heart swell. And as they ate, Billy gazed at each one of them to memorize their faces at this happy moment— saving up this feeling of glad anticipation and promise, for days when he'd eat his meals alone in a sad old house that so badly needed to become a home again.

It was Mercy's expression that made his heart clutch: she was acting happy, but the tears rolled down her face anyway—a face so full of a mother's love, he almost ran to her, to feel the same strength and courage he'd drawn upon since he'd come here as an abandoned boy.

But he was putting away childish things, wasn't he? And her tremulous smile said she knew that, and she was proud of the man he'd become.

As he and Malloy fed and watered the horses, as he'd done hundreds of mornings, it struck him that he was giving up one dream for another. Hadn't he always dreamed of training fine horses on a successful spread like the Triple M? But Michael was quick to dispel his doubts.

"It'll all work out now, son," he said as they pitched hay into the mangers. "You've had your share of trials—by fire and brimstone, some of them—and you've come through with a new vision. We're nothing without a vision, Billy.

"I've seen this day coming. Always believed you'd return to claim your birthright, when it was time." Michael clapped his hands on Billy's shoulders, his tawny eyes bright with both hope and sadness. "Go with God, son. I know how difficult this is—and how you want to be on your way now—so you might as well get this leave-taking started. It's one of the hardest things we do, leaving the ones we love."

"Thanks, Michael. Couldn't have had a better father if I'd picked him myself."

Billy turned toward the house before Malloy could see his eyes go wet.

It was almost humbling, how few things he had to pack: some clothes, mementos of Christmases past—and Eve's painting, of course. He'd been with the Malloys so long, he didn't even have a trunk; Christine had taken the ones they'd left Richmond with.

While Mercy was insisting he take one of her trunks, she was folding the patchwork quilt she'd made for his sister one Christmas—the one he'd had on his bed ever since Christine left it behind.

"This has seen a lot of wear, but it'll still keep you warm—and remind you of us," she mused. "I'll get you some towels and sheets, too, dear. I can't imagine anything you'll find in that poor, abused house will be fit to use now."

Why did her thoughtfulness make this so much more difficult? Billy could see Malloy's point: better to keep this process rolling now that he'd put it in motion. Their noon meal tugged at him, because the three girls had spent their morning with Temple, writing him letters they'd sealed for him to open when he arrived in Richmond.

Somehow he ate. Somehow he loaded his belongings on the buckboard and hitched Pete to it. Snowy and Spot panted, pacing behind the seat: They knew things were changing in a big way when they sniffed the trunk, and saw everyone else getting into the carriage for a ride to town. They knew, too, that Boots and Hattie were locked in the shed: the other two dogs howled their protest as the buckboard rolled toward the road, so they yipped in reply.

Asa rode with him—maybe the most difficult thing of all, even though each separate piece of his departure had hit him hard.

"You's on your way now, Billy," the old man murmured when they were rolling down the road. "I always knowed you'd do us all proud, 'cause you's got the heart of Jesus hisself a-beatin' in your chest. I told myself, that night your brother come at you a-shootin', that if you didn't make it, well, I didn't want to, neither. Too durn old to be losin' you thatta way, you see."

"Too feisty is more like it," Billy quipped, but his heart was in his throat. The old man was looking like a sock doll, worn out from loving and giving. But his eyes crinkled when he grinned.

"*Feisty* ain't a bad thing," Asa said, chuckling. "Where would Miss Eve and her baby be if she weren't a feisty one?"

The question kicked him in the heart: Eve Massena

had come to Abilene on just the strength of her belief that he'd do the right thing on her behalf.

And here he was. Telling himself he was going home, to that place she'd painted, when the Malloys all knew *why* he was headed there.

Somehow he said good-bye to them all at the train station, hugging them hard. It was a blur, this process, and Billy suspected that was the only way he got through it.

Somehow he got the buckboard, Pete, and the dogs situated in a stock car—and got the collies to quit barking. Now that he'd made this life-altering decision, he wished some of Spot and Snowy's exuberance would rub off on him. He hoped that someday soon, he'd smile again and know he'd really done the right thing.

And then, somehow, he sat in his seat on the train, waving through the dusty window at those faces he'd see in his dreams and fondest thoughts, no matter how far apart they were: Mercy in red calico, her brown hair tied back, her face alight with the afternoon sun and an inner glow that had always been his guide . . . Solace standing with her feet shoulder-width apart and her arms crossed, staunchly refusing to wave good-bye, beside Lily, who held Grace's hand as they both wiggled their fingers at him . . . Temple, behind them, her chocolate face a beacon of hope and faith . . . Asa who alternated between waving and wiping his wet face with his shirtsleeve.

And Michael. The man who'd stood in as his father so willingly and stalwartly; the best friend and teacher and benefactor he'd ever had. Michael Malloy just watched him with those haunting eyes, clasping his hands in front of him, until the train carried him out of sight.

Billy pulled Pete to a halt at the end of the lane that evening, quivering on this brink of a dream come true—a dream that remained as hazy and mysterious as the twilight in the overgrown trees ahead. Though he wasn't one to imagine ghosts—and he had no reason to believe Wesley's disgruntled friends were lying in wait for him—driving up to the dark, deserted house made his heart pound.

He was glad Snowy and Spot were with him. As though they knew they'd reached their destination, the dogs hopped down from the buckboard and circled the yard, sniffing the weeds and the old piles of horse manure. Out of habit, Billy went around to the back to enter through the kitchen. The border collies trotted through the shadowy rooms ahead of him, alert to strange new scents, glancing back now and again to be sure he was coming.

His footsteps echoed in the empty rooms as he found lamps and lit them. He hauled his trunk up the carpet runner of the staircase and entered the bedroom he and his brother had shared for half their lives—where Wesley had hidden to shoot at him and Eve. The window was broken—the room was a mess, like the entire downstairs—but Billy was too weary to worry about any of that right now. He stripped his bed and made it up with the sheets Mercy had sent along. The clean scent of Kansas sunshine and her kindness soothed him after a painful day.

He made the other bunk up, too, and then tossed Wesley's filthy sheets—and the whiskey bottles under his bed—out the hall window.

The room felt a lot homier then. And when Spot and Snowy hopped onto that other bunk, he smiled.

"We're gonna make it, pups," he said, scratching both of their heads. "Get a good night's sleep, 'cause we've got a lot to do tomorrow."

When he took off his shirt, the stiffness of its pocket reminded him of the letters the girls had written for him. Billy hesitated, holding the three folded pages in his hands, knowing these messages would probably make him miss the Malloys and their home more than he already did. Maybe he'd endured enough for one day—

Oh, just one. They made a special effort on these. Solace and Lily and Grace are kneeling at their bedsides right now, praying for you.

He opened the one on top and recognized Lily's delicate penmanship; imagined her studious expression as she composed this note while Temple smiled over her shoulder.

> *Dearest Billy,*
>
> *We'll miss you so much! But when I feel sad about it, I'll send my angels to check on you and report back to me. I don't tell everyone about them—their names, or how many there are. But I know you'll believe that they're real, and that they'll be our guides—just as you have been my very own angel all my life.*

Dang . . . already the tears were running down his face! He wiped his nose on his sleeve and kept reading, although the words looked cloudy now.

> *Take good care of yourself, Billy. I know you'll watch over Eve and Olivia, too! You'll be in my prayers, every single day. I'll ask God to shine a light on your path when you feel lost, and I'll ask Him to hold you in His strong, tender hands as you bring life back to your boyhood home.*
>
> *We hope to see you again very soon!*
>
> *Love, Lily*

Billy let out a long sigh. He closed his eyes and imagined Lily's sweet smile and golden hair—her astounding voice when she sang at the wedding and read at Wesley's graveside.

Goose bumps ran up his arms. He detected a flicker of movement near the ceiling—her angel, come to check on him? Or was it because the lamp oil was old? Because he had moisture in his eyes?

He smiled. What would it hurt to believe in Lily's vision of things unseen? If angels could tolerate this house right now, well—he could use their heavenly company!

Quickly, before he lost his nerve, he unfolded the next note. Just the sight of Solace's bold, squarish letters perked him up:

Dear Billy,

Well, I'll be stuck here without you and Joel. Good thing I've got Emma's dogs. I fully intend to come to your place and help out someday real soon. Don't forget! You promised to pick me out a good yearling and help me train it! I'm holding you to that!

Don't worry about me, I'll be fine. But it's already slow here and you haven't even left yet. Your Solace

His chuckle made the dogs raise their heads to look at him. "Well, pups, we never doubt what *that* girl's thinking, 'cause she pretty much blurts it out!" he told them. "Soon as we get things squared away here, I need to find her that horse. Can't let those girls think I've forgotten 'em. Can't let Solace settle for just any ole yearling . . ."

Your Solace, he read again. And yes, she would be. When things didn't go well here, or when he had doubts about this overwhelming task he'd taken on, recalling that tomboy's grin and husky voice—the sight of her standing on Mr. Lincoln's bare back while he cantered around the corral—would give him the strength to pick up and go on.

Again Billy mopped his face. Then he opened the last note.

I love you, Billy. Gracie.

That did it. He slumped forward, elbows on his knees, and gave in to the tiredness and the tears. Spot and Snowy hopped off the bed to nudge him, bright-eyed and whimpering. He blinked his eyes clear, stroking their silky ears.

"Well, there's no gettin' Grace wrong, is there?" he murmured.

Snowy's mostly white face eased into a grin that meant she was way ahead of him, but that he'd finally figured out something important.

Billy chuckled, at himself mostly. Good thing he *knew* he couldn't mess up God's grace, no matter how he bungled things. The thought made him smile as he tucked those precious notes into the night stand drawer. He felt completely wrung out now, but there was one more thing he wanted to see before he turned in.

Billy propped Eve's painting on the nightstand between the two narrow beds. He studied it by the lamp's light, his pulse pumping steadily as he gazed at the trumpet vines growing up the proud white porch pillars. It was too late in the season to know if those fiery-red poppies had survived the years of neglect, and would greet him next spring. Just another thing he'd have to take on faith—or fix, if it didn't turn out the way he was hoping.

There might be a lot of things that didn't turn out.

"But I'm back," he said as he snuffed out the light. "And someday this place is gonna look like a home again."

Chapter Twenty-nine

"Eve, I—I can't thank you enough," Virgilia breathed. She gazed at the framed painting of her former home as though she yearned to walk inside and find it the way she'd left it—with her family and furnishings intact, as they'd been before the war.

Eve certainly appreciated that sentiment. Even if life wasn't really simpler before they'd all been upended by Border Ruffians and tragedy and scandal, it seemed that way in light of what they'd endured since.

"Someday the place will look this perfect again, sweetheart." Carlton Harte spoke with the confidence of a man who saw his promises through. "With Billy back, and with our help, this proud house will be a *home* again."

"Billy's back?" Eve shifted the baby onto her other shoulder to cover her amazement. Her . . . disappointment. "I—I thought he would've come to see—how long's he been in town?"

Carlton's grin told her he'd let a cat out of the bag. Accidentally on purpose.

"About a week now," his redheaded wife replied with a feline smile. "He wanted to get things cleared away before you found him out. He didn't tell *me*, either, dear," she added demurely. "Carlton saw him at the bank, discussing the details of who owns the Bristol place now that . . . Wesley's gone."

"It's all taken care of."

Harte smiled as though he, too, could accomplish things without telling all he knew. He took a money clip from his coat pocket. "And it's my pleasure to be the first purchaser of your paintings, Miss Eve. I'm spreading the word about your talent and your new studio, so it won't be long before you have clients waiting in line for your work! Why—"

Her new studio! Eve couldn't stop grinning every time she thought of it: The Hartes had allotted her a small room at the front of the hotel they'd just purchased. It had windows to let in the light—and so passersby could see enough of her work on the walls, or in progress, to pique their interest from the sidewalk.

"—the new president at the bank saw this painting of the Bristol place, and wants to surprise his wife with one of their home," Virgilia's husband went on. "It'll soon be all the rage to have an Eve Massena work on the wall!"

She gaped at the money as he counted it into her hand. "But Mr. Harte, I only charged you—"

"Never you mind, my dear. You underestimate the value of your work—and I consider this an investment in my granddaughter's security."

"Listen to him!" Virgilia teased, tweaking Olivia's nose. "We all know Grandma was behind this, so she could play with you while your mama paints!"

Eve chuckled, tucking the money into her reticule. It was wonderful to see this woman dealing with the death of her son by diving into a fresh endeavor: Virgilia had honored Carlton's request to keep her colorful clothes, and was hiring painters and a new staff to run the hotel they'd renamed The Crystal Inn. She was a woman with a purpose now—as though entertaining Olivia wasn't a full-time pursuit—and Eve felt inspired by the way she defied convention to live life on *her* terms.

"And have you seen Billy?" she asked, trying not to sound too eager. "If he's there alone, I'm sure—"

"I'm trying very hard not to interfere with his plans—"

"She means *take over*," Carlton teased.

"—and frankly, I can't bear to set foot in that house again until he's set it to rights." Virgilia's expression tightened with her effort not to cry. "I have a new life now, with a wonderful man and an inn to revive, and there's no going back. Billy's there with my blessings."

Blessings. Now there was a word Eve had never expected from Billy's mother—a word that applied to her own life, of late, as well. Though living with her mother again—having a baby in the house—wasn't always as orderly or harmonious as either of them liked, she at least had a place to stay until she could move out on her own.

Or into the Bristol place. As the new Mrs. Bristol.

She blinked. That idea had hovered in the back of her mind for weeks, but she hadn't seen much hope for it until . . . but it was too soon to think seriously about Billy. She had a daughter to care for—paintings to plan! Carlton and Virgilia were walking with her toward the door.

"I'm so glad you like the watercolor," she repeated—and on impulse, she waved Olivia's little arm at them. "Tell Grandma and Grandpa we'll see them tomorrow when Mama comes to do her painting."

The baby bumped against her, chuffing, as though she wanted to play with her grandparents *now*.

Once the door closed behind her, however, Eve let the news about Billy's return tingle through her. She stood in front of the hotel for a few moments, wondering what to do about it: If Billy was intending this as a surprise for her, she didn't want to spoil it. Mother's lectures about proper deportment concerning men rang in her ears, warning her to be patient this time—to let Billy come to her, instead of egging him on, the way she had Wesley.

After all, Billy was crazy about Olivia. Sheer loneliness would bring him to see the baby pretty soon.

But Eve wanted him to want *her!* And she wanted to share her news about the studio and her paintings, without someone—namely Virgilia—beating her to the punch. There were just times when Billy Bristol, dear man that he was, needed a little nudge!

And as she walked down the sidewalk, she saw the enticement that would guarantee his attention: Beulah Mae's pie shop!

One step inside the door, and she closed her eyes. The aromas of warm fruit and sugar and cinnamon took her back to when the cook had made the Bristol house smell this heavenly every day. Eve just stood there, inhaling the dear, familiar scents. Her mother had never been one for sweets, and she herself had spent little time in the kitchen, so fresh-baked pies seldom graced their table.

"Well, now! If that ain't the cutest little baby I's ever seen!"

Eve burst into a smile. Beulah Mae was coming out of her back room, looking as if she'd just stepped to the Bristols' cookstove to take her pies from the oven: a broad, substantial woman still, she wore a flour-sack apron pinned to the ample bosom of her red dress, and the red plaid kerchief tied around her head looked crisp and neat.

"Beulah Mae! It's been so long—"

"Oh my gracious! Why, you's the Massena girl, ain'tcha?" Eyes the color of chocolate pie widened as the woman grinned at her. "And my stars, but that baby's the very likeness of—"

"Wesley Bristol. A—a mistake on my part, but I wouldn't trade this baby for the world now," she replied quickly. "I guess you heard we—we buried him a couple weeks ago?"

"Oh, my—I's so sorry, missy. Always afraid that boy would come to a sorry end, 'specially after he started runnin' with the likes of them James brothers," she murmured. "Never knew when to quit with his orneriness, even when they's kids."

Beulah Mae wiped her hands on a towel, and then held them out toward Olivia. "But this little red-haired angel, why, she reminds me more of Billy! Look at that precious face—and that dimple!" she exclaimed. "Sweet Jesus, this takes me back a lotta years, I can tellya."

"About twenty."

"Lordy, but I misses that family." The old woman laughed when the baby hiccuped and gurgled at her. "I's heard some wild stories 'bout Virgilia, but now I sees she's back with a new husband, settlin' in to run the hotel. And you tells me Wesley's passed now. But what about my Billy? And Miss Christine? She was a firecracker, that's for sure!"

"She lives in San Francisco with her husband. Designs gowns for wealthy ladies—"

"Who'd've b'lieved that!"

"—and has twins named Rachel and Rebecca, and a third one on the way. But—but it's Billy I'd like to talk to you about!" she confessed. "I just have to have one of your pies, Beulah Mae, because—"

"Because you's sweet on him. Like you always was."

Eve blinked.

The old cook's bosom shook as her laughter filled the fragrant bakery. "Oh, you and Wesley traded insults, and you always knew how to get 'im riled up over some little thing," she said with a fond shake of her head. "But ole Beulah Mae seen the way you and Mister Billy set in the porch swing together, and told each other your troubles. Cain't do that with just any man, no matter how old—or young—he is."

Eve nipped her lip. This woman's assessment of their childhood times together rang true, even after all that had happened to the three of them these past few years. Yes, it was Wesley she'd enjoyed setting off— just as it was Billy she'd gone to when her kitten died—

And when Olivia was born.

—because Billy understood how to console her, and how to steer her clear of bad choices, and—

"So he's back in town, too, is he? If you be needin' a pie, he cain't be far away."

Eve saw tears in the old cook's eyes as she nuzzled Olivia's cheek. "He's moved back into the Bristol place, Beulah Mae. I'm not supposed to know that, but—"

"But a pie'll be *your* surprise to make him forget you's walkin' in on *his*." She handed Olivia back with a fond swat on her bottom. Then the creases around her eyes deepened. "You's too late for a pie today, missy, but tomorrow I'll make you up—"

"But there's a pie right there in your case!"

"—a *punkin* pie, 'cause that was always the fastest way to Mr. Billy's heart," Beulah Mae continued. She raised an eyebrow, assessing Eve. "And I won't charge you nothin' for it, if I can go out there with you, so's I can see that boy again. I's heard some terrible stories 'bout what his brother done to that house. Just so happens I's got lots of time to help him there . . . if he wants me to."

Eve glanced around the little shop, confused. "You'd leave your shop to—it's going to be a long, hard job—"

"Come Saturday, I won't be here, Miss Eve. Owner of

this buildin's got him a tenant a-wantin' this little place. A white woman he's been lookin' after, if you see what I's sayin'."

"But you seem to be doing so well, I never dreamed—"

"Well, I mighta dreamed," Beulah Mae said with a heavy sigh, "but I shoulda knowed it could come to a screechin' halt when the landlord caught a whiff of a different kinda sugar."

The old woman had lost her sparkle now. She looked so disappointed, Eve couldn't possibly turn her down. "Of course you can go!" she said softly. "Come by the Crystal Inn when you've closed up for the day, and we'll head out there. Billy'll be so excited to see you!"

The old cook's chuckle followed her to the door. "You do carry on so, child. It's *you* he'll be excited to see. And that sweet little Olivia, of course."

"Dammit, call off your dogs, Bristol! When'd you get these mangy mutts, anyway?"

Billy took his time dropping an armload of rotted fence boards beside the lane, trying to recall who that reedy voice belonged to. Since his barking border collies were excellent judges of character—and since this visitor thought he was Wesley—it might pay to get his thoughts together before he replied. He was exhausted after another morning of mending fences; alone and easy prey, if one of his brother's outlaw cohorts had come here to cause trouble.

Slowly, he rose to his full height, taking in horse and rider from beneath his hat brim. "Snowy! Spot! Sit down, pups."

"Snowy? What kind of sissy-butt name is—"

"If you want to find out what kind of *sissy* that dog is, keep insultin' her," Billy said in a coiled voice. "Otherwise, just state your business. I've got work to do."

The fellow's eyes widened. Then they narrowed into

a weasely expression Billy remembered quite well. "You ain't Wesley—"

"Nope. But you're Jared Mayhew. One of his *associates*, I take it."

"Wanna make somethin' of it, little Billy? I came by for what your brother owes me, but I can just as well beat it outta *you*!"

Billy didn't let his gaze waver, but he was wishing he'd worn his pistol today, just for show. "Can't help you with that—and neither can Wes," he said in the most confident voice he could call up. "He's right over there, inside that iron fence now. Beside our daddy."

Mayhew's nostrils flared. He glanced to where Billy pointed, but looked back fast—as though the smoothed-over rectangle of bare dirt spooked him. "Don't think for a minute you'll worm outta this!" he jeered. "Wesley got this place in trade for a job we pulled for Leland Massena, and the rest of us has a right to our shares! He said he was gonna *pay* us, dammit!"

Sensing those others might be watching from the hedgerow, or laying low behind the house, Billy considered his next steps carefully. He would not lose his life over his brother's criminal career, or because of his own stupidity.

"You should've thought of that a while back, I guess. What with Massena and my brother both gone now—"

"You never were the brightest candle in the pack, Billy. Maybe I'll just have to—"

When the thug went for his pistol, Spot let out a menacing bark and Snowy lunged for Mayhew's leg. A wild shot rang out as the horse skittered backwards, wide-eyed, while the dogs circled and barked, nipping at its knees.

"Helloooo there, Mr. Bristol! Hope I haven't come at an inconvenient time!" somebody called from farther down the lane.

He'd never been happier to see anybody in his life:

Carlton Harte's top hat and fine frock coat smacked of a covert strategy Billy knew not to betray. The detective slowed his mount to a walk, poised to draw and shoot even though he was dressed like a professional gentleman.

Billy cleared his throat. "No, sir, I just came up from fixin' fence—"

"Brought the deed to your place. Paid in full—signed, sealed, and delivered." Harte leveled his purposeful gaze on Billy as he reached into his inside jacket pocket. "The new bank president was glad to have this matter settled properly, considering the way your brother came into the property."

"Lemme see that!" Mayhew grabbed for the document in Harte's hand, but the detective deftly dodged his move—and caught him by the wrist. "I don't believe we've met, sir."

"This is Jared Mayhew," Billy put in. With a pointed look, he shushed the barking dogs. "Says he came to collect on one of Wesley's debts—"

A flash of gleaming metal caught the sunlight, and then two quick *clicks* had the outlaw cussing. "You've got no call to—"

"I'm placing you under arrest, Mr. Mayhew!" Carlton announced, brandishing the arm that was now handcuffed to his. "No sense in fighting me, or doing anything stupid, because the two men who were hiding in the house and down the lane are already on their way to jail."

"You can't tell me—"

"No?" Harte challenged. "Well, maybe if you tell *me* the whereabouts of the Younger boys, or Frank and Jesse James, things'll go a little easier with the judge. Now drop the gun."

Harte's folded paper had fluttered to the ground, and Billy picked it up cautiously. There was still a chance Jared would shoot him instead of following orders.

"This is the biggest—falsified—you've got nothin' on me!"

Billy unfolded the document, his heart pounding with excitement now. "Looks pretty official to me, Jared," he said, holding it up. "Says I'm now the legal owner of this spread. Since you can't collect from a dead man—and I don't owe you anything—I'm gonna let this fella escort you off my property."

"He's just some high-and-mighty guard you've hired!" Mayhew protested. He was trying to slip free of the metal cuffs, but the agitated movements of his horse kept him off-balance. "You always had to hide behind *somebody*."

"And this time it's the law," Harte replied smartly. "We've been waiting for you boys to make a stupid move, and today's our day! Let's go, Mayhew. Billy has enough cleaning up to do here, without having *your* sorry carcass in his way."

Billy stood in the shade of the huge old maple trees, removing his straw hat to scratch his sweaty head. Jared Mayhew was cussing Carlton every step of the way. He grinned at how his dogs were herding them off the property: Snowy and Spot already knew this was their new domain.

When the black-and-white dogs loped back toward him, he crouched with his arms open wide. Spot licked his face, letting out little *woofs*, while Snowy leaned against him, insisting he scratch her backside.

"You saved my neck, ya know it?" he crooned to his collies. "And no matter what Wesley's old buddies wanna believe, the place is *ours!* I've got my land back, pups!"

His heart pounded as the reality of that hit him. After ten years away, and being abandoned, and then nearly getting shot down by his brother, he—Billy Bristol—had finally come *home!*

A feeling of inexplicable peace settled over him, as

though invisible angels hovered in the trees, flapping their gauzy wings to cool and comfort him—standing guard, like that fiery-sworded sentinel at the gate to the Garden of Eden, to preserve him from further harm. He felt as if he'd passed some sort of test, and had just received the keys to the kingdom.

He lifted his face to the sun, closing his eyes. "Thank you, Lord, for bringin' me through this time of trial," he murmured, "and for bringin' me home again, like I've always dreamed about. And thank you for givin' me the faith to see it all through.

"But I could really use some help with that poor old house," he added tiredly. "Mendin' fences and raisin' horses is what I'm cut out to do, Lord, but when it comes to—"

The thunder of hooves roused him from his prayer, and when the two dogs took off toward the road, Billy's jaw dropped.

If he hadn't recognized those sturdy brown Morgans, he would've thought he was being stampeded. But no! That was Reuben Gates on one side of the herd's dust cloud, whistling and funneling them down the driveway! Boots and Hattie were nipping at them, running along the other side to keep them moving.

And that was Mike Malloy's hat on the other side—

And if that wasn't Mr. Lincoln—with Solace—

"Hope you've got your fences fixed, Billy Bristol," she hollered, " 'cause here we come!"

Chapter Thirty

He ran ahead of them to throw open the white plank pasture gate he'd repaired and painted only yesterday. How was it that everything was falling into place for him now, happening at just the right time?

It's the answer to your prayers, Billy. It's the good seeds you've sown, bearing fruit.

Billy shook his head, wondering if he'd been out in the sun too much. That voice in his mind seemed more insistent these days, sometimes sounding like Judd Monroe and sometimes more like Michael. But he'd learned to welcome it—and to believe in it. Some folks might call it intuition, but he knew it as Divine Wisdom.

And as he stood to the side holding the gate, counting off a full dozen yearlings plus three mares and a stallion he'd raised and trained himself, Billy felt ready to burst. These sturdy horses didn't look as fancy as the thoroughbreds his daddy had raised, but they were solid. Dependable.

Just like the man who rode up beside him to watch the horses explore the pasture.

"Good to see you, Billy! I figured you'd have this place shaped up for your horses, so here they are!"

"And they already act like they b'long here, too," Reuben Gates joined in. He looked the place over from the top of his tall mount, then smiled. "Mr. Billy, I can sure understand why you was called back to this fine ranch. Look there! They's already found the stream, down by them walnut trees, 'cause the dogs knows their scent—and knows their job!"

Billy grinned, shaking his head: the four border collies were frolicking in the pasture now, while Solace was giving Mr. Lincoln his head. The sight of them racing hellbent-for-leather over the rolling green hills brought back many a fond memory—more than his heart could hold.

"Michael, you shouldn't have—I never intended for you to bring me—"

"Oh, but I figured on it all along, son." Malloy's mustache twitched with his grin. "Call it an early birthday present if it makes you feel better, but you earned every one of those Morgans."

"But what about *your* ranch?" he protested. "This has to be a third of your herd!"

The slender man swung down from his mount to shut the gate, looking it over closely. "Fine job on this repair, Billy—like I knew it would be. You never do anything halfway."

His hazel eyes shone with pride as he clapped Billy on the back. "Reuben and I talked about how things'll be, now that you've got a place of your own, and we've moved the horses from Mercy's homestead into our stables. We're going to take down those outbuildings, and the ones on the Clark place, and plow that into crop land. I've been thinking that's the way to go for a long while now. Less upkeep—with less help. More to send to market."

Billy blinked. "There's no way I can repay, or thank you enough for—"

"Well, here comes the rest of 'em, finally!" Solace cried,

pointing toward the lane. "Took 'em long enough!"

Billy turned, and took off at a trot. Asa was driving a new buckboard, which was loaded with building materials and supplies, and behind him came the carriage. Mercy and Sedalia Gates were in that driver's seat, with Lily and Grace hanging out the windows, waving wildly at him.

"Surprise, Billy!" the blonde's melodious voice rang out. "We brought you a whole housewarming party!"

"And lunch! From uptown!" Gracie crowed.

"Yessir, you's got yer work cut out for ya now," Asa teased. He halted his horse and sat there for a moment, grinning down at Billy. "After the funeral, when Mercy and me seen what your house was like, we knew exactly what we wanted to do for ya. We's brought paint, and cleanin' supplies—"

"And lots of little hands to help!"

Gracie ran at him. Billy caught her up in a hug before raising her above his head to make her shriek. Then he grabbed Lily—who wore calico today, but it was pink calico!—and grinned at Temple.

"You all are a sight for sore, tired eyes!" he rasped. "I've gotten a lot done outside, but that poor house—"

"Mama made lists for each of us," the little blonde informed him. "She says it's good practice for when we have homes and husbands of our own."

For just a moment, he gazed at these dear little girls—and Solace, who was running toward him in her dusty pants and plaid shirt—and imagined what fine young women they would become someday. Each had different gifts and talents, but they'd been raised by parents who'd shown them the same love and devotion every day of their lives.

"You'd better believe I'm gonna check those fellas over before I let you marry 'em!" he teased.

"Marry 'em?" Solace threw herself against him,

wrapping her arms tightly around his waist. "I thought you and me—"

"You and *I*," Lily corrected primly.

"—were gonna be a team, Billy! So's I won't have to get married and wear one of those sissy white dresses!"

Mercy laughed as she came up to him. She kissed his cheek loudly, swatting his backside. "Heaven forbid that Solace Monroe would wear lace or pull her hair up and curl it! I have to warn you, Billy, she's been threatening to stay here at your place—"

"Because she thinks you won't make her do any school work!" Gracie flashed him an impish grin. "I've learned all the books of the Bible now, Billy. Wanna hear them? Genesis, Exodus, Leviticus, Numbers, Deuteronomy—"

As he gazed around him, at Sedalia and Temple laughing as they handed boxes down to the men—at the wide smiles this family wore because they enjoyed bringing him this surprise—at the little girls who adored him with all their hearts—at the sheer amount of food and supplies the Malloys had brought him—Billy felt speechless. Oh, he'd labored well enough alone, and he'd had the dogs for company, and he'd resigned himself to several weeks of work before things would look good enough for Mama and Eve to see.

But *this*. This happy family gathering—to help *him*!

And to think he would've missed it—the Malloys' boundless love—if he'd never had to leave this place as a boy of ten.

He'd come so far. He'd gained so much. It came over him in a big rush, how God had taken all those hard, sorry parts of his boyhood after his daddy died, and worked them into a fine life that had now come full circle.

To everything there is a season, and a time for every purpose under heaven.

The words Lily had read over his brother's grave came back to him now, with more strength and power—more meaning—than those verses had held for him before. It was more than he'd dared to ask for, this display of love from the Malloys. And certainly more than he deserved.

"All right, girls, you know our plan!" Mercy sang out. "We'll put down the quilts under these trees, and enjoy our picnic lunch. And then it's work, work, work!"

A picnic lunch, too? Billy's stomach rumbled as familiar hampers came out of the carriage. It boggled his mind, all the planning Mercy had done, to travel from Abilene with supplies and food and then buy the rest of the meal in town, after they'd arrived. And it had taken plenty of organization on Michael's part, too: getting the Morgans and the loaded wagons on the train, and herding those horses here from the Lexington station.

But then, the Malloys had always been pretty good at miracles. The everyday kind of miracles that were woven into God's magnificent plan over the years.

He grabbed a crockery water pot—the one Asa always used for lemonade—and carried it to where the ladies were arranging their dinner. Sedalia was unwrapping a package of sliced ham, and her husband was hoisting a crate that held dishes and silverware.

Mercy smiled at him. "We thought you might like some plates and cups, dear. I didn't imagine that your brother left you too many."

"And I made the cookies!" Lily said.

"And I helped Temple stir the cornbread!" little Grace joined in proudly. "And I reminded them how you'd be wanting honey to drizzle over yours."

Solace sauntered up to him, carrying a big box that smelled like fried chicken, still warm, from a restaurant in town. "I made sure Asa put *lots* of cherries in the pies, just like you like 'em, Billy."

"I hope he made a whole one for me," Billy teased,

"'cause I haven't seen a spread like this since—well, since I left your place to come here."

"Sit by *me*, Billy!"

Gracie plopped down on the edge of the quilt, patting the spot beside her, and the two other girls took places nearby. After a few minutes of shifting themselves and rearranging the food in the center, everyone was seated in the shade and looking up at Michael.

"Let's pray," he invited them, and as he removed his dusty hat, the rest of the men did the same. Malloy gazed around them, at the lush trees, and the pasture where the Morgans now grazed, and the white house with its pillared porch, smiling, nodding.

"Lord, we thank You for the beauty of this day, and this land, and this fine occasion, as they're but small examples of the many gifts You give us all our lives," he began quietly. "We thank You, as well, for our safe journey here, and for blessing us with so many good crops and horses that we could share what You've given us with Billy."

Billy shifted, the way he always did when Michael prayed for him. Was that a horse and wagon he heard coming down the lane?

"We ask You now for your blessing on this food, and Your guidance as we work today," he went on more urgently, "and we ask Your very special blessing on Billy Bristol as he starts his new life here. Guide him in the way You'd have him go, and watch over him. Bring the people and gifts he needs to better accomplish Your purpose—"

"Looky there! It's Eve coming—with Olivia and—"

"Shh! We're still praying, Gracie!" Lily whispered.

"—as he brings this fine home back to life with Your love. For we ask these things—"

"But who's that with her?" Grace whispered back. Then she elbowed Billy. "That's the biggest old Negro lady I've ever seen!"

He couldn't resist sneaking a peek. And then his jaw dropped.

"—in the name of Your son, Jesus. Amen."

"Beulah Mae!" Billy cried, scrambling off the quilt to run to her. "Lordy, but it's been too long—and Eve! How'd you know to—"

"It's the answer to our prayers," Lily pronounced. But she was grinning, taking in every detail of the way Billy reached for Eve first, held on to her for a moment after her feet found the ground. . . .

"Amen! Let's eat!" Gracie squealed.

Chapter Thirty-one

Eve held her breath, unable to look away from Billy's blue, blue eyes. She felt as if he was devouring her with his happy gaze. "I—I hope we're not intruding on—I had no idea the Malloys were—"

"Yeah, they surprised me, too, Peaches. But you're just in time to join us!" His head was spinning so fast, he wasn't sure the words were coming out right. But all of a sudden this day felt complete.

He reached up to assist Beulah Mae, who beamed at him from the wagon seat, shaking her head as though she didn't believe what she was seeing.

"Billy, Billy, Billy!" she said with a fond cackle. "When they tole me you was back, fixin' up this house, why—"

She stepped down carefully. Her cocoa eyes widened as Billy caught her full weight and set her down.

"When did you get to be so big and strong? Look at you, all growed up into a *fine*-lookin' man!" Her ample bosom shook with laughter. "But don't you go thinkin' ole Beulah Mae still cain't take a broom to ya, if you go sneakin' pie!"

Fleshy arms pressed him against a girth as warm and full of love as he remembered from being her Billy boy. He squeezed her back, awash in this woman's familiar sound and scent. To him, Beulah Mae had been the very symbol of comfort and stability during his boyhood.

"I brung you a punkin pie, honey," she crooned, rocking him side to side. "And I's here to help you settle this house—'cept it looks like you's already got plenty of—"

"Never enough help, Beulah Mae," he murmured against her soft neck. "And don't you ever go thinkin' I don't need you! Even if you hadn't brought me a pie."

He took her by the hand, amazed that his fingers were so much longer than hers now—that he stood tall enough to look down into those kind brown eyes—although he would never look down at *her*.

"You'd better meet all these folks, and help us eat this meal! Can you *believe* this spread?" he asked, gesturing toward the food and the smiling faces. "They brought supplies and this picnic, for *me*! And those horses in the pasture? I raised 'em, Beulah Mae! And I trained 'em—and—and Michael here is lettin' me start up my own ranch with 'em!"

"I's so happy that God's been good to you, child," she murmured, swiping at her eyes. "Weren't nobody more worried for you than ole Beulah Mae, after your mama took out with you kids!

"But we's back now!" she said with an emphatic nod. "We's together again! And I already knows I'm gonna love every person I sees sittin' under this shade tree!"

Eve wandered over to stand behind the girls, handing Olivia to Mercy when she opened her arms. Her heart hopscotched. As she looked at each familiar face during the introductions Billy made, she realized that *yes*—he *was* excited! She'd always admired his quiet strength, and had never doubted his loyalty to the Malloys, but Eve could see a big difference in him now.

His shirt looked dirty and his pants bagged—probably he hadn't taken time to eat. No doubt he couldn't cook much, and didn't spend time in the restaurants uptown because so much here needed fixing. He hadn't shaved for a while, which gave his face a darker, more alluring edge. Although his auburn hair needed trimming, Billy still had a reputable look about him: his entire being brimmed over with patience and generosity and steadfast faith.

Integrity. That's what she saw in his open smile, and heard in the voice that couldn't disguise his real feelings. Even when he'd told Emma Clark the wedding was off—and that he was truly sorry for it—Eve knew Billy Bristol took his promises seriously. He'd suffered for the way he'd hurt his bride-to-be.

Unlike his lawless brother, who'd never shed a tear for anybody. Wesley thought feelings were things only silly females displayed, and couldn't have cared less about her, except to toy with her. Humiliate her, as the final way to drag her family's reputation through the mud.

But as she heard the warm greetings everyone had for Beulah Mae, simply because Billy had always loved her, Eve thanked her lucky stars—and God, even—that she'd brought the old cook out here. She walked toward the wagon, thinking it was a good time for the rest of her surprise.

"And this here's Asa," Billy said as he came to the end of the family circle. "And I gotta tellya, he makes a pie *almost* as fine as yours, Beulah Mae."

"I's mighty pleased to meet you," the old man replied. There was a lilt in his voice, and Eve saw a litheness in that bent old body as Asa stood up to reach out his hand.

She grinned. They looked like Mr. and Mrs. Jack Spratt, from the nursery rhyme about the skinny little man and his oversized wife. And wasn't *that* an interesting idea!

"Mister Billy tole me early on about your pies, Beulah Mae—"

"We've *all* had to live up to your ways in the kitchen!" Mercy added with a laugh.

"—and I did my very best over the years to take care of 'im, like I knowed you woulda done," Asa continued. He was still holding her plump hand between his—gawking at her like a puppy begging for a pat on the head.

"And I wants you to know that our boy is one of the finest young men to ever walk on God's green earth," he insisted. "And I's proud to be a part of that—and so pleased to meet *you*, Beulah Mae. 'Cause I know you's always loved this redheaded boy like he was your own."

"You done said it all. And just right, too!" Beulah Mae replied with a chuckle. Then she narrowed those bright brown eyes, still clutching Asa's hand. "You and me'll get along just fine, long as you tells me I makes the best pie you's ever ate—and I tells you the same thing!"

Eve joined in the Malloys' laughter, lifting the thickest pumpkin pie she'd ever seen from the floor of the wagon. She also picked up a slender package, hoping this was the right time to present it.

"Here, Billy—you'd better take this," she said. "You should get the first piece, since Beulah Mae made it especially for you."

His tanned face lit up at the sight of the pumpkin pie: Eve thought he was going to kiss her, he looked so happy! Everyone was shifting so Beulah Mae could sit down beside Asa—making a place for her, as well—but she felt so fluttery, it took a moment before she could speak again.

"This is for you, too," she murmured. "I—I thought you might like to look at it now and again, and remember, well—you'll see! Just open it!"

The Malloys were passing the food, watching them

covertly while they filled their plates, but Eve didn't care. Dinner was the last thing on her mind. She noticed that Billy's fingers shook as he undid the ribbon she'd tied around the tissue paper.

"Don't think I can recall a day when I got so many—well, would you look at *that*." His bronzed face went tight as he stared at the framed canvas. "Eve, this is—why, it's just—look at this, everybody! Lookit at what Eve's painted for me!"

She felt like a girl who'd just won first prize at the fair: for a breath-defying moment, she thought he'd grab her up and kiss her. Billy rushed over to show his painting to the Malloys, and his joy—even more than their immediate approval—was the finest gift she'd ever received.

"It's *home!*" Gracie cried. "And there's us, Lily! On the porch with Joel!"

"And me, on Mr. Lincoln—and Billy on Pete!" Solace chimed in. She stood up, her tanned face aglow. "That's some picture, Miss Eve! Will you paint one like it for us?"

"Yes, please do!" Mercy handed the baby to Temple so she could stand up and take a closer look. "All my children—and the home Michael built for us, right down to those triple M's on the porch pillars! What a wonderful talent you have, dear."

Eve's knees quivered beneath her skirt, as the others echoed Mercy's praise for her painting. "Thank you so much," she murmured. "I have a studio now, thanks to Billy's mother, in the front of their hotel. I—I thought Billy would like to remember all the years he spent with you Malloys."

"Couldn't have said that better myself." Michael, too, was studying the painting with an awed expression that made her giddy. "We cherish that portrait you did of Lily, but if you could paint one similar to this sometime, it would be a way for us to remember our time with *you*, Eve."

As he reached into his pocket, his tender smile made her realize how very handsome he was—how lucky Mercy was, to have a fine, steadfast man like Michael as the head of her family.

"This is a just a deposit," he said, handing her some folded bills. "Don't short yourself on pay, honey, because I'm proud of the way you've pulled yourself together. You've been a fine example to my girls, about how a woman can use her God-given talents to make a life for herself. God bless you, Eve."

Suddenly she was crying. Throwing herself at Mike Malloy. He wasn't nearly old enough to be her father, but how wise he was! What an inspiration he'd been! Such a comfort, after the shame she'd suffered . . . the way she'd disrupted Billy's wedding to have her baby, and then abandoned Olivia . . . knowing Michael and Mercy would raise her as part of their patchwork family.

What an ungrateful guest she'd been. What a foolish, spoiled girl, expecting Billy and the Malloys to right all her wrongs.

She wiped her eyes, squeezing the greenbacks . . . thinking how she could buy new brushes—fresh paints—an easel.

"I can't accept this," she rasped, thrusting the money at him. "When I walked away from your house—and my daughter—I'd sunk so low I stole money from your kitchen. Yet you welcomed me back. Never a word about my being a thief, let alone an unfit mother."

The glimmer in Mercy's eyes made her heart throb. That was empathy she saw; the deepest kind of understanding. "You were confused, dear. Not feeling well after—"

"I was selfish! Only concerned with my own comfort, and vengeance against Wesley." She curled Michael's warm hand around the money. "Your home will be the next picture I paint, knowing my work falls far short of repayment. Thank you so much," she said with a hitch in her voice. "You and your family were so good to me, when you could've thrown me out—"

"Oh, that would never happen," Temple spoke up. She was rocking Olivia on her shoulder, beaming with the conviction she brought to everything she did. "These Malloys, they not only talk about their faith— they live it and share it. Same thing applies to your Billy. He's the hero, when it comes to accepting the destiny the Lord had waiting for him."

Your Billy. Had he caught that?

Eve glanced sideways, dabbing at her eyes as she slipped from Mike's embrace. In the afternoon sunlight, Billy's hair shone like rich, fiery copper and his blue eyes sparkled—at her! There was an expectant silence, while everyone waited for either her or Billy to respond to Temple's high praises.

"Well, I can see my Billy's been in the best of hands," Beulah Mae remarked. "And I wants y'all to know how I appreciate that. My prayers for this boy has all been answered today, now that I's seen how good he's done—and that he's come back home."

"Sit down here and eat, Billy! You, too, Eve!" Gracie insisted. "Mama won't let us have dessert 'til everybody's finished, and I want a *big* ole piece of that pumpkin pie!"

It was an invitation she couldn't refuse. Eve settled herself on the quilt, aware of what a joy it was to be smack in the middle of this family and their food again. The meals weren't fancy, but she always got her fill—as much from their company as from what came to her plate. That didn't happen at Mother's.

Sitting beside Billy filled her, too. The sensations of having him this close again, where she could watch the tendons ripple in his hands and hear the rolling rhythms in his speech, were a welcome change from the somber house she stayed in now. He was warm and strong, taking such enjoyment from this meal—from everything he did.

"How's your mama?" he asked between mouthfuls of chicken and cornbread. "Everything goin' all right, havin' the baby there?"

She sighed before she could catch herself. He was being polite, but there were so many more enthralling subjects to ask about. "Mother's not one for making a joyful noise, but you were right," she admitted. "Olivia's been the key to her heart. Still, it's very quiet there. The studio will save my sanity, I'm sure."

He nodded, scraping the last of the honey-drenched cornbread from his plate. Eve sounded awfully pleased about spending her days painting. Had he made a big mistake already, not going to see her? "I figured on droppin' by the house to visit with you ladies—"

"Oh, I wish you would!"

"—but I wanted to have things squared away here." He brushed crumbs from his lap. He had to say this next part right, or he'd be stepping in it, for sure.

"This house—comin' back to this place—was the dream that kept me goin' after Mama abandoned Christine and me," he explained softly. "And once I saw what Wesley had done to it—what he was gonna do to *me*—well, puttin' things back to rights has been my way of handlin' how he died."

Eve reached for his hand. "I still can't believe he came at you with that shotgun! I'm so sorry I provoked him—"

"Wasn't your fault, any more than mine. So let's leave Wesley out of this, shall we?"

The hand in his felt so fragile, yet so strong. With each stroke of her brushes, Eve was taking charge of her new life—proving herself, in a town where snooty old ladies would whisper behind their hands about what a harlot she was, how she'd led Wesley on, to spite her widowed mother, no doubt. She'd always been a little too bold—

And when she leaned in to kiss him, Billy loved her

for that. He was kissing her back, angling his face for the best taste of lips he'd felt in his dreams. She pulled away with a gasp.

"I—forgot myself—in front of every—"

"Well, you're not gonna forget *this*."

His hand slipped around her neck and Billy pressed his mouth to hers, urgently, daring her to answer him back. Eve's soft moans had nothing to do with modesty, or fear, or his brother this time: She was pouring out her artist's soul, showing another talent he wanted to explore in the coming weeks. Kissing. This woman liked it a whole lot more than Emma had.

When he finally released her, with a last little peck that made her giggle, he felt he'd made up for some lost time. Billy smiled at the folks who were watching them, and then gazed into Eve's eyes—eyes a deep, soothing green like this leafy shade they sat in.

"Just wanted you to know how I felt," he said. His declaration made him jittery—in the best of ways—but he wasn't going to repeat the mistakes he'd made with Emma Clark. "Everybody here's been hintin' about you and me for a long time, so now they know I've been *listenin'* to them, and to my heart, Peaches. I just had to say it my way, and in my own good time."

Eve's smile quivered and she looked ready to cry again. But she seemed happier than he'd ever seen her. Dewy-eyed, with roses in her cheeks.

"Oh, Billy, you do go on so!" Beulah Mae said with a chortle. "Why, your mama and I had you two matched up from the time you's babies. Just took you twenty years to figger it out, is all!"

Everyone laughed, now that their lovestruck moment had passed. Solace rolled her eyes, while Lily wore a wistful look, gazing openly at them.

Grace, however, banged her plate with her fork. "Are you gonna cut that pie, Billy? Or do I have to help myself?"

Billy felt a welling up, a rightness about this day, as he sliced into the thick, spicy-sweet filling Beulah Mae still made like nobody else. He wouldn't tell Asa that, of course.

But then, Asa was exchanging Billy stories with Beulah Mae, who laughed and batted her big brown eyes at him, and then told a *better* Billy story. As he lifted a slice of pie to his lips—no fork, because pumpkin pie was made just so he could eat it this way—Billy felt all the important pieces of his life falling into place.

It was a miracle, delicious and sweet. And it had his name all over it.

Beulah Mae was more than a fabulous cook: She was the undisputed queen of how the housecleaning should go, which suited the other ladies fine. While he and the men trimmed bushes and repaired broken windows, he could hear feminine voices inside—the swish of scrub brushes and the clanging of pans being washed in the kitchen. The scent of lemon wax brought back memories, too, and the sense of order Mama had insisted upon in her home.

By nightfall, it was another miracle, what they'd accomplished: The Bristol home place was getting its shine back, along with its pride. While the ladies occupied the beds, Billy, Michael, Reuben, and Asa stretched out on quilts beneath the trees. He slept like a baby—like a boy come home, to awaken as a man. But not alone anymore.

The fragrance of bacon and coffee and biscuits drifted out from the kitchen as the sun brushed the sky with shades of pink and peach. Billy savored breakfast around the big table in the dining room, which was a little the worse for wear, but still a place for gathering these people he loved. Their chatter filled the room, shooing away the sadness and sense of neglect that had gathered here with the dust.

And by the end of their second day, fresh paint graced most of the rooms, and Reuben had rebuilt the front steps. The salvageable furniture was arranged much as it had been when he was a boy, on freshened rugs and glossy wood floors. The kitchen gleamed, and the food the Malloys had brought filled the pantry shelves.

"It's been a wonderful surprise, and I thank you all," he said when they'd loaded their wagon and carriage to leave. "You've brought this place to life again. I could never've done all this, even with months of—"

"We wouldn't have it any other way, Billy." Michael stepped up to grip his hand, his eyes alight with love and sadness. He gazed out over the pasture, where the Morgans already looked right at home. "Come and see us when you can, son. Bring your family."

"Y-you, too," he replied, knowing Michael wasn't just talking about Mama and Carlton. "I hope you hear about Joel soon. I know his leavin' bothers you."

"I believe, because you spent so much time with him when he wouldn't listen to me, he's got half a chance," Malloy said with a sigh. "I'm betting he sends us a telegram from someplace far away. He's always seen the grass on the other man's side as greener."

"If you'll keep him in your prayers, Billy, I'm sure God will listen." Mercy hugged him tight, pouring all her love and hope for him into an embrace that made him reel. In many ways, she'd been his mother, the woman he'd looked to for love and advice during the most impressionable years of his life. "Take care of yourself, Billy Bristol, because when I leave, a big piece of my heart's staying here with you."

He closed his eyes, nodding because he couldn't talk.

Then she turned to Eve, who stood beside him with Olivia. "Don't be strangers, you two. I can't wait to see the family portrait you're painting, Eve!

"And you, little girl," she added in a higher voice,

touching the baby's chubby, pink cheeks, "you're taking *another* chunk of my heart! What'll I have left, unless you come to see me real soon?"

Eve, too, seemed moved by the Malloys' departure. As the carriage started off, followed by the rumbling buckboard, she stood beside him waving, until they disappeared down the tree-lined lane. His arm found her waist and she leaned into him, watching until the vehicles had rolled down the road.

It seemed so natural, to be standing on the porch together, as though this were their home and they were already a family. Billy liked the feel of that. He turned to say something about it, but Eve's kiss met his mouth before he could get the words out. Then rational thought left him altogether.

He pulled her close and continued the kiss, reveling in the way she felt so soft and sweet. Olivia let out a happy squawk on her shoulder, and behind them they heard solid footfalls.

"Beulah Mae needs your help in the house, little girl," the old cook said. "You come with me, sweet pea, 'cause this ole lady ain't held a baby for way too long now. Got somethin' for ya, too!"

Billy's cheeks tingled. He stepped back enough to let his former nursemaid take Olivia, smiling at the joy on that old brown face. "No doubt she's a Bristol, Mama said."

"That's why, when I found your matched cradles in the attic, I got one down for her," Beulah Mae replied softly. "Seemed like the right thing to do."

"Are you serious, about stayin' on? Can't pay you much, 'til I get my horse business—"

"Won't be doin' it for the pay, honey." The old woman's eyes shone with relief. "This still feels like home to me, and I's happy to help out. Got no family left, and I knows you'll take care of me, just like you stepped in when Miss Eve and this sweet child needed ya. You're just made that-a way."

Once she went inside, they heard kissy noises and silly talk—songs sung by a mellow voice that made memories well up from deep inside him.

"You *are* made that way, Billy," Eve repeated. "But don't think you have to take care of Olivia and me, just because—"

Billy hushed her with a long kiss, wondering why he'd waited so long to share these feelings he had. But in matters of the heart—as with everything—there was a season.

"I *want* to," he whispered. "I want *you*, Eve. We'll take our time, though, workin' Wesley out of our systems. It's gotta be right for both of us."

Eve threw her arms around his neck, and Billy felt a power bubbling up inside him, but coming at him from all directions, as well. She was an angel, this pretty woman, and her embrace raised him up. Her wings weren't spotless, because she'd been splattered on one of life's muddier roads. But Eve Massena had now chosen a higher path—and she wanted him to go with her.

When he kissed her again, he knew that path had led them both home.

Chapter Thirty-two

Two months later, October 1876

Billy stepped out onto the wide, shaded porch and grinned at his guests. "Well, folks, I think the bride is finally ready."

He felt that an idiot grin had taken over his face, but he didn't care. It was no sin to be happy—certainly a good sign that this wedding was meant to take place, because it was at the right time and with the right woman.

To everything there is a season . . .

As Florence Massena played a showy fanfare on the piano in the parlor, he took his place at the bottom of the porch steps. He smiled at Mama, arrayed like a peacock in a new gown of brilliant blue and a matching hat with feathers in its band. Standing beside Carlton, holding her granddaughter—who wore the long beaded gown his sister Christine was christened in— she looked happier than he'd ever seen her.

And that was saying something.

A time to plant, and a time to pluck what is planted . . .

"You nervous, son?" Malloy came up beside him with a Bible, placing a hand on his shoulders.

"Nope. This is how it's s'posed to be."

Billy smiled at Gabe, who'd come in from St. Louis to be his best man—again. He looked scholarly in his frock coat and new spectacles, but his grin brought back the boy Billy had met ten years earlier. "You don't suppose Emma has somehow found out, and will show up when the preacher asks for objections?" he teased quietly.

"Well, in a way she is here," Billy replied. "After she and her daddy left their place, we found her weddin' dress hangin' in her room . . . like she didn't want any reminders of me. But since Mercy had made it—and Eve thought it was the prettiest thing she'd ever seen—"

A heartfelt *ahhhhhh!* made him look up. Lily, Solace, and Grace, dressed in identical gowns of cornflower blue, scattered the last roses from the gardens, along with maple leaves of brilliant reds and golds, as they came across the porch. When she went to stand beside Temple, Solace flashed him a wink.

A time to weep, and a time to laugh . . .

That tomboy had undergone the ultimate torture, wearing such a fancy dress for him today. She'd never let him forget it, either! Already, she had her eye on one of his Morgans . . .

It was now Lily's turn to shine, to grace this gathering with her special light. She stood proudly, clasping Grace's hand, and as they listened to the piano's familiar introduction, Mercy came out from the parlor to sing with them.

Billy beamed: "Whispering Hope" was one of his favorite songs, and he already missed hearing it in the Malloys' sunlit parlor on Sunday afternoons.

"Soft as the voice of an angel . . . breathing a lesson unheard . . ."

Lily sang the solo with a gentle clarity that floated over them, her face radiant with confidence, as Grace and her mother hummed along.

He let his gaze wander with the music, to where Asa was standing beside Beulah Mae. The old man's white-sprigged head barely came to her shoulder, but she didn't seem to notice—and was secretly clasping his hand behind her big, billowy skirts!

"Whispering hope . . . oh how welcome thy voice!" came the chorus. Everyone around him smiled at the waltz-time rhythm, soothed by the three-part harmony Mercy and her girls had been practicing ever since they'd realized Gracie had an ear for it. It was a brief song, so they repeated the chorus with extra fervor, slowing at the end.

"Making my heart . . . in its sorrow rejoice."

Sighs of pleasure rose around him, and Billy realized then that this beloved song was all about what he and Eve had gone through together: how they'd made mistakes and apologies . . . endured gossip and hostility. And yet because they'd never lost *hope*, they were here today. Surrounded by families who wished them all the best.

Mercy came down the steps with the girls, to stand proudly beside Michael. The smile she gave him—the tracks of happy tears on her radiant face—well, Billy couldn't help himself. He stepped over to hug her, hard, for all the ways she'd made this day happen for him and Eve.

Mercy squeezed him back, and then turned toward the doorway. The piano was louder and more glorious, announcing the bride.

Billy's jaw dropped.

Eve Massena, in a gown of flowing ivory with layers of fabric so soft they drifted on the autumn breeze, caught his eye and held it, straight-on. The biddies in church had tried to make mincemeat of her when she wanted the ceremony there: a harlot covering herself in bridal white, they'd called her.

But Eve had circumvented convention by inviting Reverend Searcy and their families *here*—where everyone felt welcome, no matter what color their skin, and where love overruled petty gossip. It was far more beautiful out here on this perfect autumn day, anyway.

But not like *she* was beautiful. The little beads on her bodice caught the afternoon sunlight and shimmered as she walked serenely toward him, her footsteps matching the piano's beat. Her glossy brown hair was swept up into her veil, which cascaded down her back instead of over her face.

And he liked that. She wasn't feigning innocence, nor was she hiding from anybody. She was just Eve, and she was just about to be his.

Billy stepped up to take her hand, to steady her on the stairs as she let the full skirts of her gown billow ahead of her feet. They turned, and as Eve slipped her hand under his elbow, her mother came out, accompanied by Reverend Searcy.

In his dark frock coat and monocle, the preacher looked much the same as when he'd chided Billy and Wes for playing hide-and-seek around the church pews. When Florence Massena had taken her place beside Mama, he cleared his throat ceremoniously.

"Dearly beloved, we are gathered here to celebrate the uniting in Holy Matrimony of Miss Eve Maureen Massena and Mister William Henry Bristol," he began. He stood three steps up from the ground, where he could survey the guests. "Matrimony is a sacred act, holy in the eyes of God, and not to be entered into lightly. Therefore, if anyone here knows any reason this man and this woman should *not* be joined in marriage, let him speak now . . . or forever hold his peace."

The breeze whispered in the leaves, like the rustling of angels' wings.

It seemed to Billy the preacher waited a while, as though he anticipated a last-minute interruption of their nuptials. He felt Eve grinning at him, thinking the same thing—about how *she'd* been the one to cry out from the back of the crowd, the last time he'd tried this.

"You were my angel of mercy that day," he whispered, gazing into her shining eyes. "I had no idea what love was. No idea I was goin' the wrong way—'til I met you again."

"Billy and Eve have asked Michael Malloy to grace us with today's Scripture reading," Reverend Searcy went on. "Let us listen to the word of the Lord."

How many times had he seen this man riffle through the pages of that well-thumbed Bible, at weddings and funerals, and at the close of every day?

While he himself had learned to give a respectable reading, by following Michael's example, Billy felt more blessed by the presence of God when it was this man's voice delivering the message—this man paraphrasing the difficult passages, often from memory, so that every listener could better understand it.

Malloy looked up at the crowd, his mustache curving inward with his grin. "We often overlook the Song of Solomon as a book that doesn't seem to fit with the rest of the Old Testament," he began. "But what better time to delight in love letters from God's word than at a wedding? These passages are from the second chapter, reminding us that, yes, our Lord sanctifies even our physical pleasures in one another, when we abide in Him.

" 'My beloved spoke, and said to me: 'Rise up, my love, my fair one, and come away. For lo, the winter is past, the rain is over and gone. The flowers appear on the earth; the time of singing has come, and the voice of the turtledove is heard in our land.' "

He spoke eloquently, smiling at Billy and Eve. " 'Oh, my dove, in the clefts of the rock, in the secret places of the cliff, let me see your face, let me hear your voice; for your voice is sweet and your face is lovely. . . . I charge you, Oh daughters of Jerusalem . . . do not stir up nor awaken love until it pleases.' "

Reverend Searcy's puckered expression almost made Billy laugh out loud. It was a sure bet this preacher had never read those passages in public, so he and Eve shared a smile—promises that the physical pleasures would come in their own good time. And soon.

"And from the Gospel of John, these familiar yet compelling words of Jesus about love, and where it comes from, and what it all means," Michael went on. He flipped to the ribbon marker, but then lifted his eyes to survey the guests.

" 'Already you are clean because of the word that I have spoken to you,' " he began, as though assuring Billy and Eve of his approval. " 'Abide in me, and I in you. As the branch cannot bear fruit by itself, unless it abides in the vine, neither can you, unless you abide in me. I am the vine; you are the branches. Whoever abides in me and I in him, he it is that bears much fruit, for apart from me you can do nothing.' "

Michael paused, his expression solemn. "Every one of us would do well to remember this, because I assure you that my successes—my home, my marriage, my business—would never have borne fruit without guidance from the Master's hand."

"Amen to that," Asa said softly.

Mercy beamed at her husband, sharing her joy with Billy and Eve, too.

" 'If you abide in me, and my words abide in you, ask *whatever you wish*, and it will be done for you,' " Malloy went on fervently. " 'As the Father has loved me, so have I loved you. Abide in my love. If you keep my commandments, you will abide in my love, just as I have kept my Father's commandments and abide in His love.' "

He looked directly at Billy and Eve then, a father pronouncing his blessing on them. "'These things I have spoken to you, that my joy may be in you, and that your joy may be full.'"

From there, for Eve, the ceremony was a blur. She could only gaze at Billy, at the love light in his beautiful blue eyes, and realize yet again how many wonderful things had come into her life because this fine man had rescued her—from disgrace, yes, but mostly from herself. Because Billy Bristol had believed in her, and because his family had loved her and Olivia unconditionally, she'd found a whole new life. A life as full and exciting as her renewed pursuit of painting.

"—and by the powers vested in me, I now pronounce you man and wife," Reverend Searcy said with thundering authority. "You may kiss your bride."

Billy swept her into his embrace and their mouths met with playful abandon—until muffled coughs brought them back to the ceremony at hand. Then she turned to Virgilia and took Olivia. Her red-haired daughter looked like a little cherub in the christening gown that had been her friend Christine's. She'd never known a prouder moment.

"It will be my distinct pleasure, on this sacred occasion, to christen Eve's child—the grandchild of Florence Massena and Virgilia Bristol Harte, two longtime members of my congregation," the preacher went on.

Eve smiled tightly, wondering if someone here had slipped him a generous donation. He'd balked when she'd first asked him to baptize Olivia: wouldn't perform that sacrament, in public or privately, because her daughter had no daddy.

But that was rectified now. Billy beamed at the baby, proudly answering the questions and repeating the vows with her. Olivia, bless her heart, gaped peacefully up at the preacher; had the good grace to flash him a toothless grin when the water met her scalp. Reverend Searcy actually kissed her cheek!

"I now present to you the Bristol family—Billy, Eve, and little Olivia," he announced from the step, "united and sanctified this day by the grace of our Lord. What God has joined, let no man put asunder!"

Applause broke out around them, and as she and Billy turned to accept everyone's congratulations, Eve felt waves of joy and heavenly sunshine washing over her. Behind them, her mother played a postlude on the piano, which had been tuned as Mercy's special gift to them, while Gabe was grinning at her over the top of his spectacles.

"What a day! And what a fine celebration," he said, pumping Billy's hand before pressing her cheek with a kiss. "It's good to know about weddings—what takes place when the bride and groom actually go through with it!" he teased. "Might be inviting you to one myself, one of these days."

"Oh, yeah?" Billy raised an eyebrow. "Gonna tell me about her?"

"All in good time. Right now, I'm headed for a glass of that punch."

Eve looked toward the long table set up in the shade, draped with an embroidered linen tablecloth of Virgilia's, which they'd found in the sideboard. Beulah Mae had mixed up a pretty peach punch and made pastries, and beside her, Asa was ready to cut the two-tiered wedding cake he'd created.

"If I were a bettin' man, I'd guess those two'll be tyin' the knot pretty quick," Billy murmured beside her. "It'd be good to have 'em both here, if Michael can spare Asa."

"What's that?" Malloy turned from talking with the minister to grin at them. "If you're thinking Asa wants to latch onto your cook, you're a couple months late, son. He spoke to me about it on our way home from cleaning this place. And she's already said yes!"

Eve chortled. "She's never let on! I—"

"Beulah Mae has always done exactly as she pleased," Billy's mother chimed in. "I may have been the mistress of this house, but make no mistake—my cook was always in charge!"

Virgilia gazed around at the lawn, where the girls were releasing some pent-up energy with the dogs— where the trimmed bushes and freshly painted walls bespoke a home of long-standing distinction. She made a pretty picture in peacock blue, with the red, orange, and golden leaves of the maple trees as a backdrop.

"I can't thank you enough for restoring this house . . . these grounds," she said softly, her hand on Billy's arm. "It brings me real peace—real joy—to return here now, where Owen and I began our life together and had our family."

She smiled warmly at Eve. "And I'm glad you've decided to come to your studio just one or two days a week, dear. This place needs a firm hand like yours to keep it running, so Billy can raise horses like his daddy did. It—it's a proud day. For all of us."

Eve kissed her cheek and passed her a sleepy Olivia. "We need a bite of that cake and some punch, Mister Billy. The voice of the turtledove is calling my name, you know."

Her new husband—her new *husband!*—grinned. "Michael didn't have to read that passage for *me*, 'cause I already know your voice is sweet, and your face is lovely."

Lovely. Not a word she'd heard in Billy's vocabulary before, rough-and-tumble rancher that he was. But his eyes told her he meant it, just as he meant everything he said. And, after all, *lovely* was based on the word *love*—and he knew plenty about that!

As they reached the cake table, the three girls gath-

ered around him, ready for Asa's dessert. Billy brought
the light to their faces with his smile; made them hoot
and holler when he kissed her, his bride, on a double-
dog dare from Solace about how long they could
hold on.

It was a glorious kiss, too, sweet with punch and
frosting—sweet with the promise of a love that would
only grow stronger in the coming days and years. How
far she'd come from resenting the Malloys for making
her a charity case. How much she'd learned about how
it was blessed to receive as well as to give, for the gifts
of their love had changed her entire life. She had asked,
and they had given—just as Michael had quoted in today's Scripture.

"I love you so much . . . I *owe* you so much, Billy," she
breathed, watching the way his lips moved around a
bite of white, frosted cake.

He held a forkful in front of her then, coaxing her
mouth open with a callused hand that caressed her
cheek, as though he had ideas about doing that later,
when they were alone.

"I love *you*, Eve—and I'm gonna make you pay up
every single day, too," he teased softly. "Pay and pay
and pay, until it's me indebted to you, Peaches. And then
I guess we'll have to start all over again, won't we?"

Eve took the cake—and his kiss—closing her eyes.

Life was sweet. Life was sweet indeed.

A Patchwork Family

CHARLOTTE HUBBARD

Meet Mercy Malloy. No matter what she does, God's love fills her life. So when two orphaned children appear on her doorstep, she hesitates only a moment before opening her heart and her home to them. Perhaps this is the Lord's way of sending her and Judd the babies they've prayed for.

Out on the Kansas plains the years bring hardship and heartache—Indian attacks, a runaway daughter, an abandoned baby in a basket—but also precious new life and the unlooked for joy of a surprise love. Through it all, Mercy's faith holds her family together, creating a patchwork of strength and beauty.

Journey to Love

Charlotte Hubbard

Christine Bristol is sick of waiting. For three years she's done as everyone tells her, putting aside dreams of the handsome photographer who captured her girlish fancy, trying to forget the mother who abandoned her on the stage to Abilene. Now she doesn't care who gets hurt in her desperate bid to follow her heart. Heading across the prairie in a cramped, horse-drawn wagon, Christine discovers that much of the bitterness she's known comes from her own lack of faith. On her journey of discovery to San Francisco, Christine finds a love that reunites her with her real family, puts her in touch with her true self, and brings her back to the simple Kansas homestead.
